Valerie Wood was born in Yorkshire and now lives in a village near the east coast. She is the author of *The Hungry Tide*, winner of the Catherine Cookson Prize for Fiction, *Annie, Children of the Tide, The Romany Girl, Emily, Going Home, Rosa's Island* and *The Doorstep Girls*, all available in Corgi paperback.

Find out more about Valerie Wood's novels by visiting her website on www.valeriewood.co.uk

T0204626

Also by Valerie Wood

THE HUNGRY TIDE
ANNIE
CHILDREN OF THE TIDE
EMILY
GOING HOME
ROSA'S ISLAND
THE DOORSTEP GIRLS

and published by Corgi Books

The Romany Girl

Valerie Wood

CORGI BOOKS

THE ROMANY GIRL
A CORGI BOOK : 0 552 14640 4

Originally published in Great Britain by Bantam Press,
a division of Transworld Publishers

PRINTING HISTORY
Bantam Press edition published 1998
Corgi edition published 1998

3 5 7 9 10 8 6 4 2

Set in 11/12pt New Baskerville by
Phoenix Typesetting, Burley-in-Wharfedale, West Yorkshire.

Corgi Books are published by Transworld Publishers,
61–63 Uxbridge Road, London W5 5SA,
a division of The Random House Group Ltd,
in Australia by Random House Australia (Pty) Ltd,
20 Alfred Street, Milsons Point, Sydney, NSW 2061, Australia,
and in New Zealand by Random House New Zealand Ltd,
18 Poland Road, Glenfield, Auckland 10, New Zealand
and in South Africa by Random House (Pty) Ltd,
Endulini, 5a Jubilee Road, Parktown 2193, South Africa.

Printed and bound in Great Britain by
Cox & Wyman Ltd, Reading, Berkshire.

Papers used by Transworld Publishers are natural, recyclable
products made from wood grown in sustainable forests.
The manufacturing processes conform to the environmental
regulations of the country of origin.

For my family with love

Acknowledgements

My thanks to:
Peter Burgess for invaluable research material into the fairs, circuses and portable theatres;
Vanessa Toulmin, Fairground Archivist, Sheffield University Library;
Chris Ketchell, Local History Unit, Park Street College, Hull, for information on the nineteenth-century Hull workhouse;
Pauline Falkner, speech and language therapist, East Yorkshire Community Healthcare, Victoria House, Park Street, Hull;
my daughter Catherine for her patience in reading the manuscript.

General reading sources:
Owen's New Book of Fairs (James Cornish, 297 High Holborn, London WC, 1859–60)

Romano Lavo-Lil: Word Book of the Romany, by George Borrow, 1873 (John Murray, Albemarle Street, London, 1907)

The Victoria History of the County of York, East Riding

Living and Dying: A Picture of Hull in the Nineteenth Century, by Bernard Foster (Printed by Abbotsgate Printers, Hull)

Memoirs of Bartholomew Fair, by Henry Morley (George Routledge & Sons Ltd, London, 1892)

English Fairs and Markets, by Wm Addison (BT Batsford Ltd, London, 1953)

Yorkshire Gypsy Fairs, Customs and Caravans, by Alan Jones (Hutton Press Ltd, Cherry Burton, Beverley, East Yorkshire, 1986)

Part One

1

The boy pulled the thin blanket closer to his body and shuffled deeper into the corner by the gate. A cold, damp mist was descending, drifting in from the river and settling with vaporous fingers in every corner of the town. Jonty shivered. You could always tell when it was Hull Fair time. The weather always told. Rarely in that festive week did the autumn show itself in crisp golden colours, when the entertainers, the sellers of good fortune – 'only a penny to change your luck' – the cheap-jacks with their golden rings, and the itinerant horse traders descended on the town, but it drizzled with wet, murky rain which chilled the bones and soaked thin boots, and yet did nothing to dispel the enthusiasm which the townspeople felt towards the most important annual event in their dreary lives.

But now the fair was over for another year. During each of the last two nights Jonty had heard the clop of horse beats as carts and waggons pulled the cages of wild animals, the dancing dogs and the freaks of nature, out of the town towards a resting place for the winter where waggons and booths would be repaired and painted, money would be counted and new ideas thought up for the following year, for the ancient Hull Fair was the last big fair of the year.

He stirred on the hard stone of the yard as he heard the sound of wooden wheels and recognized the vibrating wobble of Old Boney's cart, as it trundled with a lopsided pitch on the cobbled stones of Whitefriargate towards the workhouse. He raised himself and moved with swift yet awkward step to peer through the hole in the gate. It was Old Boney and his cart was laden, piled high with sacks and bundles; whether it was old clothing and rags, bits of metal, firewood or a cask of smuggled spirit for the Master, Jonty couldn't tell, for the lamp outside the gate had gone out and the street was shrouded in darkness.

He reached for a stick, kept for the purpose, and knocked back the bolt at the top of the gate, then bent to do the same at the bottom and swung open the gate to admit the laden cart and its driver.

'Shut 'gate, I'm not going out again, and fetch 'Master. Look sharp about it.' The instructions were terse, but no more so than Jonty expected. In all of his seven years he had been at everyone's beck and call and expected nothing else, but Old Boney never cuffed him as most other adults did.

''M-Master's out, 'M-Matron's in,' he volunteered reluctantly. He didn't speak unless it was absolutely necessary for very few people understood him.

'Fetch her then. Wake her up if needs be.'

Jonty ran. He moved swiftly in spite of his shortened leg and bent back and could outrun all of the other children in the workhouse; he had to to keep out of trouble. Some of them, he had decided, were jealous of his special privileges. He didn't have to sleep in the overcrowded dormitories as they did, though he could share a bed if he wanted to; he could sleep in the woodstore, where he stacked the wood for the stove, he could sleep in the old hayloft, which was warm but had much company of rats and mice, or he could sleep outside in the yard, which he preferred to the damp and stinking building, and listen to the sounds of the night.

He had the run of the whole of the old, decrepit building. He knew every loose window and unlocked door and could creep into the kitchen and warm himself on a winter's night. He was small enough too to climb through the larder window, though there was little food left about on the stone shelves save an odd crust or a bowl of gruel. What food there was was locked away in the cupboards, and he had to be careful that the food he was taking wasn't meant for the cook's own consumption.

He climbed the creaking stairs, approached the door next to the girls' dormitory and tapped gingerly. 'Mrs Pincher!' he spluttered. He put his ear to the door and heard the snoring and knocked again a little harder, but not too hard to waken her too hastily or she would be in an ill humour.

There was a sudden snort and he knocked again. 'Mrs Pincher,' he repeated and took a deep breath to form the words. 'Come! Owd Boney's here.'

He heard the shuffling of slippers on the floorboards and the door opened a crack. He blinked.

Mrs Pincher in creased voluminous bedgown and a cap askew on her head was not an appealing sight. She gazed glassily at him. 'What's he brought?' She hawked to clear her throat. 'It's 'middle of 'night!'

Jonty shook his head. No use guessing. If he guessed wrong, he would get a cuff and if he guessed right he would still get a cuff for being nosey. 'He say – come.'

'Go on then, don't stand there gawping. I'll be down in a jiff when I'm decent.'

He sped down the rickety stairs again and out of the door into the yard. Old Boney was letting down the backboard of the cart and handing down a woman, who was holding on to a large bundle and a carpet bag. She swayed as her feet touched the floor and fell into a heap, where she lay very still. Jonty bent over her and wondered why Old Boney had brought this woman in his cart, for there were plenty of others waiting outside, hoping to be admitted. 'M-Matron's coming,' he mumbled.

He was always aroused by the sight of the women who came here. It was usually their last act of despair and the pain of it showed on their faces, the pale, set expression of acceptance that they could fall no further. He searched deeply into their eyes wondering if this was how his own mother had looked when she was brought here, for he didn't remember her; he had been born in the workhouse and she had died within an hour of his birth. He was a workhouse brat and knew no other life; this was his home and because he was so useful to those in control here he would stay, for ever if need be. He had the satisfaction of security, such as it was.

The woman stirred and groaned and looked up

at him. 'I'm dying,' she whispered. 'Who will look after my child?'

He bent over her. 'M-Matron's coming,' he stammered, unwilling to enter into conversation, for when he did, strangers drew back from him, thinking him a lunatic like the ones who were locked up in the back room of the workhouse building.

'Dear child,' she said, grasping his hand, 'you have a kind face. Will you take care of her for me?'

Dear child! Kind face! He was astonished. Never had anyone said such words to him. Imbecile. Cripple. Dummy! All of these had been applied to him, but never words so sweet. He gazed at the woman, etched her fine features into his memory and loved her. He nodded his head. Yes he would, for as long as he could, for how was he to know if the workhouse would keep the child or send her off elsewhere? If she didn't belong in the district she would be shunted off to another authority.

'Her name is—' The woman broke off in a paroxysm of coughing as she gave the child's name and Jonty saw a froth of blood on her lips. The bundle beside her began to cry and pull off the shawl covering her to reveal a small girl, her head thick with dark curls and her thumb in her pouting mouth.

Her mother shushed her. 'Here is a friend for you, my darling, someone to play with.' She pulled Jonty closer and whispering into his ear pressed a small silk purse into his hand. 'This is for her when she is old enough to wear it. I have nothing else. I beg you to keep it for her.'

Jonty pushed the purse into his shirt as he saw

Matron purposefully crossing the yard and moved to one side as she took charge, admonishing Old Boney for bringing in yet another pauper when she hadn't yet dealt with yesterday's admittance; then, mollified as he lifted the corner of a blanket to reveal a cask, she ordered him to help the woman and, scooping up the crying child with one hand and the carpet bag with the other, she marched them inside and closed the door behind them.

Though Mrs Pincher was a strict disciplinarian and there appeared to be not a drop of human kindness within her soul, Jonty had much to thank her for. She it was who had ordered that he be removed from the lunatic ward, where he had been placed aged three when it was discovered that he was unable to speak coherently. 'He's a dumb mute,' the governors had declared, and added as they examined his crooked body, 'an imbecile. He has no intelligence nor ever will have. Lock him up so he can do no harm to himself or others.'

Two whole years he stayed with the lunatics. Some had been moved there from the House of Correction, men who had been violent or thieves, others who were chained to the walls and babbled and rocked in their own excreta; but there were some who were misplaced, men whose businesses had failed and who had attempted to end their lives, young mothers who nursed lost babies on empty laps and who took Jonty on their knees until he tired of their nursing and turned to play games with the men. Men who played chess and crib and one man in particular called Samuel, a morose, tired-looking man who on occasions fell on to the floor in fits and had to be sat upon until he recovered, but who on his sane days taught Jonty numbers and letters and seemed to understand his mumbling speech.

Mrs Pincher had found him one day playing cards with Samuel as she was doing her rounds in the company of her husband, the Master. Mr Pincher generally visited the locked rooms with the added protection of two paupers and his assistant, Mr Bertram, but on this day Mr Bertram had gone off on some other mission and Mrs Pincher had taken his place.

'Can this be 'mute child?' she had asked, observing him counting the score in his hand. 'They said he was a babbling idiot.'

'So he is, Mrs Pincher,' the Master asserted. 'The governors said as much, so that is what he is.'

Jonty gazed up at her with wide eyes and she had taken his chin and lifted it and, forcing his lips apart, had searched with her thick fingers inside his mouth so that he almost choked. 'He's got a hole in 'roof of his mouth. That's why he can't talk! Can you hear what I say?' she shouted at him.

He nodded. Everyone but Samuel shouted at him, but he could hear perfectly clearly.

'Tell me your name,' she shouted again.

'Jonty,' he mumbled. His name was Jonathon. He had been told that his mother had chosen the name when he was born, but he couldn't say it.

'Get him out of here, Mr Pincher. He doesn't belong in here, he's as sane as I am.' She glowered at her husband, who was frowning disapprovingly. 'As sane as you or me. I'll tek responsibility for him. I'll speak to 'governors.'

Whether she ever did speak to the governors Jonty never knew, though he was never called before the Board to answer to them, and for that he was relieved, for speaking to strangers was an ordeal he dreaded. Mrs Pincher began to understand him better, though her husband had no patience and the other children in the workhouse only laughed at his efforts and called him names and he became the butt of their own frustrations.

He revelled in the freedom he now enjoyed for no-one seemed to be in charge of him, though he missed the company of Samuel, who had shaken him solemnly by the hand and advised him not to forget his teaching, which he didn't, for as soon as he was able to reach the small window of the locked ward he climbed in and continued his lessons with his friend. But in response to Mrs Pincher's effort to release him from the lunatic ward, he became useful to her, fetching and carrying, making sure that she had sufficient wood for the fire in her room, running errands into the town with such speed that she was amazed, and she in turn would not tolerate anyone mistreating him in her presence, though she often cuffed him herself when she thought he had transgressed, or even if he hadn't.

The morning after the arrival of the woman and child he went into the building in search of Mrs Pincher, ostensibly to ask if she needed any errands running, but in fact to find out what had happened to the new inmates.

He threaded his way through the maze of shabby rooms and corridors, pushing through the crowds of inmates who milled about, some of whom were making their way to the oakum room, where they would spend the day picking at the old rope with their raw and bleeding fingers, and others who just hung around waiting for the day to end, and came out again into the open yard at the back. Sitting on a stool in the middle of the yard with her hands over her eyes was the little girl, her shoulders heaving with sobs as one of the inmates cut her long hair to above her ears.

'Mrs Pincher?' he mumbled at the woman. She shrugged and then with a toss of her head towards an upstairs window said, 'Seeing to a birthing and a deeing, folks keep coming and going. Come on lass, let's have thee under 'pump, Matron's orders.'

The little girl started to scream and flail her arms as the woman worked the pump handle, forcing her under, and Jonty jumped forward in alarm. He shook the woman off and indicating that he would help pushed his own head under the gushing water, shaking his head like a dog until the little girl stopped crying, laughed at his antics, joined in the game and splashed in the water too until they were both soaked.

Mrs Pincher came marching into the yard to find out what the noise was about and on seeing Jonty called to him, 'Now then my lad, Old Boney said 'woman last night was talking to you. Did she tell her name or where she came from?'

Jonty shook his head.

'Nowt at all?' Mrs Pincher persisted. 'She didn't give no note or letter?'

Again he shook his head.

'Then he must have been mistaken.' She eyed him keenly. 'So what was she saying if she didn't tell her name? She wasn't talking about 'weather!'

Jonty hesitated. He'd have to say something, but he wouldn't tell about the purse, for he'd have to give it up and he doubted that the little girl would ever get it back.

'She'll have to leave here if she doesn't belong in these parts.' Mrs Pincher observed the child, her now short curls dark and wet. She frowned. 'She looks like a Gypsy child to me, though her ma was no Gypsy.' She leaned over her. 'What's your name?'

The little girl shook her head and turned away from Mrs Pincher, standing closer to Jonty, who shuffled his feet, opened and closed his mouth and prepared to speak.

'Spit it out, then!' Mrs Pincher barked. 'If tha's summat to say, then say it!'

He tried, he really tried, but it was impossible. He could never say his Ls, and Mrs Pincher became exasperated and cuffed his ear. 'For Heaven's sake, dunderhead! Try again.'

He flinched and tried once more but with little success.

'Poor Ena! Is that what tha's saying? Emmalina? Poor Anna? Why is she poor? She could be lying dead in 'gutter!'

He clenched his mouth and rocked in exasperation and implored with his eyes for Mrs Pincher to understand.

'Polly Anna? Is that it? That's it, isn't it?'

He beamed. It was near enough. He looked down at the small girl who was only half his age, who took her thumb out of her mouth and smiled at him.

Polly Anna. It suited her. He'd never be able to say her name except in his head and perhaps one day when he knew enough letters, Samuel would show him how to write it.

2

Polly Anna had pushed the woman's breast away from her face and wriggled off her knee. Her milk smelt sour, not sweet and warm as her mother's had been, though she had not nursed her for many months. She was a big girl of nearly four, she had told her, no longer an infant to want her mother's breast, though her lap and arms were always soft and welcoming.

Her mama was kind and loving, with a face so beautiful and a smile so sweet, though lately on their long journey she had cried and been unhappy, and had called for Polly Anna's papa in such despair that Polly Anna too had cried. But now she had disappeared. She had been spirited away by the woman who had greeted them on their arrival in this dreadful place; she who had put her in a small, hard bed in a room full of other children with sores on their faces and running noses, who had gathered around her to stare after the woman had gone, taking her mama with her.

And now this other horrid woman had slapped her when she cried, had cut off her hair and told her that her mama was dead, so no use crying! What was dead? Was it like when her kitten had gone to sleep and she and papa had wrapped it in a cloth and buried it in the ground? Her mama wouldn't like that, she was convinced. But who to ask in this dark and dreary place, where there were no friendly faces at all except for this boy with the gentle face and strange voice who ran like Morgan's monkey.

'Keep an eye on her, Jonty,' Mrs Pincher was saying to the boy. 'I've got to find out what's what. She'll have to stay I expect,' she muttered, 'now that her ma's dead.'

That word again. Polly Anna started to cry again, but Jonty took her by the hand and led her out of the yard and into the building and through other rooms and doorways until once more they were outside in the small yard which they had entered last night. This seemed to be his own playground for there were no other children here, they were inside, they'd passed them as they came through the building, all busy with tasks; some were washing floors, some were sewing, some in the big kitchen with their hands in the sink. None were playing.

But Jonty played. To amuse her he turned somersaults, over and over. He hid behind barrels of sawdust and then jumped out quite unexpectedly from some other corner; he swung on a rope which hung from a wall until at last she forgot her misery and joined in the fun. Eventually they both tired and Jonty led her up some steps to a warm and dark hayloft, where they sat on a bale and looked down through the open doorway.

Jonty put his hand into his pocket and pulled out a soft sweet biscuit and offered it to her. Eagerly she took it, for she had not been given breakfast but had been handed over to the woman whose sour breasts she had scorned.

'Jonty! Where is my mama?' She sucked on the biscuit to make it last. 'Mrs Pincher took her away.'

Jonty looked startled, a flush came to his cheek and he bowed his head. She bent her own head to look him in the eyes. 'Why are you doing that? Are you hiding?'

He nodded but didn't answer. 'Tell me, where is my mama?' she said querulously, tears beginning to fall.

Jonty mumbled something she couldn't understand and then pointed down to the gate. Mr Pincher was opening it to allow the entry of a cart. Not the cart they had had a ride in last night, when the old man had stopped at her mother's entreaty to help them for pity's sake, but a larger cart painted black and with a plain wooden box in the back.

Jonty gazed out at the cart for a moment and then impulsively got up and closed the door, leaving them in semi-darkness. Even though he had seen hundreds of coffins leaving the workhouse it was still a desolate sight. Rarely were there any mourners to accompany them on their journey to the paupers' graveyard, unlike the ceremonial processions he had seen of other funerals of worthy citizens of this town, when plumed black horses pulled shiny carriages and mourners dressed in fine black clothes followed the top-hatted mutes to church. No, this was not the way for Polly Anna to remember her mother on her last journey.

Polly Anna licked the crumbs from her fingers.

'I'm hungry,' she groused. 'Mama and I went on a long walk and had nothing to eat. We went to see grandmother, only she wasn't there. Only Aunt Wena was there and she wouldn't let us in, even though mama begged her. She said', she hesitated, wrinkling her forehead, 'that mama had to lie on her bed!'

Jonty deliberated, it was hours before dinner-time. Today was Wednesday so it would be a bowl of soup and one slice of bread; he had had his breakfast of bread and milk and had managed to steal a sausage from the larder when he had helped to clear away the dishes. There had been five sausages on the plate and he reckoned that one wouldn't be missed, but could he get back into the kitchen to steal another?

He jabbed his finger at the bale of straw, indicating that Polly Anna should stay there; he then pointed at himself, then the door and put his finger to his lips. Polly Anna giggled, put her thumb in her mouth and curled up on the straw. He slipped out of the loft, closing the door behind him, and down the steps and across the yard as the cart and coffin trundled out into the street.

There was an empty pail outside the kitchen door and he picked it up and carried it out to the back yard and half-filled it with fresh water from the pump. It didn't do to look idle or otherwise a job would be found for him. He carried it back to the kitchen, taking care not to slosh water on the floor, and handed it to the cook, who looked at him in some surprise.

'Well, tha's a marvel, Jonty. Not as daft as tha looks. I was just going to send Billy out to 'pump.

Now then, fetch them 'taties from 'sack and start scrubbing.'

The sacks of potatoes were stacked beneath the shelves near the back door; on the shelves were boxes of carrots and swedes, most of which were black spotted and sprouting in the damp kitchen. Jonty surreptitiously slid a carrot into his pocket and hastily looking round to see if Cook was looking in his direction, he pushed over a sack and scattered potatoes all over the floor.

'Blockhead! What's tha doing? Just look at 'floor!' Cook shrieked at him as he stood in mock terror in front of her. 'Go fetch a broom and clean it up. Look sharp, dummy, I haven't got all day! Billy, fetch them spuds here and start scrubbing.'

As the cook supervised Billy and the potatoes, Jonty rushed to fetch a broom which was leaning near the larder door. He slipped into the larder, brushed away the flies and as his hand was closing over a sausage, he was gripped firmly by the scruff of his neck.

'I thought tha was up to summat.' Cook nodded her big head, keeping her hand on his collar and pulling on the short hairs on the back of his neck. 'Coming in here pretending to be helpful,' she sneered. ''Matron's little toady. Well, tha doesn't fool me.'

The kitchen door swung open and Mrs Pincher appeared. She seemed to have a knack of turning up whenever there was any sort of trouble. 'He's been caught thieving, Matron,' Cook blurted out before Jonty could draw breath. 'Caught him pinching sausages.'

'Sausages! How come there's sausages?' Mrs

Pincher demanded. 'Today's Wednesday. There's no meat Monday, Tuesday or Wednesday. Sunday was meat day!'

Cook flushed and Jonty felt a moment of triumph. She had kept the sausages back for herself, taking them from the mouths of the paupers, whose stomachs rumbled with hunger even after they had eaten.

'There was just a few left over,' she mumbled. 'I was going to put them in 'broth at dinnertime.'

Mrs Pincher peered into the larder. 'Two sausages?' she said. 'They won't make any taste at all. Put them on a plate and Mr Pincher and me'll have 'em for us dinner.'

Two sausages! There had been four left this morning. Jonty glanced across at Billy, who looked uneasy. Then he flinched from a blow across his head as Mrs Pincher clouted him. 'Don't let me catch you thieving again or you'll go without any dinner for a week. Now come with me, I want you to run into town.'

Thankful to have escaped so lightly from the cook's clutches, he followed Mrs Pincher out of the kitchen, down a corridor and into a small room which served as the office. A fire was burning low in the grate and he bent to put on more wood from the wood basket. As he straightened up he glanced at Mrs Pincher, who was taking a bite from one of the sausages. She screwed up her mouth as she chewed and then took another smaller bite. 'They're off!' She stuck her nose against it and sniffed. 'Rancid, I'd say.'

Jonty stared at the remaining sausage on the plate and licked his lips. No worse than the one he had eaten this morning. He had never tasted fresh meat and what came on the plate on a Sunday and Thursday was mostly fat and gristle which he couldn't chew anyway. Still it was food, and that was why so many people queued outside begging to be admitted; starvation was outside the gate of the workhouse for those who had no other means.

'I want you to run to 'butchers' shambles and ask for Mr Fox. Get him personally, on his own; he knows you doesn't he?'

Jonty nodded. He had been sent on numerous errands to Mr Fox, always with a note, for he couldn't make the butcher understand what he said, but Mrs Pincher didn't know that he could read most of what was written on the message and it was nearly always, 'a nice bit o' mutton', or 'a fresh kidney and piece of beef steak'. And often written at the bottom, 'I'll see you right.'

Money never changed hands as far as he knew, but Mr Fox had the contract to supply the meat to the workhouse and therefore, Jonty supposed, he would want to look after Mr and Mrs Pincher.

Today as he loped across the town, the note read, 'a nice meat pye, a piece o' bacon and a string of pork sausages'. It was written in pencil with a dull stub so that the writing wasn't clear. Jonty slipped down an alleyway and perused it. It would be easy enough to alter, except that he hadn't a pencil. He glanced around the alleyway, no pencils lying around here, only rubbish and dust and soot from the chimneys.

He scoured the debris with the toe of his boot, then bent to retrieve a thin sliver of twig. He peeled off the bark and dug his fingernails into the pappy stem to split it and make it narrower. Then salivating as hard as he could he spat several times into the dust, stirring it with the twig to make a viscous paste. He spread the note out on the wall and shaking off the excess mud from the twig he carefully altered the note to read, '2 nice meat pyes, a piece o' bacon and a string of pork sausages', and crumpled it up and put it in his pocket.

'Here! Where's this been? Dirty little toad! What 'you got in your pocket?' Mr Fox handled the crumpled scrap of paper with distaste.

Jonty pulled out the lining of his pockets to show they were empty and then mumbled long and incomprehensibly, though mentioning Mrs Pincher's name several times, just to confuse the man.

'Yes, yes. Jabber, jabber, jabber! Shut your face while I get this order. Don't know why she uses you when nobody can understand a word you say!'

'Cos I can't tell, thought Jonty as he waited for the parcel. That's why. He watched as the butcher cut a thick joint of bacon and curled up the string of sausages, and waited anxiously as he peered again at the note. 'Two meat pies? Is she expecting company?'

Jonty didn't answer, he wouldn't be expected to know of Mr or Mrs Pincher's social activities, though he often knew when the vagrant officer called and had a spot of supper with them, or when one of the guardians came unexpectedly and Mrs Pincher would bring out the cake tin. He saw much of who came and went from his corner by the gate or his bed in the straw.

'There you are, me lad. Carry it careful and don't

spill gravy out of them pies.' Mr Fox placed two bags in Jonty's hands, one with the sausages and bacon, and another with the warm pies, which shed a rich aroma making Jonty's mouth water.

He ran as fast as he could back towards the workhouse and heard jeers and laughter following him as he darted in and out of the crowds in the Market Place. His gait was lopsided and peculiar, but he could run faster than anyone else he knew. He slipped quietly through the gate; there were a few people hanging around in the yard, but no-one took any notice of him as he ran up the stairs to the hay store.

Polly Anna was still curled up on the straw bale where he had left her, but in a deep sleep. He took one of the meat pies from the bag and licking the spilt gravy from his fingers he climbed up on the bales and reached to put it up on a rafter. There was a risk the mice would find it, but it was away from prying eyes should anyone come up, and he went out again in search of Mrs Pincher.

'Didn't see anybody, did you?' Mrs Pincher took the bags from him. 'Not one of 'governors or anybody?' she questioned.

Jonty put on a vacant look and shook his head and looked longingly across the table, where the sausage still lay on its plate.

'Go on then, tek it,' Mrs Pincher consented generously. 'Mr Pincher won't want it if it's off.'

Polly Anna was still sleeping as he climbed up on the bale beside her. He stretched out on the straw and putting his arms above his head gave a sigh of satisfaction. Not a bad sort of morning, he mused, with an unfamiliar contentment running through him, as he realized that his actions had been entirely for the sake of someone else. He might well have taken the risk of pilfering a meat pie for himself, but it was much more gratifying, he decided, to know that little Polly Anna would not go hungry today.

3

The small boy wriggled his fingers as his nurse clutched tighter to his hand. 'Keep close by me, Master Richard,' she said. 'Yon Gypsies are allus on look out for bonny bairns like thee.'

'Why would they do that, Jinny?' He tipped up his fair head to look at her. 'They seem to have plenty of children of their own.'

'Never mind why,' she said sharply. 'Everybody knows that they do, that's all, so stay close by me or tha might never see home again.'

He looked across at the group of Gypsies gathered in an encampment just outside the fairground area. Their faces were very dark and to him they didn't look very clean, but that, he thought, was probably because they were always crouched over smoky fires, cooking their sausages or stews. The idea of not washing and cooking over an open fire appealed to him greatly. He didn't enjoy having to be bathed and dressed in clean clothes, which as soon as they were in the least soiled must be changed again before he could be presented to his mama and papa.

'St Bartholomew Fair must be the biggest fair in the whole world, Jinny,' he said as they walked amongst the crowded stalls and the glittering booths and hovered over the hot gingerbread and cheap sweets.

She pulled him away. 'Hmph. They say it's t'biggest in England, but tha should see Hull Fair! There's nowt to beat it, and I'll be bound it'll be still there when St Bartlemey's long gone. Why, when I was a young lass—'

He smiled and listened to her prattling away. He loved to hear her talk in her strange northern accent of the fair which she remembered from her youth, of the barges which came up the river to bring the booths and dancing saloons, of the circus and menageries, of tightrope walkers and clowns. No matter that they had them all here too at St Bartholomew's, in Jinny's eyes there was no better fair than Hull Fair.

'Perhaps Aunt Mary and Uncle Charles will have news of the fair, Jinny, when they arrive for their visit and will tell you about it.'

'Oh.' The nurse suddenly remembered her errand. To keep Master Richard occupied whilst his mother's older sister and her husband arrived from Yorkshire on a visit. Richard would be joining them for supper. It was considered that he was now old enough at seven years old to eat with his elders. 'Aye, we must be getting back. They'll have arrived by now. It'll soon be getting dark and Mistress will be anxious.'

'She'll think we've gone off with the Gypsies, Jinny,' he joked, but Jinny was cross and chastised him for such a remark and made him promise that he wouldn't ever repeat such a thing, especially not in front of his aunt and uncle.

He was very fond of his Aunt Mary, though a trifle in awe of Uncle Charles, and always enjoyed their visits. After supper he played on the rug in front of the fire with the farm animals that his aunt had brought him and knew if he kept quiet and didn't interrupt their conversation then he wouldn't be sent upstairs. So he arranged the sheep in their folds and placed the cattle in groups and jumped the horses over the fences and idly listened to the talk of farming and the price of wool, and wished that he could live in the country and play in the fields and have his own horse now rather than waiting until he was older, and then only riding in the park.

I could live like the Gypsies, he thought, and make a fire and cook sausages over it and never get washed; and as he mused over the idea, the conversation of his elders passed him by as they spoke in whispers of an unresolved 'great scandal' and 'such a waste' and of a beautiful young woman who had run away from home. His eyes started to close as the lateness of the hour and the warmth of the fire made him sleepy, and as one of the footmen carried him up to bed he dreamt he was whirling on a roundabout which was being pushed by a group of Gypsy children with black hair and dirty faces.

4

Jonty found Billy standing in a corner outside the dining room, his face pale and set as he watched others shuffling in for their bowl of soup and bread. His mouth turned down as he saw Jonty, who with Polly Anna by his side joined the queue at the door.

'What's up?' Jonty mumbled as he passed him.

'Cook said I couldn't have no dinner on account of them missing sausages and I have to stand here and watch 'others go in.' His mouth trembled as he spoke and his eyes filled with tears. 'It's thy fault. She'd not have known but for thee!'

Jonty felt a pang of conscience, though he wondered why he did so. Billy, after all, must have eaten well on two sausages, whilst he had had only one. But nevertheless his own hunger was blunted for he and Polly Anna had shared the meat pie, he had given her a larger half with almost all of the meat, whilst he had had the pastry with the gravy. He had sucked on a piece of meat all the morning until all the taste was gone and then had spat it out. Polly Anna had also eaten the carrot, but didn't want the sausage. She had pulled a face and said it was nasty. He didn't want it either and had put it back in his pocket. When they heard the dinner bell ringing he had insisted, as best he could, that she should eat what was offered to her; on no account should she refuse it but if necessary put the bread inside her dress to save until later.

He supped his thin soup and nibbled a small amount of bread, and then slipped the remainder up his sleeve and felt the silk bag which Polly Anna's mother had given to him, still nestling there. Polly Anna, he noticed, as she sat with the other small children on another table, was tucking into her bread and soup, though pulling a wry expression as she did so. He discerned the difference between her plump cheeks and the faces of the other children who sat beside her. Rarely did people who entered the workhouse look as well as she did; most were gaunt and thin and suffering from disease. She still had the smooth skin of infancy and had yet to acquire the grey workhouse pallor and she still looked clean and neat in her own velvet dress and petticoats.

Billy had gone from his place when Jonty came out and neither did he find Polly Anna again until suppertime. He didn't recognize her at first as her back was turned from him as she queued to go in for her bowl of bread and milk. Then he saw her head of short dark curly hair and realized that she had now been given the regulation dress of the workhouse.

All the little girls wore blue serge dresses and cotton aprons with black boots upon their feet; as they got older they were given heavy coarse aprons to protect their clothing while they did their everyday tasks. The boys wore rough breeches which scratched their legs and made them sore, and striped shirts, or sometimes thick white cotton ones if the governors were inspecting.

Polly Anna was holding the hand of another small girl, one with fair hair and a pale face and a racking cough which Jonty could hear from the other end of the corridor, and he saw her put her arm around the little girl and pat her on the back. Mrs Pincher marched by and Polly Anna jumped out of her place and approached her. He couldn't hear what she said, but everyone peered forward in curiosity, for no-one spoke to Matron unless requested to do so in answer to a question.

Mrs Pincher looked startled for a moment and raised her eyebrows, then peremptorily pushed Polly Anna back into her place. After supper they passed their empty bowls down the wooden tables and in some trepidation gazed silently as Mrs Pincher mounted the platform at the end of the room and, raising her voice, ordered them to sit still and not move from their places. As if pre-arranged, one of the women paupers sought out Polly Anna and taking her roughly by the arm escorted her up to the platform, where she pushed her in front of the matron.

'Turn around, girl, so that everyone can see your face and know you,' Mrs Pincher boomed.

Polly Anna did so and Jonty felt a sickly apprehension in his stomach. Had she told about the pie?

'This child!' Mrs Pincher put her hand roughly on Polly Anna's head. 'This child would like to be matron here!' There was a buzz of nervous laughter. 'Isn't that so?' she said, looking down at her.

Polly Anna stuck out a trembling bottom lip, but said nothing.

'She thinks she knows better than Matron or Master!' Mrs Pincher observed them all with narrowed eyes and there was an impressive gasp of astonishment that anyone should have such temerity. 'Better, even, than the doctor who calls so regularly, or the nurse who tends the sick in the infirmary.'

Polly Anna looked bewildered as if she didn't know what she was talking about and suddenly cried out, 'I want my mama!'

There was a great hoot of laughter and voices cried out mockingly, 'She wants her mama. She wants her mama,' and Jonty watched the jeering faces and longed to rescue poor Polly Anna from the indignity of the ridicule.

'That's enough,' Mrs Pincher bellowed after letting them have their fun for a moment. 'This child,' she looked down again at Polly Anna and a frown passed over her face, 'this – young Gypsy – had the temerity to tell me that another child needed medicine for her cough.'

The bewilderment cleared from Polly Anna's face and she piped, 'But—'

'Quiet! What are the rules of this establishment?' Matron demanded of the rest. 'Only speak when—?'

'Spoken to,' everyone chorused.

'Quite right,' she said resolutely. 'We cannot have everyone speaking their minds all of the time. If something needs to be attended to,' Master or me will do it. That is why we are here. To take care of you. This we do', she added pompously, 'out of 'goodness and charity of our hearts.'

She folded her arms across her ample chest and gazed at the upturned faces, awaiting their nods of approval and having received them she dismissed them back to their work or duties. Polly Anna turned to go too, but was held back by Mrs Pincher's firm grip. 'Not you, my girl, you come with me until I decide on what to do with you. You must learn 'rules, young as you are, or you'll grow up to be a delinquent.'

Jonty watched them go, Polly Anna being urged on by Mrs Pincher. He knew where she was being taken, where all children who misbehaved were taken until their punishment was decided, where he had been confined quite often. To the Black Box. The small dark room, not much more than a cupboard, at the far end of the building where the only door opened out into the rear yard.

This yard, confined by high walls, was much larger than the one at the front and was a place where the inmates of the workhouse took their exercise, where they could stretch their limbs and breathe in the air, which was marginally fresher than the putrid stench inside the building.

The main concern of the children who were locked up in the Black Box was not the darkness or the beetles or mice which scuttled about, for they were quite used to those in their everyday existence, but the fear that they would be forgotten: for instance, if it was raining or snowing, when few people would venture out for their sport but would stay indoors in the damp and leaking building and therefore wouldn't hear their cries.

Jonty had once spent three days in the Black Box when the Master had put him there, and who then went about some business or other and forgot to inform anyone that Jonty was there. Some of the other children had looked through a hole in the door and laughed and mimicked his cries and called to others to come and look at the monkey in the cage. Only one boy, who had since died, had commiserated with him, but dared not tell anyone in view of the rule of only speaking when spoken to, in case he too should be given the same punishment.

Jonty followed the matron and Polly Anna, who was being prodded along in front of Mrs Pincher as she marched down the building, passing the work rooms, the sewing room, the infirmary and the oakum room, where the only window was boarded up and the door was kept open to let out the stench of sweating bodies and old rope and tar and to let in some little air, for the room was filled to capacity with men, women and children bent to their tasks.

He ran out of the door and into the yard and whilst Mrs Pincher's back was turned he hid behind a barrel as she fumbled in her pocket for the large iron key.

She unlocked the door of the cupboard and Billy fell out, blinking in the light. 'Who put you in there?' she demanded. 'What crime did you commit?'

'Cook, ma'am. 'Cos of them sausages that I took.' Billy's fawning expression implied that he would have kissed Matron's feet if necessary, in order to reduce his punishment; but as this appeal would have resulted in a blow from those same leather-encased feet, he put on his most engaging look, which was quite lost on Mrs Pincher as she pondered his spotty face and her predicament. There wasn't room for two in the cupboard. Besides, solitude was essential for miscreants to ponder on their misdeeds, to bring them to their senses and ensure their future behaviour and subordination.

'Come on out, and no dinner tomorrow!'

'I had no dinner today, Matron, nor any supper yesterday!' Billy ventured and licked his dry lips.

'A slice of bread tomorrow, but no meat. Tell Cook I said so.'

Grateful for such magnanimity, Billy slunk away and Jonty, in hiding, vowed that he would give him the sausage which was still in his pocket, gathering up bits of fluff and dust but edible nevertheless.

Polly Anna cried and kicked at Mrs Pincher as she forced her into the cupboard, but only succeeded in increasing her anger. 'I'll show thee tha young peazan, who's in charge here. Make no mistake about it, it's me!' She locked the door and marched off muttering about 'bairns knowing better than their elders', passing Jonty by inches and slamming the door behind her as she went back inside the building.

Jonty waited a moment and then ran across the yard to the cupboard, where Polly Anna was banging on the door as hard as she could with her small fists. 'Don't cry! Don't cry!' he said, and tried to tell her that Matron wouldn't leave her for long in the Black Box, she never did with the small children, maybe only an hour or so, just to frighten them and make them obedient, but his words were jumbled and distorted and as he stared through the keyhole he could see Polly Anna's eyes were wide and frightened.

'I want to come out,' she wept. 'Jonty, tell her to let me out!'

'Sit down, sit down,' he urged. 'She come soon. She come soon.' He sat down next to the door and gently tapped it to let her know that he was still there, and eventually her sobs decreased, though she still snuffled, and she replied by tapping back from her side of the door. He looked around the yard and amongst the dust and litter he saw a feral pigeon feather, the quill sharp and pearly white, the feather pale grey. He picked it up and smoothed its softness with his fingers.

'Polly Anna,' he whispered, though it sounded to his ears nothing like her name. 'A present!' There was a crack in the wooden door, not wide enough for his finger but wide enough to force the quill through. Polly Anna took hold of it and held it and Jonty held the feather, and the contact quivered through as if the children were holding hands and so they stayed until Mrs Pincher returned to release them.

'I hate her, I hate her.' Polly Anna screwed up her face as she sat in the comfort of the hayloft. 'I'll tell my papa—' She hesitated, then shook her head. 'Only I don't know where he is, Mama said he was lost.' She started to cry. 'I don't want to stay here. I want my mama.'

Jonty was at a loss to know what to do. He had entertained her as best he could, he'd fed her on biscuits which he had stolen from Mrs Pincher's cupboard, and still she was unhappy; bliss as far as he was concerned was in having enough to eat, it was in avoiding the strap or a beating, it was the comfort of the hayloft, which he regarded as his private domain, and, he mused thoughtfully, it was in having his lessons with Samuel, which he had missed since Polly Anna's arrival.

Perhaps, he thought, I could show Polly Anna how to do numbers and letters, though I don't know them all. He reached up to the beam which was his own private place for keeping his treasures – a length of string, a small knife, a stub of pencil, a ribbon which he had found out in the street, and a pack of playing cards which Samuel had given him.

'Let's pretend it's your birthday, Jonty,' his friend had said when he gave them to him and Jonty had received them with such delight. Never in his life had he been given a present and he didn't know when it was his birthday, although each year Mrs Pincher had remarked to him, 'Now you are six', and then, 'Now you are seven', and he knew each time she made the remark that more was expected of him in the way of work and responsibilities, and soon when he was eight, he would be expected to pick oakum along with all the others.

He opened up the box and shuffled the cards. They were pretty cards, some with pictures of kings and queens, others with a joker wearing a funny hat and carrying a stick with a bell on it. He wondered if the king portrayed was the old King George who had died that summer or the new King William IV. He had asked Samuel, who said it could be either for there was no difference between them, but that

43

the joker was certainly the Duke of Wellington. Then he raised his tin mug of water and said, 'God bless them all and their kin', but in such a manner that Jonty felt that he didn't really mean it.

Jonty pulled out the eight of hearts and started to count aloud; he was not so shy of speaking to Polly Anna now, some of her speech was babyish and she couldn't pronounce all of her words, which made him feel very superior, for although he couldn't say them himself he knew whether they were right or wrong.

'Seven – eight,' he counted.

'I can count up to twenty,' she said and took the pack from him. 'Listen.' She started to count the cards and reached twenty, but then became distracted by the pictures on the cards and exclaimed about the pretty lady and the funny man. 'My mama taught me to count and I know some of my letters,' she said. 'I would show you, Jonty, but I haven't a book. I left it behind in our little house.' Her expression became vague. 'When I go home again I will show it to you.'

They hadn't heard the foot on the stair and so both were startled as the door was pulled open and the Master, Mr Pincher, stood there, his face red from the exertion of climbing the steep stairs and angry at finding two children there. 'You.' He pointed a finger at Jonty. 'I might have known I'd find you skulking here. And why is that child here? Who is she? Is she an orphan?'

He saw the cards in Polly Anna's hands and snatched them from her. 'Where did you get these? Did you steal them?'

Polly Anna burst into tears and Jonty put his arm

44

around her. 'Mine, mine,' he spluttered. 'Mine, not hers!'

'And where did you get them? Stole them, I don't doubt, whilst you're off on Matron's errands.'

Jonty shook his head furiously. Whatever he said wouldn't be believed or understood, and he couldn't tell that Samuel gave them to him, in case he had stolen them himself. The Black Box loomed in front of him and he stood up at the Master's orders, pulling on Polly Anna's arm to make her do the same.

They were marched down the stairs and across the yard and into the building and as they pushed their way through the crowd in the corridor, he saw Billy and remembered the sausage in his pocket. Should he now keep it for he would surely miss several dinners or should he give it to Billy as he had thought he would? Billy looked pale and miserable, a yellowish tinge to his skin, and on impulse Jonty thrust his hand into his pocket and as he passed Billy he slipped the mouldering sausage into his hand.

5

It was a pity, Mrs Pincher thought. I especially needed him today. There were several messages I wanted him to run. One to the doctor, who hadn't been in for several days. Another to Mr Fox and another to her favourite governor to warn him of some trouble which was expected. Still, if Mr Pincher says he has been thieving! Yet she was surprised to find Jonty had been stealing anything but food. I've never yet caught him thieving, though Cook said he'd pinched them sausages and I know my biscuit tin empties itself very quickly when he's around.

Though she suspected that Jonty was light fingered as far as her biscuit tin was concerned, she was quite prepared to turn a blind eye to such a small misdemeanour and in any case the biscuits were always stale: she didn't keep her best biscuits or cakes where anyone but herself could get at them; those were locked away in a cupboard and she had the only key. No, the stale biscuits were kept for the visitors or the more vigilant governors, who might complain that she and Mr Pincher ate better than the inmates of the workhouse, which was of course quite untrue.

'Better put him in 'cupboard, Mr Pincher,' she decided, 'and leave 'girl wi' me. She's obviously going to grow up to be wicked, hiding away in a loft with a – person – er, with a person who is not female like herself. She'll tread a downward path, just see if she don't.' Mrs Pincher bridled. 'I've seen young women who have started off seemingly innocent and we can see 'results every time we open 'front gate.'

'She's onny a bairn, Mrs Pincher.' Her husband fondled the top of Polly Anna's head and she shied away from his touch. 'He's 'blackguard who 'ticed her up there. Up to no good, I allus said he was. You've spoilt him,' he added maliciously, 'letting him run all over 'town. Who knows what he gets up to when he's outside our doors.'

Mrs Pincher narrowed her eyes as she gazed at her husband and thought him a fool. She knew what *he* got up to when he went into the town. What did it matter if the boy stole a piece of fruit from the market stalls, everybody did; but he wasn't yet old enough to visit the whorehouse as Mr Pincher did, nor would he ever, she surmised, for what woman would have a pauper dummy with a twisted body and no money in his pocket?

'Give me them cards,' she snapped. 'I'll find out if he stole 'em.' She took them from her husband's reluctant hand and put them on the mantelpiece and inclined her head to tell them to go. 'And no supper for him,' she shouted after them, suddenly regretting her compassionate concern for Jonty. 'Not till I find out where they belong.'

'Right, my girl. You come with me.' She marched Polly Anna out of the room and down the corridor towards the sewing room. 'We'll find you a job to do that'll keep you out of mischief. Letty!' she bellowed. 'Come here!'

The sewing room was filled with long wooden tables and benches, which were piled high with mounds of fustian sheets and shirt material. Baskets of blue serge were stacked against the damp walls and standing or sitting at every bench were women and young girls all bent over their sewing.

A thin woman with grey matted hair scurried towards them. She was wearing two threadbare coats over her thin dress, a felt hat on her head and odd boots on her feet, the same woman who had hauled Polly Anna up to the platform. She bobbed her head respectfully to the matron and looked down at Polly Anna with disapproval. 'Tha's never going to ask me to tek this bairn on, Matron? This is 'one who caused trouble afore if I'm not mistaken?'

Mrs Pincher nodded. 'Aye, she was 'one who asked for medicine for 'other little lass. She's not yet learnt 'error of her ways; she needs a firm hand. See to it, will you!'

She handed Polly Anna unceremoniously over to the woman, who took her to one of the tables, sat her on a high stool and put a piece of white cotton in one hand and a needle and thread in the other. She knotted one end of the thread and, turning over a narrow hem, pushed the needle in and out of the cloth. 'Now then,' she said roughly. 'Let's see thee do it.'

*   *   *

Mrs Pincher looked in the mirror and adjusted her bonnet; she put a dark brown cloak over her shoulders and a basket over her arm, locked the office door and sallied forth out of the gate and into the town.

The Hull workhouse, because of its situation in Whitefriargate in the centre of the town, was the cause of much controversy. Complaints were numerous: of the stench which drifted out from it, of the paupers who wandered in and out, of the wretches who slept all night on its doorstep waiting to be admitted, and of the disease, which the affluent neighbours in Parliament Street who had unfortunately to live next to it stated adamantly emanated from its walls.

The Board of Governors was constantly locked in battle, for although all agreed that the old building was in a terrible state of repair (it had previously been Charity Hall and had had additions and extensions put to it over the years), some of the Board were reluctant to spend more money on it, when, they said, it should be pulled down and a new workhouse built; whilst others complained that it was inhuman to expect poor people to live under such disgraceful conditions even when there was no likelihood of another ever being built.

Mrs Pincher walked the length of the Market Place, picking her way through the debris of fruit and rotting vegetables which lay in her path, and knocked on the door of a house in Queen Street. Mrs Pincher gave her name to the maid who answered and asked if Mr Grant was at home. She was shown into a small study at the front of the house, where she waited for Mr Grant to appear.

He came through a few minutes later, a small, portly man who rubbed his hands together and greeted her effusively. 'My dear Mrs Pincher! Such a pleasure. Such a pleasure. Shall I send for tea?'

'That would be very nice, Mr Grant, thank you. Tea would be most acceptable, it is such a grey, miserable day; we shall have a long winter I fear.'

'Indeed, indeed,' he replied solemnly. 'And pity the poor wretches who live out in it and don't have such comfort as you – and Mr Pincher, of course – can give them.'

The pleasantries over and the tea and cakes brought in – and, Mrs Pincher observed, the tea was far superior to the one enjoyed at the workhouse – she settled down to explain the purpose of her visit. She leaned forward confidentially. 'Trouble, I'm afraid, Mr Grant!'

'Oh!' His eyebrows shot up into his high domed forehead. 'What kind of trouble, Mrs Pincher?'

She pursed her lips and took a sip from her cup. 'Mrs Harmsworth,' she whispered. 'She's been noseying around again, came in one day when Mr Pincher and me were both out. Such liberty,' she complained, leaning over to select a cake, 'without so much as a do you mind, she just walked in and pottered about – had her second-best clothes on, I'll be bound, so nobody questioned her. And', she added, 'she came on a wet day when everybody was inside and not out in 'yard.'

'So what was her complaint, Mrs Pincher? Surely no complaint against you?' He appeared horrified at the notion.

'Not exactly.' Mrs Pincher daintily wiped her mouth with an embroidered napkin, then placed it on her knee, where if she moved but slightly it would fall into her basket. 'Though she complained to Mr Bertram that there didn't appear to be any preparation for dinner. Cook had gone off somewhere', she added, 'and was late back. But what she did say was, that she was going to write to 'newspapers, yet again.' She sniffed. 'To complain of 'overcrowding and of 'men, women and children being herded together like animals in a pen. Her words, Mr Grant,' she said caustically. 'Not mine.'

Mr Grant took a breath. 'And, as I said to her,' she continued, 'that's got nothing to do with me. I don't control 'numbers who come in, it's 'Board of Governors who do that, I turn away as many as I can from 'gate, but still they keep on coming.'

'Well, I'm pleased that you saw fit to advise me, Mrs Pincher. At least I shall be prepared, for if there is one letter to the papers then a flood will follow. It is a very sorry state of affairs, but what can we do? Residents of the town are reluctant to pay any more rates so where will the money come from for these persons? How many inmates at the last count?' he asked. 'A rough guess, I mean?'

'Around three hundred,' she said, helping herself to another cake. 'Give or take fifteen or twenty, including infants and lunatics.'

'Mm,' he pondered, and then asked the question which was foremost in his mind. 'And the catering side? That is running smoothly I trust, everyone getting enough to eat?'

'Indeed, indeed.' She gave him a small smile. She didn't handle the bills as Mr Grant did. She simply advised the Board as to which butcher, grocer or potato merchant they should choose and as Mr

Grant was in charge of the catering accounts he generally took her advice; if these same merchants failed in some instances to supply the workhouse with the quality paid for, then they more than made up for it when handing over parcels to Mrs Pincher and Governor Grant.

''Course they don't need a great deal of food when they are sheltered and under cover,' she said, 'and they fare better inside 'workhouse than outside it. There were two bairns at 'gate this morning begging for food – walked from Beverley, they said, to look for work, onny there wasn't any. Anyway, I packed them off back to Beverley. Can't have 'em taking bread from Hull folks' mouths or I should never hear 'end of it from 'Board.

'Well, I must be off.' She brushed her skirt of crumbs and whisked the napkin into her basket. 'I have to see Mr Fox about next week's meat. I wondered, Mr Grant, if you might like to invite Mrs Harmsworth for a spot of dinner at 'workhouse, so's she can see how well we feed our inmates?'

'What an excellent idea, dear lady! I'll wait for her protest to the newspaper though, and then issue the invitation through their pages. Excellent! Excellent!'

He showed her to the door and as she was about to depart, said, 'If you have anything more to impart perhaps you would send the young mute with a message, he seems a most reliable lad. It will save you the trouble.' And it wouldn't appear that they were conniving in any way, he mused, for the messages were always burnt after he had read them.

She nodded. 'He's otherwise engaged, Mr Grant, or I should have sent him today.'

He patted her hand. 'But then we should have missed the pleasure of a chat, Mrs Pincher, which was most enjoyable, most enjoyable!'

He closed the door behind her, took out his pocket handkerchief and wiped his brow. Mrs Harmsworth, that most redoubtable campaigner for the rights of the poor, had partaken of an agreeable supper with himself and Mrs Grant only last week and had particularly praised the excellence of the leg of mutton which had been served. Now, he pondered, had her remark been double-edged and had her expression been inscrutable when she had asked Mrs Grant who was her most excellent butcher and Mrs Grant, in all innocence, had said that it was Mr Fox?

Mrs Harmsworth, in her letter to the newspaper, had not complained of the quality of the food in the workhouse, but only commented that there didn't seem to be any, at least not when she was there; what she did complain of was the overcrowding of persons in the building, which, being two hundred years old was not meant to accommodate so many people, especially when some were of the criminal class, some were insane, some were ill, some were old and some were women of ill repute, whilst the rest were young and innocent and likely to follow the path of those with whom they shared their bread and bed.

'In short,' she proclaimed, 'though the governors are worthy men and of good intent, something more must be done and quickly to alleviate the distress of these poor people.'

Whilst agreeing with all that she said, the governors said that their hands were tied. They did their best, yet what was needed was a new workhouse with separate accommodation for the insane and an infirmary for the sick of the town, for the Hull Infirmary would not take paupers, or cholera or typhus victims, all of whom came to the workhouse sick ward, which swelled the numbers even more whenever there was an epidemic.

Mrs Harmsworth came to dinner as invited, though she refused to eat the mutton on her plate, even though it was pink and tender, and ate only soup and dry bread like the inmates, for she had discovered that today was a meatless day and said that she would like to see one of the children eat it instead of her.

Mrs Pincher was thrown into a quandary as to which child she would send for to eat the delicacy, until she thought of Jonty. He had spent several days in the Black Box and bread and water had been sent in to him once a day, except one day when she had told Cook, who had forgotten, but no harm had come for he had spent the time sleeping.

He had been released this morning and had had his bread and milk for breakfast; and as Mrs Pincher explained to Mrs Harmsworth that as everyone had just partaken of soup and bread for their dinner, it was doubtful if anyone could eat any more; she also knew, which Mrs Harmsworth didn't, that with the cleft in his palate Jonty couldn't possibly chew the meat.

He stood in front of them now, Matron and Master, Mr Grant, Mr Blake, who was another guardian, and Mrs Harmsworth; he blinked with tiredness, his face pale though clean, for when summoned to come he was told to wash first under the pump.

'What is your name, child?' Mrs Harmsworth's voice was firm and clear. 'Don't be afraid, you are not in any trouble.'

'He doesn't speak much,' Mr Grant interrupted, anxious to indicate that he knew the inmates personally. 'He's a mute.'

Jonty turned to look at Mr Grant and then at Mrs Pincher and seeing her nod her head, mumbled, 'Jonty.'

'But not deaf!' Mrs Harmsworth said firmly. 'Come here, Jonty, and stand by me. Are you hungry?'

Jonty shook his head, much to everyone else's satisfaction and Mrs Harmsworth's surprise. He wasn't hungry; he had gone past hunger, though a few days ago he could have killed and eaten the rat that had shared his abode. But today he had been given breakfast and dinner and his distended stomach had grumbled. He eyed the slices of pale meat with its pink middle on the plate near him and felt nauseous. He knew what it was, it was a dead sheep like the ones he had seen in Mr Fox's shop. The meat he pushed around his dish twice a week, grey and greasy and floating in thin stew, looked nothing like this.

'Would you like to eat some meat, Jonty? There is enough left for you.' Mrs Harmsworth pointed to the plate and he shook his head again. She grew impatient. 'Is he sick? He's very pale.'

'Are you sick, Jonty?' Mrs Pincher asked. 'Do you need some medicine?'

No fear, he wanted to say. I've seen what goes into it. Stuff that makes you sleep for a week, the lunatics have it all the time and the babies. Vigorously he shook his head and attempted a grin to show how well he was.

'Where was your home, Jonty?' Mrs Harmsworth asked. 'Where do you come from?'

Jonty again looked at Mrs Pincher, who beamed at him encouragingly. He had to get this right. His future livelihood depended on it. He smiled at Mrs Harmsworth and indicated with outstretched arms. 'Here,' he whooped. 'Here, my home.'

Jonty was dismissed and, being thwarted as far as diet was concerned, Mrs Harmsworth turned her attention to the sick. 'There was a child here when I came last time who was obviously very ill, yet I was told that there wasn't a bed for her in the sick ward. Such a very small child,' she said. 'An orphan so I was told – Mary Jane Thomas is her name.'

'The workhouse is filled with orphans, madam,' Guardian Blake broke in. 'That is why they are here, no-one else will take them.'

'And they're sick when they come,' added the Master, wrinkling his mouth in distaste. 'Most folk who are admitted are already diseased, it's not our fault they die here – better dying in our beds than in some alleyway.'

Mrs Harmsworth had turned a shade paler, but she pressed gamely on. 'But the children who are sick, surely a bed can be found?'

''Beds are taken by those with infectious diseases, Mrs Harmsworth,' Mrs Pincher explained patiently. ''Little girl you are talking of has got a mere cough. 'Doctor came to her only 'other day,

56

I went for him myself 'cos I was worried about her. He said to continue with 'medicine as before. He's fair run off his feet with illness in this town, but still he comes here very regular.'

Mrs Harmsworth rose to go. She knew when she was beaten and she couldn't face up to such over-whelming odds, not alone at any rate. It meant another letter to the newspapers; everyone in the town must be made aware of the conditions these people were living under. One privy for so many people. One pump in the yard. Putrid meat hanging in the kitchen with flies swarming over it, and she was not convinced that the mutton she was offered was of the same quality as that given to the inmates; as for the child she had seen, she had consumption, she was sure of it and there was no cure for that.

'But', she began again, 'if a place could be found in the country, perhaps she would fare better.'

'Country folk are coming to town, ma'am,' Mrs Pincher said. 'There's no living for 'em in pigs and geese. But perhaps you'd like to tek her?' She eyed Mrs Harmsworth frankly. 'Or you know somebody else who would. She'd be a good little worker, not for out in 'fields but maybe in a kitchen?'

Mrs Harmsworth reacted as expected. 'I couldn't possibly! I know nothing of her, and besides she's far too young to work; what is she – five, six? How preposterous!'

'Seven,' Mrs Pincher countered, 'and she'll go to 'flax mills when she's nine.'

'If she lives so long,' Mrs Harmsworth retaliated as she swept out of the door. 'I wish you good day.'

*   *   *

Jonty burrowed further into a bale of straw and gave a sudden sneeze as the chaff irritated his nostrils. He was very cold. It had rained whilst he was in the Black Box and the roof leaked. He had curled himself into a corner to avoid the drips, but the dampness had pervaded the whole cupboard and he felt chilled through. No-one had come except to bring him bread and water and he had slept most of the time out of sheer boredom. He had counted his fingers and toes and done various abstractions, he had counted the cracks in the walls and the holes in the roof and then he had remembered the piece of bread and the purse hidden up his sleeve. He had sucked on the morsel of dry bread, which gave very little sustenance, and then opened the purse.

It was a small purse, smaller than the palm of his hand and inside it was a pocket. Inside the pocket lay a scrap of white muslin and wrapped inside it a silver chain with a tiny locket attached, which had engraved on it the scrolled letters, M W.

He'd wondered where he could keep it hidden; it wouldn't be safe on the beams of the loft for if it was knocked off then he'd never find it again amongst the loose straw. He couldn't give it to Polly Anna to wear yet as someone might see it when they changed her clothes. The safest thing, he decided, was to wear it himself.

He had undone a bootlace and pulled it out of his boot, threaded it through the chain and then fastened it around his neck so that the silver chain and locket hung low on his chest. He felt around his shirt neck to ensure that the bootlace was hidden; there was no collar on the garment and as it was too big for him it hung loosely on his neck and shoulders, but he always wore the cut-down coat that Samuel had given him, so he hoped that it wouldn't be seen.

He heard a foot on the step outside and buried himself further into the straw; if it was the Master, he would be turfed out and sent back inside. The door slowly opened but he could see no-one standing there, then he heard a whisper, 'Jonty, Jonty, where are you?' He peered above the mound of straw and gave a grin as he saw Polly Anna vainly searching for him.

'Psst, psst! Here!'

She saw him and ran towards him, jumping up on to the bale. 'Oh, Jonty, I have missed you.' She flung her arms around his neck. 'They wouldn't tell me where you were and I thought you'd gone and left me. You won't, will you Jonty?' Her lip trembled.

His heart swelled with love. He would never leave her. He had made a promise to her mother that he would take care of her and he would, for ever.

'Jonty,' she said, rubbing her cheek against his, 'when can we move on? When will we leave this place?'

6

Jonty had missed seeing Billy around since he had emerged from the Black Box. He looked in all the obvious places where he might have been working, such as the kitchen and the oakum room, for Billy was a few years older than him, nine or ten perhaps, and therefore eligible to work in the hot and stuffy room; and in the coal cellar, where he could sometimes be found shovelling coal into a barrow and transferring it to one of the stoves in the building, but he was in none of these places.

Then Jonty overheard Matron and the doctor discussing the minor epidemic of dysentery which was in progress in the workhouse. 'Keep the chronically sick away from those with dysentery,' the doctor said, 'and we might be able to control it.'

'How?' replied Mrs Pincher. 'They're all in 'same room and there's onny one privy!'

The doctor shrugged. 'I can only advise, Matron. I'll speak to the Board and tell them of the situation.'

Jonty had come across dysentery before and knew that it was bound to be unpleasant; he sought out

Polly Anna and told her to make her appearance every morning in the sewing room and then slip away to meet him when she thought that no-one would miss her. She was confused and didn't understand what he meant at first, and he had to remind himself that she was only four and not schooled in the art of guile as he was at his great age.

But she learned quickly, taking her place at the sewing table next to an accommodating woman who patted her head in a motherly fashion and who shuffled up on her stool to fill the gap when Polly Anna slipped away.

Each morning they waited until the milling crowd of vagrants and paupers were let through the gate, then together they slipped out into the town. Jonty took her hand and led her through the Market Place, where he usually managed to steal an apple or a pie and they would walk to the river and sit on the Humber wall, munching their stolen victuals and watching the world's great sailing ships as they came with billowing sails towards the port of Hull.

Samuel had told Jonty of the produce which the great ships brought from other lands into the harbour, of silks and coffee, tobacco, tea and brandy, and this Jonty tried to convey in his dysfunctional voice to Polly Anna. He pointed to a fleet coming in with creaking sail. 'Whalers from Hull bringing in their catch, dozens of whales and seals.'

Polly Anna wrinkled her forehead. 'Ways and seas!' she repeated. 'What are they, Jonty?'

He shook his head and looked down, embarrassed at having to repeat it and knowing that it still wouldn't sound right; but from the corner of his eye he saw that she was looking at him so responsively and attentively that he knew she was interested, not in *how* he was speaking but in *what* he was saying, and so he continued, feeling a warm glow in the trust of this little girl.

Three days they spent out of the workhouse, wandering around the streets, looking in shop windows, investigating hidden courts and alleyways and even strolling along the bank of the River Hull towards the Greenland Yards where the whale blubber was processed, until the stench drove them back the way they had come. One night they arrived back late and found the gate to the workhouse was locked against them, but Jonty knew of a sheltered doorway. It was a cold, misty night and the north-east wind was blowing in from the sea and they huddled together for warmth. Polly Anna had cried for her mother and Jonty was sure that he would have cried for his too if he had ever known her.

The next day they crept back through the gate, mingling with the crowd who were waiting to be admitted, climbed the steps to the hayloft and fell into the soft bales in the happy comfort of knowing they were home. The dysentery epidemic was over and they had avoided it. Jonty listened to the gossip of the inmates and heard that six people had died including two children.

'Let me look at thee, girl.' Letty took Polly Anna by the chin and lifted it. 'Where's tha been? Hast tha bin sick?'

Polly Anna obligingly nodded and looked appealingly at the woman. 'Dysentery,' she said lispingly, saying the word which Jonty had made her practise and patted her stomach.

Letty dropped her hand and indicated with her thumb that she should go. 'Clear off,' she said. 'I haven't time to be learning bairns how to sew. If Matron wants thee to be a seamstress she can learn thee hersen, but she'll be wasting her time 'cos tha's not got talent for it.'

Polly Anna wandered off in search of Jonty, but he appeared to have gone somewhere on his own or on an errand. She passed the Matron's open office door and peeped in through the door jamb. The room was empty, but a small fire burning in the grate made it look quite cosy. She looked around her down the long corridor, no-one was looking her way, so she slipped into the room and put out her hands to the flame. She turned them over and over, stretching her fingers towards the warmth for the days had turned much colder, and remembered, with a vague sadness which filled her eyes with tears, another fire in a little house which she had shared with her mother and father.

She had thought of her mama and papa several times whilst she and Jonty had wandered the streets of Hull, for some of the surrounding area had seemed familiar and she had seen the river before too, though she hadn't told Jonty this because he was so pleased and proud to be showing it to her for what he thought was the first time. But she was reminded that she had been there before when she heard a man playing on a penny whistle; the tune was jolly and she had tapped her feet and remembered someone once saying 'Bravo', and clapping their hands in applause.

She looked up at the mantelpiece just above her head, and stood on tiptoe to see what was there, a greasy comb with strands of brown and grey hair in it, a notebook and pencil, a brass candlestick with a stub of candle and Jonty's playing cards.

'Ah!' She reached up and took hold of them. Would he get them back? she wondered. She flicked through the pack and withdrew the picture of the queen of diamonds. How pretty she was, she would love to keep her. She slipped the card into her pocket and riffled through the other cards until she came to another queen. She was even prettier, with dark curls just like her own, under her crown. That too she slipped into her pocket and with it two of the handsome gentlemen and the card with the funny man with the stick. She returned the pack to the mantelpiece and walked back out of the door in search of Jonty once more.

Jonty had been on an errand into the town for Mrs Pincher. She didn't seem to have missed him for the last three days, but then she had been busy with the sick and with dealing with the irate residents of Parliament Street, who were complaining yet again that the disease in the workhouse was being transmitted through the walls to their own staff. But as Jonty went off she warned him not to be long as she wanted to talk to him when he came back about the playing cards and where they had come from. He had mulled long and hard over this problem, but couldn't come up with any solution. Nothing would persuade him to tell that his friend Samuel had given them to him.

Samuel had taken them from a soft leather case but had kept the case, for sentimental reasons, he'd explained. 'They were a present to me, Jonty,' he'd said softly, and Jonty had known that Samuel's mood indicated the arrival of a great sadness and despair which came over him from time to time. 'But let's pretend that it's your birthday and I will give them to you as a present.'

When he got back from the town the first person he saw was Billy. His face was thinner and his jacket hung loosely around him. 'I've been sick,' he said without preamble. 'Quack said I was at Death's door but I've made a miraculous recovery.' He preened. It was the most important thing that had ever happened to him in his life, the fact that he had almost lost it.

Jonty was impressed. Billy had singled him out to impart the news and though he wasn't a particular friend of his, of all the children in the workhouse he was one of the few who didn't mock or chase him.

'Dysentery! That's what I had,' Billy said proudly. 'Doc said it was summat that I ate, probably some bad meat, he said, but I told him we didn't get much of that and he laughed as if it was a great joke!' He leant forward and whispered. 'Tha knows that little lass that Polly Anna got into trouble over wi' asking for medicine and got locked in 'Black Box? Polly Anna did, I mean, not 'little lass!'

Jonty gazed at him. Billy often had trouble stringing his words together.

'Well, she's snuffed it! She was at Death's door same as me, onny she went through it and I didn't.' He nodded significantly. 'They're tekking her to 'burial ground today. I might stop and watch her go and think on how it might have been me!'

Jonty turned away. He wouldn't tell Polly Anna the news, he would keep her occupied and hope that she wouldn't miss her little friend just yet and that the memory of her would simply fade.

Mrs Pincher was sitting at her table with the playing cards in her hand when he knocked on the door. 'Now then, my lad. What about these cards? Are you going to tell me where you got them? You know what happens if any of the inmates are found stealing? They go off to 'magistrate, that's what! And,' she threatened, leaning towards him, 'if they go from bad to worse, they get hard labour or they're sent to foreign lands and never see their mother country again!'

Jonty obligingly hung his head in shame, though wondering as he gazed down at the faded rug on the floor whether or not it would be any worse in a foreign land than it was here. Samuel had told him of other countries, like Italy and Spain where he had been as a young man, where, although some of the people were very poor, the sun shone every day and it was never cold and wet as it was in England.

Slowly he lifted his head, Mrs Pincher was shuffling the cards and placing them on the table. She grunted, shuffled them again and once more put them down. 'It's not a full set,' she complained. 'There's some missing, king and queen of diamonds, queen of clubs, king of spades and a knave! Can't play a game of crib without 'em! Where did you find 'em? In 'gutter?'

He blinked innocently and nodded, trembling his lips as if he was going to cry.

'Here,' she said, handing them to him, 'take 'em. You just wanted to look at 'nice pictures, I expect?'

He beamed at her appreciatively, 'Count them,' he said, counting out the six of spades with his finger, then turning over another card did the same with the ten of clubs.

'Who showed you how to count?' She frowned at him and he worried that he was giving too much away.

'Samuel,' he muttered, 'in 'lunatic ward.'

'And you've remembered all this time?' She pondered for a while. 'He was a teacher once, I think.' She gazed at Jonty. 'He must have been a good 'un to learn a bairn like thee. Go on,' she dismissed him. 'It's nearly dinnertime.'

Mrs Pincher was always looking for ways to keep on the right side of the governors in order to keep her position as Matron and Mr Pincher's as Master. Though in her opinion Mr Pincher did nothing to warrant his position, he merely walked about the workhouse, occasionally tapping an inmate with his walking stick to show his authority, or sauntered about the town revelling in being recognized by the town's poor. Nevertheless, without him there would be no place for her as Matron.

Some of the Board of Governors were very happy with the way Mrs Pincher ran the workhouse; those who came to take their meals within the walls two or three times a week on the pretext of administering their governorship and went home with a bolt of cotton or a leg of pork or ham, and who failed to keep their accounts in order. But there were others who asked questions constantly, on the state of health of the inmates, and who complained over the lack of sanitation, who dug their fingernails into the damp walls and shook their heads despairingly, and who shepherded the children out of the oakum room when they found them exhausted and sleeping on the floor. It was these wise and caring men whom she aimed to please, and Jonty in his innocence had given her an idea.

'I've had an idea, Mr Pincher,' she said at supper. 'One that I think will please you.'

Mr Pincher looked at her without speaking, took another mouthful of pie and a deep quaff of ale, swallowed, burped and wiped his mouth with a large white napkin. 'And what would that idea be, Mrs Pincher?'

'We should get a teacher for 'bairns in here, one that can learn 'em letters and numbers.'

'Tha must be mad!' He looked at her scornfully and continued with his supper. ''Board don't have enough money to feed 'em let alone learn 'em.'

She waited for him to finish the pie and poured him more ale from the jug. 'Aye,' she sighed. 'Tha's right as usual! It's a pity though, it would go down well with Governor Johnson and Governor Armitage, they're allus saying that 'bairns have no learning. Now if we had a teacher on 'premises, one we didn't have to pay, then that would be 'solution.'

'Aye, but we haven't,' he said and, blowing out a gusty breath, undid the waistband of his breeches and bent to take his boots off. 'Not to my knowledge anyway.'

'No,' she agreed and leaned back in her chair, the conversation apparently over. Mr Pincher shuffled in his chair and stretched his stockinged feet towards the fire and gazed aimlessly into space. He was an uneducated man, not a conversationalist nor a reader of newspapers, and his evenings when not spent walking the streets for entertainment, were usually spent dozing in a chair until bedtime.

'Where's them cards?' he asked suddenly. 'They were on 'shelf this morning.'

'I gave 'em back to 'bairn,' she said. 'I counted 'em and there was some missing. He'd found 'em in gutter, not stole 'em at all.' She watched her husband craftily. 'Does tha know what he said?'

'How would I know?' he grumbled. 'I can't understand a word he says.'

'He said – tha'll laugh when tha hears this – he said he kept 'cards to count. He knows some of his numbers. He said that that Samuel in 'lunatic ward learned him when he was in there. Before I brought him out,' she couldn't help adding spitefully, 'when everybody thought him an imbecile.'

She settled back now for the information to filter through. It might take some time, she knew, for he hadn't the quickest mind she had ever known. Her first husband had been of very quick mind and intellect, so quick that he had gone off with a rich widow and left her penniless after only two years of marriage. Mr Pincher had been her only hope of salvation and she played the poor grieving widow so successfully that she had 'married' him within a year and at her prompting they obtained together the post of Master and Matron of the workhouse.

They had some compatibility, though not much. She, providing she outwitted him yet kept him fed and watered, was able to run things as she wanted, and he, able to posture in the Market Place and noddingly agree with the governors over issues which he didn't always understand, was happy to let her organize the masses of people who thronged the building.

She watched his eyes flicker as he mulled something over. 'I do believe he was a teacher,' he said, 'afore he was brought in here.'

'What was that, Mr Pincher? I didn't quite catch—'

'That Samuel – whatever his name is, did he ever give one? I think he was once a teacher.'

She agreed. 'He never did give his name, said he wouldn't shame his family by giving it. And he was a teacher, was he?' she questioned. 'Well, I never! Who would have thought it – and to finish up in here. What a waste of learning!'

'Ah, but Mrs Pincher,' her husband waved his forefinger at her, 'I've had an idea! Why don't we use Samuel to learn 'bairns to do their letters and numbers? It's not as if he's dangerous and can't be let out for an hour or two a week. Think of how pleased 'governors would be and no expense incurred!'

'Why Mr Pincher,' she sat forward in her chair, 'what a grand idea. However did you think on it?'

7

Samuel agreed to teach the children, though he insisted that a separate room should be found and that he shouldn't be expected to teach them in the lunatic ward. 'Children between seven and ten,' he said. 'Girls and boys.'

Here Mr Pincher put his foot down. 'No sense in learning lasses, they'd have no use for it. No. Onny lads. I'll speak to 'governors tomorrow and tell 'em my idea. I reckon they'll agree.'

Most of them did but with some reservations. Governor Grant thought it a waste of time altogether, Governor Blake insisted that only the orphan children should be taught and not the pauper children. 'There's a pauper school already on the Humber bank which is not well attended and those who do attend are unruly.'

'But they are punished,' Governor Armitage broke in. 'Some of the boys were given hard labour for breaking a window recently, excessive punishment I should have thought for mere children.'

'Indeed, indeed,' agreed Governor Johnson.

'But the children here will be supervised presumably? How many children should this fellow Samuel teach at a time? Could the Board agree to a number that he can control?'

They couldn't of course, but in the end the size of the room which Mrs Pincher allocated dictated the number and Samuel was told that he would teach ten different boys three times a week. Thirty orphans out of a total of ninety children. But when they came to round up these boys they found that they didn't have thirty boys between the ages of seven and ten, but only twenty-five and so Samuel and Mrs Pincher complicitly agreed that the other places would be taken by five girls.

Mr Bertram and a male pauper would sit in the room to supervise, not only the scholars but also Samuel, for he had a tendency to go into a fit and damage himself or the furniture. 'I will not require medication whilst I am teaching, Matron,' he said. 'Will you please make that clear to the doctor? I cannot teach when my brain is fuddled.'

Mrs Pincher had her doubts whether the doctor would agree. It was policy to give all the lunatics a dose of laudanum morning and night to keep them quiet. It was perfectly safe, she knew, the nursing infants in the house had a dose of Daffy's Elixir to settle them every night and she herself chewed the occasional pennyworth of opium without ill effect.

The schoolroom was bare, there were no tables or chairs for the children and they sat on the floor with their slates on their knees. Some of the boys shuffled off after the first day and didn't return unless hauled back by Mr Bertram or the pauper Marsh, a thin, shambling man with a narrow mouth and sunken eyes who delighted in his role of keeping boys in order, but who infuriated Samuel on the first day by shouting out in the middle of lessons for a boy to keep still.

'I will keep order, Mr Bertram,' he addressed the assistant Master coldly and ignored Marsh. 'I will not tolerate interference in my class.'

Mr Bertram nodded nervously. This wasn't a job he relished, being locked in a room with a lunatic and a pauper with violent tendencies, but he had no choice, no choice at all. He was as much a victim as the rest of the inmates.

Jonty sat awkwardly on the floor, one leg stretched out, the other tucked under him and waited eagerly for the lesson to begin. Samuel wouldn't expect him to repeat aloud the letters or numbers like the others, but he would put up his hand in answer to a question and write the answer on his slate. He had complete trust in Samuel not to humiliate him in front of the other scholars and when the lesson was over he had decided that he would ask if he could take the slate with him to practise what he had learned, and to show Polly Anna.

Billy had come reluctantly, lamenting that he was too old, being almost eleven, but Mrs Pincher, anxious to fill the class and so justify her proposal, took him by the ear and propelled him toward the schoolroom. It was, however, a futile exercise for he understood nothing that he was taught except the alphabet, which he repeated parrot fashion in unison with everyone else, and frequently fell asleep, only to be awakened by Marsh's boot in his back.

After a week Jonty noticed that Samuel's attitude

was changing, he was usually a quiet man, serious and patient in his dealings with Jonty, but now he was becoming increasingly irritable. He would shout at the boys when they didn't understand him and he developed a nervous shrug and when one day he spoke sharply to Jonty and told him to stand up when being spoken to, Jonty knew that something was amiss.

Mr Bertram too noticed his changing manner and told Mrs Pincher. 'I think he's heading for a fit, Matron. He'll have to be watched. I'll need another male to handle him.' Mr Bertram hated violence of any kind. He was a slight man, pale of hands and face and avoided trouble whenever he could.

''Doctor took him off his morning dose,' Mrs Pincher said. 'He's only having it at night before bed. He'll have to go back on it, no matter what he says. We can't risk an upset. Governors will be on us like a load o' coal if owt happens.'

The next morning Samuel was held down whilst a tincture of opium was administered. He sat weeping on his bed, but as the opium took effect he calmed and on being collected by Mr Bertram and Marsh went quietly to the classroom to continue the lessons. He asked Jonty to stay back after the lesson was over on the pretext of explaining something. He turned his back on Mr Bertram and Marsh and apologized to Jonty for his behaviour the previous day.

'Be warned Jonty, don't take medication in this place unless your life is in danger, nor buy a single pennyworth. It will be your downfall as it has been mine. I cannot now exist without it and I will die of its effects.' He considered for a moment. 'Still, it will be a shorter life because of it so perhaps I should be grateful for that. I wouldn't want to spend much longer in this place.' He put a hand on Jonty's shoulder. 'Without you, my dear young friend, I would be long gone.'

Jonty hadn't realized his significance in Samuel's life but only how important Samuel was to him with his kindness and patience towards his inadequacies. Samuel's irritability towards him the previous day had upset him considerably, whereas from anyone else it would have been merely shrugged away as of no consequence.

He smiled up at him. He would work hard at his lessons, Samuel would one day be proud of him.

Christmas was celebrated only by a meagre helping of stodgy plum pudding, with a surfeit of suet and little fruit. During the bitterly cold winter the population of town and workhouse fell foul of influenza. The doctors hurriedly put out a statement that it was not an epidemic but that the many deaths amongst the very old and the very young were due to bronchitis and diseases of the respiratory system.

By the spring, Polly Anna, thinner and taller than when she had first entered the workhouse, had almost forgotten her previous life; it was a mere drifting shadow in her consciousness, though she would sometimes waken from a dream in which her beloved mama was still with her. Life sped by with a monotonous regularity, broken only by her time spent with Jonty in the hayloft when he would haltingly explain the lessons he had learned. She understood most of his incoherent speech and rarely had to ask him to repeat a statement.

During the summer a special meeting of the governors was held to discuss yet another complaint from the residents of Parliament Street whose homes backed on to the walls of the workhouse. Something must be done, they insisted, before all the residents of that eminent street were removed in their coffins. The cause of this complaint was linked to the death of a servant from typhus, which, the employer of the poor man stated most emphatically, was directly attributable to the workhouse. 'It is a disease of dirt and uncleanliness,' he wrote in his letter to the Board, 'yet it spreads to those who live in immaculate homes who are unfortunate enough to live in close proximity.'

The Board convened and once more they disagreed. Money should not be spent on the old building, a new workhouse must be built. Money *must* be spent to improve the lives of the inhabitants, said others, until an alternative site was found. A site of five acres had been offered just out of the town, but the Poor Law Board refused to cooperate and so the scheme was abandoned. The wrangling went on all the summer and as the inmates sweated during the hot dusty days they listened to the rumours that they were to be moved, that they were not to be moved, that they were to be turned out into the street, that only the Irish were to be turned out, that they were to be given more food, they were to be given less food, and that the building was to be extended or demolished.

Jonty listened, he had heard all of this before and as the rumours settled, the Board's debate was less frequent and life resumed as usual and nothing was done to ease the lot of the workhouse inhabitants, who were, said one of the governors, in a far better condition of comfort than the majority of the poor living outside its walls. Jonty, listening by the door, agreed with this fact even though knowing little of the outside world; for although in his squalling infancy he might easily have been abandoned, someone had patiently fed him on milk and pap and, he thought, there was no doubt that he would not have survived anywhere else.

As October with its fine mists and smells of smoky fires drew on, he dashed up the steps of the hayloft one evening in search of Polly Anna and found her sitting morosely with her chin in her hand, staring out of the open door into the dimly lit yard below. He put his head on one side and lifted his eyebrows to enquire what was the matter.

'Something,' she piped in her childish treble. 'I don't know.' She put her nose in the air and sniffed. 'There's a smell but I don't know what it means.' Something in the air was stirring memories which had been hidden away for the last year and were now evoking a sadness within her.

Jonty misunderstood her mood; he beckoned eagerly for her to join him and led her down the steps to the gate, which was now locked for the night. She couldn't reach the spyhole so he fetched a box for her to stand on and standing on tiptoe, she peered out into the street and drew a gasping breath at the procession going by. A procession of carts and trailers, animals and people. A cart trundled past which held a cage with live monkeys in it, and following that came a string of white horses, their manes nodding as if in time to the tune which came from a penny-whistle man who walked behind them. She watched as a group of people, as small as Jonty, though bigger than her, skipped and tumbled and banged tambourines and laughed and joked with each other, whilst a safe distance behind them came a chained shaggy brown bear, swinging its great head from side to side as if in greeting to the crowds who were watching from the footpath.

'Wait! Wait!' she cried. 'Wait for me,' and she turned to Jonty, a question spilling from her lips, but he forestalled her. 'Fair,' he said, sniffing the air. 'Hull Fair!'

She nodded, then burst into tears. 'Jonty,' she wept, 'when can we leave this place?'

8

She asked Jonty the same question every October for the next seven years until in the year she was eleven and the young Queen Victoria came to the throne, she asked it of Samuel instead. Samuel was now grey and slightly bent and in spite of his increasing doses of opium was still teaching the children of the workhouse, those who were willing to attend, and Polly Anna was one of them. She listened intently to all he taught her and she listened too to the sound of his voice and precise manner of speech, so different from the coarse language of the Pinchers, and unconsciously she copied him.

On the days when she could escape from her work in the sewing room, Polly Anna slipped into the schoolroom, even though she was now above the age limit of ten. She had rebelled against the hated sewing until she was threatened with the oakum room and, having seen the men, women and children sweating over the cast-iron buckets and tubs in the steaming, stinking, boiling room, decided that stitching coarse serge and flannel was the lesser of the two evils.

'When can we leave this place, Samuel?' She was the only pupil left, the others had scooted off, leaving just her and Mr Bertram, who was dozing on a hard wooden chair at the back of the room. The fair had arrived and the children were anxious to see it, even though they had no money to pay for its pleasures. 'I keep asking Jonty, but he will never say.'

He shook his head, 'Jonty, like me, will never leave this place, Polly Anna. I, because I cannot be trusted to behave. I should be thrown in jail within minutes of leaving the premises, and Jonty – well, Jonty knows no other life but this one, he feels safe within these walls even though he sometimes escapes from them.'

She pondered on this statement; it was true that whenever she suggested that they should run away, Jonty always found a reason for returning. 'But, Samuel,' she smiled, 'why should you be put into jail? You don't get into trouble – not like me, I'm always in trouble especially with Matron.'

He patted her head. 'That's because you've got spirit, my child, just as I once had. Mine has lain dormant for many years, but I fear it would return if I should leave these workhouse walls and see the conditions of the poor living outside them.'

'Is that why you are here?' she asked with a puzzled frown. 'Did you say something you shouldn't? But even if you had I don't see why you should be locked in the lunatic ward. You are clearly not off your head!'

'It's a long story, my dear.' He cast an eye at Mr

Bertram, who was stretching himself. 'I will perhaps tell it to you one day.'

Mr Bertram ushered her out and, locking the door behind them, left Samuel in the classroom whilst he went to fetch the Master to escort the schoolteacher back to the locked ward.

'Everything all right, Mr Bertram?' Mr Pincher wheezed; these damp autumn days always affected his chest.

'Yes, sir, everything is fine, though the attendance was down again; the only regular attender is the girl, Polly Anna, and she always stays back 'till 'last.'

'Does she? Why is that then, Mr Bertram?'

'Well, I suppose she is anxious for learning, Mr Pincher, there can be no other reason.'

Mr Pincher paused before opening the schoolroom door. 'Don't be too sure of that, Mr Bertram, these young lasses—!' He winked an eye.

Mr Bertram was taken aback. 'I don't quite follow your meaning, sir. You're not suggesting any impropriety on my part?'

The Master laughed. 'You! Certainly not, what an idea! No. Samuel! He used to be a Reformer you know! Smooth tongued, good with words, meddling in politics. There was a hint of scandal but I don't know what. He's 'sort to turn a young girl's head, especially one such as that Polly Anna.' He licked his lips as he turned the key. She was a bit young yet, but shaping up nicely, and spirited, he'd say that for her. He'd had a sore shin for days just for putting his arm around her in a perfectly friendly manner. Still, that didn't matter, he'd get round her eventually, one or two presents, a bit of ribbon and such, that would work, it usually did.

After supper Polly Anna searched for Jonty and found him just as he was coming down the hayloft steps. He'd banned her from sleeping there six months ago, much to her dismay, and had explained that if she was found there with him he would be beaten. 'I'm nearly a man,' he said quite clearly. 'Ask Samuel.'

So she had asked Samuel, who had confirmed that on no account should she stay there and that it was he who had told Jonty that she should no longer sleep in the hayloft. 'Jonty is fourteen and a man to all intents, even though he looks a child and is to you a brother and your best friend. But what is more, Polly Anna, you are seen as a female and not an innocent child.'

She'd gazed up at him, not really understanding but accepting his word, and dejectedly returned to her bed in the dormitory.

'Jonty,' she said now, 'where are you going?' He had a scarf around his neck which denoted a trip into the town, yet the gate was locked for the night.

He pointed to the gate.

'Can I come?'

He shook his head and indicated with a sweeping movement of his hand that he was going to climb over the gate.

'I can climb, you know that I can.' She could climb as well as he could. He didn't want her to come, that's what it was. He'd been strange lately, not always wanting her with him and other times seeking her out. 'I'm coming anyway.'

He shrugged, feigning indifference and casting a glance around the empty yard he took a running jump and nimbly sought a foothold on the gate panels and hoisted himself up and over the gate.

'Wait for me, Jonty,' she called in a hoarse whisper, fearful that anyone should hear and keep her back. She ran to the back of the yard, where they had coiled a rope on a hook. She loosened it and checking that it was secure she pulled back as far as she could and swung, pushing her body and legs with a great vigour to carry her up to the top of the gate. She scrambled over the top and hung the rope over, hoping that no-one would notice it draped there, better there than hanging down for all to see, she thought as she dropped with a thud on to the road below.

'God Almighty!' A voice spoke from beside the gate. 'It must be bad in there, folks are escaping and here am I waiting to be let in!'

A dishevelled bundle of rags sat hunched by the wall and Polly Anna couldn't tell if it was man or woman, but she didn't stop to enquire as she saw Jonty heading off down the street and indicating for her to hurry.

'Where are we going? What's happening?'

He sped down Silver Street and she thought that she would love to stop and look in the shop windows, at the silver and gold which was glinting in the darkness, but Jonty was in a hurry to get to his destination. 'Fair,' he said. 'Come on!'

The long street of the Market Place was packed with stalls, some spilling over into the shadow of the Holy Trinity Church. Traders of every description were there, some selling silks from abroad, some with their stalls piled high with toys and trinkets from foreign countries. Nodding dogs sat next to painted dolls and stringed puppets. Wooden hobby-horses and windmills on sticks were held up for all to see, their vendor emphasizing their valuable worth as compared with his neighbours' cheap and worthless goods.

Polly Anna paused to look and reached out a finger to touch the satin dress of a dark-haired doll. 'Get your dirty fingers off,' shouted the trader. 'Don't touch unless you're going to buy. Not you, of course, madam,' he fawned to a nicely dressed woman with a neat little girl by her side. 'Let the little lady hold the dolly.' He passed the doll over to the child, who stroked the satin dress and then looked sideways at Polly Anna.

Polly Anna stuck her tongue out at the trader and at the child and ran off to join Jonty, who was hovering by the hot pea stall. 'Oh, Jonty! Couldn't you just eat a dish of those?' The mouth-watering smell whetted their taste-buds, but they moved away; they hadn't any money and it wasn't possible to steal a helping of peas.

He nudged her. A brazier was glowing next to the pea stall and from it came the smell of baking potatoes, their skins slightly singeing. The trader turned them over and then went back to his stall to serve some customers. Polly Anna joined the queue. 'Hey, mister. How much are your hot peas?' she asked as her turn came. He glanced at her and then over his shoulder at Jonty, nonchalantly waiting by the brazier.

'More than you can pay,' he said. 'Go on, clear off!'

She pulled a pet lip. 'My mama gave me some

money,' she said plaintively. 'Not much, but perhaps enough.'

He hesitated and then said, 'Penny a bag. Let's see your money.'

She made a great show of delving into her pocket and then jumped back as if dropping it. 'My penny!' She scrabbled around on the ground and the trader too bent down to look under the stall.

'It ain't here; sorry, no money no peas.' The trader dismissed her with a wave of his hand and turned to serve another customer with money waiting in his hand. She started to cry quietly and the waiting customer looked down on her. 'Give her a bag, you'll find 'money when you pack up,' he urged. 'She looks half starved.'

'You give her a bag!' the trader answered. 'I've seen all 'tricks of workhouse brats and that's one of 'em.'

The customer wasn't convinced. 'Here.' He called Polly Anna back, 'Have this one, I'll get another.'

She smiled appealingly, wiping away her tears with her fingertips. 'Thank you mister,' she whispered. 'You're very kind.'

The man smiled beneficently down at her and she joined Jonty as they walked away to share the peas, greedily scooping them out with their fingers whilst Jonty's pocket exuded great heat from the hot potato concealed there.

They wandered down Castle Street, halving the potato, Jonty eating most of the fleshy white pulp whilst Polly Anna chewed on the skin, and came into the area known as Dock Green, where most of the entertainment was taking place. Springthorpe's Waxworks had a central place and they watched in fascination as the automated figures performed outside, enticing the revellers to enter the curtained doors.

Wombwell's Menagerie advertised all manner of animals and they heard a strange mixture of sounds coming from behind the screen; roaring and whistling, barking and snarling. Next door was a whirligig of wooden elephants and horses, which was being pushed by a bevy of small children, their backs bent as they strained. Music from penny whistles, trumpets and fiddles filled the air and Polly Anna felt a vague memory stirring.

'Stop a minute, Jonty,' she implored, but he'd wandered off to look at a tent which claimed to have a two-headed pig inside. 'Jonty – wait!' She had caught sight of a small man sitting on a wooden trailer playing on a tin whistle; his skin was dark and swarthy, he had a felt hat on the back of his head and a monkey wearing a red coat and a blue fez was sitting on his shoulder.

As she watched and listened to the plaintive tune, the monkey looked up and blinked its dark eyes at her; a sudden smile lit Polly Anna's face as with a swift movement the monkey jumped down from its owner's shoulder, gave a hop and a jump and landed in her arms, chattering excitedly.

'Here! Come back here, tha little rascal.' The man stopped his playing and came across and removed the monkey from her. 'Sorry. I've not known him do that before.' He tapped it gently on the nose. 'Tha's a monkey, that's what! Now just behave.' He looked at Polly Anna, who was standing motionless. 'You all right, lassie? He wouldn't hurt you.'

She stared at the man. 'Yes,' she said vaguely. 'I'm all right.' She put out her hand to stroke the monkey, who jumped up and down and round and round on his master's shoulder. 'What's his name?'

'He doesn't have a name,' he grinned. 'He's just known as Morgan's monkey.'

She and Jonty wandered through the fairground past the entertainment and up to the outer edge of Dock Green and Polly Anna felt as if she was awaking from a dream. Illusory phantasms were vacillating, vague and insubstantial through her mind. Small smoky fires had been lit which sent up sparks into the darkness and around the fires groups of people were hunched over cooking pots and pans, and there was a tantalizing smell of sausages and meat, which dripped and sizzled on the burning wood.

As they approached nearer to the fires they saw that there were many children and young people gathered there; small children with dirty faces who were eating their supper with their fingers and boys and girls of about their age who were chatting and laughing, which at once stopped as they came near. Adults appeared from out of tents and Polly Anna and Jonty drew back as the children sat back on their haunches and silently observed them. They didn't seem hostile towards them, but neither were they welcoming; it was as if they had strayed into a private domain where they had no place to be.

They withdrew back to the main pathway, but Polly Anna, with a compulsion she didn't understand, walked away with her head constantly turning back towards them; their figures disappeared in the darkness and soon all she could see were shadows and the glow from their fires and the sparks which flew up into the night sky, but she felt that their eyes were still upon her.

When they returned to Whitefriargate there was a crowd of people sitting by the gate of the workhouse; some who by their ragged appearance and demeanour had been already to the vagrant office and had been turned away. It was starting to rain and they huddled with their heads down seeking shelter from each other.

'We can't take a running jump, Jonty. How are we going to climb the gate without falling on to these people?' Polly Anna viewed the crowd who were barring their way. She felt no emotion or pity for them, they were simply there. Every day paupers and vagrants waited by the gate and every day some were turned away. It was life as she knew it; everyone, as far as she knew, had to eke out an existence, those who were strong in spirit, able to fend for themselves, whether by fair means or not, would survive and she was determined to be one of those few, if only to get out of this hated place.

'Here!' The voice belonging to the bundle of rags who had spoken to them earlier called to them. 'I'll give you a hitch over.' The rags revealed themselves as a man, tall but very thin with deep sunken eyes in his drawn face. 'Come on. Put your foot in my hand and I'll hoist you over.'

Jonty did so first and was hoisted up to the top of the gate. He looked down anxiously at Polly Anna before jumping down on the other side.

The man bent and cupped his hands together,

then straightened up. 'Erm – tell me, little lady. Is there a man inside this handsome building by the name of Samuel? Have you heard of such a man?'

'I'm not sure,' she answered cautiously. 'There are hundreds of men.'

'Ah, but not such a one as this. This is a special kind of man.'

'What's he to you?' she asked pertly. 'Is he a friend?'

The man's face visibly brightened. 'Ah! So he is still here!' he said softly. He bent down again and cupped his hands. 'Tell him', he whispered as she put her foot in his hands and her hand on his shoulder for purchase, 'that there is to be a meeting on Dock Green on the second Sunday from now. I'll tell him myself if I can get in. But will you tell him for me, little girl, if I can't?'

'He's in the lunatic ward,' she said softly. 'But I'll try.'

The man uttered a small gasp at her statement. 'Oh! Well tell him he still has friends who believe in him.'

She nodded. 'I'll tell him,' she promised as he heaved her up the gate. 'Be sure that I will.'

'Jonty!' she called softly through the door of the hayloft. 'I can't get in. The door's locked and the window is closed. I'll have to stay in here, it's starting to rain.'

Jonty's head peered above the bales. 'Come on then,' he muttered. There was nowhere else she could go, they would just have to risk it, but he was worried, the Master had taken it upon himself to inspect the hayloft quite frequently. It was as if he was looking for something in particular.

She climbed in beside him and heaved a sigh. 'It's much better in here than inside the building. Warmer, more comfortable and I do miss you, Jonty.' She snuggled down next to him. She had had such strange feelings tonight at the fair, vague feelings that she now wanted to consider, to try to understand what they meant; but the hour was late and her eyes started to close and she fell asleep to images and sounds of penny whistles and dancing dogs and chattering monkeys who were trying to tell her something in words she couldn't understand, and of dancing around a smoky fire dressed in white satin.

Jonty looked down at her as she slept. Though her face was thinner than when she had first arrived at the workhouse seven years before, she hadn't any spots and sores which so many of the children had and which Jonty too was now developing. Her skin was still clear though slightly olive coloured and her lashes were dark against her cheeks.

'You mustn't let her stay in the hayloft,' Samuel had insisted to him. 'She is only a child, but you are not. She will develop a reputation if you are found out and innocence is not an alibi.'

He trusted Samuel to know what was right and it was true that he felt different now from when he was a child; he had sudden powerful emotions which he couldn't understand, and sometimes he felt angry with Polly Anna though he didn't know why, and sometimes anxious and protective as tonight when he had mistakenly gone first over the gate and left her below talking to the stranger.

He gave a deep sigh and covered her over with a blanket which they had removed from the storeroom and picking up his own thin, threadbare blanket, he draped it around his shoulders and stepping out of the door and down the steps he made his way through the puddles across to his old corner by the gate.

9

'How can I get out?' Samuel had been anxious and disturbed when she had whispered the stranger's message in his ear and she had seen Mr Bertram look suspiciously at them from his seat by the door.

'I'll ask Jonty, he'll know.' She was keyed up and buoyant at the thought of helping Samuel escape from the locked ward to go to the Sunday meeting. She hadn't seen the stranger since and assumed that he had been unable to enter the workhouse. Perhaps he had a coin or two in his pocket, she mused, for only those who were completely destitute were able to come in, but then, Samuel had told her, that only those with no hope at all would sink so low as to throw themselves into the tender arms of the parish.

'What is the meeting about?' she questioned during the lessons when no-one else appeared to be attending.

'Reform,' he said and threaded into the lesson his hatred of the class system. 'The division between the population, on one side the rich and on the other the poor. Mark my words,' he rose to his feet, 'there is a time coming when our gentle Queen will see blood shed in her land.'

Polly Anna stared, she had never seen him so animated, and Mr Bertram too, stood up and hesitated, his hand on the door.

'Have no fear, Mr Bertram.' Samuel gave a small thin smile. 'I am merely giving a history lesson. A history lesson of the future, when men like you and me – yes and women too – will have a voice to decide what happens in their lives.'

Mr Bertram nodded nervously. 'I think it would be safer to continue with learning them to read and write. Master will be along in a minute. We don't want any trouble.'

'Ah! The Master! Yes, of course! That intelligent, erudite creature who manages our day. The Master, who decides what is best for us. Of course we mustn't give him any trouble. We mustn't tax him too much for fear his brain might explode!' Samuel sat down abruptly, his face pale and his hands trembling. 'I have finished for today. You may all leave.'

'So how can we get him out, Jonty?' she asked later. 'I told him that you would think of something.'

'Me!' he grumbled. 'How?'

'Because you can go anywhere! Nobody questions you,' she answered sharply. 'You have to help him, no-one else can.' She glared at him, defying him to cross her.

He was considered by the inmates to be one of the staff of the workhouse, even though he wasn't paid a wage. He was given his bed and board and for that, he had been told by the Master, he should be grateful, for no-one else would employ him. Mrs

Pincher occasionally gave him a sixpence or two and he was useful, as he had always been to her, but he also helped out in a general way in the running of the workhouse. He fetched and carried and supervised the delivery of goods, flour and coal, and ticked off on a list the names of those entering the workhouse and of those leaving it, either voluntarily, forcibly, or by wooden casket.

He was of more use even than Mr Bertram, who because of his delicate constitution was unable to lift or carry or run errands as swiftly as Jonty, nor was his memory as good and he was liable to forgetfulness.

'You help with breakfast on a Sunday,' she urged. 'Perhaps you could get hold of the key then!'

Jonty groaned. No use struggling to argue, she wouldn't listen to him. If she had an idea in her head then she persisted until she got her own way. She thinks I can do anything! But he grinned: noone else had such faith in him. He nodded. 'Maybe!'

Mr Bertram always attended church on a Sunday morning. It was his right, and the one thing on which he insisted, even though the Master did his best to dissuade him, for it meant that he had to supervise breakfast in the lunatic ward himself, instead of Mr Bertram, whilst Mrs Pincher was busy with other duties. But now that Jonty had taken on extra functions Mr Pincher occasionally stayed in bed; his Saturday nights were often very late and his head very thick the next morning, and after the first occasion, when he had overslept and found later that Jonty had supervised the morning meal without mishap, he often turned over in his sheets confident that the day could start just as well without him.

The fair had gone. Polly Anna and Jonty had watched from their spyhole in the gate and Polly Anna felt a tinge of sadness creep over her as the horses, lions and dwarfs departed; a sadness which came along with the damp and cold which filtered through the building, cloaking them all with the knowledge that winter was on its way bringing with it bronchitis, influenza and all other ailments which the inmates in their weakened state were prone to.

'I wish we could go with them, Jonty.' She had pressed her eye close to the aperture, anxious not to miss one drum-beat or trill of the penny whistle, nor a single person or animal as they trundled by. 'They look so much happier than we are. Shall we?' she turned to him eagerly. 'Shall we run away and join them?'

He had shaken his head. 'Won't want us.' The fair people and the travellers were different from them, he knew that. They were like one large family, they wouldn't want strangers. Besides they earned their living and what could he and Polly Anna offer? He changed the subject. 'What about Samuel?'

'Oh, yes. Samuel! The meeting! It's this Sunday, now that the fair has gone from Dock Green. We must get him there, he's depending on us.'

Jonty watched Mr Pincher roll through the gate late on the Saturday night and obligingly helped him indoors. 'Oh, you're not such a bad sort of fellow, Jonty,' Mr Pincher hiccupped. 'Just a pity you're an idiot. Still, you can't help that, I suppose. We're not all blessed with brains.'

Jonty noddingly agreed with him and unlaced the Master's boots. He had had the forethought to build up the fire and the room was warm.

'Shame to leave that fire and go to a cold bed.' Mr Pincher leaned forward from his chair and gazed into the flames. Then he turned to Jonty and waved a wavering finger at him. 'No comfort in my bed, I can tell thee.' He put his fingers into his coat pocket and, pulling out a set of keys, he dropped them on the floor at Jonty's feet. 'Take that little key and open 'cupboard door. I'll have a dram before I go on up.'

Jonty took the keys and opened the cupboard. There were two bottles on the shelf, one with clear liquid, one with amber, both three-quarters full. He took down the amber one. Mrs Pincher liked a drop of gin now and again and he guessed that she might be displeased if she found the contents were lower than she remembered. No use in upsetting her, he decided. He took a glass from the shelf, sniffed the bottle and thought it smelt of medicine, but poured a large measure.

Mr Pincher sat back and appreciatively sipped, then drawing in a pursing breath at the strength, winked an eye. 'Drop of good stuff, this. Brought over special if you understand my meaning.' He tapped the side of his nose. 'Just between you and me – ha, not that you could tell anybody even if they asked, but you can't beat a drop of run brandy for strength and quality.'

Again Jonty nodded in agreement. He lifted the bottle again and signalled should he pour a drop more. 'Well, go on then, twist my arm, I'll just have another drop. Then get off to bed if you like.'

Jonty put the bottle away and locked the cupboard door, then looked at the keys in his hand. They were all there, the front door, the office, the cellar, the sewing room, the lunatic ward. He jingled them in his hand and then pointing at himself and then at the Master, he indicated that he would help him up the stairs.

'No. No, I can manage!' Mr Pincher insisted and draining his glass attempted to get to his feet. 'Wh – oops! Well – maybe not. Give me a hand, lad.'

With some difficulty, Jonty helped him up the dark staircase, pushing him from behind as he swayed from one step to another. He wanted to shush him, to tell him to be quiet and not wake Mrs Pincher who was on the next landing, but he dared not for Mr Pincher was now in full song.

'I've got an extra little drop under 'bed,' Mr Pincher said confidingly as they reached the top, and put his finger to his lips. 'Onny don't tell Mrs Pincher.'

Jonty dangled the keys in front of him. 'Breakfast!' he said.

Mr Pincher shook his head and both his hands emphatically. 'Shan't want any!'

'No! Sunday.' He indicated the key for the locked ward and moved his hand in an opening gesture.

The Master peered at his hand uncomprehendingly. 'Don't bother me now, boy. Tell Bertram.' He put his hand on his door and felt around for the knob. Jonty reached over him and opened the door and pushed him inside. The room was dimly lit by an oil lamp and Mr Pincher collapsed on to the bed. 'Pass me 'bottle,' he slurred and promptly fell asleep, his mouth wide open. Jonty turned off the lamp and felt in the darkness towards the door. He put out his hand when he thought he had reached it and felt a large warm mass in front of him.

'Ah!' He jumped back in fright.

'What you up to?' Mrs Pincher's hoarse whisper greeted him. 'Is he drunk?'

Jonty followed her out on to the landing and shrugged at her question, folding his hand over the keys.

'He'll be fit for nowt tomorrow,' she rasped. 'Go on, get back to bed, and be up early in 'morning! Some of us shan't have 'luxury of a lie in.'

It was already past three o'clock, he had heard a clock strike as Mr Pincher came through the gate. Two more hours and he would have to be up. He stood pondering at the outer door. If he went to his bed now he might well oversleep. The building was quiet, everyone else would be asleep, with the exception of Mrs Pincher. He sat down in a corner and waited. He waited until such time as he thought she might have fallen asleep again, then rising to his feet he tiptoed down the corridor to the locked ward at the back of the building.

There was never anyone on duty at night. If the inmates wanted anything then they had to wait until the morning. He turned the key and silently entered the room, which was lit by rush lights set high on the walls. Samuel's bed was on the far side of the room, near to the other door behind which were those who were insane and were chained to the wall or their beds. He hoped that Samuel wouldn't make a noise when he woke him, for the slightest disturbance would set off the lunatics wailing and rattling their chains. He could hear some of them now, chanting and whimpering.

He located Samuel's bed and gently patted his face. 'S-Sam—', he began in a whisper and Samuel with a start sat up, his eyes blinking, his pupils dilated. 'Ssh. Ssh!' Jonty put his fingers over Samuel's mouth. 'Come! Sunday!'

He took Samuel's hand and, collecting his jacket which was draped over the iron bed end, led him out of the room and locked the door behind them. He had no need to explain that he must make no noise for he could see that Samuel was afraid. This would be the first time that he had been out of the building in over twelve years.

He took him up to the hayloft and here Samuel put on his jacket, though he was without boots or stockings. He shivered. 'No matter, Jonty,' he said in a hoarse voice, 'there will be others there who will be barefoot too. Today will be a good day, no matter what the consequences. I have waited for this for a long time. I hope, I only hope that I haven't been forgotten, that people will remember me.'

Jonty wondered how anyone could forget him, for he had shown him much kindness, but he knew nothing of Samuel's past life and had only gleaned in conversation and lately from what Polly Anna had told him, that he wanted the poor to have a say in their lives and not to remain downtrodden. Though how that could be achieved he had no idea and many doubts.

'Should I slip away now before daybreak, do you think?' Samuel had suddenly become anxious again, unused after so long to making decisions for himself.

Jonty agreed that he should. 'Master sleeping,' he said, laying his cheek on to his hands.

'What about breakfast? What about my dose? Who'll be there? They'll miss me!'

'Me! Me!' He attempted to calm him. He would create a disturbance if necessary, if Mrs Pincher came round with the medication; the Master, he was sure, would sleep until dinnertime.

He crept down the stairs of the hayloft and gently eased back the bolts of the gate. Then, ascertaining that there was no-one watching, he waved to Samuel to come and pushed him out of the gate. He hoped that he would remember the way to Dock Green as Polly Anna had explained it to him.

'Go. Go!' He whispered urgently as Samuel hesitated, and watched him as with nervous step he shuffled along the wall of the building, his hand clinging to the brickwork as if not daring to let go. He watched him as he went, not the way they had gone towards the Market Place and Myton Gate where the stalls and entertainment had been, but towards the Junction Dock at the west end of Whitefriargate. Samuel stood for a moment as if the road in front of him were an abyss, then, with a glance over his shoulder at Jonty watching from the gate, took a determined step forward.

10

The Junction Dock hadn't been built when Samuel was committed to the lunatic ward in the workhouse, although the land had already been sold to the Dock Company in preparation for the third dock in the town. Proposals and plans were made and then dropped and it was whilst Samuel was incarcerated that the dock had finally been built and opened. He had heard the festivities through the window as the crowds flocked to see the Whitefriargate lock gate open to let the Trinity House yacht through as it sailed through the ring of docks and into the old Harbour and out again into the Humber.

'So much has happened,' he muttered as he gazed down into the dark water, 'and I have missed it.' Should I have stayed quiet? he wondered. I would have had a good life, a profession, a wife, children perhaps. He thought of Jonty and Polly Anna. Surrogate children for the ones I might have had.

Bitterness washed over him as he thought of the woman he had once loved and whom he thought had loved him, but who proved to be false. She wasn't going to wait for him, the man whose ideals, she'd said, were stronger than his love for her, and so she had married another.

I didn't do anything so bad, did I? Merely stood up to be counted, to speak for my fellow men who couldn't or wouldn't speak for themselves. But those same fellow men disappeared like snow in sunshine at the first sign of trouble, apart from one or two, men like Goddard, who had sent the message with Polly Anna and who over the years had delivered other messages to tell him that their cause to help the poor and oppressed was continuing.

Samuel sat amongst cargo in a loading shed and waited for the dawn, which was breaking the dark sky with a milky hue. He was cold and his hands were trembling and he knew that soon his body would start to shake with the craving for his dose of opium. I must beat it, he thought, or I shall finish up in the dock.

He dozed for a while and was barely conscious of the gentle wash of water, of footsteps going past him, of church clocks striking and the occasional hoot of a ship's horn. It was Sunday and the day was quiet, too early yet for the devout to make their way to church or chapel; the only people about at that hour were those such as himself, homeless or vagrant. He opened his eyes and blinked as a flash of sunlight lit upon him and he stretched and then shivered and decided to move on towards his destination.

There was a group of Gypsies gathered beneath trees in the farthest corner of Dock Green; a dog was lying on the ground beside their fire and two tethered horses were cropping the sparse grass behind the waggon. Something was cooking on the fire and a smell of meat drifted across to him, making him lick his lips and give a dry swallow. There was no-one else about yet, only a man on a horse riding across the grass towards the Gypsies. Samuel sat down with his back to a tree and idly watched him as he dismounted and spoke to one of the men. The Gypsy shook his head and pointed across the town. The horseman stayed a few minutes longer then remounted and rode in the direction of the town, passing within a few yards of Samuel.

He reined in and called to him. 'Are you from the fair? Are you a traveller?' His voice was educated and authoritative.

'No,' Samuel called back. 'I am not.'

The man hesitated for a second and then rode nearer and looked down at him, puzzled perhaps by the difference in his tone of voice and his manner of dress.

'I am no-one,' Samuel answered an unspoken question. 'No-one at all.'

'Do you need money?'

'No,' Samuel replied. 'I don't. But if you have any to spare, then give it to the poor.'

The man, middle aged and well dressed in country style, gave a slight smile, touched his hat in a salute and rode away.

The morning wore on and people started to appear on the Green; some were taking their morning exercise, some walking purposefully as if on an errand. A group of Trinity House schoolboys came with a ball, for this was their playground, and kicked it around. The Gypsies stamped out their fire, packed their belongings into the waggon and hitched one of the horses into the shafts, tied the other at the rear and climbed in. The women and children sat at the back and the men on the driving bench and with the dog running behind they moved off. They too, looked down at Samuel as they passed; they didn't speak but one of the men nodded in greeting.

Towards noon, the few groups of people scattered about swelled to a crowd. Samuel stood up, the better to see, and noticed that a platform had been built out of boxes and planks and a few men were gathered near it, talking earnestly. He moved forward slowly. He had started to tremble, with nerves as well as with hunger and his need for opium.

'Samuel!' Someone called his name. 'Samuel!'

It was Goddard and he moved away from a group of men and came across to him. 'You came! You got my message?'

Samuel nodded as he looked at his former colleague. Polly Anna had said that the man who had spoken to her at the workhouse gate was ragged and ill fed, but now he wasn't. Goddard was simply dressed, but his coat was of good cloth and though he was thin, as he had always been, he was plainly not starving.

'They said – they said – they thought you were appealing to the parish,' he began.

'I was trying to get in,' Goddard explained with a grin. 'I'd muddied my face, worn torn clothes. I wanted to meet you, to tell you about this meeting. Henry Vincent is to speak.'

'Henry Vincent? Do I know him?' Samuel's mind was befuddled, the noise of the crowd was getting to him.

'You know *of* him, Samuel. You must do! I've sent in pamphlets to you, he is a Radical as we are. He has been honoured by associations all over the country for his speeches against the Poor Law.'

'Indeed, indeed. Then I must meet him!' This was a subject close to his heart; he too had printed leaflets and pamphlets and spoken against the injustices towards the poor, the misery which massive unemployment brought and the bribery at elections; but his speeches had been called inflammatory, his pamphlets were seized and his meetings broken up by the military under the accusing eye of the aldermen and burgesses of the town. He had been put into jail, accused of false reporting and libel, and because of these charges he had lost his position as a teacher.

'An agitator,' he muttered. 'That's what they said of me, yet I was speaking only for others.'

'Yes, yes,' Goddard said uneasily. 'You have paid the price. We know that well enough.'

And the Reform Act, when it came, meant nothing to him, for the authorities in their wisdom decided that what he thought and acted upon was the result of a diseased mind and transferred him from the comparative comfort of the jail to the inhospitable lunatic ward in the workhouse.

'I want you to stand here, next to the platform,' Goddard was talking to him, 'and when Vincent has finished speaking, I shall say a few words about you and then bring you up to speak for yourself.'

Samuel began to shake violently. I can't speak.

What shall I say? I have nothing to say. His thoughts tumbled one over another and he barely heard what Vincent was saying on universal suffrage and the treachery of those who had brought in the Poor Law. He appealed too to the women in the crowd, which by now filled the whole of Dock Green and spilled over into the area beyond.

Goddard rose to speak. He was speaking of a man who had been imprisoned for his beliefs. 'Locked away. Incarcerated for life because he spoke honestly and of what he believed. A man, broken in mind, body and spirit, yet who has risked more punishment to be here today. I bring you that man now,' he held out his hand to Samuel, who realized with dismay that he was speaking of him. 'Let him speak to you, as best he can, of what has happened to him.'

Samuel shuffled on to the platform and the crowd grew silent as they saw his difficulty in placing one foot in front of the other. He is using me, he thought, as Goddard put an arm around his bent shoulders. He is using me, as of course he always did. I was the one who went to prison and yet Goddard spoke on the same platform.

He looked down at the crowd, poor people most of them, a weary look upon their faces. He began to speak, but his voice, unused to much talking was weak and his vocabulary, once so literate, deserted him, so that he merely mumbled over his words. He wanted to tell them of their rights as human beings, that the country was divided between rich and poor. But he couldn't. His mind vacillated between one subject and another and he lost his train of thought. The crowd began to fidget, their attention wavering and Goddard, anxious not to lose them, though having gained the required effect, stepped forward.

'Wait!' Samuel suddenly found his voice and held Goddard back. Down there in the front of the crowd he saw the upturned, eager and expectant faces of Jonty and Polly Anna. His children. His children, though not born of him. 'Wait,' he thundered. 'Let me tell you of my children, of *your* children. The children who must live in the workhouse because there is no other place for them. The children all over the country who work long hours in factories, mills and mines because their fathers and mothers cannot afford to keep them.'

He pointed indiscriminately into the crowd. '*You* know of a family like that! And you! And you!'

The crowd nodded and a ripple of agreement ran through the crowd. 'The Poor Law is a failure,' he shouted. 'Every workhouse pauper over the age of seven must work. Parents cannot see their children. Married couples cannot live together. We who have nothing – are nothing! We are mere sweepings in the gutter! What kind of society do we call this?'

Goddard hustled him off the platform as the crowd roared its approval. 'You did well, old fellow, but that's enough for now. We don't want the authorities here. This is a peaceable demonstration.'

Samuel shook off his arm. He felt drained and empty. All he wanted was to get back to his bed, to close his eyes and let blackness drift over him. 'What did it cost you, Goddard?' he asked.

'What?' Goddard frowned.

'What did it cost you to bribe the authorities to

stay away? They knew of the meeting, why were they not here?'

'Come along, old fellow. You're imagining things. The day has been too much for you. It was simply a peaceable demonstration. Nothing more.'

Polly Anna and Jonty appeared by his side. 'We'll look after him.' Polly Anna took hold of his arm. 'We'll take him back.'

'Take him back? Take him back? No. He is to come with us. We shall tour the country, Samuel, and show the people how you have been treated.'

Samuel shook his head and gave a slight ironic smile. And then I shall be abandoned, just as before. Ideas will be fed to me, my fervour will be whipped up. They all know how much I care, how honest I am, unlike you, my friend; and then when my usefulness is over I shall once more be locked away. The taste of freedom bitter in my mouth. 'I'm not coming,' he said and took hold of Polly Anna and Jonty for support. 'I'm going home.'

He leaned heavily against them as they walked back along the dockside, stopping now and again so that he could rest. They had both saved bread for him and he chewed on it gratefully. He felt faint with hunger and thirst and he sat down suddenly as his legs gave way beneath him.

'Have I been missed, Jonty? Will I get back in?' A fear developed. What if the door was locked against him? Where would he go? What would he do?

Polly Anna hushed him. 'It's all right. Jonty saw to everything, didn't you, Jonty?'

Jonty nodded. It had been relatively easy. Mr Pincher, as he had thought he would, stayed in bed until dinnertime, and Mrs Pincher was caught with a sudden emergency when it was discovered that two females had died during the night. One of the male inmates came to help Jonty with the breakfast in the locked ward and as he hadn't done it before, he didn't realize that anyone was missing, and Samuel's portion of bread went into Jonty's pocket. It would be more difficult to get him back in, but Jonty had no fears, he would hide him in the hayloft if necessary.

There was a heavy tread of boots behind them and Samuel looked around nervously. A gang of men were heading towards them. 'Are they coming for me?' He stumbled to his feet. 'You must run!'

'No, no.' Polly Anna reassured him again. 'They're seamen coming off the ships.'

He wasn't convinced. There were so many of them, yet they were different in character and dress from the crowd he had seen on Dock Green. Then he saw more of them, streaming down the gang-planks of the ships moored in the dock. Foreign ships from distant lands, English frigates, paddle steamers, fishing cutters and barges. 'Where are they going?'

Polly Anna shook her head, she didn't know, but Jonty did and pointed towards the Old Dock. In the distant sky amongst the tall masts there was one which flew the Bethel flag and it was towards this that the seamen and some of their wives were heading.

'*Valiant!*' Jonty said with difficulty. 'Seamen's chapel.' The *Valiant*, a former Dutch merchantman converted and refitted into a floating chapel, was moored in the dock for the benefit of seamen who wanted to attend divine service.

Samuel contemplated the day's events, of politics and bribery, of poverty and injustice; and of seamen too who had fought long and hard for their country, of fishermen who sailed in dangerous waters to bring in their catch and yet still were considered by some to be immoral and depraved.

He watched them as they overtook them, walking purposefully towards the lantern which shone in the gathering darkness. 'God help them,' he said wistfully, 'for no-one else can.'

11

It was dusk by the time the horseman reached the high Wolds. He was weary with the day's travelling. I'm getting too old for this journey, he reflected. I could be doing far more with my time, even though it gives me an opportunity to see my other sister.

He crossed the estate of his deceased brother-in-law and reckoned that a man had a large burden in life with two older widowed sisters to consider. Especially when one is so demanding and inconsiderate as to insist on my going on this wild goose chase, year in year out, simply because I promised in a moment of weakness that I would search for her daughter. He rode up the long drive to the old stone house and noted the work that needed to be done, the dead trees to be felled this winter, the shrubs to be pruned, the leaves on the lawns which had not yet been collected and he resolved to tell Harriet to chastise the gardeners.

His niece came to meet him in the hall as the maid opened the door to admit him. He nodded to her as she greeted him in her usual manner. 'Another wasted journey, I suppose, Uncle

Charles? I don't know why you do it!'

'I do it, Rowena, because it makes your mother happier than she would be if I didn't,' he replied testily, forgetting that a short time ago he had been echoing the same sentiments, yet annoyed that she should voice them.

'Mother is waiting for you. She was getting anxious. I told her that you were late because it takes you longer every year.'

'Thank you, Rowena. I'm pleased that you are so concerned about my great age!'

He didn't know why Rowena irritated him, but she always did and she always had. Even when she was a girl she had never seemed happy, always expressing disapproval or with a misery to relate.

'Harriet!' He greeted his sister, who waited for him in the drawing room, and gratefully sank into a chair and took the brandy which a footman offered him. 'The journey gets longer every year. I had forgotten, you know, just how long I had been doing this until Cecily reminded me. Ten years, she said.' He took a sip of brandy and stretched his legs. 'Ten years! It seems twice as long.'

'And how is our sister?' Mrs Winthrop boomed. 'Still doing her good works?'

'Indeed she is. She likes to stir things up, get things moving.' He took another sip. 'Yes, she's got wind of something going on at the workhouse, some deceit or malpractice that she was out to stop. She left the house before me this morning, determined to catch some blackguard or other.'

Mrs Winthrop tutted. 'Mixing with such people! She'll be murdered in her bed if she's not careful and then she'll be sorry!'

'If she's dead in her bed she's hardly likely to know whether to be glad or sorry, will she?' he said sourly. 'Anyway it fills her life, she feels that she is doing something useful.'

His elder sister gazed at him and he thought how old she looked. Her face was lined and her eyes were tired, and although she didn't complain, he knew that she was not well. 'And', she enquired, 'is there any other news?'

He shook his head wearily. 'You know that there isn't, Harriet. Wouldn't I have burst through the door in my eagerness to tell you if there had been?'

She turned her head away. 'I live always in hope, but I am just a silly old woman with this worry constantly on my mind.' She turned back to him. 'Are you sure you explored every avenue? You asked the Gypsies?' Her mouth turned down as she spoke.

'I asked the Gypsies, as I have done every year for the last ten years. They know nothing, or they say they don't.'

'Except that one time all those years ago,' she murmured, 'when one of them said that she had been there, but then had left!'

'Yes,' he said, pondering on the Gypsy woman who had sought him out and told him that Madeleine had been there, but had gone back to her own people. It hadn't made sense then and it still didn't. 'They haven't seen her since. My dear,' he leant forward and spoke earnestly, 'if she had wanted to come home she would have done so.'

'It is my own fault,' Harriet said plainly. 'When she wrote to me that she had married him and was expecting his child, I wanted no more to do with

113

her and I wrote and told her so. And I have regretted it ever since,' she added softly.

'There should be no regrets, Mother.' Rowena spoke from the window, where she was gazing out across the dark meadow, the lamps from the room reflected in the glass. '*She* chose to live that life! A life of a wandering Gypsy,' she said scathingly. 'She has ruined her life and ours by her impetuousness!'

And you have never been impetuous in your life, thought her uncle as he heard her harsh and bitter words. You have never loved enough to give up everything else, no loving words even, to give to your lost sister who has gone from our lives. He rose to his feet. 'I must go home. I am very tired. I cannot undertake this journey again, Harriet.'

Distress showed on his sister's face. 'But who will go? Someone must! I have to know, Charles, before I die, whether my daughter is dead or alive. And the child,' she said. 'We don't know whether or not it survived.'

'Does it matter?' Rowena said sharply. 'If the child survived, she will be living a life of a Gypsy, living in a tent, cooking over an open fire, just as her mother chose to do!'

Charles looked across at his niece. A slip of the tongue perhaps? His sister hadn't noticed anything, yet Rowena's use of the female gender when speaking of the child was given with such surety, that it was as if she knew with certainty that it was a girl child. Yet she couldn't know, for no-one had seen Madeleine since the day she had left home to meet the Gypsy at Hull Fair.

'I must go,' he repeated. 'Mary's nephew is expected, he is to stay with us for a while. I need to discuss the estate with him, the farms and so on.'

'He will come to live with you, I expect?' Harriet asked.

'He will. His parents are willing. I shall adopt him, of course, as he is to be my heir. Nice young fellow,' he added. 'I think we shall get along and Mary has always been fond of him.' He took his sister's hand. 'I'm sorry, Harriet, that there isn't better news. I think you should prepare yourself to believe that Madeleine won't be coming back. Not after all this time. It has been too long, my dear.'

He took his leave of them, bidding a cursory goodbye to Rowena and set off home, accompanied this time as it was very dark by one of the grooms from his sister's house.

'No luck then, sir?' Jennings asked, helping him to mount a fresh horse. 'Nobody seen her?' Jennings had been with the family for a lot of years and knew of his annual journey.

''Fraid not, Jennings. It's a bad business.'

'That it is, sir.' Jennings led the way down the drive and across the lane towards the neighbouring estate which belonged to Charles Dowson. 'I reckon it's time missus gave up. Miss Madeleine would have been back if she'd wanted to be. She wouldn't have stopped with them Gyppos if she hadn't been happy. Though he was an 'andsome fellow all right,' he added. 'I remember him well.'

'Do you, Jennings? How's that?'

'Why, don't you remember, sir? I went with owd Parker and Miss Madeleine and Miss Rowena to Appleby Fair, to buy some hosses for t'farm. That's where she first met him.' He grinned in the darkness. 'I thought at first it was Miss Rowena that had taken a fancy to him, but it was Miss Madeleine that took his eye, fair bowled over he was, I could tell that straight away. Beggin' tha pardon, sir.' He stopped abruptly. 'I wasn't meaning to be disrespectful to t'young ladies.'

'I'm sure you were not, Jennings. But it was a long time ago.' He sighed. 'Best forgotten now. It's over.'

His wife was entertaining her nephew, Richard Crossley, but they had waited supper until Charles arrived. Richard rose to greet his uncle, giving him a small bow before shaking his proffered hand. 'It's good to see you again, sir. I'm very glad to be here.'

'Well, I'm glad to hear it,' his uncle replied. 'Your father will have outlined all the plans I expect, but I want you to be sure that it's what you want. Your life will be very different here in East Yorkshire from that in London.'

'I know, sir, but I am prepared for it. I have been prepared for it for a long time and can't wait to come.' He stood tall and slim, a young man of nearly twenty and smiled at his aunt and uncle. 'I have always felt at home here ever since I was a small boy and was delighted when I knew I was to be your chosen heir.'

Later after supper they discussed the implications, but Charles was satisfied that he had made the right decision over his wife's sister's son. Richard was more than eager to embrace life in the country.

'I'm happy to settle in Yorkshire, sir, to work the estate and see it prosper. I have plenty of energy and I have not been idle since the matter was first broached. I have researched and studied farming methods. I am, I think I could say, a reasonable judge of horse flesh and I have attended cattle and sheep markets with a friend of my father's who says I have a good eye for a bullock or ewe.'

He asked his uncle how his journey into the flatlands of Hull had gone. 'Aunt Mary explained your mission. It would seem that it was not a successful journey?'

'It was not. And this time it was a particularly tiring one. I do not think I shall make it again, though my sister will be disappointed. She wants, you see, Richard, to make up for her former hastiness in barring her daughter from the house after she married the Gypsy. She has regretted it since, and I think too', he pondered, 'that she wants to see her grandchild.'

He gazed into the heart of the fire against which the two of them sat. 'A worry, of course, for Rowena if it was a male child, for he would come into the estate and she would be dependent on him for her surety. If it was a girl, then the estate would come to me as Harriet's only brother.' He looked across at his nephew, 'And then, of course, to you.'

Richard was intrigued by the story which his aunt had related; of the youngest daughter of a wealthy woman who had given up a life of ease and riches, of dances and parties and of eligible young men, and had thrown it all away because of her love for a Gypsy. It appealed to his romantic nature and he was curious as to what had happened to her and the infant who by now, he reckoned, would no longer be a child but would be entering early adulthood.

'And will you continue your search, sir?'

Charles Dowson shook his head. 'No. Harriet must accept that Madeleine won't come back. Not now. A pity. But it's over. Finished.'

12

'I'm sick of him, forever pawing and patting me! If he does it once more I'll— I'll—' Polly Anna's face was flushed with indignation as she spat out her fury to Jonty over Mr Pincher's behaviour.

Jonty tried to calm her. It would be worse for her if she made a fuss; he had seen the master's sly hand reaching for other females and he too had wanted to punch him. Keep away from him, that was best.

'How can I keep away from him? He's forever following me about! I'd tell Mrs Pincher, only she wouldn't believe me. She doesn't like me, never did.' She grinned at him. 'She's jealous I think, because you're my friend!'

She ducked from his friendly blow, but he caught her wrist and held it. 'Careful,' he said. 'Be careful.'

He was always warning her. He was cautious in his deviousness, but she was hot-headed, not willing to be put down, always standing up for others whom she thought were being mistreated or put upon, always taking risks.

'I shall leave this place, Jonty. I keep telling you and you don't believe me. But I shall go, sooner or later!' She smiled and patted his face. 'And you must come with me. To look after me,' she added.

He sighed. At fourteen she was well able to look after herself. Ten years of survival in the workhouse had not bowed her spirit, rather they had, over those years, made it stronger, made her more determined to get out. 'Samuel needs me.'

She was silent and a disconsolate expression passed over her face. 'Yes,' she said quietly. 'I know.'

Samuel had not been out of the workhouse again since the meeting on Dock Green. He had almost seemed glad to be back as they smuggled him in late that night. He was still teaching some of the boys in the workhouse, but the numbers had dwindled and his standards had dropped now that he no longer had either Jonty or Polly Anna for pupils. He was apathetic and slow and Polly Anna never saw him but only heard of him from Jonty, who went in every day, being now in charge of the locked room, giving out meals and medication.

'Don't be tempted to take it, Jonty.' Samuel, though totally dependent himself, was constantly badgering him as he gave him his tincture of opium. 'It is a great temptation for a young man to dabble, especially if you are feeling low.'

But Jonty wasn't low, as he was at great pains to point out. He now had a position of trust, he was an asset, and even Mr Pincher didn't call him names any more. At least not to his face.

'Can't leave Samuel!'

'Then I shall have to go alone.' She watched him steadily for his reaction. 'Samuel doesn't need me.'

But I do, he wanted to say. She was part of his life

and he didn't want her to leave, though he knew one day, when she was ready, that she would.

Mrs Harmsworth came into the yard as he was checking off some goods which had been delivered. She was still as positive as ever in her campaigning, still complaining to the newspapers and arranging meetings and inspections. 'So what is being delivered today? What luxuries have the guardians ordered for the inmates?'

He smiled at her. He liked Mrs Harmsworth, no longer afraid that he would get into trouble because of her enquiries. 'Keep her sweet, Jonty,' Mrs Pincher had told him. 'Let her see how happy you are. Let her see how well you have got on here at 'workhouse.'

He showed her his list. Ten stone of flour at two shillings a stone. Two stone of oatmeal. Six sacks of potatoes. She handed it back to him. 'What a splendid repast that will make. I could almost wish I was coming to eat with you, Jonty.'

He grinned. He knew that she was on the look-out for some discrepancy, some proof that the guardians and Master or Matron were making a profit, as they were, he had seen it with his own eyes. A side of bacon which was extra to the order. A box of stockings which never reached the inmates, but the goods disappeared so fast that no-one else ever saw them.

The butcher's cart arrived whilst she was still there. A youth climbed down and whistling noisily picked up a sack and put it over his shoulder. 'Leg o' mutton, shoulder o' mutton, belly pork, three ham shanks! Is tha Jonty?'

He nodded, he hadn't seen this errand lad

before. 'Then tha's to sign for it.' He handed a slip of paper to Jonty.

He looked down at it and thought it unfortunate that Mrs Harmsworth was looking over his shoulder, for written on the paper was merely a shoulder of mutton, which was indeed in the sack, but with no mention of the other items. If I sign this, then I could be accused of stealing these other items. Mr Fox doesn't know I can read.

Mrs Harmsworth was looking at him. 'I wouldn't sign that if I were you, Jonty,' she said pleasantly. 'It seems to me that there has been a mistake.' She turned to the delivery boy. 'It appears that you have got your orders mixed up.'

'No, ma'am. I don't think so. Mr Fox does all 'orders himself. This one, he said to be sure to bring here to 'workhouse.'

The door to the main building opened and Mrs Pincher came out. She's been watching through the window, Jonty surmised as he saw the flush on her cheeks. Now what's she going to do?

'G'morning, Mrs Harmsworth. What brings you to these parts? Ah, is that 'meat delivery? We're waiting on that. Better get it inside for Cook, Jonty.' She looked inside the sack. 'Why! What's this? I never ordered all this! Ha! Would that I could with my budget.'

She turned to the lad. 'Tha'll have to take it back. Tell Mr Fox there's been a mistake, shoulder o' mutton is what was ordered.' She took out the joint of fatty meat and handed the sack back to the boy. 'Off you go, then. Don't hang about. Somebody might be waiting on that for their dinner.'

Jonty watched the two women, who were eyeing

each other, both faces expressionless; yet Mrs Harmsworth's eyes held a gleam which said she knew she had almost been triumphant, and that next time she would catch Mrs Pincher out.

'I'm going to the fair, Jonty. Are you coming?' She had tracked him down in the woodshed, where he was filling a basket for Mrs Pincher's fire. She wasn't sure whether or not to ask him and neither did she know whether to be pleased or sorry when he shook his head in answer.

Not yet. He hadn't finished all of his tasks. Mr Pincher had had him running here, there, and everywhere all day and he still had to check the storeroom, give out the medication and serve supper.

He looked anxiously at Polly Anna. She looked tired, her face was paler than usual and her eyes were red with sitting over the stitching, but she had decided some years before that sewing was preferable to picking oakum or going out to the flax mills, where the hours were long and the work arduous. She had made a determined effort to becoming reasonably expert at cutting out shirts, skirts and breeches.

'You all right?' he asked. 'Sick?'

'No. I'm all right.' She had thought that she was dying that morning when she had risen from her bed and found the blood. She had been stricken with severe stomach cramps and had bent in agony over the sewing table. One of the older women had come across to her and asked her if it was the time of her flux. She didn't know what she meant and the woman had at first laughed at her ignorance but then thinking better of it, explained.

'Tha'll have to watch it now girl. No going with lads or tha'll get pregnant. Tha's a woman now.'

No going out with lads? Did that mean Jonty? What would happen if she did? She had no female friends in the workhouse that she could ask. She never had cultivated friendship. Only once, when she was very young she had had a friend and she had disappeared, just as her mama had done. Had her young friend died too? She had never asked, not wanting to hear the answer. And she never struck up friendship with anyone else in case they too vanished or died.

'Jonty! I'm a woman now! Do you know what that means?'

He looked startled for a moment and then a flush burnt his face and neck. He nodded. He knew. He had heard the lewd talk that went on between men, and women too. But he knew that Polly Anna didn't know about these things, she didn't mix with the other inmates and was therefore still a child. But no, not now. Now she said she was a woman. He reached out to squeeze her hand, but she drew back from him.

'I have to keep away from men,' she said, putting her hands protectively beneath her armpits. 'And you're a man, Jonty. I might get pregnant and have a baby otherwise.'

He turned his head: she could read his face so well. 'Not me. Safe with me.'

She heaved a sigh of relief. 'Oh good! Will you come to the fair then?'

'Busy. Come after work. Wait for me?'

'No. I want to go now. I'm tired of being cooped

up. I'll maybe see you there.' She scowled. 'I haven't any money, though. Mrs Pincher said I wasn't due any even though I did extra sewing.'

He felt deep down into his breeches pocket where he kept the purse. He didn't have much, but sometimes he was given a tip by tradesmen; he looked younger than his seventeen years because he was so small and bent and they would pat his head and give him a copper or sometimes sixpence, which he rarely spent but put it with his small hoard.

He turned away from Polly Anna and brought out the purse, fishing out a sixpence, but curiously she reached over to look.

'What have you got there? Oh, let me look! How pretty. Where did you get it? Did you steal it?'

'No. No!' He shook his head furiously. He had kept it secret from her all these years and now he had been careless, so anxious was he to please her.

She prised it from his thin fingers. 'Let me look. Please. I'll give it back.'

Reluctantly he yielded and she stroked its softness with her fingers. 'It's beautiful. Why haven't I seen it before?'

He hesitated. Should he tell her? This was as good a time as ever, he supposed. What had her mother said as she had given him the purse with the silver necklace? He thought back over the years. Keep it for her, she'd said, until she's old enough to wear it. She was old enough now. Now that she was a woman. 'Not here. Wait for me. Then I say.'

Yet still she wouldn't wait, even though she was curious about the purse and just a little cross with him for not showing it to her before. He always was giving her things, a piece of ribbon found in the gutter, a glove or handkerchief, yet he hadn't shown her the pretty purse which he must surely have known she would love to have had above all else. So she didn't wait and told him that she would meet him near Alger's Dancing Saloon. There were times when she couldn't bear to be indoors a minute longer, when she craved to be outside and feel the wind or the rain on her face. And especially at Hull Fair time she was seized by a desire to escape the confining walls of the workhouse and join the seething throng heading down to the Market Place, to Castle Street or Dock Green. She couldn't explain the longing which came over her when she heard the music of a flute, the clip-clop of hoof-beat, the roll of a drum or the cries of the entertainers beseeching all to come, but she only knew that the call was irresistible.

She wandered around the sideshows listening to the cries of the showmen inducing the crowd to come in to see the dancing bear, the five-legged dog, the man who ate fire, and they beat on their gongs as they tried to drown out their neighbours' cries; she heard the trumpeting of elephants at the wild beast show and caught a glimpse of the huge beast through a crack in the canvas; she kept a tight hold of the sixpence that Jonty had given her as the professional beggars whined from the pitch which they occupied year by year; and then made her way to Dock Green to stand outside Alger's Dancing Saloon, whose huge structure had been brought by steamship from London.

Two young women on the open stage were tapping their feet, swaying their hips and waving their hands to the men in the crowd to come in; they wore spangled dresses short enough to see their coloured petticoats beneath, silver slippers on their feet and sparkling coronets in their hair. Polly Anna watched in fascination, won over by the glitter, the music and the jollity.

So caught up was she that she failed to notice those around her and in particular one man who had noticed her, until she felt an arm creep around her waist. 'Polly Anna! What a nice surprise, finding you here.'

She jumped back from Mr Pincher's grasp and turned in distaste from his beery breath as he leered at her. 'Do you want to come in? Have a little dance or a glass of wine? Bet tha's never tasted wine, Polly Anna!'

'No, no, I haven't. But I don't want to come. I – I'm waiting for someone.'

'Not that little half-wit?' He swayed unsteadily. 'Not yon dummy that Mrs Pincher's so fond on?'

She didn't answer him. She wouldn't give him the satisfaction of a discussion. He had no idea of Jonty's intelligence, nor of how Jonty manipulated both him and Matron to achieve his own aims.

He came towards her again and attempted to put his arms around her. 'Get off me!' She pushed him away, but he grabbed at her and held her fast.

'Come on,' he slurred. 'Come and have a little dance, I'll treat you right; give thee some money, how about that?' His small eyes glittered and he suddenly pulled her away from the front of the platform and from the lamps and crowds, down the side of the saloon into the darkness.

She tried to scream, but he put his hand over her

mouth and with his other he started to lift her skirt. She clamped her teeth over his hand and he pushed her down on to the ground as she kicked out at him. 'Little bitch, you don't know what's good for you.'

She kicked out again and as he stumbled she scrambled through his legs and back into the glare of the naphtha lamps and the safety of the crowd.

'Polly Anna! What is it? What is it?' Jonty caught her as she ran.

'Come quick. Come quick. It's Mr Pincher!' She caught hold of his arm and dragged him along with her. 'Don't let him see us.'

They sat behind a waggon and Polly Anna angrily burst out what had happened. 'He's horrible, Jonty. He's evil. I wish he was dead!' She put her hand over her mouth as the words spilled out. Did she mean that? Should she have said it? But she could still smell the sour staleness of him as his plump hands had strayed over her and she knew that she did.

'He's spoilt everything! We were going to have such a good time. What am I to do, Jonty? I'll be scared of bumping into him now, I'll be watching over my shoulder all of the time.'

Jonty didn't think that the Master would bother her during the day at the workhouse, he would be too afraid of Mrs Pincher seeing him for one thing and he wouldn't dare to go near the female dormitories, there were too many fierce and loose women up there who would think it great sport to debag him if they found him wandering in places where he shouldn't be.

'I'll take care of you.' He put his arm around her.

'I know you will,' she snuffled. 'But you might not always be there, just as you weren't tonight.'

'I'll be there,' he promised. 'Always.'

13

'You said you'd tell me where you got the purse.'
They were sitting, the following day, halfway up the
steps to the hayloft, away from the inmates who
were milling around in the yard waiting for the
strident ring of the supper bell.

He pulled the purse out of his pocket and
handed it to her. 'Yours.'

'Mine? Are you giving it to me?' She opened it,
admired it, then reluctantly gave it back. 'No. You
keep it, Jonty. You always give me things. I never
give you anything.'

Only your friendship and that means more to me
than the whole world. Only he didn't say it. How
could he? He only hoped that she would know it.
He handed it back to her. 'Yours. Your mother's!'

She stared at him open mouthed. 'My mother's?
What? How?'

'Gave it me. Keep for you.' He put his hands
behind his neck to unfasten the bootlace which
held the necklace. He had never taken it off and the
knot had tightened. 'Help me.'

Polly Anna was holding the purse as if it was made of fragile glass, turning it over so tenderly. 'I don't understand. Why have you had it all this time and not told me? Did it really belong to Mama?'

He nodded and struggled with the knot. 'Help me. Then I say.'

She turned to see what he was doing. 'What is this bit of old bootlace for? You always wear it.' She pulled on the knot with her fingernails and prised it loose.

Jonty looked around the yard to see if anyone was watching, then carefully pulled out the chain and locket from beneath his shirt. He handed it to her. 'Yours!'

She slid the chain through her fingers and placed the locket in the palm of her hand. She ran her forefinger over the scrolled letters, M W and suddenly felt very sad, though she didn't know why; she hadn't as far as she knew, ever seen the necklace before. 'Where did you get it?'

'Your mama. She asked me, keep it safe for you.'

'You remember her?' Tears gathered in her eyes and spilled down her cheeks.

He nodded and took hold of her hand. ''Night you came.'

'What was she like?' she whispered.

'Beautiful. Like you.' His own eyes were wet and he leaned his head against hers. 'She asked, would I care for you, and I said yes.'

'And so you do, Jonty,' she wept. 'So you do. I just wish – I just wish that I could remember her too.'

'Try,' he urged. 'Owd Boney brought you in. You cried.'

She shook her head. Her memories were locked deep down. She couldn't pull them out, not in this hated place.

'Put it on,' he whispered. 'Don't let Matron see.'

Her fingers trembled as she threaded the boot-lace through the chain again as Jonty had done, and placed it around her neck, where he fastened it. 'You keep the purse for me. It'll be safer with you. Women are so nosey, someone might see it. Besides,' she gave a wavering smile, 'I'd never have any money to put in it.'

He transferred his remaining coins from his pocket back into the purse and they were sitting quietly, not speaking, when the supper bell rang, making them both jump.

'You go, Jonty, I'll be along in a minute. I just want to sit here and think for a bit.'

'Don't miss supper. Must eat.'

She nodded. He always insisted that she ate everything that was offered, though sometimes the sight of the lumpy gruel or greasy stew made her want to retch. He hurried off, he had to feed the inmates of the lunatic ward before he could have his own supper and Polly Anna sat on the steps meditating over her fate. She badly wanted to know about her past life and of her mother and father, yet there was some sadness locked in, impeding her memory.

She lost track of time until she heard the sound of boots in the empty yard below and saw a lantern swinging. She kept very still, hardly daring to breathe as in the glow of the light she saw the short, stocky figure of Mr Pincher. He was dressed to go out in his cape and beaver hat and he reached up to hang the lantern on a nail in the wall. A shadow drifted about the yard and he paused and took the lamp down again and looked around the yard, inspecting each corner. He looked up towards the hayloft steps and lifted the lantern. 'Who's there? Somebody's up there!'

She didn't want him climbing up the steps towards her so she called back, 'It's only me, Polly Anna.'

'Oh! Polly Anna is it? And what 'you doing up there? Is that whelp with you?' He put down the lantern at the bottom of the steps and started to climb. 'Having a bit of a romp in 'hay, is that it?' he jibed.

She stood up. 'Jonty isn't here if that's who you mean, and please don't call him names. He's worth far more than you!'

'Is he, by God! We'll see about that, you little drab. I'll show you who's best.' He continued to climb, though he had to hold on to the rail as the steps were steep. She stepped back on to the top step and stood quite still. She was higher than him and so had the advantage. Or so she thought, for she was unprepared for the blow that he gave her in her midriff which knocked her clean off her feet and into the hayloft.

Billy raced down the corridor in search of Jonty. He opened doors and looked in the supper room, where the inmates were still sitting, and finally found him as he was locking the door of the lunatic ward.

'Come quick! Mr Pincher's got Polly Anna in 'hayloft. He's hurting her. I could hear her yelling.'

Jonty dropped the tray he was carrying and chased out of the building and into the yard, with

Billy running behind. He shouted, though his words made no sense and he cursed his impediment. He took the steps two at a time and burst through the door and saw Polly Anna on the straw-strewn floor, struggling to move Mr Pincher's heavy weight from the top of her.

'Get him off me, Jonty! He's crazy!'

He took hold of the Master's collar and tugged, tightening it around his neck so that he started to splutter and released his hold on Polly Anna, only to scrabble to his feet and attack Jonty. 'You runt! You jabbering toad. I'll drive thee out of here. Tha can fall in 'gutter and I'll stride over thee. And tha can tek this hussy with thee. I'll tell 'governors what tha gets up to in here!' With one hand he held Jonty away from him and with the other slapped him around his face.

'Let go of him.' Polly Anna grabbed a hay fork and stood with her feet astride, threatening him with the spiked prongs. 'Let go or you'll get this in your fat belly!'

Mr Pincher dropped his hold and stepped back towards the door. 'Tha wouldn't dare!' Though the look in her eye showed that she would.

Jonty held the door open; he was trembling with anger, so much that he wanted to say, so much abuse that he wanted to heap upon this foul-mouthed devil who was bent on implying some indecency in their innocent friendship.

Mr Pincher glanced over his shoulder to judge where the steps were. 'I'm telling thee both. Tha'll be out of here by 'end of 'week. Tha can starve for all I care.' With one final defiant thrust of his fist he struck out again at Jonty, who ducked beneath his arm and felt his head hit the corpulent stomach of the Master. Jonty grabbed for the rail as he felt himself falling and reached out to catch Mr Pincher's arm as he too swayed backwards. He couldn't hold him, the Master's weight was too great and he fell with a thud down the steps and landed in the yard at Billy's feet.

'Is he dead, does tha think?' Billy whispered, looking down at the Master.

'I don't know.' He was lying very still, but Jonty thought that he didn't look like any of the dead bodies that he had seen. But then, they had been ill with disease or starvation and it showed on their cold white faces. If he was dead, they were in trouble. And if he wasn't dead they would be in even more trouble when he recovered.

'Is he dead?' Polly Anna came down the steps and remembered her wish that the Master was dead. She wouldn't be sorry, she considered. Nobody would miss him, not even Mrs Pincher, though she would probably lose her job as Matron.

Mr Pincher groaned and they all started. 'He's not dead then!' Billy said gloomily. 'Does tha think it would be a good idea to finish him off? We could hit him wi' a stick or summat. Tha'll be in right trouble, Jonty, when he comes round. He'll be sure to blame thee for pushing him!'

'No! No!' He didn't push him. Though perhaps it looked like that from where Billy was standing.

'Oh, I won't say owt! Tha can rely on me. I'll tell 'em that he was chasin' Polly Anna. I saw him, I was down here in 'yard. I saw him go on up after her. That's why I run to fetch thee, Jonty, I knew tha'd be mad wi' him.'

Every word that Billy uttered made it appear worse and Jonty and Polly Anna exchanged anxious glances. Billy would make it seem worse if he was questioned, for in his desire to please and to bask in some kind of notoriety for himself, he would become confused and say everything wrong.

'Let's put him over in this corner whilst we think what to do,' Polly Anna whispered. 'Nobody will miss him yet, he was on his way out. Billy, you go back inside and don't say a word to anybody. Do you hear? Not a word.'

Billy seemed slightly disappointed that he wasn't going to be involved in the discussion, but he took heart in manhandling the Master into a dark corner of the yard, secure in the knowledge that he wouldn't remember him being there when he woke up.

'We have to leave, Jonty,' she spoke softly and urgently when he had gone. 'We can't stay. He'll tell the authorities that we pushed him. We might go to jail!'

But it will seem as if we are guilty if we run away, he thought. And where will we go? He had a few coins, but Polly Anna had nothing. How would they live?

'Samuel!' he said.

'You have to think of yourself now, not Samuel,' she said crossly. 'The magistrates will be told and how will you explain that it was an accident?'

'No,' he retaliated. 'Ask Samuel! For advice!'

'Oh! Yes. Yes, let's do that.' They were both getting nervous, not thinking rationally. 'Can you get back in? Can I come with you?'

He nodded. They would risk it. Polly Anna could

explain more clearly, more quickly than he could what had happened and he still had the key to the locked room in his pocket, he hadn't had time to hang it in the usual place when Billy had come looking for him.

The corridors were crowded with people; there were rumblings of discontent as apparently there hadn't been enough bread to go round. Some of the inmates were complaining that they hadn't had a piece of bread all day.

They slipped into the locked ward and Jonty turned the key behind them. Polly Anna kept close to him, she didn't know what to expect, there were so many rumours of what went on behind the locked door, though Jonty had always told her that the stories were exaggerated. A man shambled up to her and grinned and patted her on the shoulder, but Jonty pointed to his bed and obediently he went away.

Samuel was sitting at a table writing on a scrap of paper and didn't look up as the door opened, but only when they stood beside him. His face was yellow and lined and Polly Anna thought how old and ill he seemed since she had last seen him.

'Samuel,' she said, 'we're in trouble.'

'Trouble? What has happened?'

She explained quickly and urgently. 'I think that we have to go away. Mr Pincher is getting at Jonty now because of me.'

Samuel agreed. 'He has needed an excuse to be rid of him. You are far too useful, Jonty, and he doesn't like it!' He pondered. 'You say he was on his way out?'

'Yes, I was watching him. He was about to go out

of the gate when he heard something, it must have been Billy. Then he saw me.'

'Going drinking,' Jonty broke in. 'And to meet women.' He had seen him so many times, followed him too on some occasions, curious to know where he went, and he knew that he travelled into some sordid areas of the town.

'When he recovers from the fall he is going to be very angry.' Samuel's face creased with anxiety as he pondered on the implications. 'Polly Anna is right, Jonty. You will have to leave, who knows what will happen otherwise? But where will you go? How will you live? You must try for another workhouse in another area – another town,' he said, searching around for a solution and they both stared at him. He wasn't able to help them, he had no influence, nor after all this time in the workhouse any ideas on how they would survive. 'You could try Sculcoates or Beverley ward, but you may have to lie, don't tell them that you have only come from Hull or they will send you back here. Tell them – tell them that you have been travelling and have fallen on hard times, yes, that's it,' he pursed his lips and nodded. 'But go as far as you can in case word gets out and the Master sends the law after you.'

'Thank you, Samuel.' Polly Anna turned to leave. 'You have been very helpful, we're grateful, and we shall miss you. Come Jonty, we'd better go quickly.'

Jonty hesitated, reluctant to leave Samuel, uncertain whether this was the right thing to do and afraid to venture into another life.

'Go on, Jonty.' Samuel seemed to understand his thoughts as he had so often in the past. 'There is nothing more for you here. Go where life takes you and don't be afraid. I wish that I was strong enough to come with you.'

They both turned to look back as they reached the door, but Samuel had his head bent again over his writing and didn't look up. Jonty closed the door and locked it and they slipped once again into the milling crowd in the corridor.

'Come on.' Polly Anna took his hand, anxious to be off. 'We must go before Mr Pincher comes round and remembers what happened.'

'Jonty!' Mrs Pincher's screeching voice echoed down the corridor. 'Jonty! Anybody seen that lad?'

'Go!' he said urgently. 'Go now.' Mrs Pincher hadn't seen him yet, but another moment and she would. He'd have to stay, attend to her wishes and perhaps by doing so she wouldn't suspect him of any duplicity.

'Jonty!' Polly Anna was alarmed. 'You'll come? You will come?'

'Yes. Yes! But go!' He pushed her away.

She turned a doubting face towards him. 'I *am* going. I always intended to, but I want you to come too. Don't let me down, Jonty. I'll meet you at the fair.'

He could hear Mrs Pincher's voice calling to him as he watched Polly Anna race down the corridor and out of the door. The fair! That was where she was going. Where she had always wanted to go. He could hear the memory of her voice echoing back throughout the years. 'Let's run away and join them, Jonty,' she used to say in her childish voice. 'They have more fun than we do.'

'Jonty! Are you going deaf? I'm calling and calling. Come wi' me, there's some trouble in 'supper room. Some of folks won't move out till they've had more bread. And there isn't any.'

A group of men sat around a long table, their hands still clutching their empty plates. One of them stood up as Mrs Pincher and Jonty came into the room. 'We've not had any bread for two days, Matron. We're not out to cause trouble, we onny want our rights.'

'Your rights?' Mrs Pincher spluttered. 'I can't buy any more of your rights if my budget doesn't run to it! There was enough bread bought to go round, somebody else must have had your share.'

'Aye, and who would that be, I wonder?' another man broke in. 'I wouldn't mind tekking a look in thy cupboard.'

Mrs Pincher continued to argue even though they had a mean look about them. She gave them a lecture on how lucky they were to be here and not starving outside, but they were not convinced and sat solidly down, staring her out. So what to do? There wasn't any more bread delivered until the morning.

Jonty touched her arm. 'Baker,' he whispered. 'Send to baker for more bread.'

'Aye,' she said. 'That's it. He'll have summat left over I don't doubt. You go, Jonty. Ask him for two penny loaves, don't matter if they're stale. It'll keep 'em quiet till morning.'

I didn't mean for me to go, he contended. But then who else can she ask? He realized quite forcibly that Mrs Pincher would miss him if he went away; who else would run at her constant beck and call? Billy! He would ask Billy to go, and maybe Billy would find himself being useful at last.

The door burst open almost knocking him over as he went toward it. 'Where's Mrs Pincher?' Mr Bertram stood there, his face flushed and his coat half undone. 'Is she here?'

Jonty pointed behind him. 'Mrs Pincher – Matron!' Mr Bertram gasped. 'Come quickly. Oh dear. How embarrassing! Mr Pincher, he's out in the yard. You'd better come.'

'What's going on?' Mrs Pincher bustled up.

'Please come at once. Oh dear!'

They followed Mr Bertram out of the building and into the front yard and Jonty prepared himself for an onslaught of accusations from Mr Pincher, who presumably was now recovered.

'I had just been out on an errand and as I entered through the gate I saw the lantern,' Mr Bertram explained, 'and on investigation found Mr Pincher propped up against the wall. He – erm, seems to be in a state of intoxication I fear.'

Oh, Polly Anna! What have you done? Jonty put his hand to his mouth to cover a smile, but not so the group of inmates who had followed them out, including the men who had demanded more bread. They burst into a howling gale of ribaldry as they viewed the Master, well lit by the lantern hanging above his head and seemingly in a drunken stupor, with a clump of straw tied to his head, a hayfork in his hand, his shirt flapping around his nether regions and his breeches around his ankles.

14

Polly Anna huddled in a doorway opposite the workhouse waiting for Jonty to appear, but when he didn't come and she saw the stooped figure of Mr Bertram coming down the street she knew it would only be a short time before Mr Pincher was discovered. She had carefully placed the lantern where it would shed maximum light on him, so that anyone entering the gate would have an immediate view.

She waited until Mr Bertram entered the gate and then took to her heels down Whitefriargate, turning into Trinity House Lane, past the almshouses and inns, and skirted the Holy Trinity Church down its north side and its conglomeration of market stalls, mingling with the crowds who were heading the same way as she was, towards the Market Place and the sounds of the fair.

She lingered for a while listening to the cries of the traders and joined the crowd who were gathered about an apothecary, who was displaying a table full of magical potions guaranteed to cure any ills.

'*Charlatan*,' she heard someone cry. 'He cannot cure. You are all doomed. Give up this night of evil and debauchery and return to your Saviour.' A man dressed in black and carrying a board with a poster on it, claiming that the fair was the work of the devil, was parading up and down the road. 'You are entering a hotbed of vice, do not go any further. Turn back now before it's too late!'

The crowd turned their backs on the apothecary and heckled the preacher. 'Show us which booth 'vice is in, wilt tha,' someone called, 'and I'll gladly pay my penny!' The apothecary raised his voice and continued his patter to bring them back. 'A potion here to relieve your aches and pains of the body or the mind. My word of honour that it will cure all ill humours.'

'Tha'd better sell some to yon preacher then,' a man shouted. 'He's got worse humour than any I've seen.'

Polly Anna moved on. Every shop doorway was taken up by a trader and every lamppost by a poster advertising a circus, theatrical shows or menagerie. Hotels proclaimed that you could Dine, Eat or Sleep in their establishments or partake of their Excellent Shilling Dinners, for the town was filled to capacity with visitors to the fair who travelled from Leeds to Selby by train and continued their journey downriver by steamboat; from Grimsby, Gainsborough and Thorne they came by packet or barge, by coach from York or by waggon or cart from the surrounding country districts.

Sheep and goats were penned in areas around the church, Gypsies ran with their ponies to show their paces down the middle of the road and mingling with the smell of animals and the doubtful odour of the crowd was the sweet aroma of gingerbread, sugar sticks and honeycomb toffee.

Polly Anna glanced over her shoulder from time to time as she looked for Jonty, but the crowd was very great and his small height, she realized, would be hidden from view. The booths and stalls were sprawled over a vast area around the town and spreading almost to the Humber Basin, but she crossed through to Castle Street between the Junction and Humber Docks and continued on to Dock Green, where the circus and theatres and live shows were based and where she hoped that Jonty would meet her.

Rain started to drizzle down and she heard the grumbles of the crowd as they complained that it always rained for the fair. She began to shiver; she had no coat, only her coarse serge workhouse skirt and shirt to cover her. There were ash and sawdust scattered over the ground, but as the rain increased this turned to slippery ankle-deep mud and her toes squelched inside her thin boots.

'Roll up! Roll up! Come to the circus. See the tumblers. See the dwarfs as they ride the giant elephants. See the painted Indians as they perform their war dance. See the sword swallower. Roll up! Roll up! Come along, ladies and gentlemen, come to the greatest show on earth!' The drums rolled, the gongs were banged, the Indians thrust their arrowheads skywards, stamped their feet and chanted wild, threatening cries as the ringmaster dressed in red coat, black breeches and boots cracked his whip and led the customers up the steps and behind the curtained booth to savour the entertainment within.

Polly Anna longed to go inside; she was pent up with the excitement and glitter of it all and even though the rain was now running down her face yet still she stood watching. She could hear the music from inside, the neighing of horses and the trumpeting of the elephants and was filled with longing. Presently when she became too cold she moved on again and came to the edge of the Green where she and Jonty had once walked before, and again she saw the sparks and smoke of wood fires and the glow of lamps illuminating the darkness.

She was drawn towards the firelight and the warmth and stood a little way off from the group surrounding it, until at last they noticed her. They turned towards her but didn't speak, just stood watching her. She moved towards them. 'Could I warm myself by your fire?' No-one answered. They were all young people, younger than her by far, except for one girl of about her age who held a baby on her lap.

She put her hand out towards the flame and felt the heat. 'I haven't a coat,' she explained. Still they didn't answer, but kept their dark eyes upon her. 'Is your mother here?'

She directed her question at the girl with the baby, who pointed to a tent and said softly, 'She's in the bender.'

'Could I speak to her, do you think?'

The girl inclined her head to one of the small boys, who on glancing first at Polly Anna got up from his place by the fire and disappeared inside the tent.

He emerged a few minutes later, followed by a Gypsy woman dressed in a long dark skirt and embroidered blouse, with a coloured shawl about her dark head and shoulders. 'Yes,' her voice was sullen, 'what is it you want?'

'I wondered – I wondered.' What did she want? She wasn't sure. 'Could I travel with you a little way? I have no home, no money, but I'd work to earn my keep.'

The Gypsy shook her head. 'We don't take in strangers. We look after our own kind.'

'I could help on the booths or the stalls,' she began.

'We're not fairground folk!' The woman was angry. 'We're Romano! Nothing to do with them!' She tossed her head in the direction of the booths and sideshows, the noise and music.

'I'm sorry, I thought—', Polly Anna stammered as she realized she had made a blunder, but the Gypsy turned her back and went inside the tent.

'I didn't know,' she said to the girl, 'you're always here. I thought—'

The girl shook her head. 'We always follow the fairs, but we're not fairfolk, we don't belong. We sell things, lace and ribbon and pegs and our men sell horses. That's really why we're here, for the horses and ponies.'

'Kisaiya!' The girl was summoned from inside the tent and she rose immediately, nestling the baby on her shoulder. 'Try some of the sideshows,' she said softly. 'Sometimes they want extra help.'

Some of the traders whose business had slowed down were packing up their belongings, for this was the last night of the fair. If Jonty doesn't come soon we shall be too late to go with them, Polly Anna worried. And if he doesn't come, shall I go alone? And how? Or who with?

She approached a stallholder and asked him if he could give her a job. 'Doing what?' he laughed. 'You onny need a tail and you'd look like a drowning mermaid! Try the sideshows.'

So she tried the sideshows, but they were all too busy to talk to her, too busy by far making the most of the last evening and cajoling the customers to come in out of the rain and enjoy the fun. She slipped down the side of one of the tented booths and tried to creep beneath the canvas, but as her head protruded through the other side she looked up to see a man looking down at her. The look on his face was enough to deter her from venturing further and she backed out again.

It was close on midnight, the crowds were leaving and the tired showmen were taking down their booths, coaxing animals into pens and packing up their stuff into waggons and carts ready for an early start the next morning.

'Can I help you? Can I come with you?' Polly Anna was getting desperate. Jonty hadn't come. For whatever reason, she decided, he had chosen to stay at the workhouse. Perhaps, she thought, when Mr Pincher had been discovered, the accusing finger had been pointed at her alone. Mrs Pincher would be happy to blame her for any misdoing and there would be no reason for Jonty to be implicated if Mr Pincher hadn't complained of him.

She was given short shrift by most of the traders and the showpeople merely shook their heads as she approached them, so disconsolately she sat down on the wet ground between two empty waggons and wondered what to do. For the first time in her life she had to make a decision and she didn't know how. I can't go back, that's for certain, and I don't want to go to another workhouse like Samuel suggested. She was adamant about that. I want – I want, I want to go with the fair! That's what I want. Only they don't want me!

She leaned back against the waggon wheel and closed her eyes. She was tired but too cold and hungry to let sleep steal over her, but she sat quite still and listened to the hammering and shouting and whistling and all the sounds of the men, women and children as they packed their belongings ready for the road.

Presently another voice sounded above the others and she sat up eagerly, perhaps it was Jonty after all. But no, the voice was calling. 'Where are you, you *beti* rascal! Come on, come on. Come to Dado.'

She sighed. It wasn't Jonty. But a second later she sat up with a start as a small furry creature dressed in coat and fez pounced upon her, chattering excitedly.

'Morgan's monkey!' she breathed in delight. 'Can it be you? Do you remember me?'

The monkey scratched its head as if pondering and then did a circular dance on her lap two or three times, then with its bright eyes upon her sat shaking its head.

'I remember you,' she murmured. 'You used to make me laugh. But when?' A chink of light was filtering through, opening up a doorway into her memory. It was three years since she had last seen the monkey, but there was some other time.

'Where are you, you rascal?' The voice called again and the monkey jumped down from her lap and scolded her.

'You'd better go home,' she said reluctantly. 'Morgan's looking for you.'

The creature looked up at her and put its hand out towards her. She took it and felt the fur and the nails and memory stirred again. It pulled on her hand and she got to her feet. 'All right,' she said. 'I'll come with you. I have nowhere else to go.'

She called to the man, who had his back to her as he shouted for his monkey. 'Morgan! Here he is.'

He turned and the monkey dropped her hand and ran to him, running up his leg and on to his shoulder, snuggling comfortably against his neck. 'Thanks miss. I thought I'd lost him.' Morgan looked at her. 'How do you know my name?'

'I saw you a few years ago when I came to the fair. You told me he was known as Morgan's monkey.'

'So he is, *beti* rascal. Nobody else would have him.' He scratched the monkey on his ear. 'Nobody at all.'

'I don't suppose,' she began, 'I don't suppose I could ride along with you?'

'Ride along wi' me?' He seemed astonished at the thought. 'Why would you want to do that?'

'I've nowhere else to go, I want to join the fair.'

Morgan pushed back his black felt hat and scratched his head, looking very like his monkey. 'Well,' he pondered. 'I don't know. I don't know at all. It's very hard work you know, is travelling. On 'road for weeks sometimes, no money coming in, wondering where you'll get your next hunk o' bread. It's not an easy life.' He glanced at her as she stood with her drenched hair and wet clothes clinging to her and a small frown furrowed above

149

his nose. 'You'd maybe be better getting off home to your ma and da.'

'I have no ma or da. They're both dead. There's no-one who would care what I did or where I went.' I thought that Jonty cared, she contemplated, but where is he?

'Well, I'll tell you what,' he considered. 'Come and have a cup o' tea wi' me and my missus and we'll have a chat about it and see what she thinks. You look half starved. Come on, have a bit o' gingerbread, a nice pot o' tea and maybe you'll think better on it.'

She followed him between stalls and waggons and the stamping feet and warm breath of horses and ponies until he reached a small tent pitched at the side of a cart. There was a fire burning by the mouth of the tent and a pan, with its lid rattling, was placed on a kettle iron above the flames.

'Amy! Amy! Come on gal. Where 'you hiding yourself?' As he called, a child came out of the tent. She was small enough not to have to bend her head as she came out. 'I've brought us a visitor, come for a sup o' tea.'

The child looked up and Polly Anna saw then that she wasn't a child at all, but a grown woman with a pretty, adult face but a body as small as a child's.

'This is my *beti* missus,' Morgan said. 'And what's your name, my dear?'

'Polly Anna,' she said, staring at the childwoman, and thinking that she had never seen anyone quite as small, not even Jonty, though Jonty would be as tall as herself, they had decided long ago, if his legs were not so crooked.

'Well, lassie. Have you not seen such a little lady afore?' Amy spoke up and her voice was adult.

'Sorry. I didn't mean to stare,' Polly Anna apologized, 'but no, I don't think so.'

'Everybody stares 'first time,' Morgan said. 'Till they realize that she's just 'same as everybody else, better even,' he added. 'Nobody makes a pie as well as my Amy.'

He seemed inordinately proud of his tiny wife and beamed at her. 'Shall we have 'kettle on then?'

Amy stood in front of Polly Anna and looked up. 'It seems to me', she said, 'that she might want something more sustaining than tea. How about a bowl o' stew, dearie? How would that suit?'

Polly Anna sank to her knees. She suddenly felt ill, faint with cold and hunger and overcome with emotion that she had found kindness in this strange couple, led to them by Morgan's monkey.

15

Jonty watched as Mr Bertram struggled, Marsh heaved and two other inmates grappled with the inert form of Mr Pincher. He groaned as they banged his head on the wall, but it evoked no sympathetic response, rather the inmates guffawed and coarsely commented on Mr Pincher's predicament, and rough-handled him up the stairs to his room.

'There's been some mischief here,' Mrs Pincher muttered. 'Some trick. I'll get to 'bottom o' this!'

Billy watching from the crowd of onlookers opened his mouth to speak, but a warning glance from Jonty made him think better of it and he closed it again.

'Come wi' me, Jonty. There's an errand or two to be run.' He followed her to the office, where she handed him two envelopes. 'There's one for Councillor Grant and one for Councillor Blake. Be sure to deliver them into their own hands. Nobody else's, do you hear? Then come straight back here, no sneaking off to 'fair.'

There was no name on the envelopes so he

assumed the messages were the same and as soon as he got outside he raced up the hayloft steps and carefully opened one of them. It was a full sheet of paper but all it said was 'Delivery in Morning'. He pondered. They were halfway through the month, they had taken delivery of groceries and the meat came every week, so perhaps the butcher and grocer were bringing extras, extras which were destined for the governors and the Pinchers.

He stuck the envelope down again and reached up on the beam for his belongings. The piece of string, a stub of pencil and his playing cards. He stored them away in his breeches' pocket and then sat down on a straw bale and gazed meditatively into space. It wasn't right he thought, that food should be taken from the paupers' mouths by deception. Neither was it right that the ratepayers of Hull should pay for victuals that weren't reaching the paupers. That's corruption, he decided; that much he had learned from Samuel. Though, he contemplated, some of the governors were very honest and were following the rules, others were not following them at all, but simply lining their own pockets.

He sighed and dug into his pocket and brought out the pencil. He felt quite attached to Mrs Pincher and would be sorry if anything bad happened to her, but nevertheless he re-opened the envelope, took out the sheet of paper and creasing it with his fingernail, tore off a piece from the bottom and started to write, returning the original message back to the envelope again.

The church clock was striking ten by the time he had delivered the two messages and he headed across town towards the house of Mrs Harmsworth. He went to the kitchen door and was shooed away by the kitchen maid, who thought he was begging, but he stood his ground and showed her the back of the piece of paper on which he had written Mrs Harmsworth's name. She closed the door in his face, but returned a moment later with a man dressed in black with a high white collar who asked him in, took the note from him and told him to wait. He returned presently and motioned him to go with him. Jonty scraped his boots on the mat and followed him up a narrow staircase and into a wide hall, where Mrs Harmsworth was waiting for him, having left her supper and a relative on an annual visit, so intrigued was she at Jonty's appearance at her door.

'Is this your writing, Jonty? I didn't realise you knew your letters. So what is this about?'

He shook his head. He had said enough, he thought, in the note.

'Come early in the morning,' she read. 'No later than six! What can it mean?'

He took the note from her and fished again in his pocket for the pencil. 'Delivery', he wrote.

'Delivery! Of what I wonder?' She patted her fingers to her lips as she pondered. 'I take it no-one knows you are here?'

Again he shook his head and reached to take the note back from her. She held it for a moment. 'And what does this mean? 'Please look after Samuel?' Is he a friend?'

Yes, a very great friend, he nodded, and taking the note from her he screwed it up and returned it to his pocket. He brought out a playing card, the knave, and handed it to her. 'For Samuel,' he croaked. 'My friend.'

'Bring me my writing case, Walters,' she said, 'and give the young man some supper before he leaves.'

Jonty walked slowly back to the workhouse, full of oxtail broth and bread which he had dipped into it. His coat pocket too was bulging with cake which the cook had wrapped in a white cloth and which he had decided to save for Polly Anna when he caught up with her. The rain was pouring down and he hoped that she had been able to find shelter for the night. He had decided that he would go back to the workhouse now and let Mrs Pincher see that he had returned. Then he would leave at first light.

As dawn broke he sat huddled in the doorway opposite the gate. He saw the two governors, Blake and Grant, hurrying down the street and slipping furtively through the workhouse gate, pushing aside with their feet two paupers who were sitting there. A few minutes later there was a rumble of cartwheels and a clop of hooves as the butcher's cart driven by Mr Fox himself and the grocery waggon came down Whitefriargate. The gate was opened by the governors and Jonty saw Mr and Mrs Pincher in the yard, Mr Pincher with a bandage around his head. The gate was left open and as Jonty was wondering why, there was a lopsided rumble as another cart came trundling down the street. Owd Boney! What's he bringing? Poor owd Boney, he'll get blamed. He'll go to jail!

Boney's cart was covered over with sacks, but Jonty could see that he wasn't carrying human cargo this time. The shapes beneath the covering showed that it was casks and boxes. Brandy, Geneva and tea, brought in from the ships on the dockside.

The gate was closed behind him and Jonty was beginning to wonder if Mrs Harmsworth would come or if she would leave it too late. It was very early in a morning to expect an old lady to be about; but as he was just beginning to think his scheming had been in vain, a carriage appeared from the direction of Junction Dock and he realized that it had probably been there waiting around the corner for some time. The workhouse gate opened and Governor Grant appeared carrying a large parcel, followed closely by Governor Blake with a sack over his shoulder.

'Good morning, governors!' Mrs Harmsworth greeted them as she was helped from the carriage by Governor Armitage and followed down by Governor Johnson. 'You are taking the air very early this morning. Good morning, Mrs Pincher – Mr Pincher.' She gave a pleasant, satisfied kind of smile. 'Shall we go back inside?'

Jonty watched them go inside and as the gate closed behind them he set off at a run towards Dock Green, racing down the dock side and across the lock gate which divided the Junction and Humber docks. As he reached Castle Street he saw a stream of waggons and carts heading out of town and he was beset by fears that Polly Anna wouldn't have waited for him, that she would have gone on alone. She would surely know that I would come, he thought breathlessly and ran alongside some of the waggons, jumping up to try and see inside.

When he reached the Green his heart sank. Everyone had gone. Only scorched earth where fires had been and patches of flattened pale grass where waggons and carts had rested, remained to show that the fair had been there.

His eyes searched the area. Only a Gypsy encampment was left. The smoke from their fire drifted across and reached his nostrils and he saw that they too were packing up to leave. He went across to them. A man was storing stuff into the cart and he could hear a woman's voice inside the tent scolding children. A girl was hanging a kettle over the fire.

The man glanced up at Jonty, but when Jonty didn't speak he looked away again and continued with his tasks, but the girl studied him as if waiting for him to say something. He stared at her not knowing which words to use which she would understand. She glanced over her shoulder towards the tent and then turned back to Jonty. She said not a word, but raised her arm and pointed. She pointed to the far end of the Green and Jonty turned and saw a donkey and laden cart driven by a small girl trundling out of the Green, another taller girl held the snaffle at the donkey's head. Behind the cart walked a man. A man with a large pack on his back, a felt hat on his head and a monkey on his shoulder. He smiled his thanks to the Gypsy girl and set off at a run.

16

'So where've you come from, Polly Anna?' Amy had questioned her as she had eaten her stew. 'Have you run away from home?' She had a different way of speaking from Morgan, who had said he was a northern man unlike Amy, whom he described affectionately as a foreigner from the south.

'I have no home.' She mopped the bread around the bowl. 'I live – lived in the workhouse. But I'm not going back,' she asserted. 'I'd rather die in the gutter than go back to that place.'

'A lot of folks do,' Morgan had said. 'Die in 'gutter, I mean. I've seen some of 'em. Nowhere to go, nowt to eat and no money in their pockets.' He gazed into the fire. 'But still, I'd feel 'same way. I'd rather die wi' wind and rain on my face than in a *choveno ker*.'

'So what can you do?' Amy persisted. 'If you want to travel along with fair folk, you've got to offer some skill or trade. They don't like strangers at the best of times, and especially not anybody who can't work.'

But I can't do anything, Polly Anna thought

dismally. What can I say that I can do?

'Can you read and write?' Amy asked. 'Can you cook or sew?'

'Yes,' she said eagerly. 'I can read and write. Samuel taught me. And I can't cook, but I can sew.' Not very well, she thought and I hate it, but I would do it if I could stay.

'Well, that's a start I suppose. Sometimes the circus or sideshows want somebody to sew costumes or write up leaflets, but it's not a lot to offer.' Amy was still dubious. 'And are you sure that nobody's going to miss you?'

'Only Jonty,' she said. 'He's my only friend and he was supposed to be coming with me.' It was then that she started to cry. How would she manage without Jonty? He had always been there, protecting, advising, for all of her life in the work-house. She could barely remember a time when he hadn't been there. And as she cried, she told the Morgans how she and Jonty used to watch the fair arriving and departing every year through the spyhole in the gate; she told them of Samuel and of Jonty's hideaway in the hayloft and she told them finally of Mr Pincher and why she had run away.

They had listened without interruption, Morgan throwing a piece of wood on to the fire every now and again, sending sparks shooting up into the night, and all over Dock Green small fires glowed as the fairfolk burned their bits of rubbish and broken chairs or cartwheels, the pungent smoke curling and drifting towards the town. The lamps and candles flared and guttered, showing up dark shadowy shapes as the travellers prepared for their journey at dawn.

But it was the sounds of the night which disturbed her, for they brought back memories that were still half-hidden, flickering like the flames of the burning fires. Memories of her mother and of a man whom she thought was her father, a man with a quick ready smile who used to toss her in the air and catch her. Other darker memories too, of someone saying, 'You can't stop here. You don't belong,' and of her mother crying.

She was frightened. The sounds she could hear, as she lay in the tent next to Amy, were strange and yet familiar. The snuffle of the donkey behind the tent, the scuffling of rats searching amongst debris, the hooting of owls from the trees around Dock Green and the clop of horses' hooves and rattle of wheels as some of the fairpeople moved off. Other sounds too, the screech of monkeys and chimpanzees, the snarl of wild beasts and trumpeting of elephants which carried through the darkness and reminded her of something, but what?

She had talked into the night in whispers with Amy whilst Morgan snored beneath a blanket at their feet, his monkey tied to the ridge pole so that he wouldn't wander, and when Amy had finally fallen asleep she lay wide awake listening. The cry of elephants came very close and she peeked out of the tent flap and saw in the darkness a herd being shepherded out of the site by four men, two at the front, two at the rear. The men had lanterns tied to sticks, which were strapped to their belts, and the glow from them swayed and bobbed as they urged the great beasts on in their slow procession.

The Morgans had agreed that she could spend the night with them and travel along in the morning. 'But we can't keep you, lassie,' Morgan had said. 'There's barely money for two of us, let alone three. What we have has to last us all 'winter, unless Amy gets taken up by 'circus again.'

'They'll want me, never fear,' Amy assured him. 'What a worrier he is,' she had added to Polly Anna. 'Plenty of work for a woman like me.'

She told her what she did in the circus, she and the other little people. 'Dwarfs, they call us, or midgets, but we don't like that name. They dress us up in fancy clothes and we turn cartwheels and chase about and ride on horses and some of us ride on elephants – only not me, 'cos I get dizzy, I can't abide heights.'

She and Morgan had been married for five years, she told Polly Anna, 'Met him at Nottingham Goose Fair. I'd heard of him, 'cos everybody knows every-body else in this business, but I'd never met him before. But I heard him playing on that old tin whistle of his and I knew that he was the one for me.' Her face took on a dreamy look, then she said cynically, ''Course I didn't know I'd have to share him with that dratted monkey.'

Morgan grinned and the monkey looked up and blinked its eyes, then turned its back on her.

'He's been with you a long time, hasn't he, Morgan?' Polly Anna had said softly.

'Aye, that he has.' He'd stroked the monkey's ears. 'A long time.'

She woke the next morning to find herself alone in the tent and when she put her head out into the cool morning air, the kettle was steaming on the fire and Amy and Morgan were loading up the cart. 'Put a pinch o' tea in the pot, will you,' Amy greeted her. 'We're almost ready for off.'

Dock Green was half empty and a stream of waggons, carts and cages were trundling away. Only a few stragglers remained and groups of men, women, children and the little people whom once she had thought of as children were heading out of the fairground with packs on their backs following the cavalcade.

She looked up as a cry sounded over her head and a flock of long-necked geese flew over.

'Greylags,' Morgan said. 'They allus see us off.'

'Where are they going?' she asked.

'Winter feeding ground. All travellers need one, just like us.'

'So where are we going, Morgan?'

'Wakefield Winter Fair. Circus'll be there and there'll be work for both of us. There's not many fairs in winter, unless they're Stattis.'

'Stattis? What's that?'

'Statute Fairs. Hiring day. You might get a job there, you know, at one of 'markets, if you don't tek to travelling. You could maybe be a kitchen maid if you've a mind for it.'

She took a deep breath. Her first taste of freedom. There was a smoky, pungent aroma in the air: a mixture of woodsmoke from the damped-down fires; the oily smell of blubber, which always pervaded the whaling town; the salty smell of the estuary and a touch of autumn aroma as the crisp mottled leaves from sycamore and horse chestnut trees drifted down.

I should feel happy, she thought as she brewed the tea to Amy's instructions. I'm free, but I'm afraid and I'm sad because Jonty isn't here. Why didn't he come? He said he would always be there for me!

They drank their tea, poured the slops under a bush, emptied the kettle and packed it and Morgan stamped out the fire, scattering the ash with his boots. Then he dismantled the tent, putting the canvas over the donkey's back and packing the poles and withies into the back of the cart. He hoisted a pack on to his back, his monkey jumped on to his shoulder and Amy got into the driving seat. Polly Anna stood and watched them, uncertain what to do, or what part she should play.

'Come on then, lassie.' Morgan handed her a supple twig. 'Tek hold of yon Bess; she'll not move without a bit of encouragement or a thwack on her rear.'

She smiled at him and took hold of the donkey's snaffle and pulled. The donkey curled its lips, showing large yellow teeth, but she pulled again and swished the twig in front of its nose and it moved off. She turned as they reached the road; they were the last to leave, only the Gypsy encampment was left at the far end. She could see figures moving around as if they too were about to depart. Soon Dock Green would be empty again, given back to the town for other activities, for a meeting place such as Samuel had spoken at, for the ball games that men and boys played, for the Trinity House schoolboys who claimed it as their own.

She turned determinedly in the other direction. 'Goodbye,' she whispered. Perhaps I will be back next year in a different sort of life. Goodbye old life. Goodbye Jonty. She had a lump in her throat that was hard to swallow. Try not to forget me. Don't forget your Polly Anna.

'Polly Anna! Polly Anna.' The cry was distorted but she knew it was her name that was being hailed and that it came from no-one else but Jonty. 'Wait! Wait!'

She turned and saw his lopsided run and leaving hold of the donkey ran towards him, her arms outstretched. 'Oh, Jonty! Wherever have you been?'

It was all right, the Morgans said, for Jonty to travel along too, or at least as far as Brough on the Humber, which was the route they would take, and then they would discuss what was to be done.

Polly Anna watched the ships, the cutters and schooners, sailing towards Hull as they trudged along the path by the river. The tide was full and churning crests washed over the shore, glistening the white pebbles with an iridescence as the early autumn sun broke through. She was filled with excitement as she observed this great expanse of new world which was opening up in front of her; the banks of Lincolnshire beckoned on the other side of the water, and onwards beyond Ferriby and Brough who knew what awaited them?

Their feet were sore and their legs ached before they were halfway to Brough, for they were un-used to walking and they lagged behind Morgan, who strode along behind the donkey cart and who finally called to Amy to halt and give them a rest. 'But not for long,' he said, ''cos you'll stiffen up.'

They sank down on the grassy verge and undid their boots. 'No. Leave them on,' Morgan said. 'Unless you want to walk barefoot. You'll never get

164

those boots on again once you've taken them off.'

The weather was fine and Polly Anna was glad of it, for she hadn't a coat or shawl and her clothes still felt damp from the soaking she had had the day before. They sat for ten minutes and then moved on again, Amy urging the donkey on across marshy track and rough balk, for Morgan refused to use the turnpikes.

'A travelling man, that's what I am.' He stuck his chin in the air. 'No *Piker*, me. Even though some say I'm onny a half-breed,' he muttered.

'What do you mean, Morgan?' Polly Anna asked curiously.

'Why, I've got Gypsy blood in me,' he said proudly. 'My grandmother was a Romany and she married a fairman and they were ostracized by both Gypsies and gentiles. Then they had my mother, who married a fairman and then they had me, and I'm a *gry-engro* – a horse dealer, just 'same as my Gypsy ancestors.'

'But what's a *Piker*?' she asked, still curious.

'Not a real traveller. They roam about like Gypsies but they travel in comfort along 'turnpikes instead of across common land which belongs to us all.'

They stopped again just beyond the village of North Ferriby and Morgan knocked on a cottage door. A woman answered and greeted him warmly. 'Just 'man I need, Morgan. I was hoping tha'd come. My man's laid up and I need some wood chopped for 'fire and knives sharpening. Then tha'd like a bite o'summat I expect.'

'Just water today, mum. We're travelling wi' company and we can't expect no more'n that.'

'Come wi' me then, onny leave 'monkey behind. He allus frightens dogs.'

He gave the monkey to Polly Anna and it jumped into her arms, chattering and scolding as Morgan disappeared round the back of the cottage. After a moment's hesitation Jonty followed him.

'There's allus somebody who'll give you a drink or a bite to eat,' Morgan told him as the woman went inside, 'and you'll soon find them as is willing, but you have to repay – in kind, if you haven't any money.'

Jonty nodded and surveyed the pile of wood. Chopping wood was no hardship, he'd done it every day since he was big enough to hold an axe. His legs ached with the walking, but his arms were strong. Morgan picked up the axe leaning against the wall, but Jonty took it from him and swung it, splitting the wood into manageable pieces which the old woman could burn.

'Well done, lad, but give it here, I'll finish.' The woodpile was three-quarters chopped and Morgan did the rest, swinging the axe with powerful strokes from his muscular arms.

They went back to the front of the cottage, where Amy and Polly Anna were sitting on the grass and the donkey was grazing. 'Jonty, taste that!' Polly Anna handed him a cup. She had a white smear around her lips. 'It's milk!'

Jonty gingerly tasted it. He had trouble with eating and drinking as Polly Anna well knew. But this liquid slipped down, coating his throat with a creamy texture. 'Not milk!' He shook his head. He knew what milk was. It was white but thin and taste-less, he'd often stolen a drink of it from the kitchen when he'd been thirsty. It was nothing like this.

'It's milk all right.' The old woman came to him with a jug and topped up the cup. 'Come wi' me and I'll show thee.'

He followed her again to the back of the cottage and into a byre whose smell reminded him of the hayloft. 'Come on then, Daisy.' The woman spoke to a brown-spotted cow, which lifted its head at her. 'Let's have a drop more for this young fella.' She pulled a three-legged stool towards her and sat down by the cow's udders and started to milk into a bucket.

Jonty stared in stupefaction, then raced round to fetch Polly Anna to look. They both stood in amazement and the woman started to laugh. 'Don't tell me tha's never seen a coo milked afore?'

They shook their heads and then, at the woman's invitation, dipped their cup into the bucket and tasted the creamy milk fresh from the cow. 'It's beautiful!' Polly Anna said. 'I've never tasted anything like it before.'

The woman crinkled her forehead. She obviously couldn't understand their ignorance. She stood up and beckoned them into her kitchen. 'Then tha'd better tek a morsel o' my cheese wi' thee. It'll taste good between two pieces o' bread.'

They moved on, their energy refuelled after the rest and the refreshment and arrived in Brough by midday. 'We'll pitch by 'river,' Morgan decided. 'We'll be handy for water and we'll see who else comes by.' He rubbed his chin and looked at Jonty. 'There'll not be room for four in 'bender. Somebody'll have to sleep in 'cart – or else – have you any money, Jonty?'

Jonty nodded and dug into his pocket to bring out the purse. 'Well, what I was thinking,' Morgan continued, 'was that you and me could go and buy a bit o' canvas from 'shipyard and find a strong ridge pole and I'll show you how to make a bender – a tent,' he added as he saw Jonty's puzzled expression. 'How would that be?'

Jonty agreed and whilst he and Morgan went towards the haven, Polly Anna gathered sticks and twigs for kindling and Amy showed her how to make a fire; she collected water from the river and by the time Morgan and Jonty came back, the kettle was swinging from the kettle iron and boiling for tea.

They drank their steaming tea, then Morgan stood up. He reached for a wicker basket and stick of blackthorn from the back of the cart. 'I won't be long,' he said. 'I'll just go and get our dinner.'

Polly Anna and Jonty exchanged glances and Jonty wondered why Morgan hadn't bought food when they went for the canvas, but ten minutes later he came back with a basketful of mushrooms, a tin box filled with blackberries and the warm body of a plump rabbit tied to his stick.

'Blackberries are all but finished,' he said as he started to skin the rabbit, 'but these are all right, they're not maggoty. Here, try 'em.' He handed them over to Polly Anna and Jonty. 'Finest thing for giving you energy, them and rose hips, but missels have had a good feed on 'em already.'

They popped the blue-black fruit of the bramble into their mouths, Polly Anna being the first to try and nodding to Jonty as the sweet juice met with her approval. 'Will you show us, Morgan, so that we know?'

'Aye. Plenty of food about if you know where to look and know what's good and what's not. No need for folks to starve.'

Whilst Amy put the rabbit pieces into a pot over the fire, he showed them how to put up the tent, cutting first some supple willow branches which he fixed to the ridge pole, then bent them to take the canvas which he threw over the top and pegged to the ground. 'There you are,' he said. 'There's your new home.'

'Morgan!' Polly Anna hesitated, unsure how to say what was on her mind. 'Jonty and I used to sleep in the hayloft at the workhouse, but, but – then I was told that I shouldn't any more. I'm a woman you see, and Jonty's a man, though he does still look like a boy. So, is it all right if we sleep in the same tent?'

Morgan looked enquiringly at Amy and then at the two of them. 'He's like your brother, isn't he? Always looked after you?'

'Oh, yes.' She smiled towards Jonty, who was looking down at the ground. 'Since I was very little. Since—'. Her smile faded. 'Since my mama died and left me. Jonty's always taken care of me.'

'Then that's all right. Brother and sister can share 'same bender and nobody's going to say owt about that. I reckon Jonty'll keep on looking after you, isn't that right, Jonty?'

Jonty raised his head and looked Morgan straight in the eye. 'Yes,' he said. 'Always.'

As night fell, Polly Anna, tired with the travelling and keen to sleep in her own tent said good night and curled up on the blanket which Amy had lent her, but Jonty sat outside the tent doorway listening to the wash of the river and the night-time cries and wondering what they were and thinking too of the events of the last two days and of their future. He felt insecure, not knowing what the day would bring.

Amy had also gone to bed, but Morgan with his monkey on his shoulder was smoking a pipe and gazing up into the sky. He came across to Jonty. 'It'll be another fine day tomorrow,' he said. 'We'll have a good day for travelling.'

Jonty nodded. Would he be welcomed along as Polly Anna had been? Nothing had been said, no arrangements made. Morgan and his wife had been very kind, sharing their food, Morgan advising about the canvas and showing him what to do, but would they want them to continue as companions or would they be regarded as a nuisance? A liability? Jonty had always had some degree of independence even though cocooned within the workhouse walls. Now, though, he felt very vulnerable.

As if he was reading his mind, Morgan continued. 'Amy and me think it would be a good idea if you came along with us for a bit, if you want to that is. Just till you get used to travelling 'road.'

'Why?' Jonty asked. 'Why do you do this for us?'

Morgan sat cross legged beside him. 'I'm not sure,' he said, tapping out his pipe. 'But I remember you, from a few years back when you and Polly Anna came to 'fair – when my monkey recognized her from somewhere. And you've both stuck in my mind, I don't know why. You'll do all right, Jonty. Polly Anna is – I don't know, but she'll belong on 'road. And as for you, well, my *beti* Amy has had an idea for you.'

Jonty gazed at him wondering what the idea was.

'Amy thinks you should join her in a circus!'

'A circus!'

'Aye. She's been watching you moving about. She says you're as wick as can be in spite of your crooked legs. She says, and she means it as a compliment, that you're just like Morgan's monkey!'

17

Other travellers joined them on the long trail to Wakefield Winter Fair. Circus people riding in their waggons, in which they packed their baggage and equipment and also slept; theatre entertainers with packs on their backs which were stuffed with costumes, boots, shoes and wigs and who were heading for the cheapest lodgings they could find, no camping at the roadside for them; and the Gypsy folk, who travelled in families of ten or twenty carts or waggons, the children and dogs running behind with the team of horses and ponies, and who camped apart from everyone else.

'Morgan! Why don't we pitch our tent with the Gypsies or the circus people instead of on our own?' Polly Anna was curious that not everyone mixed. 'We could all share the same fire then.'

'Well, Amy belongs to 'circus and she's accepted by them, but I'm part Romany and they're a bit wary of me, though they'll buy horses from me and I'll sharpen their knives and mend their pans. And some of 'Romanies'll accept me, 'cos of my blood, though not all of them! But Amy's a *Gorgie* – a gentile. So we stay apart. We don't mind, do we Amy?'

Amy shook her head, but Polly Anna felt sad for her and wondered why it was that people should be prejudiced against others because they were different. She had noticed a tall black man, an African, Morgan said he was, who always travelled apart from the others, loping along the road with long strides, speaking to no-one and no-one speaking to him.

It was November by the time they arrived on the outskirts of the prosperous cloth town of Wakefield and during those weeks of travelling, Polly Anna had gone among the fairpeople, making herself known and asking if she could do any work for them, any washing or sewing, and some of them had agreed. Jonty too did odd jobs for them, gathering or chopping wood for fires and sometimes feeding the animals.

Polly Anna found herself drawn to the horses, those belonging to the circus and those of the Romanies. Morgan had taken her with him when one of the fairmen had called on him to give his advice on one of his mares. 'Her heels are badly cracked,' Morgan told him. 'You'll have to let her rest up a bit until they heal.'

'Can't do that,' the man said bluntly. 'I need to move on. Get me another and see if you can raise a good price for her. She's a good hoss apart from her feet.'

'But not much good without 'em!' Morgan answered. 'I'll get you another, but keep her. She'll be all right if she's kept dry and off wet pasture.'

They went then to the Romany camp to buy

another horse. Morgan wheeled and dealed, sometimes using language which Polly Anna couldn't understand as he bargained. Someone laughed and called him a *Zingaro gry-engro*, but another Romany with dark skin shook his head disparagingly and said he was a *Gorgio*. Morgan merely shrugged and continued bargaining and moving among the horses and ponies. Then one of the Romany women who was standing by a tent listening and watching, called out to him in a foreign tongue.

'What are they saying, Morgan, are they insulting you?' Polly Anna asked.

'They're taunting me because of my parentage! One said I was a mixed blood Gypsy horse dealer, the other said no, I was only a gentile. But there's no malice,' he added with a grin. 'They know me and what I am.' He hesitated. 'They're very curious, the Romanos. The woman asked about you. Who you were, where you were from. Who's the *Romani chi*? she asked – the Gypsy girl. She said that you've the look of a Romany about you.'

'A Gypsy girl!' she breathed. 'But, how can that be?'

'I don't know.' He bent to examine the feet of a Pinto, whose markings were predominantly white against brown. Then he ran his firm hand down the length of its neck and noted the small head and wide eyes. 'But there's summat.'

'That's a good hoss,' one of the Romanies said. 'Try him out on 'common tomorrow. He's nippy – very fast.'

Morgan shook his head. 'No, he's a poor specimen. Short-winded, I shouldn't wonder.'

They hummed and hawed, arguing on the merits of the animal until Morgan reluctantly capitulated. 'Aye, all right. First light?'

It was agreed and as they moved back to their own camp, she asked. 'What did you mean, Morgan? That there's something? I don't understand!'

'You have a look of 'Romany,' he said. 'I noticed it 'first time we met. But you're not true Romany, it doesn't come from your ma.'

'No. My mother was fair.' The image of her mother came back sudden and vivid and she remembered those last precious hours in her childhood when they had walked, and then finally ridden in Old Boney's cart, when she had watched her mother's face, in her innocence trying both to give and take comfort. 'She was fair,' she whispered again, and was wracked with a resurfacing sorrow which had been deeply hidden. 'Jonty remembers her too.'

She woke early the next morning and asked Morgan if she could go with him to watch him try the horse. They joined a group of Romanies who were leading horses and ponies on to the common land. They kept them on long ropes and ran beside them, showing their paces to the showmen and tradesmen of the town who had come to look and buy.

Polly Anna watched and felt a thrill of pleasure as some of the men jumped on to the horses' backs and cantered swiftly across the hillside, some of them racing each other and all of them whooping and shouting. She saw Morgan mounted on the Pinto, trotting, cantering, turning and circling, the horse keeping a smooth rhythm and obeying his commands.

'He's a good hoss isn't he?' Polly Anna turned as someone spoke to her. It was the Gypsy girl Kisaiya, who had spoken to her at Dock Green, with a baby strapped to her chest.

'Hello! I don't know. Is he?'

Kisaiya nodded. 'One of 'best. I've ridden him.'

'Does he belong to you? To your father, I mean?'

She shook her head, her shawl slipping down showing her thick, dark-brown plaited hair. 'Not mine. Jack's dad.'

'Jack? Oh. You're married then? Is this your baby?'

The girl turned her head as if she had said too much and merely nodded.

'Do you live with your husband's family?' Polly Anna persisted. She was very curious about the girl, who seemed as if she would like to be friendly but yet was holding back. 'Don't you have a bender of your own?'

'No.' Her voice was soft, but she had a clipped way of speaking. 'Jack's away. He'll catch us up. He's a tinker and often travels alone. He's a Boswell,' she added. 'My father is a Lee.'

'Ah!' There must be a difference, Polly Anna thought. I'll have to ask Morgan.

'Do you want to ride on him?' Kisaiya asked as Morgan rode up towards them. 'He's gentle, he won't throw you.'

'I don't know if I—'. Memories stirred. Had she once ridden on a pony? Had someone put a hand on her back to make her safe? 'Yes please. Can I, Morgan?'

He dismounted and she approached the horse, talking softly, praising and admiring. She stroked his strong neck and took hold of the reins and as Morgan bent to take her foot she sprang on to the saddleless horse and knew that yes, once before she had ridden on a small brown pony.

She looked down and saw Kisaiya staring at her, staring as if she was seeing something or someone else and not her.

Morgan took hold of the bridle and clicked his tongue. 'Keep your knees in tight, get into his rhythm. He's a good 'un, onny don't tell them 'Gyptians I said so.' Morgan hadn't yet started his bargaining for the buying of the horse.

She moved off and felt the sway of the horse beneath her. She nudged with her heels and he started to trot and she bounced and laughed, she nudged again and the animal swiftened his pace and she was away, across the common, leaving Morgan and Kisaiya behind, feeling the wind in her hair and remembering the sensation of the canter and of her father running beside her.

She reined in at the top of the hillside and looked down, the morning was bright and sharp, the sun breaking through the clouds and she looked down at the encampment below and remembered. My father. Papa. *Dado*. The man with the olive skin and thick dark hair who had flitted in and out of her awareness, was now clearly defined.

She trotted down to re-join Morgan and the Romanies, who were now hard bargaining with those who wished to buy. Kisaiya stood a little apart from Morgan and the Romany who was selling the horse, and whom Polly Anna now recognized as the one at the camp in Dock Green, he with the sullen wife, and she was glad that the woman wasn't Kisaiya's mother, but the mother of her husband.

She rode towards Kisaiya, reined in and looked down at her. 'Kisaiya. I have Gypsy blood!'

Kisaiya looked back at her. Her eyes were blue, as blue as the sky on a summer's day. 'I know. Welcome back, *Sister*.'

The clocks in the town struck midnight as she waited cross-legged in the tent doorway for Kisaiya to come. There had been an implicit understanding between them, though no words had passed from their lips as they came back from the common to the camp.

She had said nothing to Morgan, who had led the Pinto to the camp of the showman to tell him that he had managed to buy this wonderful horse at a bargain price. The showman would haggle as Morgan had done with the Romany, but everyone would finish up satisfied, Morgan more than most, for with this horse he knew that his reputation would increase for it was a good one, and he would have money too in his pocket, the difference between what he had paid the Romany and what the showman would pay him.

She had told Jonty, of course, for he knew from her air of pent-up excitement that something had happened. 'Mrs Pincher called you Gypsy,' he remembered.

'Yes, she did.' The Matron used the term disparagingly because of her dark hair and her skin, which was of a slightly different hue from some of the other children.

Now, Jonty was sleeping inside the tent, but she waited, a blanket wrapped around her shoulders, watching the fires dying down and the lights of the town below flickering and knowing that Kisaiya would come as soon as she could get away.

It had already struck one o'clock when she heard the pad of feet on the grass and a murmur of a voice saying, 'Don't be afraid. It's Kisaiya.'

'I knew you would come,' she said. 'I felt it.'

Kisaiya sat beside her, her baby sleeping against her breast. 'In my thoughts I told you that I would come. That is why you felt it. Our thoughts always ran the same way.'

'What do you mean? Tell me who I am, Kisaiya, and how do you know?'

'I remember you from many years ago, even though we were both only *tawnie chavvies*. We played together like sisters and I looked after you because I was older. I'm seventeen now and you are perhaps fourteen? I missed you when you went away.'

'But – but, where did I go – and why?'

'I don't know it all because I was only a *chavi* and the elders talked only in whispers about your mother. She was a lovely *rawnie*.' Her voice softened, even though she was already talking in a whisper so that no-one else should hear. 'A beautiful lady. I loved her very much.'

Polly Anna waited, eager to know, yet knowing that Kisaiya would have to tell it in her own way and in her own time.

'It was the Romany women who made her leave. They said she could no longer stay without her *rommado* – her husband. There was no place for her. She was a *Gorgie* and didn't belong.'

'I remember,' Polly Anna whispered. 'They were sitting around a fire talking and Mama and I sat in our little house waiting to hear what we should do.'

Kisaiya nodded. 'Your *dado* had built the waggon-house himself, no-one else had one like it then. He fitted it with beds and a little stove and had two horses to pull it. He said that his Leina would live in a palace.'

'Leina?'

'That was what he called your *mam*. But the women said,' she went on, 'they said that she couldn't stop, that she had to go back to her own people. Even my own *mam*', she said bitterly, 'said that it was for the best, though she said that you could stop if your mother would leave you. But of course she wouldn't.'

'But why?' Polly Anna was close to tears. 'Why did we have to leave? Where was my papa?'

'Your *dado*?' she said, as if surprised that she didn't know. 'Didn't your *mam* tell you? He died. He was killed. Run down by a runaway horse and struck his head as he fell.'

Polly Anna tried to join together all the missing pieces which puzzled her. 'I don't remember,' she said. 'Why don't I?'

'Because you weren't there,' said a man's voice which made them both jump. 'It was at 'Nottingham Goose Fair. All the women had gone *dukkering* in the town and you and your mother had gone with them to buy supplies, and it was then that it happened.' Morgan stood in the shadows. 'I was away as well and when I caught up with 'fair in

Hull I was told of the terrible thing that had happened to your *dado*. Your mother—'

'They sent her away,' Polly Anna cried. 'How could they? Do you know what happened then? We had to go to the workhouse and my mama – Mama died there.' She started to sob. 'How could they?'

Kisaiya and Morgan were both silent, then Kisaiya got to her feet. 'I must go. If Orlenda finds that I'm here, she'll be angry.'

Polly Anna looked up, her eyes streaming. 'But why? Because you are talking to me?'

'Not just you. She dislikes all *Gorgios* or those with mixed blood. Even Morgan – even though Riley does dealings with him.'

Morgan nodded in agreement. 'She's a hard woman.'

'Yet you are married to her son! You live in her tent!'

Kisaiya's face in the dim glow of the dying fire had dark shadows upon it. 'I must go,' she said. 'We will talk again. Good night, *Sister*.'

Morgan sat beside her as Kisaiya slipped away into the darkness and his monkey climbed down from his shoulder and sat on her lap just as he had done when she was a child. She stroked him, remembering, and he chattered quietly. 'Why does she call me *Sister*, Morgan? I'm an only child, I have no kin.'

He smiled as he looked at her. 'You have now, whether they like it or not. Romanies always call those of their blood, *Brother* or *Sister*. She's your cousin. Kisaiya's father James and your father were brothers. Paul Lee was his name.'

18

'Can I come and work for you?' Polly Anna had decided that boldness was the only way to obtain work, proper work, from the showfolk.

'What can you do?' It was Edgar Brown whom she had asked, the showman who had bought the Pinto from Morgan. 'Can you dance? Ride?'

'Yes,' she answered swiftly. 'I can do both of those things. I can dance like your Indian girls do, anyway.'

She had seen the young girls dancing outside his booth at Hull Fair. They had worn fringed skirts and feathers in their hair.

He gave a cynical laugh and spat out a chew of tobacco. 'Let's see you then!'

So she had danced in front of him, stamping her feet, waving her arms up in the air and chanting strange cries, then she put her hand to her mouth and yodelled, throwing her voice in a caterwauling melody.

'You a Gypsy?' he frowned. 'I've seen you wi' Morgan.'

'I'm travelling with Morgan and Amy. I want to join up with the fair.'

'Are you a Gypsy?' he persisted.

She stuck her chin in the air. 'Seems as if I am,' she said. 'My father was Paul Lee.'

His eyes moved across her face, scrutinizing, assessing. 'Paul Lee? How come we haven't seen you about afore then?'

'I've been in the workhouse,' she said simply.

His forehead creased disbelievingly. 'Never! Tell me, who was your ma?'

'They said my father called her Leina, she died when I was very young. She died in the workhouse,' she said bitterly, 'after the Romanies sent her away.'

'They onny did what was best for her. They sent her to her own folk. Some of 'Gypsies set her part of 'way, I saw 'em go. Then they burnt his waggon and everything in it.'

'Burnt his waggon?' She stared at him. 'Why did they do that?'

He shrugged. 'Tradition! Though it seems a waste of a waggon to me. Anyway, come wi' me. We'll soon see if you're Paul Lee's *chavi*.'

She followed him to a patch of rough ground where a temporary ring had been made. Inside the ring two men on horseback were galloping round and round and whooping war cries, whilst in the middle against a wooden stake a woman stood screaming.

'Can you do that?' he asked.

'Scream?' she said.

'No. Ride like them.'

She hesitated only for a second, she was sure that Morgan would teach her. 'Yes,' she said. 'I can.'

He whistled across to a boy. 'Fetch that new Pinto. Look sharp about it.'

She hid a smile. She could ride the Pinto all right, she had already proved that, but as she mounted she could tell that the horse was nervous and mettlesome. Something had upset him, maybe the other horses as they galloped round or perhaps someone had been harsh with him. She soothed him with soft words, clicking her tongue as Morgan had done and gently urging him on. She was halfway round the ring when the horse suddenly reared, throwing his forelegs in the air and whinnying loudly. She clung on, leaning forward with her weight and gripping with her knees as the horse bucked and tossed.

Eventually he quietened and she slid down. 'Something's upset him! He's been frightened.'

'It's that bit.' Morgan was standing with his arms crossed watching them. 'I told you to go gentle on his mouth.'

Brown nodded. 'Aye, maybe. We'll try another. What about this Romany *chavi*, Morgan? Can she ride as well as her *dado*?'

'I don't know. But I'll learn her if you like. If she's Paul Lee's *chavi* she'll have 'gift.'

Polly Anna looked from one to another. Then Brown said tersely, 'Gyppos and fairfolk don't usually mix, but if you can ride like your da I'll give you a job riding with 'Indians in 'booth. You'll have to dress up like a squaw and you'll have to do other jobs as well, mucking out hosses and teaching 'em tricks.'

'Thank you,' she said. 'When do I start?'

'Tomorrow after dark,' he said. 'So take 'Pinto now, change his bit and get practising, 'cos if you're no good you'll be finished after 'show tomorrow night.'

'You got a licence for this gaff?' Morgan enquired.

'No,' Brown groused. 'But I've been travelling long enough to know I can manage wi'out one.'

'Watch out for trouble then. Johnson doesn't like anybody else on his pitch.'

'I'm ready for him any time. He calls it a circus when it's no bigger than a shabby old pea stall! Anyway, I won't be near his gaff, I'm stopping in town.'

Morgan shrugged. It was nothing to do with him, and the showmen and fairground folk had always been a law unto themselves, setting up their stalls and booths in villages and towns whenever the opportunity arose. If there was a cattle or sheep fair, hiring day or feast day, there they would be, and regardless of whether or not it was a Charter Fair or Statute Fair, some of them, even if they hadn't a licence, would find a way around the law.

'What did you mean, Morgan?' Polly Anna asked as they led the horse away. She seemed to be constantly asking him questions. 'About having the gift – like my father?'

Morgan smiled. 'He was the finest horseman I ever knew, a good judge of horse flesh too. And your mother wasn't bad either, for a *Gorgie.*'

He showed her how to change the bit and fit the bridle and saddle up and then took her out on to the common. He taught her to trot and to canter and then to full gallop and the long-forgotten memory returned. Then he drew two large circles with his stick and with sharp crisp commands from him she rode a figure of eight, changing directions in the centre. The Pinto obeyed her every command and when she finally drew breathlessly to a halt, Morgan said, 'He's a circus hoss! I knew he was a good 'un. He knows exactly what to do.'

She was disappointed. 'You mean it wasn't me that was showing him? It was him showing me?'

He grinned. 'Summat like that! Just think yourself lucky. Mind you,' he added, 'you did all right.'

And that, she thought as she rode back down the hill, was praise indeed.

Jonty had been taken by Amy to meet the circus proprietor, Johnson, who was hiring her. They found him inside the booth watching a lion tamer put a scrawny old lion through his tricks. This was a small circus in comparison to some such as Wild's or Richardson's or Ogden's, which were very successful and travelled the whole of the country, unlike Johnson, who stayed in the north of England.

Johnson looked down at Jonty when Amy suggested that he come to work for him. 'Can't he speak for himself? Haven't you got a tongue in your head, lad?'

Jonty put his hand to his mouth and shook his head. Amy spoke for him. 'He doesn't talk much,' she said. 'He's got a cleft.'

Johnson surveyed him. 'One of my lads is the same,' he said. 'Onny he's got a hare lip as well. His ma was frightened by a hare when she was carrying. Can't understand a word he says, sometimes.' He shook his head. 'Sorry, lad. I can't be doing wi' two of you.'

So that was that, Jonty thought, I don't know what I shall do now, but he stayed and watched as the lion jumped through a ring or two, climbed on to a box and yawned, and then slowly jumped down and slunk out of the ring as the tamer cracked his whip. Then into the ring tumbled a crowd of dwarfs. One of them carried a ball, bigger almost than he was; he threw it to one of the others, who pretended to be bowled over by it and somersaulted over and over.

I could do that, Jonty thought, an excitement growing inside him, and he watched their antics, taking note of all they did. Someone brought in a small ladder and held it whilst another climbed up it. On reaching the top, it tipped over and he scrambled down and held it whilst the dwarf at the other side climbed up, and so they went on climbing up and down and tipping over and over all round the ring.

He saw Johnson watching them, not smiling as Jonty was doing, but merely assessing whether their new act was good enough for the next performance.

This was a small booth and there was no seating. The people who stood on the muddy ground at the back paid their sixpences and peered over the heads of those in front who had paid a shilling to see the show; but to mark the ring a raised wooden block separated the performers from the crowd. Jonty stood well back at the rear of the booth; he gave a loud whoop and saw Johnson raise his head and look in his direction. He whooped again and with a great leap forward somersaulted in the direction of the ring. He reached the wooden block and leapt upon it and somersaulted all the way around it, landing finally in the ring, where Amy and the other dwarfs were standing watching him. He stood on his hands for a moment and then with a quick change of direction he cartwheeled around the ring.

He took a deep breath as he stopped in front of Johnson. He put out his hands in front of him, then with the forefinger of his left hand he tapped it against his right palm. 'I can count,' he mumbled. 'Take money at 'door.'

'Can you, by Jove!' said Johnson. 'Right, we're here for three days. I'll try you out.'

Jonty had seen at Hull Fair that most of the performers at the circus and the side booths all had more than one job, some took money at the entrance and then disappeared inside to perform in the ring or on the platform. Others took charge of the animals, exercising or sweeping out their cages, and he knew that he would have to offer more than just clowning.

They were pent up with excitement as the day of the circus opening arrived. They had watched the booth being erected on a piece of waste land, the men working the previous day hammering and sawing as the shutters which formed the sides, the rails and rafters were put into place and the canvas tilt placed on top. But Edgar Brown had not yet built his fit-up in the streets of Wakefield.

Jonty had been given a clown's outfit which was far too big for him and Polly Anna worked swiftly, shortening the arms and legs so that it would fit him. 'I never thought', she said, as she rethreaded a needle with cotton, 'that the hated sewing at the workhouse would come in so useful.'

Jonty's thoughts too were on the workhouse or more particularly on Samuel, and he wondered how his old friend was faring and what had happened to the Pinchers.

They joined the trail of waggons, horses, bullocks and sheep in the narrow streets, for this was primarily a livestock fair. Polly Anna rode down the hillside on the back of the Pinto, with Jonty running by her side, his face painted with a white mask and a red slashed mouth. She was wearing a brown, fringed skirt and shirt, her face was darkened with dampened charcoal and Amy had pinned a false plait made from dyed sheep's wool to her hair, and fastened a leather headband around her forehead. As she passed groups of revellers making their way to the circus, she gave a loud holler and several whoops as Edgar Brown had instructed her to do, to make the crowds follow.

They parted company and wished each other luck. Jonty joined up with Amy and some of the other dwarfs and she introduced him to her sister Dolly, who was younger than her and aptly named, he thought, for she was as pretty as one of the dolls which he had seen on toy stalls. Polly Anna rode on towards the river and the Chapel bridge, where Edgar Brown and two youths were hammering the last nail into a precarious-looking booth where two of his Indians were doing their war dance.

'Ride around a bit,' Brown said. 'Go round the Bull Ring. Whoop it up. Get the folks to follow you here instead of to 'circus.'

So she set off again around the streets of

Wakefield, giving her war cries and, where space permitted, swiftly cantering, then turned back in the direction of the booth. Darkness had fallen and the booth was lit by lamps and candles and Edgar Brown was standing outside on a rickety waggon calling to those passing to come and see the drama of real Indians.

She rode around the back of the booth and slid off the horse, leading it in beneath the canvas, but was amazed to find such a small arena. There would be scarcely room for them to ride and that's why, she realized, there were only two other horseback riders, they were in great danger of crashing into each other!

Edgar Brown judged that no-one else would be coming in for the first performance and signalled for them to start. They would give a ten-minute act, each rider coming in separately and riding around the ring giving their war cries, then one of the two male Indians captured a white woman, who was a disguised Mrs Edgar Brown, dressed in a yellow gown and wearing a curly white wig; she was tied to a stake and Polly Anna and the other two riders whooped and hollered around her with blood-curdling cries, whilst she screamed and struggled to escape from the ropes which tied her. Then creeping out from the audience came her rescuer, a youth in a soldier's red uniform, who brought out his rifle and shot the Indians dead.

They all, including Polly Anna, hung over their horses' backs in various poses of death and rode out of the arena to the loud cheers of the audience as the innocent woman prisoner was released. They rode in again to take their applause and then out to tie up the horses and return to the waggon, where they did yet another war dance to entice in another audience for a second performance.

There came a heckling from a man standing outside. 'Call that a show?' he shouted. 'Come on folks, come to a real show. Come to Johnson's Circus! See the clowns. See the dwarfs, the sword-swallowers and fire-eaters. Follow me.'

Edgar Brown got down from the platform and approached the man. 'Clear off my pitch, Amos Johnson,' he threatened, 'before I fetch you one on.' The man laughed in his face and the next second was sent sprawling on the ground, his nose bleeding and his hat rolling on the floor.

'Clear off,' repeated Brown, 'and tell your dad he'll get 'same if he tries owt.'

'I'll have you for assault,' Amos Johnson spluttered as he retrieved his hat and backed away. 'You're here without a licence and I'll get you for that as well!'

Brown made a menacing gesture, and the crowd who were watching gathered closer in anticipation of seeing a bare knuckle fight free of charge. But Amos Johnson wasn't having any, he would fight back another way. 'I'm going to fetch 'constables,' he said. 'I'll have you closed down.'

And so he did. As Polly Anna and the other Indians went through their routine for the third time, a commotion was heard at the back of the booth and the constables and a clerk to the local Board arrived to order Brown to close his unlicensed show.

'I'm so disappointed,' Polly Anna complained to Jonty later that night, 'my job's finished before it started and I didn't get paid either. But it wasn't very good. There just wasn't room to do anything. I wanted to canter and maybe try some tricks. I didn't realize that the booth would be so small.'

Jonty was full of enthusiasm; he had had a marvellous time and had raised a cheer as he'd played the tumbling clown, falling over and turning somersaults when the dwarfs pushed him, and Mr Johnson had been pleased with him. 'Join 'circus with me, Polly Anna. It's fun!'

For the first time ever, people had laughed at his antics because he had encouraged them to do so. No-one had felt sorry for him, because no-one had seen his crooked legs beneath his costume and no-one had drawn away from his mumbled speech because clowns didn't have to talk. He'd mimed and gestured and with his painted face had looked sad or happy and the audience had been sad or happy with him. They were on his side. 'Join 'circus, Polly Anna,' he urged. 'Better than being Indian.'

She pursed her lips, 'But would they take me?' she asked doubtfully, her confidence ebbing away.

But they did. Amos Johnson, determined to close Brown down, asked Polly Anna and the two other Indian horseback riders to join their circus. Not because he thought they were especially good, but only because without Indian performers Brown couldn't put on another show.

'Join us,' he said persuasively, patting her shoulder. 'We're touring all 'winter. You'll have regular work if you're good enough.'

Polly Anna did a dance after he had gone. 'I will

be good enough, Jonty,' she declared. 'I'm going to learn to ride like my *dado*. I'll show the Gypsies and the *Gorgios* that I'm just as good as any of them.'

19

For three years they toured the northern region with Johnson's Circus and Polly Anna, with Morgan's tuition, became more and more proficient on horseback. She persuaded Mr Johnson, the father of Amos and Harry, and owner of the circus to try out the Indian routine, but to have the Indians winning an occasional battle rather than the soldiers; but the audience didn't like the idea of the soldiers being killed, and they booed when the Indians held up the matted wool scalps, even though they cheered when the Indian maid, played by Polly Anna, and a soldier officer rode away together on the same horse.

'It doesn't work,' Johnson said. 'They're a bloodthirsty lot but very patriotic, they like the English to win and not the foreigners, makes 'em think of our own victories.'

He'd paid her a tolerable wage because her reputation was growing and in that first bitterly cold winter, when she and Jonty, Morgan and Amy shared one tent for warmth, when they had to break the ice on river or stream for water and the wind shrieked in the tree-tops, she had bought warm clothes and blankets and was able to repay them for their kindness to her and Jonty when they had had nothing.

They missed the Hull Fair for two Octobers because Johnson knew that the Wombwell and Ogden Circuses would be there and he couldn't compete with both of them, and although Jonty was disappointed not to be going back, Polly Anna thought that perhaps it was just as well that they didn't go. 'You would be sad, Jonty,' she said, fingering her locket which she now wore openly. 'You would want to see Samuel, and if the Pinchers are still there, there could be trouble.'

Reluctantly he agreed. 'I'll write to Samuel,' he said, and he did and put a forwarding address of the next two towns where they would be visiting in the North Riding of Yorkshire, but there was no reply from his old friend.

During those years, Polly Anna occasionally saw Kisaiya; her baby was no longer tied around her but was toddling on dimpled brown legs around the campsite. 'Hello, Floure,' she greeted the little girl, who smiled shyly at her during the third spring when the circus went once more to the West Riding of Yorkshire, and they met again in the town of Boroughbridge. 'She's lovely, Kisaiya,' she said, aware, but not caring, of the disapproving glances of Orlenda. Riley, Kisaiya's father-in-law, always nodded and greeted her but never made any conversation, and neither did Jack, Kisaiya's husband, who seemed as sullen as his mother was.

'I want you to come and meet *Mam* and *Dado*,' Kisaiya said. 'They're here and I've told them about you. You must come now because tomorrow we're travelling to Appleby and we shan't meet again until Hull Fair.'

They walked to the Gypsy camp with Floure between them and Kisaiya called to her mother, who was inside their tent. She opened the flap and looked out and put out her arms to Floure, who ran to her. 'Come here my *tawnie chavi*.' She kissed the child warmly on each cheek and tucking her comfortably against her chest, she greeted Kisaiya, who said, '*Mam*, this is Polly Anna that I was telling you about. Leina's *chavi*. This is my *mam*, Polly Anna, Shuri Lee.'

Polly Anna saw the likeness between Kisaiya and her mother. Her skin was olive and she wore her dark shiny hair in a long plait as her daughter did, a black straw hat was on her head and gold rings in her ears. 'Hello, Mrs Lee. I'm glad to meet you.'

Shuri Lee put down the child and came to Polly Anna. She touched her gently on her cheek and to Polly Anna's surprise she saw tears in her eyes. 'Welcome, *Sister*,' she said softly. 'I can see who you are. Who your mother was and your father. Aye, I knows it well enough.' She called to her husband, lifting up her voice and calling, for he was tending to some horses on the grassy wayside. When he joined them, she said nothing but simply put out her hand towards Polly Anna. He stood for a moment and looked at her, then put out his hand. She put hers into his and he held it close with both of his. 'Paul's *chavi* sure enough,' he said huskily. 'Welcome, *Sister*.'

They invited her to sit down by the fire and they were joined by Kisaiya's younger sister, Narilla, a

196

pretty girl with a shy smile. Conversation was stilted at first, for Polly Anna didn't know what to say to these relatives who had sent her mother away just when she most needed them, but the opportunity to ask them why, came when they asked her how she came to be in the workhouse, the dreaded *choveno ker.*

'There was no other place we could go, I suppose,' she said, thinking back into her past. 'My mother was ill. I can remember her crying as we travelled, and then, and then – yes! She said, we must go to Hull to find them before it is too late, before they are gone.'

Shuri and her husband looked at each other. 'She must have been making her way to Hull Fair,' he murmured. 'We'd been at Nottingham Goose Fair and she'd know that we always went on to Hull after. It's a good hoss fair.'

'Why?' She was suddenly angry. 'Why did you send her away? When she had nowhere else to go?'

'Paulina!' Shuri said gently. 'Why do you blame us? Why do you not think of your mother's people? She was going back to them!'

Polly Anna blinked back her tears. What was Shuri saying? What people? Why had she not thought of her mother's family before? Why had she only thought of her father's and why did Shuri call her by that name?

Shuri touched the locket around Polly Anna's neck, then took hold of her hand and turning it over gently stroked her palm. 'You have other family somewhere. Once, many years ago, a *Gorgio rye* came looking for your mother and I told him that she'd gone. I don't know if he ever came again,

197

but', she gave a small shrug of her shoulders, 'there would have been nothing else we could tell him.'

Polly Anna stared at her. 'You called me Paulina,' she said. 'Was that my name?'

'Yes.' Shuri smiled at her. 'It was the name they chose. It was the joining of Paul and Leina. Don't you remember, Kisaiya?'

'Now I knows it,' she nodded, 'but I'd forgotten. Polly Anna seemed right.'

'It was Jonty who named me,' Polly Anna said. 'He can't speak properly. But I do remember now.' Her voice dropped to a whisper. 'That is what my mama called me.'

'Yes.' Jonty nodded when she told him. 'I tried to say Po—'. Her name came out as Po-y-ena. 'Mrs Pincher mistook!' He put his hand into an inside pocket of his coat and brought out a scrap of paper and handed it to Polly Anna. On it in childish writing was written, Paul Lena, and underneath in Samuel's unmistakable writing was written Paulina. 'Samuel showed me how to spell it.'

'But by then I was known as Polly Anna?' she smiled.

He nodded and took her hand. 'That's who you are.'

She thought he looked sad and she leaned forward and kissed his cheek and to her surprise felt a tremor in him. 'Don't you like me to kiss you any more, Jonty?'

He looked at her, perusing her face, then lifted her hand to his lips and kissed it. 'Yes,' he murmured. 'I do.'

*   *   *

Through the summer they travelled the villages and small towns wherever Johnson had obtained a licence and sometimes when he hadn't. The smaller villages were glad to see them there and the ploughmen and farm labourers would appear to help them put up the booth and get ready for a performance and sometimes invite them to stay overnight in their homes. They spent a week in Seamer and Polly Anna and Jonty saw their first sight of the sea when, before the show started, they rode into the town of Scarborough, just a few miles away.

Jonty rode behind Polly Anna and Amy rode behind Morgan. 'Look!' Polly Anna shouted. 'Look at all that water! And what's that smell? Oh, it's wonderful!'

She slipped down from the horse's back, breathed in the salty smell of the sea and stared across the wide yellow sands and the great expanse of grey-blue white-flecked ocean; her gaze took in the cliffs and the castle, the pier and the lighthouse and the harbour filled with fishing cobbles and herring drifters, and she thought she had never seen anything more beautiful.

In August they travelled to the ancient fair at Ripon and watched as a horseman dressed as St Wilfred and accompanied by henchmen opened the fair to much cheering and handclapping. This old custom was enacted every year to remind the townspeople of St Wilfred's return to his monastery after his exile in Rome.

Amos Johnson came up behind her as she watched the ceremony and casually put his hand on her shoulder. 'This is a good fair. We should do well here.'

She moved away slightly so that his hand slipped off. Lately he seemed to be making a habit of seeking her out, adjusting her head-dress before a performance or helping her to mount before she went into the ring.

'There's a coffee shop just round 'corner,' he said. 'Do you want to come?'

'No, thank you,' she said. 'I'm meeting Jonty in a minute.'

'Is he your fella? You're allus with him.'

She considered. 'He's my best friend,' she said simply. 'We've always been together, since we were children.'

His mouth twitched. 'Like brother and sister? I'll bet he doesn't think so! Not a great-looking lass like you.' He put his hand back on her shoulder. 'He's spoiling your chances, you know that don't you? Allus hanging round you, you'll never get another fella when he's around.'

'I don't want a fellow, thank you very much,' she retorted. 'And I'll thank you to mind your own business.'

He flushed and backed away. 'Now then! That's enough of that. Don't forget I can give you notice whenever I want.'

'What do you mean? I'm doing the act all right, aren't I? There are no complaints?'

'No,' he said softly. 'But you could do better if you were nice to me.'

She swore at him, a fat juicy word which she had overheard from some of the circus men. 'If you threaten me again I'll tell your father,' she warned. 'It's his circus, not yours, and what's more,' she pointed a finger at him, 'I'll get Jonty and all the

200

dwarfs and everybody to back me up. They'll believe me if I tell them what you've been saying.'

He sneered. 'Scared for your virtue are you? What – and you with black blood? – *kaulo ratti*! That's what they say anyroad,' he added lamely as he saw the anger on her face.

'Yes, I have Romany blood.' She put her hands on her hips and stared him in the face, 'And I'm not ashamed of it. I am what I am.'

But his words and actions stirred something within her. She had entered womanhood and found it amusing that Amy was constantly warning her about the men, both in the audience and those working in the circus, who waited for her outside the booth, asking her if she would meet them for a talk or a walk or go with them to the dancing booths, and although she was flattered, she simply smiled sweetly but always refused.

She had lived in the tent with Amy and Morgan for a while when Jonty had said he wanted to have his own bender, but she felt this was unfair on them because, as she told them, she wasn't family, even though they treated her and Jonty as such. So now she had her own bender, tucked between the Morgans' and Jonty's so that she would be safe.

But as she lay under her blanket during the Ripon Fair, she pondered on Amos Johnson's remark about her 'black blood', implying that the Romany women were wanton, which was quite untrue. The Romany women that she had met were quiet and modest where men were concerned, the young girls were kept under the watchful eyes of their parents and not allowed to mingle with young men unless there was serious intent of marriage.

But what of her mother? What kind of woman had she been? A lady, Morgan and Kisaiya had both said. But where had she come from? And how had she come to meet and marry a Romany? And who was the gentleman who had come looking for her? The questions jumbled around in her head, keeping her awake, tossing and turning from one side to another on her mattress. She was so hot. Her hair was sticking to the back of her neck and she sat up and removed her shift. As she did so, she heard a sound, a shuffling on the grass outside. Cats, she thought, then curled up her toes, or rats!

She heard a scratching on the canvas of her tent and she pulled the blanket around her. 'Jonty? Is that you?'

'No, me Gypsy lass, it's not Jonty.' A hoarse whisper came back through the tent flap. 'It's Amos.' She saw his fingers coming through the flap as he strove to undo the cords. 'Let me in, will you? Just for a minute! I just want to talk to you.'

From his slurred speech he was plainly worse for drink and she picked up one of her boots and hurled it towards the flap. 'Get away! Leave me alone.'

He pulled on a cord and the flap opened and he poked his head through. 'Come on, pretty Polly,' he persuaded thickly. 'Let me in. Let's have a bit o' Gypsy passion!'

She started to shout. 'Jonty! Morgan!'

'They're not there, me darlin'. They're having a bit of a chin wag with some of 'other folk. I've just left 'em. I thought I'd come and keep you company, seeing as you were on your own.'

She had forgotten. Jonty had said that he was going to talk to the dwarfs and the Thin Man after the show to discuss a new act that they were going to use at Nottingham. Morgan must have gone over with Amy and decided to stay.

She shouted again as he pushed his way further into the tent. She heard an answering screech of monkeys and a muffled roar of lions from the cages at the other side of the field, and she knew if she shouted loud enough she would waken all the animals who would set off a cacophony of noise loud enough to attract the keepers, who would go running to see what was amiss. But as he lurched in he put his hand to her mouth. 'Shut up, you little fool.'

With one hand she hung on to the blanket which covered her nakedness and with the other she lashed out at him. 'Help.' Her call was muffled as he tightened his grip on her mouth. She bared her lips and bit, nipping the flesh between her teeth and as he let go she kicked him, knocking him off balance and sprang away.

She almost fell over the small furry creature who leapt through the tent flap and threw itself on to Amos Johnson's head, clinging to his hair.

'Get it off! Get it off! I can't stand monkeys. Get it off me!' He scrabbled with his hands to remove Morgan's monkey from his head, but the animal clung on pulling on his hair and screeching at an ear-piercing pitch.

Polly Anna crawled out of the tent. 'Help! Somebody!' She could hear Amos crashing around inside the tent as he tried to remove the monkey from his head and she started to run towards the glow of a fire, but her cries had been heard; there was an answering roar of lions and a pad of running feet and she shouted again. 'Help me, somebody. Come quick.'

An army of small people surrounded Polly Anna's tent as Amos, his face and hands covered in scratches, and Morgan's monkey still clinging to him, crawled out and clambered to his feet. The dwarfs stood in a circle surrounding him, their eyes lifted to his face in silent disapproval. Behind them stood Jonty and Morgan, the Thin Man, the Fire-eater and the Fat Lady, watching his squirming humiliation, but saying nothing.

'What's going on?' A voice thundered out behind them and they all turned to see Mr Johnson standing there. 'We shall have all of Ripon here with this racket, and if townsfolk start complaining we'll have the law here before morning!' He peered towards his son. 'Amos? What you doing here, mush?' He glared around at the crowd. 'Whose bender is this?'

Polly Anna pulled her blanket closer around her. 'It's mine, Mr Johnson.'

He narrowed his eyes and indicated with his thumb towards his son. 'And did you invite him in? 'Cos if you did you're off this gaff right now. I'll not have that sort of thing going on in my fit-up.'

She shook her head and started to cry and Amy came across to her and patted her arm. 'No, she never, Mr Johnson. She's a decent lass is Polly Anna. Your lad's been following her about for ages, he's allus bothering her.'

'Aye, he has. We've seen him.' There was general agreement, much nodding of heads by the dwarfs, and the Thin Man leant across and poked a stabbing finger at Amos Johnson's chest.

'What?' Mr Johnson roared. 'You've been bothering this young lass, have you, mush?'

Amos swayed on his feet, the alcohol, the scratching monkey and the crowd of onlookers becoming too much for him. 'She asked me in,' he began. 'You knows what these Gyppos is like. She's been giving me the eye—'. His words were no sooner out than he keeled over, crashing backwards into the tent and pulling it on top of him as Jonty hurled himself at him and smashed his fist into his chin.

It took three dwarfs and Morgan to pull him off before Jonty, red-faced and babbling incoherently, finally let go of Amos, and Morgan's monkey was safely back on his master's shoulder.

'His father'll turn him off 'gaff now as well as giving him a black eye,' Morgan said later as he and Jonty re-erected Polly Anna's tent. 'He'll not stand for it. He's nowt but trouble anyway and he never does any work.'

Polly Anna stayed the rest of the night in the Morgans' tent, for she was very shaken over the events, and lay thinking of how much less complicated childhood was than being grown up, when all you had to worry about was being hungry; and yet how lucky she was that brave and loving Jonty was still taking care of her.

20

Richard Crossley rode up the drive towards Mrs Winthrop's house. It was a solid, square country house which had the advantage of overlooking some of the most beautiful views of the Wolds, standing as it did at the head of a dale. Below him sheep grazed on the grassy hillside and rabbits scampered, the hawthorn hedges and wild apple trees were white with spring blossom and the air was filled with birdsong.

He had become a frequent visitor to the home of Harriet Winthrop and her daughter Rowena, and although he found the old lady quite intimidating with her peppery manner, and Rowena inclined to be rather dowly, he was inclined to think that they were growing fond of him since he had come to live with his uncle and aunt Dowson on their neighbouring estate.

Today, though, wasn't a mere courtesy call for he had a special reason for visiting. He wanted to ask a favour. He rang the bell and the maid who answered the door said that Mrs Winthrop was not receiving company today but was resting, but that Miss Winthrop would receive him.

'Good morning, Miss Winthrop.' He gave her a formal bow as the maid led him into the morning room. 'I trust you are well and your mother also? I understand Mrs Winthrop is resting – nothing amiss, I hope?'

She indicated that he should take a seat opposite her and replied that her mother was quite well. 'She occasionally has a touch of malaise at this time of year and takes to her bed, but it is nothing to worry about.' Her lips tightened. 'We all have sombre thoughts from time to time and would wish to change matters, but some things cannot be changed and we must get on with the business of living.'

He raised his eyebrows and murmured some agreement. He hardly ever had sombre thoughts, life was too full, too busy, though he wondered how Rowena's and her mother's life could be called living, for it rather seemed to him that they did nothing with it, apart from play the piano, sew or take tea with neighbours and have an annual holiday in Harrogate or Scarborough.

'I wanted to ask your mother a favour, Miss Winthrop, but perhaps I should call another day when she is up and about?'

'A favour, Richard?' Rowena gave him a rare smile and he thought that perhaps she had been a fine-looking woman in her younger days and he wondered why she hadn't married; she would have been most eligible with such a large estate as her fortune. 'Perhaps I can grant it for you?'

'Well!' He relaxed and smiled back at her. 'I wanted to know if I could steal Jennings from you,

Miss Winthrop – just for a week or so, not permanently.'

'Steal Jennings! And do call me Rowena. We have known you long enough and we are practically related.' He had rarely known her to be so affable. 'And what do you want with Jennings when you and Uncle Charles have a perfectly good man of your own?'

'Ah, but Jennings is a good judge of horse flesh, much better than Smithson, and as I have my uncle's permission to build up the stables and buy some more horses for the estate, I wondered if I could take Jennings with me to the horse sales to give me his advice.'

'What a good idea! And perhaps he would look out another mount for me. Poor old Star is not fit to ride, he ought to be put out to pasture.'

'Do you care to ride, Miss Winthrop – Rowena? I didn't know that you did.'

'Why yes!' she said. 'Once I rode every day and all day.' Then she added caustically, 'But not any more. There is no fun in it now that I am old and I must confine myself to a carriage or trap!'

He laughed. 'Do not think of yourself as old, Miss Rowena. There is much to do in life. Perhaps if we get you a suitable mount you would care to ride with me?'

Her manner lightened again. 'That would be very pleasant. I should like that very much. So, where do you intend buying your new stock? You have missed Malton. Driffield perhaps or York? Yes – York would be best.'

'No. I had in mind to visit Appleby. That is the one I most favour.'

Her face paled. 'Appleby?' Her voice dropped to a whisper. 'But – that is the Gypsy horse fair!'

'I know,' he said cheerfully. 'But Appleby is the very best or so I'm told; it seems there are fine horses both for work and for carriages as well as for riding. And,' he added, blundering on, 'there's no finer judge of horses than the Gyp—!' He stopped, realizing his error, but not knowing if she was aware that he knew the story of her sister and the Gypsy.

'Er – are you unwell, Miss Rowena? Can I get you something – shall I summon the maid?'

'No. Certainly not! I am quite all right.' She squared her shoulders and sat back in her chair. 'The name of Appleby simply brought back unpleasant memories. Memories which I prefer to forget.'

'I'm so sorry,' he stammered. 'I had no idea, I would not have brought up the subject had I known.'

'Of course you didn't know,' she said sharply. 'How could you? It was all a long time ago, you would have been a mere child. How could you know?' she repeated as if to herself and bent her head, drumming her fingers across her brow. 'How would anyone know?'

He sat silently for a while then, clearing his throat, said, 'Perhaps I had better go. I take it that you would rather I didn't take Jennings with me?'

'Not take Jennings!' Her eyes flashed with anger. 'Why of course you must take Jennings if you intend going. It is essential that you take him! You'll be robbed and swindled if you don't. You can't trust the Gypsies! Take my word for it, Richard, I know. They will steal your purse, your horse, your sister –

your life – if you are not very careful. Take my word for it. I know.'

He stared at her, confused by her last abrupt hissing words. It was almost as if she had taken leave of her senses; she had a bright gleam in her eyes indicating some kind of madness. But then she blinked and stared back at him. 'I'm sorry. I didn't mean to startle you. I am affected you see, by the same malady as my mother. At this time of the year we always think of my sister.'

Her lip curled and he saw again the disgruntled woman that he was used to. 'You will have heard that she ran away with a Gypsy! She chose to live the life of a traveller, eating berries from the hedgerow, skinning rabbits for the pot and baking hedgehogs in the fire! That's what they do, you know.' She gave a derisive snort. 'And all for the love of a Gypsy.'

'But,' he said softly, 'it was a long time ago. Can you not find it in your heart to forgive? She might be very happy in her chosen life.'

She looked away from him, out of the window and down the green valley. 'I don't think so. She will have been punished for the upset she has caused, she and her child.'

'The child survived?'

'Yes – at least – I don't know. She wrote to my mother that she was expecting a child.'

'So – you don't know where they are? Do they never come to see you? I have seen Romanies in the village sometimes.'

She didn't want to say any more, he could tell, but yet he persisted. The story had always intrigued him and he wanted to know what had happened to them, the Gypsy and the lady and their child.

'Where do you think they are now, all these years on?'

'I don't know,' she almost shouted. 'I don't know! I only know that my life is ruined because of her. Who would take a woman in marriage who had a sister wedded to a Gypsy? Such shame! Don't you understand?'

He looked at this middle-aged woman and felt sad for her in her bitterness, yet he felt that there was something more behind the words that she was saying. 'And – and so, how did they come to meet?'

She turned towards him and raised her head but her look was far away as she whispered, 'They met at Appleby Fair.'

'Aye, it'll be nigh on twenty years since I were in Appleby. Mistress would never hear of me going again, not after what happened to Miss Madeleine.' Jennings was happy to talk as they set out on their long journey to Westmoreland. 'Can't think why she agreed to it this time.'

She had agreed to it because she had asked Richard to make enquiries about her lost daughter. 'This will be the very last time,' she had said. 'If there is no news then I shall give up for good.'

Richard had requested that they use the old roads, the drover roads and tracks over hillside and common whenever they could, rather than use the faster tollroads. 'We're not in a hurry,' he said. 'The weather is good and we can use the village inns and hostelries for our accommodation. Besides, the Gypsies travel this way and we can take a look at the horses before we get to Appleby.'

Though they had taken two other fresh horses

they were several days travelling and as they neared Westmoreland the roads were filled with waggons and carts and strings of horses as Romanies and traders rallied to the great horse fair. 'Let's sleep out, Jennings!' Richard said enthusiastically as they estimated that the next day they would reach the outskirts of Appleby.

'Sleep out, sir? Whatever do you mean?' Jennings viewed him in concern. 'You're not suggesting—?'

'Yes! Like the Gypsies. The weather is warm.' He looked up at the evening sky. 'There won't be rain, and we have blankets.'

'But – my rheumatism, sir! It won't stand for t'damp!' Jennings had enjoyed his sojourn in the inns, where he had eaten well and partaken of the local ale with enthusiasm, something he had not been able to do on his last journey to Appleby, when he had been responsible for the two young ladies and a maid. 'If my back plays me up I'll not be able to try out hosses.'

'Oh.' Richard was disappointed. He'd rather fancied sleeping out beneath the stars. 'Well, I'll tell you what, Jennings. We'll find you accommodation at some hostelry and then after supper I'll come back here. This is such a perfect spot.'

There was a small copse of ash and hazel with an undercrop of blackthorn to his back, whilst below him a brook sang its way down the hillside towards the River Eden. Beside the brook, groups of Gypsies had placed their tents and lit fires for cooking and their horses grazed nearby. He could hear a low buzz of conversation as they called across to each other, but he couldn't make out what they were saying, for they seemed to be speaking in a foreign tongue. They were neither rowdy or rough, but appeared to be getting on with the serious business of discussing horseflesh as first one then another would inspect the horses, then nodding their heads would briskly slap hands and walk away to another group. The women stirred the pots over the fires or nursed babies and chatted quietly to each other.

'They'll not want you up here looking down on 'em, sir, if that's what you're thinking. And neither would I be happy about leaving you alone without even the protection of a tent. No, sir, I'd lose my job. Mrs Winthrop can be a tartar when she wants. I wouldn't want to risk it.'

'Oh, very well!' His eye was caught by a young Gypsy girl who was chasing after a small child; she picked her up and swung her up in the air, swinging her round and round. A male Gypsy standing by a tent, whom Richard hadn't noticed before, called abruptly to her and sharply indicated that she should come inside. She glanced up the hillside to where Richard was standing as if he had been pointed out and for a brief moment she stared at him, then quickly turning away she scurried inside out of view.

'They don't like anybody looking at their women-folk, sir. It's as well to remember.'

'Yet they will look at ours. Isn't that what happened with Miss Madeleine, Jennings?'

'Well sir, it was like this.' Jennings brought out his tobacco pouch and proceeded to fill his pipe and light it. 'We'd brought t'coach to Appleby on account of 'maid didn't ride. The two young ladies had wanted to come across country as we've done this time. They were both good horsewomen so it would have been all right, but Mrs Winthrop insisted that Jinny came with us, so t'coach it had to be. But because of that, we were a bit conspicuous like. We had t'coachie and t'post boy and me and Parker riding alongside. And t'Gypsies were forever bothering us, the women *dukkering* or wanting to sell a bit o' lace or summat.'

'*Dukkering*?' Richard laughed. 'What's that?'

'Fortune telling, sir. And that's where 'trouble started. Whenever 'young ladies went out they were surrounded by these Gypsy women, all pleasant like, but persistent, or so Jinny said—'

'Jinny! I used to have a nursemaid called Jinny.'

'Aye, same one, sir. She couldn't endure staying on after what happened, so Mrs Winthrop and Mrs Dowson arranged with your mother that she should go to London to look after you.'

Richard shook his head in amazement. How very odd that he had never been told.

'Anyway.' Jennings shook out the moisture in his pipe. 'Where was I? Ah, yes. Jinny said that this Gyppo came up and told all the women off for bothering t'young ladies and so they went away, all but one woman who kept hanging around after this Gypsy. Jinny said he was right handsome – tall, and thick black hair and a real way with words, and he chatted with Miss Rowena first until he caught sight of Miss Maddy, and then she said, Jinny that is – she said that it was as if there was a spark which flew between them. 'Course!', he gave a short laugh, 'that's just women's talk, I expect. They're inclined to be a bit romantic aren't they, sir.'

Richard agreed. 'Yes, I suppose they are. Come on then, Jennings, let's go and get our supper,' and gathering their things together they mounted and rode off down the hill towards the nearest hostelry.

By noon the next day they arrived above Appleby and looked down at the crowded roads and lanes leading towards the town. Every inch of space in field and meadow was taken up by horses and waggons as traders and farmers, farriers and gentlemen gathered together waiting for the next day when the fair was officially opened and they could do business together. Richard left Jennings with the horses and strode into the town to try and book a room for himself and a place for Jennings and the horses, but everywhere was full and he realized that he might well get his wish to sleep out. In every inn or hostelry yard, trestle tables were set up and men were drinking ale and smoking their pipes or trenching on beef puddings and apple tarts, and there came echoing through the streets, great shouts of conversation and laughter as they discussed the price of horseflesh, bullocks, sheep, corn and the weather.

He wandered by the River Eden, where already some of the Gypsies were washing their horses, a bunch of soapwort in their hands as they scrubbed away the dust of several days and even weeks of travel, for to this famous fair came Gypsies and travellers from all over the country.

'Tell your fortune, sir?' A Gypsy woman accosted him. 'You have a lucky face; good fortune is following you.'

He grinned at her and was about to refuse politely when he saw, hovering behind her, and holding her child by the hand, the young Gypsy girl he had seen the previous day. 'Well! All right then, but only if you will answer a question of mine.'

'I'll try, sir. Will you buy a piece of Romany lace for your lady?'

'Maybe. But I wondered if you ever knew of a lady – a lady who married one of your race? Her name was Madeleine Winthrop.'

The Gypsy drew back, her eyes hard and her smile fading. 'True Romanies don't marry out, sir. We only marry our own.'

'Oh, come!' he said in a jocular manner. 'Sometimes you do. I know of one for certain. She had a child who would be about the same age as your own daughter here,' he nodded towards the Gypsy girl.

'Then you knows more than me, sir.' She turned away and signalled to the girl to come.

'Oh. But what about my fortune?'

She hesitated as if the sight of a coin would persuade her. He jingled his pocket and she turned back and took his hand, opening out his fingers. She gazed down into his palm, her face expressionless. 'You are young sir, there is not much written yet. But you will have good fortune; a happy marriage, children.' She put out her own hand for the shilling he was offering and slipped it through a slit in her skirt to a pocket beneath. 'I wish you good day, sir.'

What tosh, he thought as he watched her walk away. A happy marriage and children. That is what everyone expects and hopefully will get. Could she not see anything more, no adventure or excitement?

It was a dry warm night and they slept beneath the trees, much to Jennings's dismay and discomfort.

The next day they rode down into Appleby along with hundreds of others to inspect the Gypsy horses and those of other horse dealers who were there to sell and buy. Mine owners from the Yorkshire pits were there to buy their ponies, farmers and butchers buying for plough and dray and gentlemen looking for fine-bred colts not yet broken in, and steeds which were powerful and spirited, for their own personal use. They watched the horses being put through their paces down on the Sands, some moving with swift hard pace, others, with nervous high-bred temperament, their ears trembling and nostrils quivering, were bucking and lunging at every obstacle.

Richard left Jennings haggling over a carriage horse and went to look for a mount suitable for Rowena. He stood with his hands in his pockets as a long-necked grey mare with short and sturdy back was trotted along the road and he mused that she had a quiet and steady temperament and seemed a suitable mount for a lady, when he felt someone brush against his jacket. He immediately felt for his pocket book, but it was safe and as he turned he saw the Gypsy girl walking away from him but with her head turned towards him. She gave a slight indication as if he should follow her. He put his finger to his chest. 'Me?' he mouthed and she gave a slight nod.

He strolled nonchalantly, stopping now and again beside a crowd of buyers and dealers but keeping her in sight, when he suddenly bethought himself that perhaps he was walking towards trouble. Her husband, who had seen him watching her on the hillside, could be waiting around a corner to give him a warning. Jennings had said that they didn't like anyone looking at their women. Or her mother could have told someone of him making enquiries of the Gypsy and Madeleine. They were private people, he did believe, not accustomed to being questioned. All of this he had in mind, and yet still he followed her, away from the site by the river and towards and around the lanes of Appleby until finally she stopped behind a blacksmith's forge. She glanced around, put her finger to her lips and bade him stay, then slipped away around a corner and out of sight.

Well! He leaned against the wall of the forge, I had hoped for excitement, perhaps I am about to get it. There was no-one about apart from an apprentice, who was inside the forge stoking up a fire, for the blacksmiths and farriers were all up on the field by the river, trimming and shoeing as required; and that made him tense, for if a gang of Gypsies should come along, he pondered, then I won't stand much of a chance against them.

A lone Gypsy woman strolled along the lane in his direction, she looked neither to left nor right but straight towards him. 'Tell your fortune, sir?' she asked as she drew abreast.

'No, thank you.' He gave her hardly a glance. 'I had it told yesterday.'

'But not as I would tell it, sir. You were misled, I fear, by one of my *Sisters.*'

He turned and gave her his full attention. He saw that she was a handsome woman, very striking looking, with a long dark plait down her back, gold earrings and a straw hat upon her head. 'What do you mean that I was misled?'

'You are searching for someone? A lady who married a Romany?'

'That's right. But the other Gypsy said that she did not know of anyone.'

'She has her reasons for not speaking of it, sir. But it is the truth that there was such a marriage. You may take my word as a Romany.'

He nodded. He knew that it was the truth without her oath. 'Where are they now, do you know? They had a child I understand?'

'They are gone from this place. To a happier one I trust.'

'You mean – that they are dead?' He was shocked. This wasn't something that he had envisaged. He had had a romantic vision that they were living an idyllic existence, the Gypsy and his lady, out on a hillside of green grass and meadow flowers, their child or children playing at their feet whilst they chatted quietly by their glowing fire, their horses grazing nearby.

She nodded. 'Many years ago.' She moved towards him. 'May I read your palm, sir? I want no money.'

Without thinking, he held out his palm and the woman took it, smoothing it with her fingers. A small smile played around his lips. 'You're not going to tell me I'll have a good fortune and a happy marriage?'

'You will have that, sir, but not yet. There are other obstacles to be overcome first. And first you must find the one you are seeking.'

'But, but you said she was dead!'

'There is someone else that you must look for. That person has the key to your future.'

'And is this person something to do with the Gypsies?'

'Yes. That much I can tell you.' She gathered her shawl about her and prepared to move away. 'Nothing more. God bless you, sir.'

He watched her as she walked away. He hadn't offered her money but then, she had said she didn't want any, so why did she want to read his palm? How very strange.

The young Gypsy girl suddenly appeared by his side and he wondered where she had been hiding. 'That's your mother, isn't it?' he asked. 'Not the other one?'

'Yes,' she said softly. 'You can trust her. She will tell you the truth.'

'So, what do I do now?' He muttered almost to himself. 'If Madeleine really is dead, do I tell her mother and sister? And what about the child?' He cursed himself. I didn't ask about the child – did she mean that it too was dead?

The girl touched his arm. 'You must go to Hull, sir. You will find the answer there.'

He walked slowly back to find Jennings. What am I about? What will I find in the streets of Hull? Am I on a wild-goose chase? Will Mrs Winthrop and Rowena want to know about the child? How stupid I am, why didn't I ask if it was a girl or a boy?

He mingled with the crowd as he searched for Jennings, a myriad of questions running through his head. When he finally found him, Jennings was jubilant, having done a good deal with the horses. 'Just one to find for Miss Rowena, then that should do us.'

That night after supper, he left Jennings chatting

with other grooms and waggoners and took a walk up the hillside. He wasn't tired, rather his mind was full of images of Gypsies and horses and fortune telling. The night was still and a moon was just rising and there seemed to be a magic in the air as he looked down at the camps by the river and in the meadows. Dozens of fires were lit, there was a smell of food cooking, rabbit or some other game, and there was music from fiddles and tambourines and the lilting sound of singing.

The Gypsy women had put on their finery, bright flowing skirts and lacy blouses, gold rings in their ears and on their fingers, bangles on their wrists and necklaces around their throats. Some of the Gypsy men were dancing, their felt hats on the back of their heads and their heels clicking and Richard wondered if some of them were of foreign extraction, Spanish perhaps or Irish.

He wandered down, skirting the edges of the groups so as not to intrude, though there were other curious non-Gypsies like himself, also enjoying the scene. He looked when he could, without appearing too curious, inside the bender tents. They seemed to him to be cosy and inviting, little furniture, merely a mattress or two half hidden behind curtains, and wooden boxes which appeared to serve a dual purpose of seating and storage. Children played on blankets or outside the tent but within the watchful eye of parents and grandparents.

They nodded and smiled as he walked by and he greeted them in return and he looked for the Gypsy girl or her mother but saw neither.

When he returned to their site Jennings was

already beneath his blanket and grumbling at the hardness of the ground. He crouched beside him. 'Jennings! What would I find in the town of Hull if I should go? Do you know it?'

'Not well, sir, I don't often need to go. But there's a fine estuary, a great whaling and fishing industry. It's a busy town, full of seamen from other lands, industrialists and such. Your uncle has another sister living there. Why, sir, are you thinking of visiting?'

'I might,' he said, 'if I thought it was worthwhile. And is there anything more that might tempt me?'

Jennings pursed his lips. 'Well, onny t'fair, sir. It's a good hoss fair, allus was, though myself I don't think it comes up to Appleby or Brough Hill. But they do say that Hull Fair is t'best in t'land for entertainment – side shows and circuses an' that.'

'Hull Fair,' he breathed. Of course! That was what the Gypsy girl had meant. Yet his uncle had visited many times and found nothing. What could he expect to find? But perhaps I might go anyway. It could be great fun. What was it that Jinny had said all those years ago? There's nowt to beat it, she had said in her broad northern accent. Hull Fair. 'Biggest and 'best.

21

The open forests and parklands around
Nottingham were dotted with old thorn trees which
hung with clusters of mistletoe; ancient oaks, birch
and sweet chestnut spread their branches and
beneath them the grasses, heath and bracken were
turning to a golden hue as they arrived for the fair
at the beginning of October.

Polly Anna tried to picture how it would have
been when she had been there with her parents.
She wandered down Long Row and Bridlesmith
Gate and Vault Lane trying to relive a memory, but
she had no recollection, none at all. It had been
blotted out. She realized that her parents would not
have been involved with the pleasure fair; as a
Romany her father would have been there only for
horse trading and the Romany women to sell their
lace, trinkets and bunches of wild flowers, but she
wondered what her mother had done.

Now the streets of Nottingham were filled with
stalls and booths just as at Hull Fair and the sights
and sounds filled her with excitement, more so now
that she was part of it than when she had been an

onlooker without money to spend on its pleasures. She loved the clamour of the drums and tin trumpets and the showmen calling to the crowd; the crack of rifle shot in the shooting gallery; the cry of the elephants and the roar of tigers as they paced in their cages; and she laughed with glee when havoc erupted as sheep and goats escaped from their pens and raced down the streets with the farmers in pursuit, whilst the gooseherd with his crook drove his flock through Goose Gate into the town from Lincolnshire and the Fens to be sold in the market place.

What she didn't like to see were the freak of nature shows, when the showman would call out, 'Come and see the Living Skeleton,' or, 'See the Man with Two Heads,' or 'the Dog with Five Legs'. She would scurry past these sideshows averting her eyes, and yet, strangely, she had never seen any of these so-called monstrosities when the shows were packed up and moving on to another town, and she wondered where they hid themselves or if they really were dead and pickled in spirit as Jonty said they were.

She stood and watched as the large booth belonging to Wombwell Circus was being erected and couldn't help wishing that she could join that troupe instead of Johnson's. 'I'd like to do something more exciting,' she complained. 'All I ever do is ride round and round and whoop and holler. It's very boring!'

Jonty commiserated. He, if he wanted to, could change his act, even going into the audience if he felt like it and pretend to 'kidnap' someone and take him into the ring, which the audience loved.

But Polly Anna had to remain an Indian because that was what Mr Johnson wanted.

She had another worry also. She had overheard Mr Johnson and his other son Harry, arguing one day. Harry was the son with a harelip and often couldn't be understood, but Polly Anna could understand him, being used as she was to Jonty's speech, and on this day she had heard Harry complaining bitterly over his father's apparent agreement to allow Amos back. 'If you don't like it, then you can hop it, mush,' said his father. 'I'll not have any arguments about what goes on in my fit-up.'

And so that was it, she thought. What Mr Johnson said, goes, and if Amos was back in favour then it didn't bode well for her. 'Mr Johnson?' she called to him, 'do you think we could change the routine, seeing as Wombwell's is here? We've been doing the Indian one for a long time.'

'Aye, but we haven't done it here or in Hull. It was Brown who did it then and you can't compare his show with ours. No, we'll give Wombwell's a run for their money, and they're not going to Hull so we'll be all right there.' He looked at her keenly. 'Getting fed up with it are you? I can soon get another rider.'

'Oh, no,' she said hastily, 'not a bit. I was only thinking about the competition.'

'Don't you worry your pretty head about that, chavi, that's my affair. You'll have heard Amos is coming back?'

'Yes, I had heard,' she said nervously.

'Then just watch out. I'll not have any goings on in my circus, not even if it's with one of my own sons. You'll be out on your ear if I hear of owt again. Do you hear me?'

Numbly she nodded. It didn't seem to matter that it hadn't been her fault, she had just been given a warning.

But Amos ignored her presence and though she felt nervous when he was around, he didn't approach her or even speak very much. He seemed preoccupied now with the animosity of his brother Harry, who hadn't wanted him to come back and harsh words and blows often came between them.

'It's Hull next.' Jonty, in his clown costume and painted face, was jubilant at the end of the last night of the fair. He had received a tremendous ovation from the circus audience as he'd finished his act and Polly Anna was so proud of him. 'You'll be the most famous clown in the world, Jonty. Won't he, Dolly?' she added to Amy's sister, who was standing nearby.

Dolly smiled. 'He's the best in the business,' she said. 'I just hope he doesn't go away and leave us.'

'Oh! But why would he do that?'

'Ogden's Circus will be in Hull. They're always looking for somebody special. And Jonty is very special,' she said, looking shyly at him.

I do believe she is taken with Jonty, Polly Anna thought mischievously; she is looking at him so adoringly, and she too looked at Jonty with fresh eyes and saw, not her faithful friend but a young man, who it was true had a twisted body, but who to the tiny Dolly was tall and fair, with a kind face and caring nature.

'You've got an admirer, Jonty,' she said later as she watched him wipe off his mask.

He turned to look at her, one eye and cheek were clean, the other still painted, a rosy round spot on his white cheek and a glossy teardrop below his eye. 'Who?'

'Can't you guess,' she teased.

'Not you!' One side of his face smiled, the other remained sad.

'Not me! Of course not!' She waited for him to laugh but when he didn't, she said, 'But of course I admire you, Jonty, you're the best person in the world and I love you more than anyone, you know that! But this is someone else.' She leaned forward and whispered. 'It's Dolly!'

'Phew!' He blew a raspberry. 'Silly!' He turned away, embarrassed, she thought and she reached out and tickled him in the ribs.

'Don't!' His manner was sharp, so unlike Jonty that she was taken aback.

'But – I'm sorry. What's the matter, Jonty? Why are you cross with me?'

'Not cross. Go now. I want to change.'

Puzzled, she left him and went to take off her own make-up and change her costume and then go back to help pack up the circus, feed and settle the horses and prepare to take the road again; this time back to Hull, to the streets which she had so willingly left and yet, for reasons she couldn't explain, was now so excited to return to.

That's why Jonty is so crotchety, she mused. He's thinking about going back. He'll want to see Samuel, but he'll be worried about going into the workhouse and what he will find. She gave a sudden shiver as the remembrance of those lost years of childhood came back to her. What would I have done without Jonty? How would I have survived? She thought of the times when she had felt so hemmed in and confined and realized now that it was probably due to her Romany blood, for the Romanies hated walls surrounding them.

She looked up from her task of clearing the horse stalls and saw Jonty watching her. 'Jonty,' she said, putting down the hay fork, 'I didn't mean to tease you. I'm sorry. Are you worried about going back to Hull?'

He came towards her, his face was clean and washed and his eyes seemed unusually bright. He put both arms around her and gave her a squeeze, then kissed her cheek. 'No. Not worried about that.'

'What then? Tell me.'

'Nothing to tell,' he smiled, yet still she felt he was sad.

They had to make haste to be on the road, for the Hull Fair started the following week and there was much clattering and banging, cursing and shouting as the showmen took down their fit-ups and stalls. Some of the townspeople were glad to see them go, as they often were in other towns, and groups of people stood around to see them off and grumbled about the mess and mud that was left behind. 'Don't come back,' shouted one man. 'Dirty Gypsies! Bringing dirt and disease to a respectable town.' Yet another complained abut the drunkenness, fighting and immorality which went on when the fair was there.

'Not us – it's your lot!' Mr Johnson shouted back. 'And don't call us Gypsies! We're fairground folk!' He looked as if he was prepared to get off his waggon and fight with the man over the issue, but was restrained by his son Harry.

Polly Anna waved from the top of a waggon to another crowd of onlookers, who were shouting, 'See you next year,' and she gave an Indian whoop, to which the children in the crowd responded and chased after them. The long trail began, the donkey carts laden with canvas tilts and costumes, the horse waggons piled with wooden elephants and horses from the roundabouts, the drays with the swings, wooden boards and cross beams, and show folk striding out on foot with packs on their backs on to their next gaff. Hull Fair.

The fair folk who arrived in Hull scrambled to find the best pitch for their booths, sideshows or circuses; they not only had to compete with each other but also with the travelling theatres which came to Hull especially at fair time and which set up their portable booths to take advantage of the thousands of people who flocked into the town for their annual pleasure. Many used their waggons as a stage and erected a simple booth with painted screens depicting mountains and castles, or sailing ships on turbulent oceans as a backcloth to the actors' performance.

Any building, hall or room at an inn which was large enough to hold a melodrama, play, farce or burletta was rented and posters put up on every lamppost and window advertising these splendid events. When Polly Anna and Jonty had finished their tasks for Johnson they set off into the town and read of the presentations about to begin.

'Look, Jonty – *The Captive Queen,* at Lawrence's

Theatre, and then after, a comic pantomime, *The Clown's Disasters*. And here – at Rickatson's Theatre, *Portas' Gardens*—'

'Come on. Come on!' Jonty was anxious to be off; they were on their way to the workhouse to try and see Samuel.

But Polly Anna hung back, still reading the posters: *The Fairy of the Mountain* or *Harlequin Runaway, The Sailor's Return*. What magical titles, how she wished that she could join a company which put on such grand events as these. Then her eye was caught by another poster advertising Ogden's Circus, which opened the next day with his famous clowns and trapeze artists and highly acclaimed French Equilibrist, Mme Gabrielle.

'An equilibrist, Jonty! That's what I am.'

Jonty gazed at her impatiently. 'What 'you talking about?'

'It means someone who can balance – like a tightrope walker or standing on a horse,' she said excitedly.

'Can you stand on a horse? I've never seen you!'

'Well, I can! I've tried it – ask Morgan, he'll tell you.'

Jonty shrugged. 'I'm going. You coming or not?'

Reluctantly she followed him across the town, through crowded Cambridge Street, St Luke Street and Osborne Street, where the fairmen were erecting their fit-ups and palaces of entertainment, and her spirits sank as they left the bustle and noise of preparation and approached Whitefriargate and the gloomy building of the workhouse.

'I'm scared, Jonty.' She hung back at the gate. 'I daren't go in. What if we get into trouble?'

'You stay here. I'll go first. See who's there.'

'No! Don't leave me. We'll go together. We didn't do anything wrong! We could leave if we wanted to.' Brave words which hung on her lips, but she was churning with fear at the thought of meeting up with Mr Pincher after she had humiliated him so publicly.

Jonty pushed on the gate, which wasn't locked, and cautiously walked inside the yard. Nothing seemed to have changed except that, as they looked up, the hayloft door had a bar and padlock across it. There were a few people hanging around in the yard and the door to the building was ajar. They stepped inside and it seemed to Polly Anna that the building had shrunk in size, its grim walls leaning in to trap her, and that it was meaner and shabbier than when she had last seen it. And there was a smell which she had either forgotten or not been aware of previously, a smell of rank decay, of boiled cabbage and unwashed bodies.

She started to shake. 'Don't let's stay, Jonty!' She swallowed, her throat dry. 'I'm frightened. It's horrible. I can't bear it.'

'We must. We must find Samuel.' He took her hand. 'Don't be frightened.'

Dear Jonty. How brave he was. Yes, they must look for Samuel. 'Jonty!' She clung to him as they walked through the corridor. 'Let's see if we can get him out! Like we did before. We could take him with us, he could live in your bender. We earn enough money between us to keep him!'

Jonty nodded. 'Yes. We'll try.'

They threaded their way through to the back of the building, but changes had been made: some of the rooms had been divided into two and seemed to be used for different purposes from previously and they couldn't locate the lunatic ward. Jonty opened the rear door leading into the yard and looked out; it was darker and gloomier than before and he lifted his head and saw that the high wall surrounding the yard had been made higher still, trapping in the darkness and stench of the building and keeping out any light or air.

'Hey! What's tha up to?'

They both jumped at the voice; a tall thin youth was coming determinedly towards them. Then he slowed down. 'Jonty? Is it thee?' It was Billy. Taller, thinner and spottier than he had been, but unmistakably him.

Jonty nodded at him and Polly Anna greeted him with relief. 'Hello, Billy. You're still here then!'

'Aye.' He drew himself up taller. 'I took over thy job, Jonty, when tha left – where did tha go? I looked all over town for thee.'

Jonty didn't answer his question, remembering Billy's loose tongue. 'Where's Samuel?'

'And the Pinchers,' Polly Anna questioned anxiously, 'where are they?'

Billy drew in a gasping astonished breath. 'Didn't tha hear? By heck, what a to do! Mrs 'Armsworth and some of 'governors caught 'Pinchers redhanded with stuff from 'butcher and 'grocer – and then at 'same time Owd Boney came in with run goods off 'ships. Constables were here and 'magistrate and they were all taken off to jail – not Mrs 'Armsworth and governors, I don't mean, though two of 'em were, Blake and Grant, 'cos they were in on it as well. By, tha should have been here to see it.' His look commiserated with them that they had missed such an event. 'Somebody had tipped 'em off,' he whispered, 'onny they don't know who. Mrs 'Armsworth knows, that's my bet, 'cos she was first here, onny she's not telling, her lips are sealed!'

Polly Anna and Jonty glanced with some relief at one another. 'And where are they now, Billy?' Polly Anna asked, knowing of old that only a direct question would get a straight answer from him.

'Pinchers are still in jail and two governors – in York – and they might get hung yet,' he added, ''cos of all 'crepancies that came to light, and Owd Boney died, it was 'shock I expect of going to jail.'

Polly Anna felt a fleeting stab of sympathy for the old man who had rescued her and her mother from the streets of Hull, even though she couldn't remember ever having any words or greeting from him since that day, but she felt nothing for the Pinchers.

'Samuel. Where is he?' Jonty's voice was urgent.

'Tha doesn't talk any better, does tha, Jonty? Though tha's grown a bit. Where's tha been?'

'Samuel – from the lunatic ward, Billy,' Polly Anna pressed, seeing Jonty's frustration, 'do you know where he is? We can't find the locked room.'

'Oh, it's up at 'top of 'building. There's been some changes made,' he said proprietorially. 'We've had 'wall built up at 'back to keep stink from them in Parliament Street, and lunatics have been put up at 'top so nobody can hear 'em. But Samuel's not there,' he added. 'He's been long gone.'

'Gone where?' Jonty asked. 'Where's he gone?'

Billy shrugged. 'Don't know. There was such a commotion going on, what wi' constables here and then a new board of governors and a new master coming, I didn't notice he was gone until they started to use 'schoolroom for summat else.'

'Perhaps he was let out and is with the other men.' Polly Anna could see that Jonty was depressed over the fate of his old friend.

'No, he's not. I would have seen him. Maybe he's snuffed it,' Billy added cheerfully. 'Owd folk don't last long in here.'

'Samuel did,' Jonty said slowly. 'He'd been here a long time. Maybe he just gave up after we'd gone.'

'You mustn't blame yourself, Jonty.' Polly Anna became the comforter as they hurried away from the workhouse and its tainted memories. 'Samuel urged us to go, he would have wanted us to have a better life.'

Jonty said nothing although he knew she was right. There is nothing for you here, Samuel had said. Go where life takes you and don't be afraid. He wasn't afraid. His life had changed and for the better, but he would have given so much to know that his old friend had had a peaceful end to his life and had not just withered away, wracked by the torment of opium addiction in the cold and friend-less lunatic ward of the workhouse.

22

'So Richard, you have taken over the mission of my brother, have you? I told him many years ago that he was on a fool's errand.' Mrs Harmsworth sat across her dining table from Richard. 'If Madeleine had wanted to return to her family she would have done so.'

'I'm sure you are right, Mrs Harmsworth.' Richard wondered whether or not to confide that he had heard of Madeleine's death, but as he had not yet told Mrs Winthrop or Rowena, he decided against it. 'But your sister is very dismal and not well, and I rather think it is preying on her mind.'

'Hmph. On her conscience more likely! She shouldn't have been so implacable in the first place. The whole affair would probably have faded away if she hadn't been so impossible about it. Madeleine was quite headstrong, in spite of looking like an angel, but she would have given up this Gypsy fellow eventually. But I suppose once she had made a stand against her mother she had to go through with it.' She took a sip of wine. 'And I suppose you are fascinated with the whole situation? You probably think it most romantic?'

'Well, yes, I suppose so,' he admitted. 'It does intrigue me, I must say. What I don't understand, though, is Miss Rowena's attitude towards her sister. She is very bitter and quite uncharitable, though perhaps I shouldn't say so.'

'Well, of course her own marriage prospects were ruined once the news got out, but Rowena was always jealous of Madeleine, even when they were very young. Madeleine had a very sunny nature, kind and good with people. Her mother and sister were always more interested in sheep and corn than in people. I find that people are so very interesting, don't you agree?' she added.

He was about to concur when she continued. 'For instance, I am involved with the local workhouse in Hull and you wouldn't believe the diversity of characters who are admitted there. I am now on the Board of Governors and I assure you that my eyes have been opened! It is a pity that I was born a woman, for I assure you that had I been a man, I would surely have been a Radical!'

They were dining alone; she had no other visitor staying, and, because when he had met her at Mrs Winthrop's previously she had invited him to stay should he ever visit Hull, he had written to ask her if he might take up her invitation during the week of Hull Fair.

After supper they withdrew from the dining room and sat by the fire in her drawing room. 'Yes, you see,' Mrs Harmsworth settled herself back into her chair, 'I have been a widow for a long time, and I knew that I would need some cause to fill my life, and although women of my station can visit the poor and hand out food parcels and do "good works", I wanted to be more involved than that, and as I cannot be in politics I thought I would make my presence known in other areas.'

Richard murmured something in response. He was tired after his ride to Hull, the fire was warm, the supper had been satisfactory and he felt pleasantly sleepy and quite willing for his hostess to talk, for she didn't seem to require any response from him.

'There was one man', she continued, 'who really shouldn't have been there at all, in my opinion. I was told of this Samuel and asked to seek him out by a young crippled lad from the workhouse. Jonty subsequently disappeared, but that is another story altogether. Samuel had been involved in politics many years ago – from a good family, I do believe, although not a gentleman, and he had taken up the profession of teaching. However, he had been declared insane and locked up in the lunatic ward of the workhouse.'

Richard blinked and took more interest. 'But why?'

'He had said too much, I suspect. The truth, no doubt, which those in authority didn't want to hear. Anyway, when I searched him out, he was dying, and I knew he was as sane as you or I, though he was inclined to have fits. He had been given opium to keep him quiet and he was well and truly addicted and dying of its effects.'

Richard pondered. He had once had a tincture of laudanum when he had been unwell, to help him sleep; it had done just that, but he had felt very strange the next day.

Mrs Harmsworth gazed into the fire and folded her hands in her lap. 'He was on my mind for days. He wasn't so old, though he looked like an old man, but he was very polite and well spoken and I decided that I would, after all, do a good deed that would be not only charitable, but make up for my having so much and others so little, for believe me, Richard, my conscience has been troubled over the inequalities of life.'

'So what did you do, Mrs Harmsworth?'

'There is a new Master at the workhouse, and I persuaded him to let this Samuel go to a woman who kept a lodging house and I would pay his expenses; he took little persuasion as you can imagine. It was a clean and respectable place, warm with reasonable linen on the beds and substantial fare on the table, not that he could eat much by then, for he had a poor appetite.' She paused, lost in thought, then she sighed. 'I visited him every day, just sitting by his bedside or reading a little, and I do believe he was comforted by my being there. Then, on the day before he died, he gave me this back.'

She got up and going to her secretaire opened a drawer. She handed him a playing card, a card with a jester on it. 'It belonged to the young boy who had asked me to visit Samuel. I don't know what it meant, but it was some kind of symbol between them, and Samuel said would I keep it in his memory.'

'Fascinating,' Richard said. 'You are so right, Mrs Harmsworth. People are much more interesting than sheep or corn.'

'Would you like to keep it, Richard? The playing

card, I mean. You get about so much more than I, and who knows, perhaps one day, you may find the other cards to match.'

The farmers were already doing business in the Market Place when he walked through the next day, for this had originally been a cattle, horse and trading fair. The entertainers and show people had followed on over the years, knowing that where people gathered in their masses, there was a living to be earned by entertaining them.

Sheep and goats were gathered in their pens, hens and geese squawked in cages and dark-skinned Gypsy men ran their horses along the road, showing off their paces to groups of potential buyers. Richard stopped to watch. One horse, a Pinto, took his eye. He looked a fine horse, not handsome but sturdy and fast and he thought he might seek out the Gypsy later and try him out; but not now, now he was on his mission, as Mrs Harmsworth called it, and perhaps it is, he mused, for the Gypsy girl told me to come.

Not all the booths were open, for the entertainment fair began in earnest in the evening when dusk had settled and the people of Hull had finished work. But the crowd was quite large nevertheless: country people had come to town for the day; seamen, foreign and English, and the local fishermen had returned from icy waters especially for the Hull Fair. There were many poor people too who wandered about, gazing longingly at the food stalls and eyeing the live fowl and baskets of eggs as if envisaging a good dinner.

Richard watched as a canvas tilt was placed on to

a frame and he wondered at its weak and slight structure and whether it would hold in a high wind; then he moved on to another area where, at Ogden's Circus, workers were putting up the hoarding advertising the night's performance. I might come to that, he thought: Chinese trapeze artists, jugglers and Mme Gabrielle, the French Equilibrist and Equestrienne.

The fair spread further than he had realized; the business and trading fair were confined to the Market Place, but the entertainments were dotted around every street, square and space that could be found. Eventually he came to a large green where most of the larger entertainment seemed to be. Roundabouts, ready and waiting beneath their covers, swing boats swaying gently on their ropes and various booths and sideshows, which although not yet open advertised their entertainment. The Pig Face Lady, he read, grimacing. The Fat Lady. The Living Skeleton. No thank you, I don't think so. He stopped at Johnson's Circus and read the hoarding. In addition to the usual animal acts, clowns and dwarfs, they were also advertising a special act, the Call of the West. See the real Wild Indians. Well, I might try sixpennyworth of that, he thought. The Americas always did attract me.

A man came out of the booth; he was sullen in appearance, but he glanced at Richard and nodded. 'Come tonight, sir, you'll not be disappointed. A real Indian squaw brought over specially from Santa Fe, pretty as a picture and a marvellous rider. Come early so as not to be disappointed.'

'Yes, I might,' he answered. 'Tell me, if I wanted

to know anything about the Gypsies, who would I ask? Do you know?'

The fairman glowered. 'Don't be mixing up 'Gypsies and fairfolk, will you, sir? None of us'll like it; we keeps separate. Gypsies is an odd bunch, private like, and won't tell you owt about themselves. What did you want to know?'

'Oh, nothing much.' He decided he didn't like the man's manner. 'I just wanted to know about a horse.'

'Best get down to 'Market Place then,' the man said dismissively. 'That's where they all are – 'cept for women,' he gave a toss of his head in the direction of the back of the green, 'and most of 'em are over there.'

Richard was walking away when a girl sauntered by. He took a quick glance at her, she was dark and pretty with a sway to her body as she walked, graceful as a cat, he thought, with a light and easy step. He smiled at her, but she merely glanced at him and didn't smile back.

'Polly Anna!' the fairman called to her. 'Where've you been? You should have been here rehearsing for tonight!'

'I don't need to rehearse,' she answered sharply. 'I know what to do. We do the same thing night after night. Anyway, I've been on an errand of my own.'

Their voices dispersed as they went into the booth and he wondered what she did in the act. I most certainly will come and find out, he decided, especially if she is in it.

As he walked back towards the Market Place he

mulled over a few ideas. If Madeleine and the Gypsy are dead and the child is a girl, it stands to reason that the Gypsy women would look after her, bring her up as their own, teach her their ways and so on, but that means that I won't be able to find her as she'll be protected, sheltered, just as Jennings said. But if it was a male child, he considered, then he would have to work as the Gypsy men do, either horse dealing or tinkering or whatever it is they do, and as he'd be about eighteen or so, he might well be here in the Market Place with the other Gypsies. So do I look for someone fair as Madeleine was, or someone who's a mixture of dark and fair?

With this in mind he perused the faces of the Gypsies that he passed, but none were fair and all were darker skinned than the average Englishman. It's impossible, he thought at last. I give up. I'll go back to Mrs Harmsworth's. Tonight I'll enjoy myself at the fair and tomorrow I shall go home.

'Sir!' Mrs Harmsworth's butler approached him after supper as he entered the hall. 'Forgive me for intruding, but I understand that you will be visiting the fair this evening.'

'Yes,' Richard smiled. 'I'm on my way now.'

'Then, sir, may I advise you to leave your pocket book and watch and chain behind? Take only loose change and perhaps wear some older clothes.'

'Pickpockets? I suppose you're right. But I haven't any older clothes with me, only my travelling wear.'

'Perhaps we could erm – lend you a jacket, sir? If you wouldn't feel too uncomfortable?'

'You're serious? You think I might get knocked down and robbed?'

'I'm perfectly serious, sir. There are villains who frequent the fair expressly for the purpose. Erm – the lowest class of women', the butler's voice dropped to a whisper, 'are there to tempt young men such as yourself; they are set up as a decoy in order to rob. Your uncle always took my advice whenever he was here, although, of course, he never went to the fair in the evening.'

So twenty minutes later Richard set off, dressed in his own travelling breeches and boots, and a flannel shirt and jacket belonging to one of the younger footmen, which was slightly short in the sleeve.

He was not familiar with the streets of Hull, but a large crowd was wending its way down the side of Junction Dock towards Castle Street and he simply followed them, glad now that he had changed clothes, for most of the crowd were poorly or simply dressed and in his own apparel he would have stood out as an easy target for anyone with criminal intentions. As it was he felt quite comfortable as he merged into the crowd.

He could hear the sounds of the fair before he could see it and as the rattle of drums, the beating of gongs and the shrill sound of tin trumpets tried to drown each other out, the conglomeration of sound seemed to infuse an excitement into the approaching crowd, and individually they raised their voices in shouts and laughter and hurried on so as not to miss a moment of the festivity.

As the evening wore on, Richard found himself buffeted from side to side as the crowd grew greater. He grew hot and sticky as the heat from the people, the smell of the gas light and naphtha lamps pervaded the air, and he realized that there was very little likelihood of finding a trace of Madeleine's child here. And in any case why should he or she be here if Gypsies and fairfolk don't mix? But, he debated, why did the Gypsy girl say I should come? It doesn't make sense!

He paid his money and went into Ogden's Circus. The trapeze artists and sword swallowers were first class, though he felt sorry for the dancing bears, who looked old and weary with torn and matted coats. The elephants lumbered in and performed dainty tricks on small stools, squirted water at the crowd and lifted young children from the crowd on to their backs and carried them around the ring. The equestrienne acts were also well trained, though he suspected that Mme Gabrielle was not all she should be, her lithe body as slim as a youth's and her long fair curls a little too perfect.

He wandered among the other shows, watched the moving waxworks, declined the offer of pleasure from a young and coarse female, and stood and watched two fighters in a boxing booth as they slugged away at each other. One, a raw country youth by his manner of dress, stood no chance at all of winning the contest as the 'Champion' hammered away at him. Richard glanced idly around at the crowd as others were exhorted to come up and chance their luck, knock out the Champ and win a shilling. They were a crowd of mostly men, but also some women, the worse for drink, who egged on the men to go and fight. Up on the stage the proprietor was bending over, talking earnestly to a man in the crowd. They finished their discussion, slapped hands and the man in the crowd turned away, revealing himself as the fairman who had spoken to him earlier in the day.

I wonder why he's not minding his own booth? Or perhaps it isn't his, although he spoke authoritatively to the girl, Richard mused, and he turned and made his way across to Dock Green, where Johnson's Circus was situated. There was a queue of people waiting to go in and he joined them and noticed that the programme had been changed for the second performance. Now it was advertising 'The Call of the West: See the Shoshone Squaw, Sacajawea, rescue her Lover from the Chinooks'.

There were no seats in this circus, but he paid extra to stand at the front and although it wasn't as professionally expert as Ogden's, he laughed at the dwarfs and clapped at the clown's antics as he tumbled and somersaulted, and then folded his arms to await the pleasure of the Wild Indians when they performed their daring feats on horseback.

Two Indians, with ochre-tinted stripes upon their faces and feathers in their hair, rode in first, giving wild cries and whoops. Then they gathered up a fair-haired woman from the edge of the crowd and tied her to a stake in the middle of the ring and proceeded to ride around her, all the time giving blood-curdling cries. An English redcoat then gave chase and sent them off with much cracking of rifle shot, and rescued the woman, who ran off; then he in turn was captured by the same Indians and tied to the stake whilst they did a war dance around him. Then to loud hollering and whooping a young Indian squaw rode into the ring, holding a rifle high in the air which she fired loudly. The Indians mounted their horses and chased her round and round the ring, while she eluded them with great dexterity. Finally she pointed her rifle at them, a great hail of shot rang out and the Indians fell dead, heads and bodies slumped down over their mounts, which cantered out of the ring.

Richard clapped enthusiastically as the squaw leapt down from her moving horse, undid the ropes holding the soldier and then sprang back on again as it cantered back. She rode round the ring once more, then held out her hand to the soldier, who vaulted up behind her.

They rode out of the ring, both with one arm held high in acknowledgement of the crowd's approval. In all the performance had lasted about fifteen minutes and there were several more performances to be given that night. Richard hung around the booth, wondering whether to see the next one, for the hoarding was being changed back to 'See the Real Wild Indians'. He wasn't keen to see the show as much as the girl who was in it, for so easy was she on horseback that she seemed to be part of her steed, moving in unison with the horse's limbs. She rides like a man, he thought, not like a woman at all; they have a different seat altogether. I wonder where she learned to ride like that?

He walked round to the back of the booth and saw some of the performers there, taking the air, for it had been stuffy inside. The dwarfs were chatting to the clown and presently the girl came out, wiping her brow with a towel. He went up to her. 'I beg your pardon for intruding,' he said, 'but I wanted to congratulate you on your riding skills.

It's most unusual for a young woman to be so adept.'

She turned to him, her skin too had been tinted with ochre and her dark hair was plaited with a leather band around her forehead. 'Thank you,' she said. 'I've had a good teacher.'

The clown came towards her, his grin looking menacing in the darkness. 'It's all right, Jonty.' Richard heard the smile in her voice. 'The gentleman isn't bothering me. He's only talking about my riding.'

The clown hesitated and came no further, but neither did he go back to join the others.

'I'm sorry,' Richard apologized. 'You perhaps get bothered by admirers?'

'Admirers?' She laughed. 'I get bothered by men wanting to take me to the dancing and drinking booths. They think that the women of the fair are loose and immoral, but the opposite is true.'

He was slightly shocked by her openness, yet admired her honesty, and, he thought, she is telling me in no uncertain manner not to bother her in that direction.

He nodded, excused himself and walked away; the clown was watching him and he felt uncomfortable under his gaze. He went again to watch the boxing whilst he waited for Johnson's next performance to begin, and it was while he was watching yet another country youth being battered by the Champion that something started to disturb his subconscious. What was it she had said? Something to the clown? But what? And why was he so protective towards her? Perhaps he was her brother, he mused. Nothing more, for although I couldn't see his face he only had the size and figure of a boy.

Jonty! That was what she had called him. The same name that Mrs Harmsworth had mentioned. That's what it was! Unusual name – but a coincidence perhaps?

23

'What do you mean you're leaving?' They were just about to start the last performance of the night and Mr Johnson glared at Amos as they stood in the empty booth. 'I've onny just taken you back on.'

'Aye, well, I've decided I'd rather start up on my own again.' Amos was truculent though a little shamefaced. His brother Harry stood listening, a frown on his forehead.

'You might have waited till we'd finished wi' this gaff,' their father said. 'You're leaving us short-handed.'

'We'll manage,' Harry said. 'Good riddance.' His words, though muttered and indistinct, were understood quite clearly by his brother.

'I'll see you outside.' Amos pointed a finger. 'I'm sick of your snide comments. You're not man enough to start up on your own.'

'There's no need for him to start on his own,' his father shouted. 'There's a good fit-up here, enough living for all of us if everybody pulls their weight.'

'Maybe,' Amos muttered, 'but I'm off. I've done a deal and that's that.'

'Who've you done a deal with?' His father's eyes narrowed. 'You'll not take any of my acts or else you'll know about it.'

'No, I won't. I'm going into 'fight game. Sharp is short of money and I'm going in with him.'

Although his father looked relieved, Harry gave a snorting laugh. 'What 'you know about fighting? He that turns and runs away—!'

Amos took a step forward, 'I've told you I'll deal wi' you outside.'

'Not now you won't,' their father roared. 'We've a show to put on. You can do your fighting later.'

But it was too late. The brothers' tempers had got the better of them and they both rushed through the flap, pushing their way through the crowd of people waiting outside and unbuttoning their coats as they went.

Jonty had appeared through the back flap of the booth and had heard something of what was going on. 'Take money?' he questioned, for Harry usually gave out the tickets at the door.

'Aye, all right, lad. Somebody's got to.' Mr Johnson handed him a tin box. 'Make sure you get 'right money,' and he went outside, climbed up on to the platform and ignoring his two sons rolling around on the muddy ground below him, he proceeded to exhort the passing crowd, 'Come and see the best circus in town. See the Wild Indians. Best show at the fair.'

Richard stepped over the two men as he queued for his ticket, as did the short stout man behind him, who remarked, "Johnson brothers! They've been fighting each other since they were little *chavvies*. Just watch, one of 'em will get up in a minute and back off.'

Richard watched and sure enough, one of them did. 'Don't think I'll forget this, Harry Johnson,' Amos shouted, ''Cos I won't.' He wiped his bleeding nose on his sleeve and backed away.

'There you are, folks,' Mr Johnson called from the platform. 'A free show of bare-knuckle fighting at no extra charge. Now, come along! Come along, the circus is about to start. Just a few places left. See the Shoshone Squaw, see the Wild Indians. See Jonty, the famous clown.' He turned and winked at Jonty. 'Internationally renowned! Roll up. Roll up!'

'That's who I want to see.' The man behind Richard nodded towards the Indian squaw who had appeared beside Johnson. 'They say she's the best equestrienne at 'fair.'

'I can believe it,' Richard agreed. 'I've seen her. I've never seen a woman ride as she does.'

'That's 'cos she takes after her *dado* – her father – or so they say.'

Richard paid the clown for his ticket and stepped inside. 'Oh? Does he ride in the circus?'

The man shook his head. 'He died some years ago. Ogden's my name, you'll have seen my fit-up. Best circus in town, ha – you might smile. I know, that's what they all say! But ask anybody; mine might not be as big as Wombwell's or Richardson's, but it's quality that counts, and I've got the best acts that money can buy and I'm always on the lookout for new talent – and from what I hear she's good.'

The drums started to roll and the dwarfs dashed

into the ring, tumbling and falling and throwing rubber balls into the crowd.

'Funny thing is', Ogden continued, watching dispassionately, 'you don't usually find Gypsies working in fit-ups like this, goes against 'grain with 'em. But I suppose as she's neither Gypsy nor gentile she doesn't belong to one or the other.'

Richard stared. 'I don't understand! What – what are you saying? That she's—?'

'They say her ma was a lady, those who remember her, 'cos word gets around even though we don't have much to do wi' Gypsies. But her *dado* was pure Romany and well known for his skill wi' hosses. Paul Lee was his name.'

Richard couldn't take his eyes from her as she went through the same routine as before. Can it really be her? It must be. But why is she here and not with her Romany family? Or perhaps they didn't want her?

So many questions buzzed through his brain that his senses reeled, yet he was sufficiently aware as he watched her that she was slipping in various other equestrienne skills, even though continuing with the same act. As she cantered around the ring she sprang from a sitting position and crouched with both feet on the horse's back and then rose to stand, holding the reins with one hand. She vaulted from one side of the horse across to the other several times in succession, barely touching the horse with her hand and with a smile acknowledged the cheers of the audience.

'I'm going to have her!' Ogden said as they filed out. 'She'll not want to stay with Johnson after I talk to her. She can tour the country wi' me, not just stay in the north with Johnson.'

Richard wanted to detain him, to ask him more about the girl. 'I think I've seen your circus at St Bartholomew's, haven't I? I remember it from when I was a child.'

'That's it,' said Ogden. 'It was my father's before it was mine. He started with just a stall, then he got a booth and then another and now – well, as I said, we've got best 'fit-up anywhere. Well, sir, I must be off. It's been nice having a chat. Not often I get 'chance to talk to a gentleman like yourself, and I hope we'll meet again. Just watch yourself now. Keep your hand on your money 'cos there's some villains about.'

He touched his hat and left and Richard smiled to himself. So much for wearing old clothes! He again wandered around the back of the booth, but it was dark, there was no lamp glowing and although he could hear voices within the booth and figures cast their shadows against the canvas, he decided that he would probably appear to be a disreputable character if he hung around waiting for the girl.

However, he stood back for a few moments where he couldn't be seen and presently he saw her come out with the clown and two of the women dwarfs, then they were joined by a man with a monkey on his shoulder. He watched them and followed a little as they made their way through the waggons and booths to the back of the green, where there were some tents pitched, though not those of the Gypsies.

'Who wants a sup of tea?' a woman's voice called

and a man answered that he did. 'Not me, Amy,' another voice answered and he was sure it was the girl. 'I'm going to bed. Good night. Good night, Morgan. Good night, Jonty.'

So where was she going? Did she live alone or was she going to the Gypsies? He followed the sound of her voice but then he lost it; he could see three tents pegged close together and outside one someone was rekindling a fire and placing a kettle over it. He heard the murmur of voices and he turned away. He didn't want to intrude. Then came the sound of someone singing in a loud drunken voice. 'Polly Anna,' he was calling. 'Come to me, my lovely, my Gypsy princess – I ado-re you!'

The other voices were stilled as if listening and the voice sang on and came nearer and presently the swaying figure of a man came into view, lit up by a lamp he was holding.

'Clear off, Amos. We don't want trouble again.' The man with the monkey rose up from beside the fire and another smaller figure also approached.

'I'm not making trouble, Morgan,' Amos Johnson hiccuped. 'I onny want to see Polly Anna. Pretty Polly,' he caterwauled, 'come on out!'

'You'll get her into trouble. You know what your father said last time.'

'My father! My father has nowt, nothing to do wi' me any more. I'm a free man.' He swayed unsteadily. 'I'm my own boss. Got my own fit-up. Got a fighting booth. Come on,' he turned in a circle, his fists raised. 'I'll tek you all on.' He turned again too swiftly and promptly fell over. 'I onny want to see Polly Anna,' he mumbled, his face in the mud. 'I want her to come wi' me to my fit-up. I don't mind that she's a Gypsy lass. All the better.'

Morgan hauled him to his feet. 'Say another word and I'll break your nose.'

'No. No. Don't!' Amos put his hand protectively over his face. 'Just tell her I want to see her.'

Morgan was struggling to keep Amos on his feet and the other figure, who, Richard saw as he stood watching from the shadows, was a slightly built youth with a limp, came forward to help. 'Help me get him back to 'booth, Jonty. It'll take two of us.'

'He's finished wi' circus,' Jonty mumbled. 'He's joined Sharp.'

Richard stepped forward. 'You appear to be having difficulties. Can I be of assistance? I erm, I lost my bearings,' he said, explaining his reason for being there. 'I thought there was a way out here.'

'No sir, there isn't. Well, not one that you'd know of. But if you're going back through 'fair, perhaps you can take this fellow's other arm. Jonty, you stay with 'women folk. I won't be long.'

'I saw him fighting with his brother earlier,' Richard remarked as they hauled the insensible Amos back through the fairground. 'They were hurling abuse at each other as well as their fists.'

'Just family squabbles I expect, sir. It happens in 'best of families.'

'Indeed it does. That is a fact.' He hesitated. 'None of my business, I know, but I couldn't help overhearing this fellow babbling – the er, young lady who appears to have excited his passion, would it be the equestrienne – the Shoshone Squaw as she is called?'

Morgan let go of Johnson's arm and his head swayed over his feet. Richard struggled to hold him

255

and then let him drop as Morgan faced him. 'Why do you ask, sir? Why would you be wanting to know?'

'I mean her no harm, I assure you. It's just that – well, she is such an excellent rider, that I am intrigued to know where she learnt the art. I overheard someone discussing her earlier. Ogden,' he mentioned the name to give credence to the discussion, 'he was most impressed.'

'Was he now?' Morgan hauled Amos to his feet again and Richard took his other arm. 'Well, well!' Morgan's monkey shuffled from one shoulder to another and reached out to scratch Richard's head. 'Stop that, you monkey! Aye, that's who Amos meant, he's allus hanging around her. Well, to answer your question, sir, Polly Anna learnt all her tricks from me. Onny – onny, she had 'gift already, it was in her blood I reckon, handed down from her *dado* – and from her ma to some extent. She was a right bonny horsewoman too.'

'Were they in the circus?' He wanted confirmation, though he knew with a rising excitement that he had it already.

'Why no, sir. Certainly not! Her ma was a lady. Her father a Romany.'

24

'Mrs Harmsworth!' He could barely contain himself until the maid had left the room. 'I've found her. I'm sure that it is her!'

'Found her? Whom?' Mrs Harmsworth had been in bed the previous evening when he had returned from the fair and he had spent a sleepless night tossing, turning and reappraising the situation and events. She put down her coffee cup. 'You can't mean – not – Madeleine?'

'Oh!' He raised his hand in denial. 'No. I'm sorry! I fear there is bad news there.'

Her face paled and he was stricken that he had blundered on in such a way instead of breaking the news more gently. He had forgotten that, although Mrs Harmsworth wasn't directly involved, she would naturally be upset to hear of her niece's death.

'I – I'm afraid that I have heard, indirectly, that Madeleine died some years ago and her husband also; although I do not know the circumstances.' He watched her carefully as she absorbed this news. He must remember to be more circumspect when telling Mrs Winthrop and Rowena. 'But, I think I have found their daughter. In fact I am sure of it.'

'A daughter?' she said slowly. 'And how can you be so sure?'

He explained the meeting with Ogden and then the man Morgan, and then as an afterthought told her about meeting the Gypsies at Appleby Fair. 'There can surely not have been more than one marriage between a lady and a Gypsy at that time. Everything fits so perfectly.'

'I wonder,' she said. 'It seems very strange that Charles never found any trace in all those years he was looking. Why was he not told of them?' She looked dubiously at him. 'Are you sure that you have not been set up by a pretty girl and her friends?'

'But, Mrs Harmsworth! They didn't know who I was. They still don't know. The girl doesn't know that I have been enquiring. And I have had only the briefest of conversations with her.'

'Nevertheless!' She shook an admonishing finger. 'They will all be in league with one another. The Gypsies are a very close-knit race, they will know that enquiries were being made. Yes,' she poured another cup of coffee and handed it to him, 'they have set you up, my dear, being a handsome, susceptible young man, which they wouldn't have done with your Uncle Charles! They've found a pretty girl and are out to make some money.'

He shook his head. 'But she's not with the Gypsies! She's with the fair people and they stay quite separate – or so I'm told,' he added, beginning to doubt just a little. 'She's an equestrienne in the circus. They said she takes after her father – and her mother.'

Mrs Harmsworth's eyes flickered slightly in interest. 'Really? Madeleine was an excellent horse-woman I have to say, even though I never did approve of such an unladylike way of getting about. But don't be too disappointed, my dear boy. Try to forget it. It's just a trick of their trade. That is what the Gypsies do, I fear. They are not well known for their honesty! They swindle and cheat unsuspecting people without them even knowing it.'

Why would they do that, he wondered, when Polly Anna didn't live among them? Perhaps he ought to seek out the Gypsy girl again, she seemed to hold the key. 'And then there's the clown,' he murmured, 'I think he might be Jonty.'

'Jonty! What do you mean?'

'There's a clown in the circus called Jonty and he might be the one you once knew. He's fairly small and if it is the same person I have seen without his costume and make up, he's lame and rather bent. And he's a friend of Polly Anna's.'

Mrs Harmsworth sat forward. 'Polly Anna? Jonty? Am I hearing you correctly?'

He nodded. 'He seems to take care of her. He's very protective towards her. I thought at first he might be her brother, but now I think perhaps not, he is fair haired and she is as dark as a – as a Gypsy!'

She was silent for a moment. Then absent-mindedly she rang the handbell for the maid to clear away and Richard realized that he had not had any breakfast. 'There is more to this than meets the eye,' she said with much determination. 'If this is the Jonty that I knew, then we shall find out from him, and', she shook her finger again, 'he did have a young friend in the workhouse who ran away at the same time. I was told of it by another lad in the workhouse. He said her name was Polly Anna.'

It took him quite some time to persuade her that she shouldn't go with him when he returned to the fair. 'I am "incognito",' he smiled, 'simply a visitor to the fair. They would surely be suspicious, ma'am, if they should meet you.'

'That is true,' she acknowledged. 'And if it is indeed the Jonty that I once knew, he may be afraid of getting into trouble. Not that he would. He did a great service to the people of this town, and I shall tell him so if ever I meet him again.'

He returned to the fair in the late afternoon. Lamps and braziers were being lit, which did a little to lighten the dull and dismal day, and Richard pulled up the collar of his borrowed coat against the drizzling rain. He passed the boxing booth and saw that Johnson now had his name up on the hoarding in addition to Sharp. On the waggon in front of the booth, two bare-chested men were dodging and weaving, feinting and shadow-boxing as Johnson called out, 'Come on now, fight the Champ. Three rounds only and win a shilling.'

'You sir,' he signalled to Richard, 'come and try your skill.'

Richard shook his head. He surely can't remember me from last night? He was blind drunk! He turned away and across the crowd he saw Polly Anna and Jonty strolling along and laughing together.

He went across to them. 'Hello!'

Jonty scrutinized him warily, but Polly Anna smiled. 'Hello,' she said. 'Thank you for your help last night. I heard the commotion and Jonty told me that you helped Morgan with Amos Johnson.'

'Why were you there?' The question from Jonty was direct, with no preamble.

'I'd lost my way,' he hedged. 'I thought I could get out that way,' and he knew that Jonty didn't believe him. 'No, that isn't the reason.'

'Ah.' The youth's face cleared. 'Told you,' he said to Polly Anna.

'So why were you there?' She too looked curiously at him. 'Were you looking for me?'

'Y–es, but not for the reasons which you might imagine.' Though that would be a consideration, he mused, she is quite lovely when seen without the paint on her face. He glanced at Jonty, who was scowling at him again. 'I wanted to talk to both of you.'

'You're not from another circus?' She put her head on one side and scrutinized him. 'You don't talk like a fairman.'

He laughed. 'No. I'm a farmer, though once I lived in a town.' Well, almost a farmer, he judged, though Uncle Charles with his vast estates wouldn't care to be described so.

'What 'you want to say?' Jonty was still obviously suspicious.

'Well.' He put his hand in his pocket and drew out the playing card and showed it to Jonty, 'several things. And this for a start.'

Jonty took it from him. 'Samuel!' he whispered. 'Where did you get this?'

'It will take some time to tell. Can we go somewhere to talk.' The rain was coming down even more heavily, but even so the crowd was increasing.

'We haven't got long,' Polly Anna said. 'Fifteen minutes at the most. We mustn't be late for the show. But come with us. We'll use my bender.'

'No,' Jonty said firmly. 'Use mine.'

He followed them to Jonty's tent and they went inside. It was sparsely furnished with a straw mattress, a wooden box, and a kettle and a pan stacked in one corner. Jonty lit a lamp, put a blanket over the mattress and invited Richard to sit down. He and Polly Anna sat on the box opposite.

'I'm not sure where to begin,' he said, 'but I will explain about the playing card first. I'm staying in Hull with a friend of my family; you might say that she is a relation of sorts. Mrs Harmsworth is her name.'

Jonty let out a gasp. 'Mrs Harmsworth!'

'Yes,' Richard beamed. 'So you are the person of whom she spoke? You once lived in the work-house?'

Jonty shuffled uncomfortably. 'Yes.'

'She speaks very highly of you.' Richard allayed his obvious apprehension. 'She says that the people of Hull have much to thank you for.'

'What of Samuel?' Jonty insisted. 'Never mind me.'

'I know little, except that he died,' Richard said quietly and saw Polly Anna put her hand into Jonty's and squeeze it. 'But not in the workhouse. Mrs Harmsworth will tell you herself that he was in comfort at the end.'

Jonty managed a smile though Richard could see that he was close to tears. 'She will tell you herself,' he repeated, 'if you would like to visit her.'

262

Jonty looked questioningly at Polly Anna, who nodded. 'Yes. You must go, Jonty. Then your mind will be at rest. Samuel was like a father to Jonty,' she added. 'And to me too. We have much to thank him for.' She toyed with a chain around her neck. 'Poor Samuel.'

'You were in the workhouse too?' Richard asked. 'For how long?'

'For ten years. From being nearly four years old until I was fourteen, when we escaped.'

'Escaped?'

'We ran away, didn't we, Jonty?' she smiled. 'To freedom – and I to my roots.'

'To your roots?' Now he was to hear it from her own lips. 'So you were from the fair?'

'No.' She was quite emphatic. 'I was not. I work in the circus to earn my living. I'm good with horses, just as my papa was.'

'Your papa?'

She put her head up proudly. 'My *dado*. He was a *Romano rye*.'

'A *Romano rye*? What is that?' he questioned.

'A Gypsy gentleman. That's what everyone says, for I barely remember him.'

'And your mother?' He lowered his voice, for he could tell that she was becoming quite emotional. 'Was she a Romany too?'

'Polly Anna. We must go.' Jonty rose to his feet. 'We have to change. Get ready. I have to give out tickets. We mustn't be late.'

'What's your name?' Polly Anna got up from her seat and faced him. She fingered the chain on her neck again and he saw that a locket was attached to it. 'And why do you ask so many questions?'

'Richard Crossley, and I'm sorry if I appear so curious, but there is a reason. Excuse me,' he reached out to touch her locket. 'But that is very pretty. Silver, I think?'

'It was my mama's. She left it in Jonty's care.'

'With Jonty? But – you were saying – was your mother not a Romany too?'

'No.' She gave a half smile and her eyes were full of tears. 'I don't ever want to forget her,' her voice trembled, 'but her memory is fading so fast.'

'Enough!' Jonty took her arm. 'She is upset. Enough!'

'I'm sorry!' Richard was contrite. 'Could I come back later?'

'No!' Jonty's word was plain.

'Yes!' Polly Anna argued. 'You must arrange to meet Mrs Harmsworth.'

'I'm going! I'll be late. Close the flap, Polly Anna.' He slipped out and they heard his lopsided run as he slopped in the mud and chased away to the booth.

'He looks after me,' she said, as she fastened up the toggle on the tent flap. 'He's my best friend in the whole world.'

'Yes. I can see that. He's very fond of you.'

'He loves me,' she said simply. 'And I love him. We've been together since we were children.'

'Ah! Like brother and sister?'

'Yes. Of course! Goodbye, Mr Crossley. I must go.'

'Oh, but! Can I come back – please?'

'All right, but you mustn't mind Jonty. He sometimes gets cross with people if he thinks they are bothering me. Men, I mean,' she said significantly.

'I understand.' He gazed at her. 'I quite understand. If I had a sister like you, I would do the same.'

'Would you?' She stood perfectly still and gazed back at him; he caught his breath and felt his blood pound. 'Would you really?'

He nodded and swallowed. 'Yes. Indeed I would.'

The rain was ever increasing, but she didn't seem to mind. Her hair started to corkscrew into curls around her forehead and droplets of rain ran down her neck. He started to take off his jacket. 'Here,' he said. 'You're going to be soaked. Put this on.'

'No.' She laughed. 'I don't mind the rain. I'm used to it. I belong to nature – to the rain and the wind, to the sun and the earth. I'm half Gypsy, born to it!'

'But what about the other half?' He lightly touched the locket on her neck and saw this time with certainty the scrolled initials M W. 'Your mama. What was she?'

'My mama?' she said with a sad smile. 'I don't really know. But she was a lady. So they say.'

25

'Kisaiya! Kisaiya! Can I talk to you?' Polly Anna called on the Gypsy girl the next day. 'Something has happened.'

Kisaiya got up from where she was crouched by the fire and glanced at her husband, who was lounging by the tent door. 'Don't be long,' he said.

Orlenda came out from behind him and muttered something to her son.

'Your husband doesn't like me, does he?' Polly Anna asked as they walked away.

Kisaiya gave an expressive shrug. 'Jack takes after his *mam*. They don't like *Gorgios*.'

'But I'm half Romany! Doesn't that make a difference?'

'Not to them.' She looked at Polly Anna and smiled. 'And when I come with you they calls me *pauno-mui*.'

'*Pauno-mui*? What's that?'

Kisaiya linked arms with Polly Anna. 'Pale face! A silly girl who likes to be with the fair gentiles instead of the dark Romanies.'

'Oh, but that's wrong!' Polly Anna protested.

'We spend little time together, and besides, I'm not fair, I'm as dark as you.'

'Your skin is fairer than mine. But they knows that I would spend more time with you, *Sister*, if I could.'

Polly Anna squeezed her arm. 'I'm so glad that I met you, Kisaiya. Now I have a family, Jonty as my brother and you as my *Sister*.'

Kisaiya nodded. 'Come. We'll go and see my *mam*. She'll know what to do. You can talk to her.'

Polly Anna stared. 'Know what to do? About what? I haven't said what I want to talk about yet.'

Kisaiya smiled. 'So you haven't.'

She led the way to the tent, where Shuri and Narilla were sitting in the open doorway. Shuri was making lace and Narilla was stitching a length of white cotton. '*Mam*. Polly Anna wants to talk to us.'

'Come in, *chavi*. Sit down and let's hear. Narilla put the kettle on the fire.'

'What are you making, Shuri? Is it a shawl?'

'It's a wedding shawl for my Narilla. Soon she'll be married to her *pireno*!'

Narilla blushed and busied herself about the fire. 'Aye,' said Shuri. 'My second daughter gone, then only my sons left.'

'I didn't know you were going to be married, Narilla. Will it be soon?'

'When the *mushipen* gets around to asking her,' Shuri interrupted with a laugh. 'I must tell his *mam* to make him hurry up.'

'Oh. Is that what happens?' Polly Anna said in surprise. 'Is it arranged?'

'No,' Shuri said. 'But when they start making moon eyes at each other, we keeps them apart until they make up their minds. Then his *dado* comes to talk to Narilla's *dado*.' She glanced across at Kisaiya. 'Then when they are wed, the woman goes to live with her *rom* and his family. It's the way it's done, isn't that so, Kisaiya?'

'That's the way it is,' Kisaiya muttered.

'Why don't you live in your own bender with Jack and Floure?' Polly Anna asked. 'Wouldn't you prefer it? It must be a bit cramped with you all together.'

'It's the way it's done,' Kisaiya repeated in a flat tone. 'I can't change it.'

'So, Paulina,' Shuri gave her her proper name as she always did, 'what is it you wants to talk about? Something troubles you.'

'It's a man,' she said. 'He came to see Jonty and me. He said that he had something to tell Jonty, which he did, only – only,' she became thoughtful, 'I don't think that was the real reason. He kept asking me questions in a casual way, but he seemed as if he wanted to know more than usual.'

'What sort of questions did this man ask?' Shuri asked as she plied the cotton between her fingers. 'Was it personal like?'

'About who my parents were, and was my mother a Romany as well as my father.' She caught a glance exchanged between Shuri and Kisaiya. 'And where did I learn to ride a horse. Things like that. Not the sort of questions that men usually ask me.' She laughed. 'Usually they ask me if I'll meet them behind the booth after the show!'

Shuri tut-tutted. 'That's why our young *chavvies* are kept apart. They're not allowed to behave like the *Gorgios*!'

'Shuri!' Polly Anna changed the subject. 'Why do you think that Orlenda and Jack don't like me? Is it because I am half *Gorgie*?'

Shuri kept her eyes on the lace in her hand. 'Jack listens to what his *mam* says. But he'll change. I tells Kisaiya that he will, if she's patient.' She looked up and her face was kind. 'Orlenda doesn't dislike you, Paulina. She doesn't like anyone very much. She's a *tippoty* woman, always has been. But it's nothing to do with you. It's to do with your *dado*.'

'My *dado*? I don't understand.'

'Well now, listen to what I tells you. When we were all young, Orlenda was very sweet on your *dado*. I knows it, James knows it, everybody knows it – all but Paul, your *dado*, knows it. And when he came to find out, he laughed. He said he wasn't going to marry Orlenda. He didn't love her and never would. He didn't love any of the *Romani chi*, he said. And so out of spite, she married Riley Boswell, poor *mush*.

'And your *dado* never did choose a *Romani chi*, even though all the women did some matchmaking with their pretty daughters. But Orlenda still hankered after him, following him about in spite of all her little *chavvies* and a good *rom*.' She gestured angrily. 'Any other man but Riley would have given her a hiding or cut off her hair. Anyhow, then Paul met your *mam* and never looked at anybody else.'

She put down her lace and gazed into space. 'She was very beautiful, so fair, so gentle; yet strong – she had to be strong to come and live among the Romanies for they didn't treat her easy. Not at first. Not until they realized that she was going to stop;

that she loved Paul enough to put up with all the trouble they caused her, and to follow the tradition of our ways as she was bid. So they came to accept her at last; all but Orlenda and she never did; never since she first set eyes on her at Appleby Fair.'

'Is that where they met?' Polly Anna was enthralled. 'My *dado* and mama?'

'Aye, that's the place. There's a lot goes on at Appleby Fair.' Shuri took up her lace again. 'More than you knows, *chavi.*'

They were silent for a while whilst Narilla gave out the tea. Shuri poured hers into a saucer and took a sip and said, 'So what else does this young gentleman ask of you, Paulina?'

'He wants us, Jonty and me, to go and meet someone that Jonty used to know – when we were in the workhouse,' she said vaguely, still thinking of her parents meeting at Appleby Fair. She wondered what her mother was doing at a Gypsy fair. Perhaps she lived at Appleby, she thought with a gathering excitement. 'Did she live there, Shuri? At Appleby?'

Shuri shook her head. 'No, she didn't. I don't know where she came from, but some of the men might, those who set her back on her way. Or perhaps the young gentleman knows. I think perhaps you could ask him.'

It wasn't until she was on the way back to her own bender that she realized what Shuri had said. How did she know that the young gentleman would know about her mother? And neither could she remember telling Shuri that he was a young gentleman. Or an old one for that matter.

When she arrived at her bender, Morgan was

standing outside it talking to another man. 'Here she is,' he said. 'Polly Anna, this is—'

'Ogden's my name, miss,' the man interrupted and touched his hat. 'You'll have seen my fit-up. Best circus in town, best in the country in my opinion. I've come to make you an offer. We tour the country, starting next week after Hull Fair closes. What do you say? Equestrienne and equilibrist. Star turn of the show!'

'What shall I do, Jonty? What shall I do? Oh, I can't go. How can I leave you? Or Amy and Morgan, and Kisaiya. I can't go.'

Jonty said nothing, he just walked with his head down as they made their way across the town towards Mrs Harmsworth's house in Albion Street; he had refused Richard Crossley's offer to take them, saying curtly that he could remember the way.

'Jonty! Speak to me! Say something.'

'Goodbye.'

'Jonty! I didn't tell him that I would go!'

'But you will.' He stopped and looked at her. 'And you should. But don't expect me to be happy about it.' He started to walk on again. 'I'll miss you, that's all.'

'And I would miss you, if I went. But – but, you wouldn't go without me, would you, Jonty, if the offer had been made to you?'

'No,' he said simply. 'I wouldn't. Couldn't. We're here.'

'What? Oh, is this it?' She looked up at the row of tall, elegant houses with their clean, scrubbed steps leading up to the front door. 'Which one?'

It had been a long time since he had last come

to warn Mrs Harmsworth of the wrongdoing at the workhouse, and then he had had to find his way to the kitchen door. But this time Richard Crossley was standing at the front door waiting for them.

They both approached rather nervously – they had neither of them been through the front portals of such a grand house before. Although Polly Anna was somewhat surprised to see Richard Crossley looking so distinguished in his dark jacket, brocaded waistcoat and narrow trousers, whereas previously he had been dressed rather ordinarily in a wool jacket and breeches, she was appeased by his relaxed and welcoming manner as he led them into a warm room off the hall, where there was a fire burning in the grate and a bowl of flowers on a polished table, and several comfortable chairs on which he invited them to sit.

Jonty perched on the edge of one of the chairs, but Polly Anna stood for a moment or two, staring wide eyed at the pictures on the wall and the clock and the ornaments on the mantelpiece.

'Mrs Harmsworth will be down in a moment.' Richard sat down too as soon as Polly Anna did. 'You – er, didn't have any trouble finding the house then?' he ventured.

'Jonty wouldn't forget,' Polly Anna said. 'He's very clever and has a good memory.'

Jonty implored with his eyes for her to be quiet, but he remained silent. He only wanted to know about Samuel and then they could be gone.

'The fair will be finished in a day or two, I believe,' Richard said, 'er, Saturday, is it?'

'Yes,' Polly Anna answered brightly. 'Saturday.'

'And, erm, what do you do then?'

Her face fell and she glanced at Jonty. 'I'm not sure,' she said uneasily. 'We haven't made up our minds.'

The door opened and Mrs Harmsworth came in; she was wearing a brown printed silk gown with velvet trimmings and leaning on an ebony walking stick. Polly Anna was glad that she and Jonty had changed into clean clothes and brushed their hair before coming. They both rose to their feet a second before Richard did and Mrs Harmsworth smiled approvingly. 'Well, Jonty. It is very nice to see you again. I must confess that I never thought that I would. I imagined you lying dead somewhere, but I should have known better,' she added. 'You have the will to survive; you must have, having been brought up in that dreadful place.'

Jonty's cheeks burned and Mrs Harmsworth turned to Polly Anna. 'And this is the young woman who ran away with you! I'm not sure if I remember seeing you before.'

'I don't think you did, ma'am, though I saw you. And Jonty used to talk about you.' Polly Anna spoke up boldly.

'Did you, Jonty?' Mrs Harmsworth raised her eyebrows. 'I wonder what you said? Ah, no, don't be embarrassed. I don't expect you to tell me.' She sat down in a chair by the window. 'Would you like some tea?'

Jonty shook his head, but Polly Anna said yes, she would, and Richard pulled a bell rope on the wall which sent a tinkling sound down the hall. She smiled at him and thought it seemed a very strange thing for him to do and why wasn't Mrs Harmsworth getting up to make the tea?

When the door opened a few minutes later, she was surprised to see a girl in a black dress and white cap and apron appear bearing a tray with the tea things on it. And exactly the right number of tea cups too, at least there would be if Jonty was having some, but of course he wouldn't. He hated eating or drinking if anyone else was around.

'I remember once asking you if you would like some extra meat, Jonty,' Mrs Harmsworth said. 'And you refused it. Why did you do that?'

'Couldn't chew it,' he mumbled.

'Hah! And that is why Mrs Pincher chose to invite you to come in. What a clever woman she was.'

Jonty nodded in agreement and watched as the maid poured the tea into china cups. He wouldn't dare to drink out of one of those. He would certainly slurp and what if he dropped it?

Mrs Harmsworth talked of Samuel whilst they had their tea and Jonty was assured that his friend had been in caring hands during his final illness. 'He is buried in the churchyard, Jonty, not in a pauper's grave. I thought it fitting.' He thanked her for her kindness and although he felt sad, he was also relieved in some measure that Samuel was no longer locked away in the workhouse.

'So, we know that Jonty was born in the work-house, but how did you come to be there, Polly Anna?' Mrs Harmsworth tapped the tips of her fingers together and gazed at her. 'What circumstances brought you to that place? Can you remember?'

She shook her head. 'I can't remember much and what I do, I think, is what Jonty told me. He remembers Mama and me arriving in Old Boney's cart.'

'Old Boney! Ah, yes, unfortunate man.' Mrs Harmsworth pursed her lips together. 'Punished for the sins of others. But how did you come to be in his cart?'

'I don't know. He picked us up somewhere, I think. Mama was crying and coughing and lying on the ground.' Her brow furrowed as she tried to remember. 'I was crying too and he heard us and told us to be quick and jump in.'

'Come over here,' the old lady commanded. 'Let me take a good look at you.'

Somewhat surprised, Polly Anna got up and stood in front of her.

'Turn sideways, in profile,' she said and as she obeyed she pulled a wry face at Jonty, who was watching with a puzzled look on his face. 'Mmm,' said Mrs Harmsworth. 'I can't see a likeness.'

Richard, who had been sitting quietly listening, stood up. 'I think that perhaps Polly Anna has a likeness of her father, Mrs Harmsworth.'

'More than likely. What was your father's name, my dear?'

'Paul Lee,' she answered, 'and I was named after both my mother and father. Why are you asking me these questions, Mrs Harmsworth?'

'How can that be if you are called Polly Anna?' Mrs Harmsworth ignored her question.

'Paulina is my proper name,' she said, 'Paul and Leina joined together.'

'So – your mother was called Leina?' Mrs Harmsworth said slowly.

'I believe so. At least that is what the Romanies said my *dado* called her. Mrs Harmsworth,' she repeated, 'we have to go now, so can you tell me why you are asking these questions?' She glanced at Richard Crossley. 'You didn't bring us here just to tell Jonty about Samuel, did you? There's something else. Something about me?'

'Yes,' he said quietly. 'Come and sit down whilst I explain. We think – I think, at least', he came and stood next to her chair, 'that we might know who your mother was and where your family, your mother's family, is now.'

A flush came to her cheeks and she looked across at Jonty, who had an anxious expression on his face. 'How?' she asked. 'How do you know or think you know?'

'For many years a family by the name of Winthrop have been looking for a young lady who ran away and married a Gypsy. They could find no trace of her at all; but then I stumbled on some information, quite by chance.' He smiled at her and was heartened to see a bright hopefulness in her face. 'It would take too long to tell of it now, but, I think, no – I am almost sure, that the young lady was your mother.'

'Where are they,' she whispered, 'this family?'

'A good way from here. A day's ride into the country.' He glanced at Mrs Harmsworth, who was sitting with her hands folded and her face expressionless. 'Mrs Harmsworth, would you admire the locket that Polly Anna is wearing? A very pretty item, I think you would agree.' He indicated that Polly Anna should show it to her and she slipped it out from beneath the neck of her shirt and went across to show her.

'And the initials, M W, what do they represent do you think?' Mrs Harmsworth's voice, though stern, wavered a little. 'They are not your initials or those of your father or mother.'

'I don't know.' She was beginning to feel agitated. 'My mama asked Jonty to look after it until I was old enough to wear it.'

'And you kept it?' Mrs Harmsworth said incredulously. 'You never tried to sell it to buy food?'

Jonty stood up. 'It wasn't mine to sell!' He was quite indignant at the idea. 'It was for Polly Anna. The only thing her mama had left.' His words were strangled and indistinct but his meaning was clear.

'I'm sorry,' Mrs Harmsworth began,' I didn't mean – it's just that so many people were starving in that place.'

Jonty shook his head. 'Not us.'

'And besides,' Polly Anna interrupted, 'if Jonty had tried to sell it, which he wouldn't have, it would have been thought that he had stolen it!'

'Of course!' Mrs Harmsworth apologized. 'Forgive me.' She gave a sigh and then said, 'And is there a picture inside the locket?'

Polly Anna looked puzzled. 'A picture?'

'Yes. It does open, I assume?'

Polly Anna looked from one to another and then

down at the locket. 'I don't know. Does it open, Jonty? I didn't know that it did!'

Jonty shrugged. He didn't know either. It had never occurred to either of them, it was just a pretty silver object on a chain.

'May I?' Richard leant forward to help her unfasten the clasp. He lifted her dark hair from the nape of her neck and slipped the catch. She turned the locket over in her hand. 'I've never taken it off since Jonty gave it to me.' She looked up at him. 'How does it open?'

He took it from her. 'Well,' he gave a slight smile, 'I don't know much about these things, but there should be a thumbnail slit at the side. Yes! It's a little tight, but – there you are!' The locket opened into two halves. Jonty came across to look and Mrs Harmsworth sat forward with interest.

'Oh!' Tears ran down Polly Anna's cheeks as she looked down at the likeness of her mother. 'Mama! You were so close to me and I never knew. And papa too.' A pencil sketch of a dark-skinned, serious-faced man faced a water-colour of his smiling, golden-haired wife. 'You were together all the time.'

Jonty looked down and nodded. He couldn't speak as he saw the likeness of Polly Anna's mother who had all those years ago called him a dear child when everyone else only called him vile names.

Richard glanced at Mrs Harmsworth and gave an indiscernible nod. He had seen a portrait of Madeleine and he knew it was the same.

'My dear child,' Mrs Harmsworth rose to her feet, 'may I see?' She took the proffered locket from Polly Anna's trembling fingers. 'Don't cry. Dry your tears. This is not a day for weeping but for rejoicing,' but as she spoke the words trembled on her lips as she looked down at her lost niece. 'Here is your mother, my sister's daughter and my own dear niece, Madeleine, come back to us at last.'

Part Two

26

'So will you come to meet your grandmother and the rest of your family, Polly Anna? We can travel there on Sunday after the fair is over. You er – you'll want to stay with the circus until then, I suppose?'

Richard looked down at her, she was obviously shocked by the revelation and Mrs Harmsworth had rung for a little brandy and water as Polly Anna sat trembling in her chair.

'Yes. I don't know! Jonty, what shall I do? I'm so confused.'

Jonty too had sat down again and had his chin in his hand as he pondered. 'You must go.' His voice cracked and he cleared his throat. 'If they're waiting for you.'

'Oh, but no-one knows yet,' Richard interrupted. 'I am simply continuing the search as my Uncle Charles did. No-one will really expect me to come back with anyone. It was always considered a hopeless task, isn't that right, Mrs Harmsworth?'

'Indeed. I will admit that I too thought it so.'

Polly Anna gazed at her. 'Mrs Harmsworth,' she spoke in a low voice, 'if my grandmother is your sister, does that mean that we are related too?'

'Why yes!' She smiled at her as if she too had only just realized the connection. 'I am your Great-aunt Cecily.'

Polly Anna got up from her chair and went across to her. 'Then I am very pleased to meet you, Great-aunt Cecily.' She gave a slight bob of her knee and put out her hand.

Mrs Harmsworth took it and drew her towards her. 'Come here child and give me a kiss. You are the only great-niece that I have, I am delighted that you are found.'

Polly Anna leant forward and gave the old lady a kiss on her cheek and saw the brightness in her eyes which set her own tears streaming again. 'Would you give Jonty a kiss too, Great-aunt Cecily? You know that he's almost my brother?'

Jonty looked very embarrassed, but Mrs Harmsworth eased his confusion by saying, 'Come here, Richard, and show Jonty what young men do when they meet a related lady.'

Richard came across to her, he put his heels together and gave a slight formal bow and took her hand which he kissed lightly, then he leaned forward and gave her a peck on her cheek. He grinned at Jonty, who didn't smile back but stepped forward nervously and repeated the procedure, but hesitated over the kiss on the cheek.

'You don't have to kiss me if you don't want to,' she smiled. 'Not everyone does.'

'I would like to,' he whispered. 'It'll be 'first time.'

He leaned forward, but instead of proffering her cheek she kissed him instead, very gently.

'Well done, Jonty,' she said softly. 'You are a real gentleman. You have taken care of Polly Anna better than anyone else could have done.'

Jonty swallowed hard and turned around to face Polly Anna. 'We have to go. And you have to tell Johnson that you're leaving.'

Polly Anna put her hand to her mouth. What would Mr Johnson have to say about her joining Ogden's Circus? And how would she get back from her grandmother's house in time to join her new company? She would have to borrow a horse.

'Send for a chair, Richard. It will be quicker for them than walking all that way.' Mrs Harmsworth rose from her chair, her gown rustling around her feet. 'I will look forward to seeing you soon, Polly Anna, and you too, Jonty.' She looked at him anxiously, as if she sensed the turmoil inside him. 'Will you be all right? What will you do?'

'Going to Bradford. With Johnson's Circus.' He answered briefly. He didn't want to think about anything else; not losing Polly Anna and certainly not thinking of her travelling alone with Richard Crossley who, when he thought he was unobserved, kept gazing at Polly Anna as if he was entranced. No need to tell me what it means, he brooded. I know well enough.

As they passed into the hall, Polly Anna glanced at her reflection in an oval mirror. She stopped and looked beyond herself to the surroundings behind her. The flowers on a table, a large urn standing in a corner, the doors leading to other rooms and the staircase sweeping up to other floors. She also saw Richard Crossley looking at her and behind him, Jonty. She saw herself and she self-consciously ran her fingers through her hair to tidy her curls. I look very shabby in this grand place; even the maid waiting to open the door is neater than me.

'Is my grandmother's house like this one?' she asked as the door was opened for her and the sedan chair waited in the street below.

'Er, similar.' Richard hesitated. 'Though rather larger. A country house, not in a town.' This is a very modest establishment in comparison, he thought. Perhaps it is as well I brought her here first, she will be at least partly prepared. He helped her into the chair and Jonty climbed in after. 'I will come for you early on Sunday morning.' He could hardly suppress his exhilaration, but he put out his hand to Jonty, who took it reluctantly, and solemnly said, 'Goodbye, Jonty. I hope to see you again.'

Polly Anna sat back with a sigh as the sedan was lifted and moved along, but Jonty wasn't comfortable being transported by two men working as donkeys and he folded his arms and stared straight ahead.

'You're not cross with me, Jonty?' Polly Anna looked at him anxiously.

He grasped her hand in his. 'No! Glad for you. Sad for me.'

'But we'll meet, Jonty. Quite often.' But will we? she wondered, Ogden said he travelled all over the country and Johnson doesn't. 'And we'll always meet at Hull Fair,' she added consolingly. She lifted the curtain and looked out at the streets and the people as they passed them by. 'I feel like a lady,' she said.

He nodded. 'Soon will be.' He squeezed her

hand. 'Fine gowns and bonnets. How pretty you'll be.'

She turned to him. Her eyes were wide and enquiring and he thought his heart would break. 'What do you mean?'

'When you're at your grandmother's house.'

She pondered. 'Do you mean – do you mean that she might want me to stay?'

He laughed. 'Of course. Silly! Of course you'll stay.'

'You mean for a visit?' Will Mr Ogden let me catch him up later? she thought, as she mulled this over.

'Not for a visit. For ever.' He looked at the expression of incredulity on her face. 'Polly Anna! Don't you understand? This is your family. They've been searching for you! Of course they'll want you to stay.' And wouldn't anyone, he thought sadly, for she is so lovely, so innocent. They'll make her into a lady and then I've lost her for good. Then he laughed in spite of himself. 'You're not thinking of going with Ogden?'

'Well – yes. I was. I didn't think – but, she might not want me to stay, not when she meets me! Look at me, Jonty. I have nothing of my mother's appearance. I'm half Gypsy. I look like a Gypsy and not everybody likes them. They think that they're vagabonds and thieves.'

He nodded. 'I know. But she'll want you to stay, once she meets you.'

'I don't know if I am well enough to travel with you, Richard, the roads are so rough and boggy at this time of the year.' Mrs Harmsworth pondered. 'You can take one of the maids and send her back the next day.'

'Oh. I hadn't thought of you going, Mrs Harmsworth! There is really no need.' He had been looking forward to the ride across country with Polly Anna, pointing out various landmarks and so on. He certainly didn't relish the thought of travelling by carriage with Mrs Harmsworth or a silent maid. 'And besides, she is an excellent rider. Better even than I am!'

She stared at him as if he had taken leave of his senses. 'I know the child has been living a singular life, but that must change now. Hmph! Can you imagine what my sister would say if I allowed the pair of you to arrive without a companion? Bad enough when she and Rowena see that she has been living a life of a Gypsy, without them having to question her virtue!'

'Not a Gypsy, Mrs Harmsworth,' he emphasized. 'She's been with the fair.'

'It's the same thing as far as I am concerned; and her father was a Gypsy, so there you are,' she concluded and he knew that that was the end of the matter.

'Well, you can't travel alone with this gentleman, Paulina.' Shuri was quite firm when Polly Anna told her and James what had happened at Mrs Harmsworth's house. 'It won't be seemly and even though you are not all Romany, as part of your *dado*'s family it is our duty to protect you, at least until you reach your *Gorgie* people.'

Polly Anna was amazed. Morgan and Amy had

said the same thing and were trying to think of someone who could go with her. Yet she had lived in her own bender and had an independent life of a sort, even though within the family of the fair people.

'Tell Kisaiya,' James said to his wife. 'She can go with her. And I'll tell Riley.'

He went out of the bender and Shuri nodded. 'Now there'll be changes,' she said. 'And all for the good.'

'She is my cousin and sister in blood,' Kisaiya said firmly as she stood to face her husband. She had found him by the fire mending pans; old pans which the fair people had thrown out before they moved on to the next gaff and which he would mend and eventually sell back to them. 'I have to go with her – and I want you to come too.'

'She's a *Gorgie*,' he said patronizingly. 'We don't mix with them.'

'Her *dado* was a well-respected *Romano rye*,' she insisted. 'He would have been a leader of the Romanies if he hadn't married out.'

'But he did! And so that's the end of it!'

'No Jack, it isn't the end of it. I knows why you hate the *Gorgios* and it's not because they're a different race. It's because Orlenda says you must. And I'll tell you why she does.'

'Get inside, *mushi*! I'll not listen to you.'

His face flushed and she knew he was angry but still she continued, 'If you don't come with me, I shall travel alone with her and take Floure.'

'Would you bring shame on me?' He lifted his

arm as if to strike her, but his arm was caught by Riley, who had come up behind him and held it fast in a hard grip.

'Never let me see or hear that you strike your woman.' His face was like thunder as he glared at his son. 'God knows I've had reason enough to strike your mother but I never did.'

Jack stared at his father. 'Are you drunk? Why are you saying this?'

'I am not drunk! I'll tell you why. Your mother craved after Paul Lee even after we were wed. She followed him about like a harlot! Everybody said I should beat her and cut off her hair, but I never did. Maybe I should have and she might have come to her senses; as it was, her bitterness turned towards the *Gorgios* because Paul married one of their race. She's wrong.' He shook his fist. 'We must try to live in harmony, even though they are different from us.'

'I didn't know.' Jack was shaken. 'Did you know, Kisaiya?'

'Aye,' she said softly, 'I did.'

'But you never said!'

'If I had been the one to tell you it would have come between us.' She looked up at him and knew that her mother had been wise. Soon everything would come right, just as she had said.

'Go clear your things from our bender,' Riley ordered, 'and get canvas for another. Then get ready for your journey.'

The conglomeration of sounds from the fair, the roar of the animals and barking of dogs, the applause of the audience in the circuses and the laughter and shrieks of the crowd hid the sound of crockery being broken, of abuse being hurled as long-held grievances echoed from the Boswell bender and around the Romany camp. The Romanies hunched silently around their fires or hushed the children on their mattresses as they tried to listen to what was being said and nodded to each other that Orlenda's reckoning had come at last.

Jack threw the canvas over the frame of their new bender and Floure gathered sticks for Kisaiya to make a fire. Soon there was a warm glow and the kettle on the kettle-iron started to steam and rattle. Floure lay down on her mattress and slept and Kisaiya covered her with a blanket and then joined Jack outside. She made the tea and handed him a cup. She said nothing, waiting for him to speak, for he had been very quiet since his father's outburst.

'Would you have gone alone, Kisaiya?' he said. 'Would you have shamed me?'

She shook her head. 'I would have gone, but I wouldn't have shamed you. I would have asked my father or yours to go with me.'

He heaved a sigh. 'I had it in my head that you thought more of your *Gorgie* friend than your husband.'

As they were under cover of darkness she put her hand into his, there should be no show of affection in front of others, that wasn't the Romany way. 'No,' she whispered. 'Never.'

He got up and stamped out the fire which she had carefully lit. 'Kisaiya,' he said, 'this is our new home. Let's go inside.'

'I need a horse, Riley.' Polly Anna caught up with Riley the next day, the last day of the fair. He was

291

beyond the camp where the horses were tethered and cropping the grass on the wayside. 'I'm going to ride to see my new family. I might also need it to catch up with Ogden.' She was so unsure of what would happen that she had simply told Ogden that she might be delayed, and he said that she could catch up with them at Sheffield, where they would be for two weeks before going on to Newark.

Riley looked at her questioningly and said, 'You'll need a good 'un then. I've got the Pinto ready for you.'

'How—?' No use asking how he knew that she would want a horse, there were so many things that the Romanies seemed to know even without being asked. 'The Pinto? Which? Not the one I used to ride?'

'Aye, he's the one. I bought him at Appleby. He'll do for you well enough.' They walked across to where the horse was cropping.

'Oh, he will!' She was so delighted she put her arms around the horse's neck and hugged him.

'Don't spoil him,' he warned. 'He's a hoss not a *chavo*! But he'll ride well on the journey.'

'I'm not sure that I can afford him though, Riley,' she said reluctantly after the initial euphoria. 'I seem to remember that Brown paid Morgan well for him.'

'Aye, he did.' Riley's normally taciturn features wrinkled into a grin. 'But the deal is struck. Finished.'

'Struck? Who by? Who struck the deal?'

He hesitated for a moment, then, 'James Lee. He said you'd be wanting a hoss, so here he is.' He grinned again and put up his hand square towards

292

her. 'You can strike again if it makes you feel better.'

She put up her own hand and slapped against his. 'Thank you, *Brother*. You're a true *Romano rye*.'

'Is it far, Riley, to my grandmother's house?' They walked back to the camp together and some instinct told her that he would know of the journey.

'We went from Nottingham last time and that was a goodly way, but we went slow because your *mam* was ill and distressed. But it's not so far from here.'

'Did you take us all the way?' She wished that she could remember.

'Right up to the edge of her village. Night was coming on and she didn't want to go up to the house in darkness. We pitched the bender in a meadow and then left. That's what your *mam* wanted. She said she wanted to do the last bit on her own, just the two of you, and that her mother wouldn't want to see her with the Romanies. We understood that.'

'And you never saw her again?'

'Never.' He patted the top of her head. 'We thought you were living a *rawnie*'s life.'

'So the Romanies don't know everything, Riley?'

He shook his head and looked sad, she thought. 'It's as well that we don't. Otherwise there'd be no peace.'

She told Mr Johnson that she was leaving and he wasn't pleased. He even offered her more money to stay, but she said no, there were other things she wanted to do. Later in the day he came looking for her; he had heard that she was going to Ogden and he was very angry. 'You'll not stay long with him.

You'll find out he's a hard taskmaster, not like me who lets you do what you want!'

'I'm sorry, Mr Johnson, but I'm leaving.'

'What about Jonty? Is he going with you? He follows you everywhere!'

'No. Jonty's staying.'

'That's all right, then.' He seemed relieved. 'He's a good fellow. I know I can trust him and he gets on with Harry.'

'I'm tired of being an Indian, Mr Johnson. That's why I'm leaving. I want to be an equestrienne.'

He nodded. 'All right. No hard feelings!'

He came back to her later in the day. 'It's going all round 'fair that you've come into a fortune and are going off to claim it.' He frowned suspiciously. 'You said you were going to Ogden's!'

'A fortune!' she said in amazement. 'It's the first I've heard of it. Who said that?'

He shook his head. 'The dwarfs, I think. You know how they chatter.'

Around the Romany camp people were gathering and gossiping that Paul Lee's *chavi* was going to join her *Gorgie* family; that she had been lost and was found again. They came to her, smiling and wishing her luck and some of them giving her lucky charms and sprigs of heather.

At the last evening of the fair the crowds poured into the town and everyone did great business. The pea stalls sold out of peas, the smell of charred potatoes filled the air, the jugglers strolled up and down the streets throwing coloured balls and striped wooden clubs up into the air, enticing the people to come and see their show. The dancers on the platforms swirled their spangled skirts and tapped their toes, the showmen banged their drums and blew whistles and shouted, 'Come along ladies and gentlemen. The last night of the fair. Don't miss it, another year to wait. Roll up! Roll up!'

Polly Anna was filled with excitement, but she tried not to show it too much as she knew that Jonty was miserable. He had painted his mouth turned down and his eyes with soulful tears and as the show opened he sat in the middle of the ring with his head between his knees.

'O-oh,' said the audience in sympathy as he looked up at them and then hid his head beneath his arm. 'Don't be sad, Jonty,' a little girl shouted. Jonty looked up, then swiftly sat up and looked around. He put his hand to his forehead as if he was searching for the child, but then as if he couldn't find her, put his head down again on his chest.

'Jonty! I'm here!' The child waved from the front row. It was Dolly dressed in a frilly pink dress and holding a large coloured ball. 'Don't be sad! Come and play!' She climbed over the board into the ring and fell flat on her face. 'O-oh,' said the audience again and suddenly the ring was filled with tumbling, skipping dwarfs, all falling over each other to help Dolly up. Jonty jumped up to join them, turning somersaults, falling over the dwarfs and tipple-tailing over them as if he was made of rubber.

Polly Anna watched him from the side of the ring. How brave he was; he wouldn't show that he would miss her, even though she knew that he would. She gave him a loving smile as he and the dwarfs passed her and she mounted her horse and prepared for her last act as an Indian squaw.

The next morning the fair people were moving off as day was breaking, but Morgan, Amy and Jonty were waiting for Richard Crossley to come before they said goodbye to Polly Anna. Kisaiya and Floure and Jack were hovering at the edge of the group, not getting too close, but near enough to move off when the time came. Morgan went across to talk to them and Floure played with the monkey.

'Now don't worry about Jonty,' Amy said to Polly Anna. 'We'll all look after him, isn't that right, Dolly?'

Dolly nodded and looked down. 'Yes,' she whispered. 'We will.'

Polly Anna bent down and gave her a kiss on her cheek. 'Then I leave him in your care, Dolly. He's very special.'

'Yes,' said Dolly. 'I know.'

'Here's the gentleman coming, Polly Anna,' Morgan called. 'That's a fine hoss he's riding, one of Riley Boswell's if I'm not mistaken.'

Kisaiya smiled. 'You know your hosses, Morgan. The gentleman bought it at Appleby Fair.'

'Ah! I thought as much.' Morgan walked across to meet Richard Crossley. ''Morning, sir. It'll be a fine morning for a ride, once 'sun is up. Polly Anna is ready and waiting for you.'

Jonty was standing nearby, folding up the canvas from his bender and he stopped what he was doing and stood watching.

'We all decided, sir,' Morgan appeared to have taken up the position of spokesman, 'that is – Polly Anna's other families – me and Amy and the Romanies here, that she should have an escort.' He indicated to where Kisaiya and Jack were mounted,

Kisaiya with Floure in front of her on a Fell pony and Jack behind on a piebald. 'We don't wish to offend you, sir, but it wouldn't be right for her to travel alone with a stranger, gentleman or not.'

He may have been surprised at the grin on Richard's face as he heard this piece of information, but he nodded approvingly as he heard him say that she wouldn't have been travelling alone, but that arrangements had already been made for her to have a female travelling companion. 'Which of course I will now cancel, for I am sure Polly Anna would rather have someone she knows with her than a stranger.'

Polly Anna looked around at the crowd gathered to see her off. The dwarfs were there and the Thin Man, they always travelled together. The Fat Lady had gone for she couldn't walk as far as the others and had to have a ride in a waggon. She saw Mr Johnson and Harry in the distance and they waved to her, and she saw Amos standing with his arms folded watching the scene as his partner struggled to take down the boxing booth.

Then she saw Jonty, a picture of abject misery. She went to him and put her arms around him. 'Just say, Jonty, and I won't go,' she whispered. 'I'll stay.'

'What?' he said, in mock astonishment and held her away from him. 'Not go? This is a new start, Polly Anna. You with your new life and new family and I – I'm going to be 'greatest clown in the country! Didn't you hear? Johnson is going to expand and give me star billing. My name will be on the posters!'

This must have been the longest speech he had ever made and Polly Anna gave him another hug.

'I didn't know that! Oh, I'm so pleased.' She gave him an anxious glance. 'So – so you won't be too unhappy when I'm gone?'

'Unhappy? Me? I'll miss you Polly Anna, you know that, but there'll be so much to do. Mustn't worry.' He kissed her on her cheek and then tenderly on her lips. He took a deep breath. 'Off you go! Mr Crossley is waiting for you. He – he'll take care of you, I've no doubt.'

She nodded and bit her lips. 'Goodbye, Jonty. We'll meet again soon, I promise.' She mounted the Pinto and looked down at him. He gave her a big smile and waved and she was reassured. He had, after all, managed without her once before. He was the one who had looked after her.

'Goodbye, Amy. Goodbye, Morgan.' She stretched out her hand to them. 'This is not for good, you know. I shall see you again soon. Goodbye, Dolly, you won't forget, will you?

'Ready Kisaiya?' she called and the Romanies trotted towards her. 'We're ready, Mr Crossley.'

He nodded and smiled and she felt a surge of excitement in the pit of her stomach; a new life, Jonty said, a new family.

Richard heeled his horse and trotted to her. He saw Jonty watching and felt a wave of, not pity exactly, for he was glad for himself that Polly Anna was by his side, but more like compassion and understanding, for the fellow undoubtedly cared for her. 'Don't worry,' he called down, 'she is in good hands, I promise. No harm will come to her. You have my word.'

Jonty put his hand on the horse's mane. He gave a thin smile and said softly, 'If harm should come to her, then you must run for your life, sir.'

Richard looked into his eyes and there was an understanding between them. He nodded. 'We're off then, the sun is almost up.' He heeled his horse again and moved forward and Polly Anna did the same, the Pinto acknowledging her light command. The Romanies held back for a moment to let the others draw ahead, then they flicked their reins and moved off.

Polly Anna turned around as she got to the edge of Dock Green. The last time she had done that she had been with Morgan and Amy, and Jonty had chased after her; that too had been the start of a new life, but this time she saw him, a lonely figure standing apart from the others with his arm held high as he bid her goodbye.

27

'We'll take the Beverley road,' Richard explained
as they trotted across the town. 'The turnpike roads
are good and we shall make better progress for the
first part of the journey. Then we'll cross country
and you'll see the beauty of the Wolds at first hand.'
He could hardly contain his enthusiasm at the
thought of giving Polly Anna her first glimpse of
the countryside which he had come to love. 'But
first we must call and leave a message for Mrs
Harmsworth to say we have no need of her
carriage.'

The Romanies hung well behind them as they
rode through the town and Richard realized that
they were doing this deliberately so as not to give
the impression that they were travelling together.
Even so, as they approached Albion Street he heard
a commotion behind them and on turning around
he saw a clergyman haranguing them and telling
them not to follow the gentleman.

He rode back and assured him that they were
doing no harm and that they were indeed travelling

together. The cleric stared incredulously, then grunted and moved away.

'Travel on to the Beverley road,' Richard instructed Jack Boswell. 'We shall be ten minutes only delivering the message and will then catch up with you.'

Kisaiya looked dubious, her instructions had been to keep Polly Anna in her sight at all times, but Jack ruled that it would be all right. 'We can't wait outside the *rawnie*'s door and besides no harm can come in ten minutes,' he said. 'The *Gorgio* will take care of her, he's smitten by her, can't you see?'

'I knows it,' Kisaiya said seriously. 'Polly Anna doesn't.'

Richard wrote a short note to Mrs Harmsworth, explaining that Polly Anna had arranged for a friend and her husband to travel with her and would not therefore need the services of the maid or carriage. He didn't feel it necessary to say that the friend was a Gypsy, but added a postscript thanking her most kindly for her hospitality and assistance in bringing a remarkable episode to a close.

He mounted the grey and glanced at Polly Anna, who was waiting for him out in the street, the Pinto's bridle held by a small boy who had come running at his whistle, glad to earn a copper by keeping guard on the young lady. 'Right. Now we really are on our way.' He couldn't help the grin which spread across his face.

'You seem very happy, Mr Crossley,' Polly Anna commented as they trotted off towards the Beverley turnpike. 'Is it because you are going home?'

'Y— yes, I suppose it is,' he agreed. 'I love it in the country. But, also, I am so pleased to be taking you with me – I mean,' he stammered self-consciously as she raised her eyebrows at the remark, 'I mean now that the search has ended. Although', he added, 'Mrs Winthrop will be sad to hear the news of your poor mother.'

'Mrs Winthrop!' She touched the locket around her neck. At last the initials meant something. They gave form and substance to her mother's former life. 'Do you think that she'll accept me, Mr Crossley?'

He wanted to ask her to call him Richard so that they could come on to a more familiar footing, but knowing Mrs Winthrop as he did, he knew that any familiarity in such a new relationship with Polly Anna, would promote distrust and indignation on Mrs Winthrop's part. There would be difficulties enough he had no doubt, no doubt at all, especially when she and Rowena saw the Romanies accompanying them.

'She is a very strict and proper lady,' he said in answer to her question, 'but she seems to have had many regrets over her behaviour towards your mother, and now, so late in her life, I think she wants to make up for that. She has been very anxious for many years, to know of her grandchild. The difficulty, I feel, may lie with your aunt, your mother's sister, who may not be so amiable towards you. My own uncle and aunt, whose home I share, however,' he added enthusiastically, 'will be delighted that you are found at last!'

'Then that's all right.' There was some relief in

her voice and he guessed that she was apprehensive. 'I shall have some friends at least.'

'Of course you will,' he said earnestly. 'And my own friendship you can rely on at all times. Miss Lee,' he added impishly, 'we must remember to be correct. You will be entering a different society from now on.'

'I'm not sure that I'll want to change, Mr Crossley.' She stared across at him, her eyes wide, and she tossed her head. 'Won't they accept me as I am?'

'I hope so, Polly Anna,' he said softly. 'I really hope so.'

They caught up with the Romanies, who once more dropped a few paces behind until they reached the tollgate at Newland when Jack rode alongside them. 'I don't agree with this,' he said. 'We don't go through tollgates!'

'Well, you have to if you're using the turnpike. It's all right, I will pay,' Richard assured him.

He shook his head. 'It's not the money. Romanies don't use 'turnpikes, those who are not true travellers use them.' There was a proud look on his face. 'We have the freedom to travel over all common land and heath. It is our right.'

Richard leaned forward in his saddle and the tollkeeper stood with his arms folded, listening. 'I agree with what you say, Boswell, but someone has to pay to keep the road in good order. It's quicker for us in this instance to use the toll road and we shall make better time than with the smaller roads. As soon as we're out of Beverley we shall cross country.'

Here was a confrontation that he hadn't

expected. The Romanies were a proud race, he decided, with as many customs and conventions as anyone he had met within his own social circle.

'Just this once we must use it,' Kisaiya whispered to Jack. 'We can't leave Polly Anna, we are charged with her safety. Our *Brothers* and *Sisters* will understand.'

He agreed, but surlily, and as Richard paid the toll for four horses, the toll keeper touched his hat. 'Never see'd a Gyppo through here afore, sir. First time ever.'

Jack Boswell scowled at him as he passed and snorted, 'And the last, *Dinnelo!*'

'*Dinnelo! Dinnelo!*' Floure shouted gleefully as they passed through the gate and Kisaiya hushed her and gave Jack a reproachful frown. He looked sheepish for a second and then gave a sudden grin at his wife's admonishment.

'That's a fine horse you're riding,' Richard commented later as they approached the outskirts of Beverley and skirted the Beck, which was crowded with shipping. 'I saw him in the Market Place and took quite a fancy to him myself.'

'I've ridden him before. He's a beauty.' Polly Anna leaned forward and stroked the horse's neck and his ears pricked.

'You'll be able to ride every day when you are at Mrs Winthrop's. She has some good land and so has my uncle. Good riding country.'

'What? You mean that they own land – oh, of course, you said that you were a farmer. I went to a farm once and watched the woman milk a cow. Does my grandmother have her own cow?'

'Er – no! They keep sheep mostly and grow some

crops, but your grandmother lets out her land to other farmers; she er – she doesn't actually do the work herself!'

'Is she rich, then, if she doesn't work or is she very old and can't do it?'

'She is old but she's also very rich, Polly Anna. Very rich indeed.' What can she know of riches? he thought. She has had to earn her own living, she can have no conception of the life she is about to enter, where ladies need do nothing more than play the piano or dabble with paints and embroidery. He suddenly felt uneasy. How will she adapt to such a life?

The prosperous, medieval town of Beverley sat in a hollow surrounded by trees and green pasture land and this Sunday morning was quiet and peaceful; only a few townspeople were about as their horses clattered over the cobbles in the narrow streets. Suddenly the peace was shattered as the bells of the ancient Minster, which dominated the town, started to peal, urging the pious and devout to come and worship; they passed the old Market Cross, where old men sat on the steps smoking their clay pipes, and rode on past the inns and shops towards the North Bar Gate, when the bells of St Mary's also began to chime calling their faithful flock to enter their doors.

The clangorous sound filled the air and conversation was impossible, but Polly Anna looked around and admired the handsome church and the timber-framed houses and fine shops as Richard pointed them out to her.

The sun came out as they passed through the hamlet of Molescroft and took the country roads through the villages of Etton, South Dalton and Bainton and rising up to Tibthorpe, the foothills of the Wolds. 'Are we almost there?' Polly Anna asked nervously. 'Is this where my grandmother lives?'

'No.' Richard shook his head. 'We are some way off yet, but we can stop and rest here if you wish. We shall start to climb soon, although but gently. There are no great heights on the Wolds but gentle rolling hills.'

So they took a rest close to a copse and Floure ran in the meadows to stretch her legs and the horses were loosed to graze. Polly Anna collected sticks and filled the kettle from a small stream. Kisaiya made a low fire and soon the kettle was boiling for tea and Richard tried to involve a taciturn Jack in conversation about horses, but to no great avail.

'I imagine that a Gypsy's life can be a good one.' Richard stretched himself out on the grass next to Polly Anna. 'No worries or cares such as those with houses and land have.'

She laughed at his ignorance. 'Except when you are moved off from the wayside in the middle of the night when it is raining or snowing and you have nowhere else to go!'

'Ah, yes.' He admitted his error. 'It seems so idyllic when the sun is shining. I have seen them, you know, at their camp at Appleby. They sang and danced and played their fiddles and seemed to be having such a merry time. I was quite envious.'

'At Appleby? You were there?'

'I was. I'd gone to buy horses.' He hesitated. 'And I discovered that Appleby was where your parents met. It is no wonder that there was a great romance for it's a magical place.' He lowered his voice and leaning on his elbow turned towards her. 'It is also the place where I met Kisaiya for the first time, and also her mother. Kisaiya told me that I should go to Hull to find whom I was seeking.'

Polly Anna was silent for a moment, but she gazed engrossed at him as if searching in his face for a solution. Then she said softly, 'And who were you seeking, Mr Crossley?'

He felt mesmerized by her gaze as her eyes held his. He hedged. 'I thought I was searching for your mother.' But of course I wasn't, he realized. I was searching for you.

Their road took them through rich pastureland where sheep grazed and rabbits nibbled the short grass and here and there, high on the chalk hill-sides, hidden springs suddenly appeared spouting crystal-clear water. There was little habitation and Polly Anna marvelled at the freshness of the air, the chorus of birdsong, and the hedges of hawthorn and blackthorn, which already wore their dress of winter red and blue-black berries. Through the village of Fridaythorpe they passed and as the sun started to slowly sink, the road snaked into Thixendale, nestling within the steep-sided valley.

'We stopped too long for our rest,' Richard murmured as they trotted onwards. 'I'd hoped to arrive before nightfall, but we still have a few miles to travel. Yet it was so pleasant there in the meadow, I could have stayed all day long.'

'Night is coming on.' A voice whispered in her head. 'I don't want to go to the house in darkness.' Polly Anna shivered. Who said that? It was a woman's voice. She turned and saw Kisaiya and Jack following and their dark figures on horseback stirred up a vague memory. So too did this stretch of countryside look strangely familiar; a meadow with three elm trees standing tall and majestic, a lone cottage with a crooked chimney spouting curling grey smoke across the night sky. Was it possible to remember it from so long ago?

'Are you all right, Polly Anna?' Richard Crossley's voice broke into her reverie. 'Are you tired? It has been a long journey.'

'A little.' Her voice was low. 'I feel very strange. It's almost as if I can remember coming here before.'

'How can that be? You have surely not been up here?'

'Yes,' she murmured, 'I have. When my papa died, it seems that mama and I were brought here by the Romanies. Mama was coming back to her own family; the Romanies said that she could no longer stay with them.'

'How cruel!' he exclaimed.

'That's what I thought at first; but then I realized that they thought it was the best for us, that Mama would want to be with her own family.'

'And didn't she?'

'I don't know,' she whispered. 'I can't remember.'

'So—?' He was puzzled. 'I don't understand! If they brought you up here, why didn't you stay?'

She shook her head. That part of her life was a blank, lost in the bygone years, obliterated by her mother's death and her own life in the workhouse.

It was getting colder on this higher ground and she pulled her shawl closer around her. They passed a dense wood of ash, elm and hazel, its outline dark against the evening sky. There was a smell of woodsmoke and damp leaves and overhead a flock of crows flew homewards. A cock pheasant croaked a raucous cry and in front of them a weasel slipped by.

Richard drew in at the top of a rise; below them the road meandered up and down the dale, the chalk road showing white in the gathering darkness. 'I've been thinking,' he deliberated. 'Your grandmother's doors will be closed for the night and the shutters drawn. They usually have an early supper and retire soon after. I was thinking that perhaps we shouldn't disturb them now, but go to my uncle's house for the night and then in the morning we will go to your grandmother's. And my uncle would probably like to accompany you, he has been very much involved in searching for you over the years.'

She was very tired, not so much with the journey, but by a heaviness which was coming over her the nearer they came to her grandmother's home, for the closer they came to it the more convinced she was that she remembered coming before. The hedgerows were familiar, the undulation of the fields and now as she looked down the winding road she knew that her journey was almost ended and she was filled with trepidation. 'Yes,' she said. 'I think that perhaps I would like to do that, if you think that your uncle and aunt won't mind. But what about Kisaiya and Jack? Where will they stay?'

'Uncle Charles and Aunt Mary will be delighted to welcome you, and the Romanies can camp in the meadow below the house. They will be happy to do that, I'm quite sure, once you are delivered safely,' he added with a smile.

They turned off the road on to a wide, well-used track which forked after about a mile. They took the left-hand fork and Polly Anna turned in the saddle and looked down the other fork and wondered if that was the way to her grandmother's. 'Does the house have a name?' she asked.

'Beck House,' he said. 'The house stands on a rise overlooking the dale and below it is a beck, one of the few which are here in the Wolds. My uncle's house is called Warren House. A whim', he explained, 'of the man who built it, for the place was overrun with rabbits, and indeed still is.'

He chatted on as they rode the final leg of their journey, not expecting any answers from her for she seemed to have become very quiet and when she did speak there was a nervousness in her voice. They turned a bend in the track and in front of them were a pair of handsome iron gates. 'Here we are, almost there.'

She turned around to look for Kisaiya. 'Kisaiya,' she called, 'come on! We're here. Stay with me. Don't go!' She felt a sudden panic that they would leave her as once the other Romanies had done.

Kisaiya trotted up alone, leaving Jack, who now had a sleepy Floure in front of him. 'I won't leave you, Polly Anna. I'll stop as long as you want me to.'

'You can camp in this bottom meadow if you want to, Kisaiya,' Richard said. 'The house is in view and no-one will disturb you, or', he said as an after-thought, 'perhaps you would prefer one of the barns?'

'No.' She shook her head. 'Not a barn, sir. They

have doors and walls. We'll pitch out here by the hedge. But first we'll come up to the house and see Polly Anna safely inside.'

They trotted up the long drive and the grey stone house stood out in the darkness. All of the windows downstairs showed a light and Polly Anna could see someone moving in one of the rooms, someone who held a lamp in her hand. 'It's a very big house for only you and your aunt and uncle,' she whispered. 'Or does someone else live there too?'

'Just the servants who look after them,' he replied. 'The cook and the maids and the footmen, then there are the grooms and the stable lads to look after the carriage and horses.'

She said nothing. She was quite overwhelmed by the enormity of it all and as she dismounted she suddenly felt weak and giddy and held on to the Pinto's saddle.

'Give me your arm, Polly Anna,' Richard said gently. 'I think you are fatigued.'

As he held her arm and propelled her to the wide steps, the door opened. A man in grey breeches and embroidered coat and waistcoat gave a slight bow and murmured a greeting, and behind him a maid bobbed her knee. Polly Anna knew she was a maid for she was dressed in cap and apron like the maid at Mrs Harmsworth's house. They entered a wide hall with carved wooden doors at the other end, which were partly opened and through which she could see a sweeping staircase. A figure was descending the stairs, a plump woman of senior years, yet dressed sprightly in a gown of dark crimson and a lace cap upon her head.

'Richard!' she exclaimed as the doors were

opened for her by an unseen hand. 'How glad I am to see you safely back. You have been so long gone I was beginning to – worry.' Her words trailed away as she saw Polly Anna holding so tightly on her nephew's arm. 'And who is this, my dear? You have brought a guest?' She drew nearer, the smile on her face turning to bewilderment and she placed her hand against her chest taking small gasping breaths.

'Charles,' she called vaguely, 'Charles. Come here! Fetch the master,' she waved her hand towards the maid. 'Be quick.'

'Richard,' she said. 'Is this—? Who is this young lady?'

Richard held firmly to Polly Anna's arm. He could feel her shaking, and drew her toward his aunt. 'Aunt Mary, may I present Miss Paulina Lee – Madeleine's daughter. Polly Anna, this is my Aunt Mary – Mrs Charles Dowson.'

28

Polly Anna's fears dispersed as Richard's Aunt Mary stepped forward and took hold of both her hands. 'My dear,' she exclaimed. 'My dear! Welcome to our home. How glad I am to meet you. Charles!' She turned to her husband, who was slowly descending the stairs. 'Charles! Here is your great niece – Paulina, did you say, Richard?'

'My name is Paulina, ma'am, but everyone calls me Polly Anna.' She bobbed her knee to Charles Dowson, who looked at her with amazement written on his face.

'I don't believe it!' he said gruffly. 'How—? Where did you find her?' He too took Polly Anna's hand in both of his and tears began to gather in her eyes, for although his voice was brusque, his welcome was genuine, though tinged with astonishment that his nephew had achieved what he was unable to. 'But – Madeleine? Your mother? Where is she? Why is she not here too?'

'Why are we standing here?' Mrs Dowson exclaimed. 'Come inside. But why is the door still open, Sanders? There is someone there, is there not?'

'Yes, ma'am.' The servant stood with his hand on the door, his face implacable. 'There is a person here. A Gypsy, ma'am.'

'It's Kisaiya,' Polly Anna said hastily. 'She is my friend and she and her husband have travelled with us.'

'As a companion, Aunt Mary,' Richard interrupted. 'The Romanies did not consider it proper that Miss Lee should travel alone without an escort.'

'And quite right too,' Aunt Mary agreed, moving towards the door. 'Will you not come inside and take a little supper?'

Kisaiya shook her head. 'No thank you, lady. But Mr Crossley said that we can pitch our tent in the meadow.'

'Yes, yes, of course.' Charles Dowson stepped forward. 'And if anyone bothers you tell them that you have my permission.'

'Don't leave, will you, Kisaiya?' Polly Anna insisted. 'You promised.'

'I promised,' Kisaiya affirmed. 'We'll stop until you tells us to go.' She gazed at Polly Anna. 'I'll not let you down, *Sister*. You knows it.'

Polly Anna nodded. 'I know it, *Sister*. Thank you.'

'Your sister?' Mrs Dowson looked bewildered as Kisaiya turned away and ran down the steps and the door was closed behind her. 'I don't understand? If she is your sister why will she not come in?'

Richard led the way into the drawing room. 'Not her real sister, Aunt Mary, but it will take a little time to explain. But we will go through everything in good time, including the fact', he said quietly, 'that Polly Anna's mother died some years ago.'

There was instant remorse, though Charles Dowson shook his head sorrowfully and vowed he had always known it. 'Otherwise she would have come back home at some time,' he muttered into his hand as he stroked his chin meditatively. 'I told Harriet as much. Madeleine wasn't the sort to hold a grudge. Not like some.'

Polly Anna stared at him. But she did come home, she wanted to tell him. Yet she remained silent, for was she sure that her mama had gone home or had she changed her mind at the last minute, turned tail and followed the Romanies on an ill-fated journey?

After supper Mrs Dowson asked Polly Anna if she would like to retire early as she had had such a long journey. 'And I do understand my dear, that you will be feeling emotional, coming back to where your mother lived as a girl. But try not to worry, Charles and I will go with you to your grand-mother's tomorrow to ease the shock of your homecoming. She is an old lady, and rather peppery,' she smiled and nodded, her double chin wobbling. 'It is a family attribute, Charles has it too, but you mustn't mind for it hides a kind heart.'

Polly Anna was taken upstairs to a bedroom and a maid came in to help her undress. She stood as if mesmerized as the girl undid her shirt and skirt and, wrapping a large sheet around her, unfas-tened her shift and let it drop to the floor without displaying her nakedness. She then gently washed her hands and face and slipped a fresh white nightgown over her head, drawing the sheet from beneath her. Then she brushed her hair, turned back the covers on the big bed and helped her in.

'Shall I draw the bedhangings, miss?' she asked. 'Or leave them open.'

Polly Anna looked up at the drapes above the bed and the curtains attached to the columns at each end. She would be completely shut in if they were drawn. 'Leave them open please,' she whispered. 'I want to see the sunlight when I wake.'

'Yes, miss.' The maid bobbed her knee. 'Will that be all, miss?'

Polly Anna nodded. 'Yes, thank you. Thank you very much.'

The maid bobbed again and left, taking Polly Anna's clothes with her and leaving her with a jumble of thoughts running through her mind: of this great house and the servants and the supper which she had eaten with such trepidation as she saw the array of cutlery in front of her, and she had watched as Richard used various knives and forks and had assiduously copied him.

She leaned back against the feather pillows and looked around at the sumptuous furnishings, then as a sudden thought struck, she jumped out of bed and ran to the window. Kisaiya! Where was she? She drew back the curtains and looked out. The night sky was clear and dotted with bright stars. She opened the window and breathed in the sharp autumn air. There was a smell of woodsmoke which was what she had hoped for and her gaze searched down past the formal lawns in front of the house, past the dark shadow of the ornamental trees which focused the eye before drawing to a long low hedge which bounded the meadow beyond.

A shower of sparks revealed where a fire burned and a curl of smoke showed her that the Romanies were there. She breathed a deep sigh. 'Good night, *Sister*. Good night, *Brother*.'

She was woken the next morning by a different maid, who greeted her with a wide smile and a breakfast tray. 'Mrs Dowson thought you might like to have breakfast in your room, miss. She said as to take your time coming down.'

She ate her breakfast of eggs and ham and fresh bread and had just finished when there was a tap on the door and yet another maid came in with her clothes; her shirt and skirt and shift freshly washed and pressed and her boots cleaned and polished. 'Shall I help you dress, miss, or will you stay abed a bit longer?'

'I can dress myself, thank you,' she said, thinking that the maids were coming in one by one just to take a look at her.

'Oh! – But, miss, I was sent up specially.' The girl was clearly flummoxed by this state of affairs. 'What'll I say to them downstairs?'

'What's your name?' Polly Anna asked as she climbed out of bed.

'Sally, miss.'

'And who helps you to dress, Sally?'

The girl laughed. 'Why nobody, miss. I don't need anybody to dress me!'

'And nor do I, Sally, thank you all the same. I've dressed myself since I was a child so I shan't be needing anybody to help me now. But you can take the breakfast tray away,' she asserted. 'I've finished with it.'

317

'Oh, I'm sorry, miss, but I'll have to leave that for Ellen; she's for t'kitchen, I'm for upstairs.'

Polly Anna sat down again on the bed after Sally had gone. She'd never get used to this. So many people to do such simple things. She washed in a bowl which had been placed on a marble table, using the jug of fresh water, and dried herself on a cream linen towel. Then she dressed quickly and went to the window. The fire in the bottom meadow was still burning and she could see the horses cropping the grass. I shouldn't doubt them, she thought. Kisaiya promised. It's just that I'm still so afraid.

Charles Dowson drove himself and his wife in the trap and Polly Anna and Richard rode in front of them, with the Romanies following behind on the short journey to Beck House. It was a fine crisp morning and the trees in the lanes glowed with rich autumn colours and thrushes and finches filled the air with their song. They turned into the lane, which continued on towards another track that opened out into an undulating meadow, but before they reached the end Richard turned into a driveway flanked by stone pillars.

'Only a little way now,' he said. 'The driveway rises and curves for half a mile to the house. The views are wonderful.'

Polly Anna nodded dumbly. Yes, she knew. She remembered the pillars with the stone balls on top and she also remembered the long walk up the drive and back again. Her heart started to pound in anticipation of what was to come; it was as if she was reliving a scene from her childhood.

The two of them reached the house first, the

horse and trap with the Dowsons coming more slowly up the steep incline and the Romanies lagging behind them. 'They've seen us coming,' Richard said. 'There's someone in the window. There's a gap in the trees where anyone approaching can be seen.'

He dismounted and put his hand up to help Polly Anna dismount, but she lithely jumped down on her own but gave him her hand. He squeezed it gently. 'Don't be nervous,' he murmured. 'No-one is going to eat you.'

She bit her lips apprehensively and mounted the steps just as the door opened. 'Good morning, sir,' the maid greeted him and then stepped aside to let her frowning mistress greet the visitors.

'Miss Winthrop,' Richard began. 'I have brought your niece, Madeleine's daughter—'

Rowena opened her mouth and swallowed but no words came out. She simply stared at Polly Anna as if she had seen a ghost.

'Hello, Aunt Wena,' Polly Anna said softly. 'Do you remember me?'

Because I remember you, she thought, as she stood in front of her in the doorway. I remember how Mama cried when you were so unkind. She recalled quite clearly what it was that her aunt had said, when such harsh words were spoken and her mother had implored Rowena to let them come in. 'Mother isn't here,' she had said. 'And if she was she wouldn't want to see you.'

There had been more, but time had eradicated it from her memory and so she stood now and waited for her aunt to speak.

Rowena drew herself up. 'Madeleine's daughter? Really? How extraordinary! But where is Madeleine to tell us that she is?'

'May we come in?' Richard asked. 'Uncle Charles and Aunt Mary are just coming; we spent the night at Warren House,' he explained, 'as it was late when we arrived.'

Rowena looked at him coldly and turned towards the morning room just off the hall. A fire was lit, but in spite of the sun streaming in through the window Polly Anna gave a shiver. The welcome here wasn't going to be as warm as at the Dowsons' home.

'Please be seated.' Rowena sat down on a gilt brocaded chair. 'And tell me why you think this young woman is Madeleine's daughter. She looks nothing like her!'

Richard looked at Rowena's severe expression. No, he thought, she probably doesn't, but if a smile lit your face occasionally, she would look like you. Rowena's once dark hair with its wings of white at her temples was thick and springy as Polly Anna's was, but tightly coiled about her ears to tame it.

The Dowsons came into the room, bursting with excitement. 'Isn't it wonderful?' exclaimed Aunt Mary. 'A miracle almost, one might say!'

'Where's Harriet?' Charles boomed. 'Now, we'd better break the news gently about Madeleine. It will hit her very hard. Is she not down yet?'

'Mother is dressing; she will be down presently. Please sit down, Aunt Mary. Uncle Charles, you too, you're making me feel quite edgy.' Rowena took a deep breath. 'Would someone please explain what this is about? What about Madeleine? Is she still playing at being a Gypsy and wandering barefoot in the grass?'

Polly Anna stood up and confronted Rowena. 'Mama is dead,' she said slowly. 'She died in the workhouse. I think her heart was broken.'

Rowena's face turned white and she placed her hands across her chest. 'The workhouse?' she breathed. 'But – I didn't—. I wasn't to—'

'Beg pardon, Miss Winthrop.' A maid hesitated at the door. 'There's some Gypsies out on t'drive. Shall I send them away?'

Rowena stared at the maid and then turned her gaze on Polly Anna. 'Are they with you?'

'Yes,' she said simply. 'They are my friends. My family.'

'What is happening here?' They all turned at the imperious voice; the maid dipped her knee to Mrs Winthrop and stood aside. 'Charles? Mary? This is an unearthly hour to be calling. Has something happened?'

'It's eleven o'clock, Harriet,' Charles bellowed. 'Not early at all.'

'Never mind that, dear,' Mary interrupted. 'Harriet, do come in and sit down, we have some momentous news for you and it is not all good.'

Harriet Winthrop gazed around at the assembled company in turn, her gaze falling on Richard and then Polly Anna. She came slowly into the room and Richard slipped behind her, spoke briefly to the maid and then closed the door.

She sat down on the nearest chair and everyone fell silent as she looked at Polly Anna, still standing by Rowena's chair. 'I feel that I should know you,' she said. 'Have we met before?'

Polly Anna dipped her knee. 'No ma'am. We haven't met. But you know – knew my mother. She was your daughter Madeleine. My name is Paulina Lee.'

The old lady put her hands to her mouth and her eyes grew wide. '*Was* my daughter, do you say? Do you mean that she is no longer my daughter?'

'It means, Harriet,' Mary interrupted softly, 'that Madeleine is no longer with us. That she has gone to a better place.'

'You mean that she is dead? Why do you not say what you mean, Mary, instead of babbling on and beating about the bush?'

Mary sighed audibly and resignedly sat back in her chair. 'I was only trying to—'

'Come here, child.' Mrs Winthrop beckoned to Polly Anna. 'Tell me yourself in plain words what has happened to my daughter.'

Polly Anna took a deep breath. This was worse than she imagined. The old lady was not going to believe her. Rowena did, she could see it in her eyes. Guilt and shame mingling with arrogance lingered there. 'My mother, who was Madeleine Winthrop before she married *Papa*, died in the workhouse fourteen years ago. We'd lived with my papa until he died in an accident and then we had to leave the Romany camp.' She glanced at Rowena. 'I can't remember much of what happened after, but we arrived in the Hull workhouse where my mother died the day after.'

'Why did you leave the camp? Why did you not stay with the Gypsies? Did they not want you?'

Again Polly Anna's glance caught Rowena's, who

was sitting on the edge of her chair. 'I – I think it's tradition that a non-Gypsy has to leave when her *rom* has died.'

'*Rom*? What does that mean?' Mrs Winthrop's voice was sharp.

'Sorry! It means husband.'

'So they did marry!' It wasn't a question, the old lady seemed to be talking to herself. 'And now she is dead.' Her mouth worked as she digested the facts. Then she drew her rounded shoulders up as straight as she could. 'Let me look at you. Come closer so that I can see.'

Polly Anna stepped forward and gazed frankly at her grandmother. So here was her other family, as different as could be from the Romanies. She felt suddenly alienated, belonging to neither one nor the other. She saw Richard's eyes on her and lifted her head up proudly and he gave her an approving smile.

Mrs Winthrop's gaze ran over her face, her hair, down to her boots and back again. 'I don't know how or where Mr Crossley found you,' she said. 'I suppose it was you?' She looked up at Richard, who affirmed it. 'No doubt it will all be told in the fullness of time. But have you any proof that you are who you say you are?'

'No, ma'am.' She suddenly wanted to cry.

'Yes! Yes, Polly Anna. You have.' Richard came towards her. 'The locket. You've forgotten the locket!'

'Oh!' She undid the clasp and handed it to her grandmother. 'This is all I have.'

Mrs Winthrop turned it over in her hand and her

323

eyes became bright. 'Yes, this was Madeleine's. It was given to her on her eighteenth birthday. Are the pictures still inside?'

'Yes, ma'am.' Polly Anna took it from her and slid her nail under the slit to open it. 'They are still here.' She gave it back to her grandmother, who looked down at it for a moment.

'And this was your father?'

'Yes.' Polly Anna suddenly realized that Mrs Winthrop would not have seen a likeness of her father before.

'And the other picture, is it still there?' Mrs Winthrop picked at the edge of her father's likeness with her fingernail. 'Did she keep it?' And lifting the pencil sketch from the locket, she gave a slight, sad smile. 'So she didn't abandon us completely, Rowena, as you said she had.' She held up the locket for all to see the miniature colouring of Rowena which had been lying beneath the likeness of Madeleine's husband, Paul Lee.

The Dowsons and Richard stayed for luncheon so that a discussion could take place over what should happen next. 'Paulina is very welcome to stay with us if it is not convenient for you just now, Harriet,' Mary said eagerly. 'I know how you like to prepare for guests.'

Harriet gave her a frosty stare. 'But she isn't a guest, is she? If she is my granddaughter as she appears to be, then this is her home and no preparation is needed apart from her room.' She looked at Polly Anna and then at a silent Rowena, who was merely toying with her food. 'I think that perhaps she could have Madeleine's old room, Rowena. What do you say?'

Rowena shrugged. 'Whatever you say, Mother.'

'Would you like that?' Mrs Winthrop asked Polly Anna. 'Would you like to have your mother's room? Sleep in her bed?'

Polly Anna burst into tears. How very cold these women were, how unfeeling. Did they have no compassion? No sorrow for a lost daughter and sister? Did they not understand how she was feeling coming back to where her mother had spent her girlhood? A thought struck her that perhaps her mother had been glad to go away, to take the chance of love when it beckoned.

Richard rose to his feet. 'Mrs Winthrop, this has been a very trying time for Polly – Miss Lee. Perhaps if I take her for a walk whilst you finish luncheon? You can then discuss arrangements between yourselves and I will ascertain what she wants to do.'

'Oh! Very well.' Mrs Winthrop seemed rather surprised at the show of emotion and he was reminded that Mrs Harmsworth had said of her sister and niece that they were more interested in sheep and corn than in people, and it seemed, he thought, that she was right.

'Don't get upset.' He took Polly Anna's arm as they walked around the garden. 'Everything must seem very strange to you, so different from what you have been used to. They are not the sort of people who display their inner feelings. They have been brought up to hold them in check; they consider it improper to demonstrate emotion in front of others.'

She lifted tear-filled eyes. 'And is this how you are, Mr Crossley? Have you been brought up the same way?'

He gazed down at her and felt a sudden lurch of protectiveness towards her. She was so vulnerable in spite of the life she had led. 'No,' he said slowly, 'though perhaps I might not always be able to say exactly what I mean. But my parents are warm-hearted and responsive. I have always felt their affection.'

'So why did you leave them?' she demanded. 'Why did you come to stay with your aunt and uncle?'

'Sometimes that is the way things are done,' he explained. 'Uncle Charles and Aunt Mary have no children, no heir to their estate, whereas my parents have two sons. I am the younger,' he added, 'and Aunt Mary always had a soft spot for me. That is why.' He looked at her and wondered about fate. 'And sometimes,' he said reflectively, 'sometimes, I think that our lives are not totally in our own hands, even though we may appear to choose our own direction.'

He took a clean handkerchief from his pocket and standing still for a moment he gently wiped the tears from her cheek. 'When I was a small boy I was taken by my nurse to St Bartholomew Fair, and she said to keep tight hold of her hand in case the Gypsies ran away with me; and when we went home I heard my family talking about a beautiful young woman who had run away with the Gypsies.'

Polly Anna felt the soft touch of his fingers on her cheek and looked wonderingly at him. 'And it was my mother they were speaking of?'

'Yes,' he said softly, 'and now here you and I are; and if I hadn't left my parents and come to live here, we would never have met. Don't you think it rather strange?'

Another tear fell and she blinked it away. 'Yes.' Her voice was a mere whisper. 'It is.'

29

Rowena looked out of the window and saw them standing close together and her lips drew in a tight line. 'Of course, Mother, the locket isn't total proof that she is Madeleine's daughter.' She turned towards her mother and relations. 'She could have found it – stolen it even. It's well known that the Gypsies are thieves.'

'From whom would she have stolen it?' Her mother demanded. 'And how would she know it came from this family?'

'And in any case it was Richard who sought her out,' Aunt Mary added firmly. 'He was quite adamant about that.'

'There is no doubt,' Mrs Winthrop stated. 'Like it or not, Rowena, anyone can see who she is.'

'What!' Rowena laughed scornfully. 'She's pure Gypsy! She has a wild look about her. She is ill bred and her manners are appalling! There is nothing of Madeleine, she was gentle and so fair!'

'And the only fair one in the family,' her mother retorted. 'Look in the mirror, Rowena, and you will see who she is like, manners or no! She is like you were, and your father, and as I was, though I was not quite so dark. Why are you so set against her? You should be glad that though Madeleine has gone we at least have her daughter.' Her bottom lip trembled a little, but she pursed her mouth tightly. 'Even though she has Gypsy blood. But we must make the best of that even though there will be talk over the whole of Yorkshire!'

'As there was before,' Rowena said bitterly. 'It seems there is to be no end to it.'

'We will overcome it,' her mother said flatly, 'as we did before.'

Polly Anna, in view of her talk with Richard, did not expect warmth or tenderness from her new family, yet as the weeks went by and she settled into the routine of the household, she began to understand her grandmother more, though Rowena rarely spoke to her and when she did it was in a brusque offhand manner as if she was speaking to an inferior. Her grandmother bid her come to her room every evening and speak of what she remembered of her mother, of her life in the workhouse and who her friends were, and without ill temper patiently corrected her unpolished speech.

'Jonty is my very best friend,' she said, and wondered where he was now. 'I wish I could see him, he'll be very worried about me.' Winter was coming on, with cold, wet, foggy November days, when the view from the house was obscured by a thick grey blanket of mist and she wondered about her fairground friends, who would be huddled inside their benders or in inferior lodging houses when they were travelling between the fairs and markets, which were fewer in winter.

'Tell me again what you remember about leaving the Gypsies,' her grandmother said, 'and arriving at the workhouse in the old man's cart. There is something missing, a void which you haven't filled in.' She shook her head sorrowfully. 'I can't believe that a daughter of mine could come to such an end. It just doesn't seem possible.'

The door opened and Rowena entered as she was speaking. 'Why didn't she come back home? Did she think I was so unfeeling that I would have turned her away? I was angry with her, yes, when she ran away with the Gypsy. I had so much planned for her; but she could have come back when she was in trouble. Why didn't she, Rowena? I don't understand.'

Rowena stared at Polly Anna as if challenging her to speak, but Polly Anna put her head down and wouldn't look at her. 'How would I know, Mother? How would I know what was in her head? Perhaps she was too ashamed!'

Polly Anna looked up. 'She wasn't ashamed of marrying my papa,' she said sharply. 'She wept all the way back to Hull. I won't ever forget that. She said her life was over without him and that she didn't know how we would manage without him; that no-one else cared.' She stared her aunt in the face until she looked away. 'And no-one else did. Not enough. Except for Jonty.'

Every evening she came to talk and little by little she and her grandmother seemed to come to an understanding and her grandmother grew at last to know of her life before, except for the blank area which she did not fill in, and told her that she couldn't remember.

Richard too questioned her about this when they rode out together on crisp cold days when the ground was hard with frost and their breath curled in opaque mist as they spoke. 'What was it you meant on the day you arrived?' he asked. 'You asked Rowena did she remember you.'

'You're mistaken, I think,' she said briefly. 'Oh, there's Kisaiya. Let's go and meet her,' and his question remained unanswered.

The Romanies were camped in a meadow belonging to Mrs Winthrop, much to Rowena's anger and disapproval, and she had given instructions to the servants that the doors were to be kept locked at all times. But Polly Anna, though at first treated with a cautious regard, had soon been welcomed by the servants, who regarded her as a breath of fresh air in this staid household, and when she asked for a little bread or good meat that was going to be thrown to the fowls they didn't ask where it was going but sometimes put a few eggs alongside in the basket also.

Jack Boswell travelled the roads around the Winthrop and Dowson estates, calling at the cottages and farmhouses and asking if they had any pans for mending. Sometimes, if the cottagers were poor, he would mend their pans and take a cabbage or a few potatoes in return, but if the farms looked prosperous he would charge them and beg a cabbage or a jug of milk as well. 'For my little *chavi*,' he would say softly, 'not for myself.'

There were no wild flowers for Kisaiya to pick and sell, and in any case she knew that these country folk knew more about herbs and flowers than she did and wouldn't buy what was on their doorstep;

but she had a good hand at lace making and had brought her cottons with her and so she sold lace trimmings and made collars to order when requested.

Polly Anna was introduced gradually to the close friends and neighbours of her grandmother, and she withstood their scrutiny and their comments on whether she had her mother's likeness, and sat silently listening as they openly discussed whether or not Mrs Winthrop had done the right thing in accepting the Gypsy's daughter. Of Rowena's friends she saw none, nor did she expect to.

Mary Dowson coached her in the intricacies of table manners and conversation and was given the task of helping to choose new clothes for her. She was always eager to invite Polly Anna to luncheons and supper parties, and although at first this was an ordeal Polly Anna endured when she realized that guests were curious to come and see this half Gypsy girl, she gradually relaxed in this genial household and with Richard by her side began to enjoy herself.

At Christmas the snow was thick on the ground and she tried to persuade the Romanies to move into a barn and escape the worst of the weather. 'Do it for Floure,' she pleaded, 'if not for yourselves.'

'She's a Romany *chavi*,' Jack grumbled, 'not a weak *Gorgie*.' But he gave in eventually when a snow-storm covered the tent, trapping them inside, and the farm labourers were sent by a frantic Polly Anna to dig them out.

As spring approached she and Richard rode out across the countryside and in her green riding dress, made especially at her request with a divided skirt for she was reluctant to ride side-saddle, she sat astride the Pinto at the top of a dale and looked down. The snow had gone, leaving the grass green and lush; buds were appearing on the willow trees, though the ash trees were still stark and bare with pale, papery wings fluttering empty in the March breeze.

'Do you like it here, Polly Anna? Are you happy?' Richard watched her as she viewed the scene. 'I mean – could you spend the rest of your life here?' He was anxious to hear the reply he so much wanted.

She hesitated. 'It's so beautiful,' she said softly. 'I feel that I could belong here, but—'

'But?' He leaned forward to watch her expression and it seemed to him that she was not totally happy.

'I'm not sure that I am welcome at my grandmother's house. I don't mean Grandmother,' she added hastily. 'We are getting to know each other. It's Aunt Rowena. She doesn't like me and I feel very uneasy because of that.'

'But if it wasn't for Rowena, then you would?' he insisted. 'I mean, do you like Uncle Charles and Aunt Mary?'

'Oh, yes,' she laughed. 'I do. I think they are dears.'

He smiled. Polly Anna was changing, she was even using different expressions and learning how to respond to the gentry she was meeting. Though I hope, he mused, that she doesn't change too much. She is perfect as she is. 'Polly Anna,' he said, 'I'm going to London to visit my parents.'

'Oh!' She turned to him in surprise. 'Will you be away long?'

'A week or so. There is something I wish to discuss with them.' He gave her an imploring glance. 'Will you miss me?'

'Yes,' she said seriously, 'I will. You have taken care of me whilst I've been here. Just as Jonty took care of me before.'

He was disappointed. 'You mean that I have taken Jonty's place?'

'Oh, no! No-one could ever do that!' She shook her head vigorously. 'Jonty will always be very special.' Her eyes smiled into his and lingered for a moment, then she dug her heels into the horse's flanks. 'But you're special too,' she called as she cantered swiftly away and his spirits lifted as he chased after her. It is enough for now. No use expecting too much too soon.

'I'm going to visit my sister, Mrs Harmsworth, for a few days, Paulina,' her grandmother said at supper the next evening. 'Rowena isn't going, so you won't be lonely.'

Polly Anna's mood sank. Bad enough that Richard was going away but Grandmother too and leaving her alone with Rowena. 'I hope you have a pleasant time, Grandmother,' she intoned politely as she had been taught.

'You and Rowena will have a chance to get to know each other better,' the old lady said. 'I have noticed that you spend little time together.'

'That's because she is always out riding with Mr Crossley,' Rowena answered sharply. 'We don't even have conversation with him these days.'

'You should come out riding with us, Aunt Rowena. Richard has asked you.'

Rowena gave her a scathing glance, but her

mother interrupted. 'Yes, you should. I thought that was why he and Jennings brought you the new horse from Appleby.'

Rowena's face tightened. 'You don't appear to mind mentioning that place any more, Mother. You seem to have forgotten the anguish it always brought us.'

Her mother reached over and patted her hand. 'Not forgotten, Rowena, but it is in the past now. We must look forward to the future, now that we have Paulina with us.'

Rowena got up from the table, pushing her chair back with such force that it fell over. Her face was white. 'I have no future, Mother! Please excuse me,' and she marched out of the room, her skirts swishing as she went.

Her mother sighed. 'I'm sorry, my dear. Rowena was always difficult and she is very bitter over lost opportunities.' She picked up her knife and began to butter her bread energetically. 'But whether it is hard for her or not, she must make the best of it. That's all there is to it.'

Rowena barely spoke to Polly Anna for the first few days when they were alone together, except in front of the servants when she maintained an icy politeness. She refused Polly Anna's invitation to ride and so Polly Anna went alone, exploring the countryside, trotting over the dales, listening to the chattering of magpies and cawing of rooks and taking in great breaths of sweet, fragrant air.

Then one morning the sky was bright with sunlight which streamed in through the breakfast-room window and Rowena changed her mind. 'Perhaps I will ride out this morning,' she said briskly, and Polly Anna sat amazed that her request, asked out of politeness more than out of desire to have her aunt's company, should have been conceded. 'Give me ten minutes to change.'

Polly Anna stood and watched out of the window as she waited. She could see the smoke from the Romanies' fire in the bottom meadow and she knew that soon she would have to make a decision about them. Jack was anxious to be off. He had stayed long enough in one place, he said, and though Kisaiya didn't press her, she knew that she too was wanting to rejoin her family. 'There is a special reason, Polly Anna,' she had said shyly. 'I shall need my *mam* later in the year.'

Polly Anna didn't at first know what she meant until Kisaiya put her hands across her belly and smiled, and Polly Anna flung her arms around her and cried, 'You're having another *chavi*!'

'Or a *chavo*,' she'd contradicted. 'Jack thinks it'll be a boy, but what would he know about it?'

'I'm so glad for you, Kisaiya,' Polly Anna said. 'Things are better between you and Jack now, aren't they?'

Kisaiya had nodded. 'Just like my *mam* said. But we had to make this journey with you before we both knowed it. And once you say that you are happy here, then we shall move on.'

They hadn't discussed it further, but Polly Anna felt comforted by the fact that Kisaiya would stay until she told her that she was settled, no longer afraid of being abandoned as she had once felt that she had been.

She turned as the door opened and Rowena came in dressed in a black riding habit and small feathered hat. 'I thought we would ride over Wharram way,' she stated. 'It was once a favourite place of ours, mine and Madeleine's.'

Polly Anna agreed, though she thought that perhaps it was a long ride for Rowena though nothing to her, and so they set off, telling the servants that they would be back late afternoon.

It was a beautiful day, the sun bright in an almost cloudless sky. The birds were busy building their nests, trailing long pieces of straw or clumps of moss in their beaks as they flew and there was a gentle hum of bees. Hares sped across the meadow and Polly Anna told Rowena that the Romanies and the fair folk said it was unlucky if a hare crossed in front of your path, to which Rowena replied that that was nonsense. Polly Anna gave a small sigh. The day was not going to be enjoyable, she could feel it. Rowena was in her usual disagreeable mood and not even the prospect of a ride across country on such a lovely sunny day was going to cheer her.

She started to think of Richard and hoped that he wouldn't be gone too long, for she missed his company. She thought that he had been a little cast down when she had told him that he couldn't take Jonty's place. But he has a place of his own in my affections, she mused. Perhaps I should have told him that. Though I have noticed that the people I am meeting now don't always say what I think they are meaning. They skirt around the subject and don't come straight to the point like the people I knew before did. Grandmother speaks of polite society. Perhaps that is why they do it. She sighed again. It was very complicated.

The area they were covering now was new to her

and she asked Rowena where they were. She gave a thin smile. 'There are places up here which are hidden away, valleys which Madeleine and I knew so well and which even Mr Crossley doesn't know about.' She turned to Polly Anna. 'Would you like to see them?'

'Places which my mother knew? Oh, yes! I would. I really would.'

'Come on then.' Rowena flicked her crop sharply and her mount broke into a swift canter, dropping down into the valley bottom and up a steep-banked track which ran between two fields and disappeared into a thick copse. The track through the copse reappeared on the crest of another valley and Polly Anna looked down, thinking with some gladness that her mother too had enjoyed the view and had heard the song of the skylark and the bleat of the sheep which roamed across the grassland.

They rode for another hour and didn't see any habitation or other sign of human life; not a cottage or farm labourer. Nothing and no-one, only rabbits and sheep and a deer drinking from a dewpond in a shallow valley.

'Just a little further,' Rowena said. 'I will show you the finest view in the whole of the county, and then we will turn back.' She led on, crossing tracks and occasionally jumping hedges, through woods filled with primroses and faded snowdrops and rising up on higher ground until at last they reached the highest point and the gradient fell away to the patchwork meadowland of the Vale of Pickering and the edge of the North Yorkshire Moors.

'I haven't been up here in nearly twenty years,' Rowena said softly as she gazed across the panorama. 'Not since Madeleine and I were here together.'

'It's beautiful,' Polly Anna whispered, overwhelmed with delight. She felt she should whisper, for only the rush of the wind broke the silence. 'Thank you so much for bringing me, Aunt Rowena. Thank you for sharing it with me.'

Rowena turned her head and looked at her through lowered lashes. She had a strange expression on her face. 'I had a reason for bringing you,' and Polly Anna suddenly felt threatened.

'A reason?' she asked. 'It was because my mother and you used to come!'

Rowena shook her head and gave a harsh laugh. 'No! I want you to prove who you say you are. Prove that you are Madeleine's daughter. Madeleine and I had a game, you see. We used to try and lose the other. We would ride to the furthest point, taking a different route each time and then see who could get home first. Before dark,' she added.

'And this is what you want to do now?' Polly Anna said slowly and Rowena nodded, a triumphant look on her face.

'But I haven't been this way before. We have taken so many different tracks.'

'That's the whole point,' Rowena said caustically. 'We'll see what you're made of, won't we? Anyway,' her voice was cutting, 'you're a Gypsy, aren't you? A traveller! You're supposed to know about these things.'

'I lived as a Romany until I was nearly four,' Polly Anna said softly, 'as you very well know. Then I lived in the workhouse. Where you sent us, my mother and me. When you turned us away from your door!'

Rowena's voice was icy. 'I don't know what you are talking about. I had never seen you before.'

'Yes. Yes you have. I remembered it so well on the day I came back with Mr Crossley. As I rode up to the house, I remembered. I remembered my mother urging me on, saying that everything would be all right. That now we were home.' Her eyes filled with tears. 'But you were the only one at home and you even opened the door to us yourself. Only, you wouldn't let us in. Not even through the door. You said – you said, you have made your bed, now you must lie on it.' She gave a small sob. 'I didn't know what it meant then, but it has stayed in my mind all of this time.'

She saw a flicker on Rowena's top lip which she turned into a sneer. 'And that is what I meant. She had made her choice and gone off with her Gypsy lover. There was no place for her with us!'

'But my papa had died! She had no-one else she could turn to for comfort; only you and grand-mother.' Polly Anna stared at her aunt and saw the cold dispassionate expression written on her face. 'You were jealous,' she exclaimed. 'You were jealous that she loved someone and he loved her.' Their eyes locked and Polly Anna knew that she had found the reason.

Rowena put her head up. 'Think what you will! She wasn't welcome and neither are you. That is something that you must either live with – or pack your bag and leave! It's up to you.' She raised her crop and for a second Polly Anna thought she was going to strike her, but she brought it down with a sharp thwack on her horse's rump. It whinnied and skittered and Rowena held it fast, but the Pinto which Polly Anna was riding, reared, almost unseating her.

'Let's see who gets back first, shall we?' Rowena shouted and struck again, breaking into a gallop down the valley. 'Let's see if you can find your way home!'

30

She sat for a moment watching as Rowena rode across the valley and out of sight, then she spurred her horse on and followed in her direction. No chance of catching her because she wouldn't think of treating her horse in such a wild manner as Rowena was doing with hers. She had more thought and consideration for its well-being than that.

She reined in at the head of the dale and ascertained her direction, then narrowing her eyes she saw a shape of horse and rider in the far distance and realizing that it was Rowena, she rode on, a sudden laugh lightening her mood as she thought of her mother and Rowena vying with each other to be home first. But Rowena wants me to get lost, she thought, her merriment subsiding. It's no longer a game to her. If I don't find my way back I could be out all night and no-one would know. Only Rowena. She would make some excuse to the servants and they would think nothing of it.

She shuddered. Why is Rowena so vindictive? I am no threat to her. She rode on, meditating on her aunt's contentious behaviour and the thought came that she didn't know if she wanted to go on struggling against it. I have the option of going. That is what she said. And I can. I can still join Ogden's Circus. If I can find it.

But the prospect didn't fill her with joy, even though once the thought of being a famous equestrienne had thrilled her. I wouldn't see Grandmother again, she thought, and I am beginning to care for her, and the Dowsons, I am fond of them too. And Richard. She analysed her feelings for him. I would miss him, I know that and not in the same way as I miss Jonty. I would miss his caring manner, his thoughtfulness towards me, which is above that of being brotherly as Jonty was. She liked the way his face would break into a sudden smile that would reach his eyes. Such blue eyes, she mused, and why would I remember them now?

She reached another rise and saw two tracks. Which should I take? She looked up into the sky; the sun which was lower now was obscured by clouds, she would have to move swiftly to be home before nightfall. Home! Was that what it was? No. It wasn't. Not if there was no love in it but only bitterness. She took a decision and veered right. The copse above her looked familiar as did the chestnut tree below it. You're a Gypsy, aren't you? Rowena had said so sneeringly. Yes, she was, and her mother was a fearless rider too if she had raced with Rowena across these valleys and hills. She would let her instinct guide her. She would not get lost. She would reach her destination.

And as the evening chill descended and dusk was beginning to fall, she reached familiar territory and skirted the village below her grandmother's house, and trotted up the lane towards the house and the meadow where Kisaiya and Jack were camped. She would visit them and tell Kisaiya that she wasn't sure if she would be staying. Though I won't make a decision until Richard returns, it's only fair that I discuss it with him first. He has been so kind.

As she approached the meadow she saw that there was no fire and her heart missed a beat, thinking that they had left, until she saw the bender there, but no sign of anyone about and the canvas flap tightly fastened. Then she heard someone shouting, screaming almost, and she saw Kisaiya running down the meadow from the direction of the house and Floure running behind her trying to keep up.

'Polly Anna! Polly Anna!' Kisaiya's voice was frantic. 'Help me, help me.'

Polly Anna slid down from the Pinto's back and rushed to catch her friend as she fell headlong into her arms. 'What is it? What's happened?'

'They've taken him.' Kisaiya could hardly speak. 'They've taken Jack. He'll die, Polly Anna. He'll die!' She collapsed in a heap and Polly Anna knelt beside her and Floure put her face in her hands and cried.

'Who's taken him? I can't help you unless you tell me.' She shook Kisaiya gently by the shoulder.

'They said he's stolen a *shoshoi*,' Kisaiya sobbed. 'They said he'll hang for it. Thieving Gypsy they called him and said they'll send him to York.' She started to wail. 'They said he'll be hanged and I've been up to Mr Dowson's house and there's nobody there, and I've been to Miss Winthrop and she won't see me.'

'Won't see you? Did you tell the servants what had happened?'

'Yes. She sent a message down for me to go away.'

Polly Anna pulled her to her feet. 'Come on. We'll go back. I'll talk to her. Where is Jack now, do you know?'

Kisaiya shook her head. 'They said they'd lock him up in the village and send him to York when the *gav-engro* was ready.'

'Who said he'd stolen the rabbit? I thought Mr Dowson said he could catch them?'

'Yes,' she sobbed. 'He did. But these were men from the village and they said he'd caught it on the road. That it wasn't Mr Dowson's rabbit.' She looked up at Polly Anna with streaming eyes. 'It's nothing to do with the *shoshoi*, I knows it. It's to do with us being Romanies. There's always some *Gorgio* who hates us and wants us out of his district. They think they can't sleep easy in their beds when we're around.'

They rode back to Beck House and whilst Polly Anna went in search of Rowena, Kisaiya and Floure waited outside the front door.

'She's in her room, Miss Paulina,' the maid replied in answer to her query. 'She said she was unwell and would take supper upstairs. We didn't expect you back yet, miss. Miss Winthrop said you'd been delayed.'

'So I was,' Polly Anna said grimly, 'but not so much as was expected.'

She knocked on Rowena's door and her aunt was obviously surprised by her sudden appearance. She

345

was lying on her bed still dressed in her riding habit and boots but with her hat on the floor where she had seemingly flung it. 'Ha!' she scoffed. 'So here you are! Did you enjoy your journey back?'

'I did, thank you.' Polly Anna didn't want to aggravate her more. She needed her help in the matter of the Romanies. 'Aunt, Jack Boswell has been locked up. It's a mistake. We need help to get him out.'

Rowena examined her fingernails. 'Jack Boswell? Do I know him?'

'Kisaiya's husband. He's been accused of stealing a rabbit.'

'The Gypsy!' Rowena tutted. 'I didn't realize they had proper names. Why are you telling me? Was it our rabbit, from our land?'

'It was caught on the road, but Kisaiya said the men who took him were only using that as an excuse.'

'They probably were,' she responded idly. 'We're all rather weary of having them around. It's about time they moved on.'

'They're only here because of me,' Polly Anna objected. 'They're not doing any harm.'

'Quite.' Rowena's manner was scathing. 'Well, if you're expecting me to go down to the parsonage to plead for him then you'd better think again.'

'But they said he could be hanged for theft! Aunt Rowena, we have to help him!'

'Then it will be one Gypsy less won't it? Now will you excuse me. I have a headache. Close the door behind you.'

Polly Anna raced down the stairs and through the open door, where the maid was still standing, uncertain whether or not to shut Kisaiya out. 'She won't help us, Kisaiya, but he's at the parsonage. We'll go and plead for him.'

Kisaiya looked up and Polly Anna followed her gaze. Rowena was standing by the window looking down at them. '*Rinkeno mui and wafodu zee,*' Kisaiya called softly as she mounted her pony. '*Kitzi's the cheeros we dicks cattanē.*'

The maid at the door gave a gasping breath and Polly Anna stared at her friend. 'Kisaiya! What does that mean? You haven't cursed her?' But Kisaiya was already riding away and didn't answer.

Polly Anna had met the parson at the Dowsons' house; he was a local magistrate and rather pompous she had thought. The parsonage was a grey stone house next to the church and they waited in the darkness outside the oak doors after pulling on the bell. Kisaiya stood well back holding the bridles of the two horses. A maid appeared holding a lamp in her hand. 'Master's at supper, miss,' she said. 'I can't disturb him.'

'Tell him it's Miss Lee, Mrs Winthrop's grand-daughter. Tell him that it's most urgent.'

The maid peered out at Kisaiya. 'The Gypsy'll have to wait at t'back door, miss. Master won't have 'em at t'front.'

Kisaiya had turned away almost before the maid had finished speaking and Polly Anna entered the wide hall, thinking that she could never learn such humility as Kisaiya had. Perhaps my mother's blood does run strong after all.

The parson came out of the dining room wiping his mouth on a linen serviette. 'Has someone died?' he grumbled. 'Not Mrs Winthrop surely?'

'No. I'm sorry to disturb you, Mr Hawgood, but I understand you have the Romany, Jack Boswell, here under arrest.'

'Yes!' The parson looked puzzled. 'That's right. The fellow was caught poaching. You surely haven't disturbed my supper because of that?'

'He has permission from Mr Dowson and Mrs Winthrop to catch rabbits, Mr Hawgood. It's a mistake. He mustn't be locked up. The Romanies can't bear to be confined.'

'You don't need to tell me that, young lady. I've never heard such a din as he was making. I had to order all the doors to be closed, he was quite spoiling my supper.' He shook a podgy finger at her. 'You are living in a different society now, Miss Lee. You must sever your association with such people. Now off you go home for your supper and leave me to mine. The constable will take him to York tomorrow and the courts will decide what is to be done. Law and order would break down if such people were allowed to do whatever they wanted.' He gazed at her. 'Of course, if Mr Dowson says it is one of his rabbits then that is a different matter, but the men said it was caught on some other land and I'd believe them before I'd believe the Gypsy.'

She turned without speaking and walked out of the door. Such prejudice! But what was she to do? She walked towards the back of the house to look for Kisaiya and heard the soft patter of footsteps behind her.

'Miss Lee!' It was one of the parson's maids. 'Go to t'back door, miss. He's locked up in a little room there. You'll find it, it's got bars on t'window.'

She scurried round and found Kisaiya with her

nose pressed against a small window next to the door. It did have bars on it and Jack Boswell's hands were tightly clasped around them. Hanging on the wall by its feet next to the window, was the ill-fated rabbit. 'Don't worry, Jack. We'll find Mr Dowson,' she whispered. 'We'll soon have you out.'

He shook the bars. 'You'd better be quick, or I'll tear this place apart. I can't stop in here much longer.'

'Don't do anything to aggravate the parson,' she urged, 'or they'll take you to York on some other charge as well as the rabbit. Be patient.'

She dragged a weeping Kisaiya away and they mounted and set off down the lane towards the Dowson house. 'We'll cut through the woods,' she said. 'It'll be quicker that way.'

It was dark in the wood and the track was uneven and in some places disappeared, for it was little used, but Polly Anna remembered it as she had been this way with Richard. I wish he was here, she thought. He would know what to do.

As they emerged from the woods behind the stables and coach house they saw the Dowsons' carriage being put away and heard the murmur of voices as the grooms settled the horses for the night. 'They're back, Kisaiya. It will be all right now. Mr Dowson will go to see the parson.'

Kisaiya shook her head. 'Not tonight he won't. He'll want his supper and Jack will have to stop locked up. He'll break out, Polly Anna. He'll break the door down rather than stop in that cell.'

The Dowsons were still in the hall divesting themselves of their outer garments when Polly Anna rang the bell and they greeted her with surprise at her late, unannounced visit. 'My dear,' said Mary, 'out alone after dark!'

'I'm not alone, Mrs Dowson. Kisaiya is with me.'

'It's the same thing, my dear. Two young women alone!' She was horrified at the idea. 'You can't be sure whether there are villains lurking even in this quiet place.'

'Mr Dowson,' she began urgently, 'something has happened and I need your help.'

'Can I have my supper first?' he said jovially. 'Or is it a matter of life or death?'

'It could be,' she said seriously. 'I wouldn't like to answer for the consequences if we don't get Jack Boswell out of the parson's cell.'

They took her through to the drawing room and listened to her story. 'And Kisaiya came to find you earlier, only you were out,' she finished, 'and Mr Hawgood wouldn't listen to me.'

Charles Dowson humphed. 'He wouldn't. He doesn't listen to anyone very much. Except Harriet. She always gives him a piece of her mind if she doesn't like his attitude or his sermons.' He rose from his chair. 'And you're sure I can't have my supper first?' he growled, but she now knew him well enough to know that he was teasing.

'Of course you can't, Charles. Don't torment the child,' Mary urged. 'Go this minute and tell the parson it is our rabbit. Whether or not it is,' she added.

Charles Dowson called for a mount and they rode back the way they had come and once more waited at the door of the parsonage. The maid looked apprehensive when she saw Polly Anna again and at the prospect of disturbing her master from his supper a second time.

'Tell the parson I need to see him at once,' Mr Dowson boomed and Polly Anna was impressed by his authority and once more Mr Hawgood appeared.

'Some tomfoolery going on about one of my rabbits, Hawgood,' Mr Dowson complained. 'Who are the scoundrels who brought in this Gypsy fellow? I'll have their hides.'

'Well – I er,' the parson blustered. 'They didn't say it was one of your rabbits, Mr Dowson! They caught the Gypsy with it; 'said he'd been poaching.'

'I'd better take a look at it then, hadn't I? Come along, I'm tired and weary. Haven't had *my* supper yet.'

Mr Hawgood apologetically wiped a crumb from his mouth and called for a maid.

'It's hanging at t'back door, sir,' she said. 'Cook was about to skin it.'

'What!' Charles Dowson exclaimed. 'Conceal the evidence! You weren't thinking of eating it, Hawgood? Before there's proof of ownership! And you a magistrate!'

'Well, I—. I didn't think that—'

They all trooped out via an inner passageway and arrived at the back door and the little room where Jack Boswell was locked up. He was no longer hammering to be let out and Polly Anna stood on tiptoe to look through the small pane of glass at the top of the door and saw him sitting morosely on a wooden bench, his head in his hands. 'Won't be long now, Jack,' she whispered encouragingly, but he didn't answer.

Charles Dowson unhooked the rabbit from the nail on the wall and held it up. 'Fetch me a light,' he demanded and the maid scurried away for a lamp. He held it this way and that beneath the beam and finally said, 'No doubt about it. It's definitely one of my rabbits.'

'But how can you tell?' The parson was unconvinced. 'They all look the same.'

'Well, you should know, Parson,' Charles Dowson said scathingly. 'You've had many a one for your supper, I'll be bound! Just look at that plump body. Fed on my land without a doubt. Let the fellow out,' he said abruptly, 'and I'll say no more about it.'

'No more about it?' Hawgood said nervously. 'No more about what?'

'About those blackguards blaming the Gypsy and bringing the spoils to you. They want them out of the village don't they? I know what they're up to.'

'Well, it's true some of the villagers are getting agitated about them being here so long,' the cleric hummed and hawed. 'Though there's others say they don't mind them.' He fished in his pocket and brought out an iron key and turned it in the lock of the door.

Jack Boswell shot out of the door and outside into the yard, nearly knocking the parson over in his hurry to regain his freedom. He stared at them all as they stood there and Charles Dowson lifted his arm still holding the rabbit.

'Here.' He threw it. 'Yours, I think.'

Jack caught it with one hand and held it up. 'Thank you, sir,' and flung it back, 'but keep it or give it to 'parson. I'll have nowt else from this village.'

He gave a sharp inclination with his head towards

Kisaiya and after a swift glance at Polly Anna, she followed him.

'Ungrateful cur,' the parson growled.

Jack turned as he reached the gate. 'Thank you, Mr Dowson, sir. We'll not forget your help this night.'

'Wait!' Polly Anna called. 'Wait for me.' She turned to Charles Dowson. 'Thank you,' she said simply. 'You have been a real friend and I won't ever forget your kindness or Mrs Dowson's.'

'Nonsense, my dear. You are welcome to any help we can give you.' He was clearly embarrassed. 'I know it can't be easy for you up there.' He pointed in the direction of Beck House. 'So any time you want to escape, you come to us. You're always welcome, especially by a certain young fellow, but I expect you know that already? Now, come along. I'll escort you back.'

'There's no need, thank you,' she said. 'I'll catch up with Kisaiya and Jack. They'll wait for me as they always have.' She put out her hand. 'Goodbye, and thank you.'

Puzzled he took her hand. 'Good night my dear, and don't forget what I said.'

They travelled in silence back to the meadow, Jack carrying Floure in his arms. 'We're not stopping any longer,' he said bluntly to Polly Anna. 'This is onny beginning. They'll find some other way of getting rid of us.'

'I know,' she said. 'But wait for me. Give me half an hour to write a note to Grandmother and get changed out of these clothes. Then we'll go.'

'Polly Anna!' Kisaiya was shocked. 'You don't have to come. What will they think up at the house?'

353

'I don't know,' she said softly, 'but I'm not wanted up there, any more than you are wanted down here, so we'll go together.'

'But Mr Crossley! What will he say? He'll miss you.'

'Perhaps he will,' she murmured. And I'll miss him. She gave a small sad smile in the darkness, but it can't be helped, as Grandmother would say.

She rode back up the drive and fastening up the Pinto to a post she went in by the kitchen door. 'Could I have a little bread and cheese to give to the Romanies?' she asked the cook. 'Or anything that's left over.'

'Miss Paulina, you've had no supper. Will you have a slice of rabbit pie?'

She gave a sudden laugh. 'I couldn't possibly face it, Cook, thank you. Just make up a parcel for the Romanies will you and leave it by the back door, and I'll take it to them.' She paused by the door. 'Where did the rabbit come from?'

'The Gypsy fellow brought it yesterday. He'd just caught it, he said. By it was a grand 'un. Firm and plump – he has a knack for catching 'em.'

Polly Anna slipped up the backstairs and along the corridor which the servants used, and into her room. There she changed out of her riding habit, taking off everything but her petticoat and boots. She searched in the bottom of her closet and brought out her old skirt which she had arrived in so many months ago, and was glad that she hadn't allowed the servants to throw it away as they had wanted to do. Her shirt though had gone, it had been threadbare and worn, and she searched through the rails for one to wear in its place. She found one in white linen, which though of a superior quality from what she had previously been used to, was plain and would be hard wearing. She pulled out a warm shawl and wrapped it around her shoulders, hastily scribbled a letter to her grandmother, who would be arriving back tomorrow, saying she was sorry to leave her. 'I'm beginning to love you, Grandmother,' she wrote, 'but I don't think that I will ever fit in here. I am a Romany's daughter and there are some who will never accept me. It will cause you conflict and pain if I should stay.'

She sealed the letter firmly and placed it on the table by the window. She wrote another letter to Richard: 'Dear Mr Crossley, I can't explain why I am leaving, but I thank you so much for your kindness and friendship towards me, and trust that you will not think too badly of me for leaving without saying goodbye. I wish you much happiness in your life. Polly Anna.'

A tight band of emotion wrapped itself around her as she wrote and she swallowed hard. This is harder even than leaving Jonty. She blinked away a tear and took a deep breath. I shall miss him more than I imagined. We have had such pleasurable times together. The rides into the country, the discussions when we discovered so many things about the other. This letter too she sealed and placed beside the other.

Again she crept down the rear staircase and past the kitchen where she could hear the kitchen staff at their supper. She picked up the parcel of food, which had been placed as she asked on a stool at the back door, unfastened the Pinto and whispering to him that soon he would have a feed and rest, she mounted and with one backward glance at the house, shrouded in darkness save for one lamp burning in Rowena's room and the flickering shadows of firelight in the downstairs rooms, she cantered away.

31

Jack had packed their belongings; the canvas which made the covering for the bender was laid across Kisaiya's pony, and their cooking pans and implements were strapped to a pack across his back. Polly Anna had nothing to carry so she took Floure up with her on the Pinto. They moved quietly off down the lane and through the village and there was not so much as a lift of a curtain or a bark of a dog as they passed.

'We'll get out of the district and travel for an hour,' Jack said, 'and then we'll pitch for the night.'

Polly Anna was grateful to rest when they did stop. The day had been long, for she had ridden all day with Rowena, neither had she eaten since breakfast and was glad of the food which she had begged from the kitchen. She curled up next to Floure and fell asleep as soon as she had eaten and drunk the tea which Kisaiya made and heard only the soft murmur of their voices.

Kisaiya shook her awake as dawn was breaking and she sat up and shivered. 'Is it time to go?'

'Jack says we must make tracks now before

anyone knows that you've gone or else they might come after you.'

Polly Anna gave a wistful grimace. 'They won't. The maids will think I am out riding. They won't miss me until at least noon. And no-one else will care,' she added softly.

'We'll still get off, anyway.' Jack stood outside the bender. 'The sooner we're out of here the better.'

'I'm sorry, Jack. It's my fault you've had this trouble.' She looked up at him through the tent flap. 'I do appreciate what you've done for me.'

'Hmph. You're beginning to sound like that lot up there! Their talk's rubbed off already.' His manner was brusque. 'You sure you want to travel wi' us?'

'Jack!' Kisaiya warned disapprovingly. 'She didn't have to come.'

'Get ready, *mushi*,' he said walking away. 'Don't waste time.'

They ate a little bread, packed up again and moved off. Yellowhammers were darting in and out of the hedgerows and a flock of geese flew over their heads heading towards the Humber, reminding Polly Anna of something that Morgan had once said when she had first met him, of all travellers needing a winter feeding ground. Well, I have been to my feeding ground, she thought, and now I must move on again. I have a living to make. I have nothing in the world, very little money, no food, the clothes I am wearing, and my only friends are the Romanies. She caught Jack looking at her and she knew that he considered her an encumbrance. Yet he would take care of her as he had promised. As he had promised Kisaiya and his father. It would be a matter of honour to him. But should she let him honour that promise? No, she decided. I think not. I have to let them go.

Ogden had told her that he was going on to Sheffield and then Newark with his circus, but that was many weeks ago, he would have moved on to other towns since then. When they stopped at noon, she asked the question. 'Jack, will you travel with me as far as Newark?' Nottingham and Newark she knew were the limit of their travelling, these Romanies rarely went out of the area and spent their year at the fairs and markets in the northern towns and villages. 'Then I'll go on after Ogden; someone will know where he is.'

Jack nodded. 'He might have been at Loughborough Winter Fair in February, somebody will know.' He looked rather relieved, she thought, at the prospect of turning back.

'Or Leicester,' Kisaiya broke in. 'There's a big fair there in March, but Polly Anna – we can't leave you alone. Come back with us. Travel with the Romanies.'

'Aye,' Jack interrupted. 'You could. It'd be all right now.' He looked away from her. 'There'd be no trouble from anybody.' Then he turned to her and gave a sudden grin, which made his usually brooding face seem quite handsome. 'We'd find you a *Romano rye* to keep you occupied!'

She laughed with them. 'No, thank you! I'm not ready yet to settle down with husband and *chavvies*. But I want you to go back soon. Kisaiya will need her mother, and I—'

Who do I need? she pondered. I don't like the thought of being alone, but there is no-one. She felt suddenly lost and vulnerable. No Jonty to care for her, no Richard to guide her through the intricacies of genteel life. No loving hand to take hers. She felt a sharp pang of envy as she saw Kisaiya and Jack standing close together with Floure holding on to her mother's skirt. 'I,' she said in a cheerful bright manner, 'I am going to be Mademoiselle Paulina, the famous equestrienne.'

'Did you have a good journey, ma'am?' A maid took Mrs Winthrop's cloak and bonnet. 'The weather is very pleasant.'

'But the roads are as bumpy as ever. My poor old bones are suffering.' Mrs Winthrop sighed. 'But it's good to be home.'

'I'll bring you a pot of chocolate, ma'am, that'll soon revive you.'

'And I'll take a drop of brandy with it,' she said as she hobbled towards the morning room where a bright fire could be seen. 'Is Miss Winthrop about? Or my granddaughter?'

'Miss Winthrop hasn't been down, ma'am. I sent luncheon up to her room and Miss Paulina must have gone out early. She wasn't in for breakfast or luncheon.'

'Well, tell my daughter that I am home and when Miss Paulina comes back tell her that I'd like to speak to her.'

She settled herself by the fire, drawing up a footstool to rest her feet and when Rowena came in ten minutes later she was sipping on a cup of hot chocolate into which she had tipped a small brandy.

Rowena gave her mother a peck on her cheek. 'A good journey, Mother? Nothing untoward?'

'Uneventful. The corn is coming up nicely I noticed and Parkinson's flock has grown considerably since I was last over that way.' She nodded complacently. 'It's good to be back, there's nothing really to notice in the town, you know, except for people and buildings, oh – and ships I suppose, in the Humber.'

'Aunt Cecily? Is she well?' Rowena asked only out of courtesy. She had nothing in common with her town aunt. 'Still doing her good works amongst the poor?'

'Yes,' her mother replied thoughtfully. 'She is. She took me to look at the Hull workhouse.'

'Why on earth would she do that?'

Her mother raised her eyebrows. 'Because I asked her to! Why else would I go?'

Rowena shuffled uneasily. 'What a very strange request.'

'Not at all,' her mother rebuked. 'The only reason I went to see Cecily was to ask if she knew anything about Madeleine being there.' She put her thin veined hand to her forehead. 'But she didn't. Such a dreadful place,' she muttered. 'I cannot believe that a daughter of mine should fall so low. Poor, poor Madeleine. Poor dear girl.' She looked across at Rowena and her eyes were moist. 'How could it happen, Rowena? Tell me, how could it?'

'How would I know, Mother?' Her voice was edgy. 'You keep asking me and I can't tell – I don't know!'

The old lady sighed. 'I'm sorry. If only I knew. Where is Paulina?' she asked abruptly. 'She wasn't in for luncheon.'

Rowena shrugged. 'I haven't seen her since

yesterday when we rode across to Wharram.'

'You rode to Wharram! Good heavens, aren't you getting too old for such a long trek?' She stared keenly at her daughter. 'That's where you and Madeleine used to ride when you were young!'

Rowena lifted her head. 'Yes. I thought I would show her our old haunts. The places where we used to ride before – before—'. She stopped abruptly. 'And no, Mother. I am not too old. I arrived back first.'

'You never left her?' Her mother's eyes flashed. 'You didn't try out that silly game that you and Madeleine—?'

Rowena gave a short laugh. 'It's all right. She found her way back.'

Mrs Winthrop sipped at her chocolate and remained silent. Then as if she had bethought herself, said, 'The Gypsies have gone. There's no fire in the meadow and no tent or horses.'

'Really! Well, thank goodness for that. There was some trouble with them yesterday, they must have decided to move off.'

'What sort of trouble? With the villagers?'

'Something to do with them stealing a rabbit.' Rowena put her hand to her mouth and yawned. 'I don't know or care.'

'But they have permission to catch rabbits, here and on Charles's land. Why would they steal someone else's?' She put down her cup, and rather unsteadily got up and looked out of the window towards the meadow. 'How very odd. Where is Paulina?' she asked for a second time and on receiving only a negative shrug from Rowena, rang the bell.

'I was just coming to tell you, ma'am.' The maid was flustered. 'I sent Sally up to Miss Paulina's room and she found these. She said she hadn't noticed them this morning.'

Mrs Winthrop put up her hand to take the envelopes and after reading the names on them opened the one addressed to her. Her face grew pale and distressed. 'She's gone,' she whispered. 'Rowena, she's gone. Where can she have gone?' She rubbed her fist across her chest as if in pain. 'Dear God,' she exclaimed. 'Not a second time. I can't bear it! Send for Mr Dowson,' she demanded. 'No – Mr Crossley – both of them! And Mrs Dowson. Tell them to come at once!'

'Yes ma'am.' The maid scurried to the door. 'But I understand that Mr Crossley is away at present.'

'Well, fetch somebody and be quick about it! We must fetch her back.'

'She may not want to come back, Mother,' Rowena said idly. 'She's probably gone off with the Gypsies; you said their camp was gone.' There was a gleam in her eye that her mother couldn't comprehend. 'Perhaps we should check the silver.'

'Check the silver?' her mother said blankly. 'You can't mean that, Rowena? Are you glad that she's gone?'

Rowena shrugged. 'I'm glad that the Gypsies have gone, anyway. They were a constant reminder of what happened before.'

'But the Gypsies were never here before.' Her mother was puzzled. 'When were they here?'

'Before Madeleine went away. I saw him in the village one day.' Rowena spoke in such a soft voice that her mother could hardly hear her. 'He'd come looking for Madeleine.'

'He?' her mother questioned.

'Paul Lee,' she whispered. 'I saw him and he saw me. I knew then that she would go with him.'

Her mother stared at her. 'There's more to this than you are saying. I think that you have driven Paulina away.' She handed the letter to her. 'Read it! It's you she's meaning when she says that there are some who will never accept her. Isn't it?' she demanded, her voice angry. 'Isn't it?'

'Yes,' she shouted. 'It is. We have built a life of sorts without Madeleine. I have come to terms with my spinsterhood, and now, she – she has come back again to ruin everything once more.'

'Come back again? I don't understand. Rowena! Come here and explain yourself.' But she had gone, sweeping out of the room and rushing up the stairs, leaving the door wide open.

They sent men out looking for her, but no-one in the village or surrounding hamlets had seen her or the Gypsies, though word was heard of a band of Gypsies travelling towards the Pocklington road. Charles Dowson sent a letter to Richard Crossley at his parents' home asking him to return immediately, but he arrived the following evening, unaware of the furore that was taking place until he stepped through the door of Warren House and his aunt greeted him with the news.

'But why should she take it into her head to go?' he asked. 'She seemed happy enough. I asked her if she could live here always and she said – she said—' He trailed off vaguely.

'What did she say, dear?' His aunt gave a little nod of encouragement. 'She didn't think you were asking—?'

'What?' His anxiety made him irritable. 'She said something about not being welcome at Beck House! Something about Rowena.'

'Ah,' his aunt said meaningfully. 'I might have known.'

He had travelled by coach from London to York and then hired a mount for the rest of the journey, he was tired and thirsty, but nevertheless called for a mount and rode off to Beck House immediately. Only Mrs Winthrop was there, Rowena had apparently kept to her room since her altercation with her mother.

'Will you speak to Rowena, Mr Crossley? I'm not blaming her for what has happened but I am angry because something has gone on between them.' The old lady was clearly upset but had rallied round, continuing as far as possible with her daily duties, and not retiring to her bed in distress as Richard thought she was quite entitled to do.

'I'll come tomorrow to speak to Miss Rowena and try to find out what happened,' he said, 'and then I'll set off to look for Polly Anna. It might take some time so you must try not to worry. I think I might know where she has gone.'

'Your friendship with my granddaughter is quite informal, Mr Crossley,' Mrs Winthrop commented, though not in a critical manner. 'You call her by her old name, the one she used in the workhouse. Does she prefer it, do you think?'

'It was the name I first knew her by.' His cheeks flushed a little at his indiscretion. 'I beg your pardon, I did not intend to be too familiar. Though', he explained, 'she isn't used to formality. It seems a little unnecessary in view of the life she has led. Whether she prefers it, I don't know. She would perhaps find it strange if perhaps you or my aunt, say, called her by that name.'

'What are your intentions, Mr Crossley?'

The question came abruptly and he was taken aback. 'I – erm, I shall ride to Pocklington and then on to—'

'I don't mean that as you very well know. I mean your intentions towards Paulina, if you should find her,' she added quietly. 'For we don't know if you will.'

'I shall find her, Mrs Winthrop. I won't come back until I do. And then – then I shall ask your permission to ask her to marry me, if she will have me. I have been to my parents' house especially to tell them.'

'And how did they react to the idea of your marrying a wild Gypsy maiden?'

He smiled at her intended witticism. 'They remembered Miss Madeleine very well. They described her as spirited, yet always a lady. They were sure that her daughter would have some of her attributes. They raised no objections.'

'And do you think that you can tame Paulina and make her a lady, should she consent to your proposal?'

He looked shocked. 'I have no intention of even trying. Her charm is in her being as she is.' His face became animated as he realized he had no longer any reason to hide his feelings. 'She is like the first breath of spring after winter.'

Mrs Winthrop gazed at him for a moment, then her rheumy old eyes became misty. 'Sweet love of youth,' she said softly. 'You do well to capture it, Mr Crossley. It is not within everyone's gift. Guard it well.'

32

The next morning he rose early and gathered together the possessions he would need. A waterproof cape in case of rain, a blanket in case of the cold, and a square of canvas to make a tent, for perhaps, he thought, as he remembered his journey to Appleby, I might not always be able to find lodgings. He searched out a woollen shirt and cord breeches such as he wore when visiting the farms on the estate, and a tweed jacket. For his head he had a felt hat with a battered and droopy brim.

He chose the mount he would need and told the stable lad to make sure it was well shod and ready for a long journey and after breakfast he mounted another and rode to Beck House to talk to Rowena.

A groom was waiting outside with a horse for Rowena; it was skittish and shied when he tied up his own horse to the rail next to it. He thought that she would be still at breakfast, but she had already taken breakfast, alone, for her mother was still in bed. She was in the morning room, fully dressed in her riding habit and drawing on her gloves to go out.

'I'm glad I've caught you,' he said pleasantly. 'I'm just off to search for Miss Paulina.'

'A party has been out already.' Her voice cut like a knife. 'They couldn't find her, why should you?'

'Because I want to find her,' he said bluntly, 'and to bring her back. If she'll come.'

She gave a sarcastic snort. 'She's like her mother, she prefers the company of Gypsies. She won't come back.'

He gazed at her. 'But her mother did, didn't she?' he asked quietly. 'Madeleine did come back and brought Polly Anna.'

Rowena's mouth dropped and her face paled. 'What do you mean? I don't know what you are talking about.'

'I think you do, Miss Winthrop. Polly Anna had been here before. That day I first brought her here I could tell by her manner that she knew you. There was something she said. Something I didn't quite catch – about you. She called you Aunt Wena, the sort of name that a child would pronounce.'

Rowena stared coldly at him. 'I think you should go, Mr Crossley. I don't know what your insinuations mean but I do not care for the implication.'

'The implication, Miss Winthrop, is that your sister came here with her child and you turned them away.' He saw her blanch and knew that his assumptions were correct. 'You turned them away and by doing so you effectively sent your sister to her death.' He was harsh but felt no sympathy for her as she stared back at him, devoid it seemed of any emotion.

'Why?' he asked passionately. 'Why did you? Were you jealous of the love she had shared with her husband?' She didn't answer and he pressed further, remembering something that Jennings had said. 'Or was it more than that? Were you jealous of her? Perhaps you wanted him for yourself? You had been there at that first meeting at Appleby.'

'How dare you?' she spat. 'How dare you?'

'I dare because I think it is true,' he said quietly, 'and I don't want the same thing to happen again, not to Polly Anna. She has had enough distress in her life.'

'Get out!' She pointed to the door. 'And don't ever come back.'

He gave a small bow and turned to go. 'I won't,' he said, 'at least not at your invitation. Nor will I bring Polly Anna here when I find her. There is a welcome for her elsewhere.'

She started at the significance of his statement, then said angrily, 'She will never be accepted in society. You will both be ostracized!'

'Only by people like you, Miss Winthrop,' he gave another small, formal bow, 'and that is of no significance whatsoever.'

She rushed to the window as he left the house and watched him mount. 'How dare he?' she stormed. 'How dare he say such things to me?'

'Because they are true, aren't they, Rowena?'

She whirled round and saw her mother standing by the door. 'I heard,' Mrs Winthrop said wearily. 'At least as much as I needed to.'

Rowena put her head up. 'Yes,' she said defiantly, 'it is true. She did come back with that child, begging to come back, and I didn't let them in! She had made her choice.'

'But the Gypsy? He was dead. Had you no feeling of compassion?'

'She had had his love! What had I had? Nothing!' Her face suddenly crumpled. 'He didn't even notice me. He only saw Madeleine.'

'But, my dear,' her mother's voice was shaky, 'you wouldn't have gone with him even if he'd asked you. You wouldn't have given up everything for love as Madeleine did. Not your comfort or your place in society.'

Rowena lowered her head, 'No. I wouldn't,' she whispered. 'But I would have liked to have been asked.'

'It wasn't to be,' her mother said gently. 'He loved Madeleine and she loved him.'

Rowena looked up. She was trembling, her face working in anguish. 'Yes,' she said. 'And now she is dead and I killed her. That's what Richard Crossley said and it's true.'

'No,' her mother cried. 'No. He didn't mean it like that. Fetch him back, Rowena. Explain how it was.'

Tears started to stream down Rowena's face. 'Explain how it was? That I was jealous of a common Gypsy who loved my sister? And be a laughing stock just as she was? Never!'

She stormed out of the door. 'Never,' she shouted and her voice echoed through the hall and around the house. 'Never! Never! Never!'

The horse reared as she snatched the reins from the groom's hand and she pushed him away as he tried to help her mount. 'I can manage,' she cried, yet mounted clumsily as the horse, unsettled by her anger, skittered and shied and the groom tried to calm him.

'Careful, Miss Winthrop. He's lively this morning.'

'Don't tell *me* how to ride! I can teach you any time and I'll teach him too.' She lifted her crop and thwacked the horse on its rump. It whinnied and reared almost unseating her. She recovered and thwacked it again, digging in her heels and setting off at a gallop. They cleared the low hedge dividing the gardens from the meadows and headed towards the beck and the hedge beyond.

The groom pushed back his hat and watched. Then he broke into a run and shouted. 'Miss! Tek it steady! They'll nivver mek it,' he muttered as he chased after her. 'That hoss don't like watter and t'beck's running strong. He'll buck at it, bet any money on it.'

Richard, trotting along the lane towards Warren House, heard the shout and looked back up the meadow. He saw the groom at the top of the meadow and Rowena galloping towards the beck. He saw the horse come to the swiftly running stream and with its forefeet firmly locked to the ground refuse the jump and Rowena thrown straight out of the saddle to land in the middle of the beck.

He jumped down and, hooking the reins around a tree branch, crashed through the hedge, feeling the sharp hawthorn catching on his clothes; it was quicker for him to cut across the meadow on foot than to ride back along the lane and up the drive again, and he reached Rowena's still form just after the groom.

'I warned her to be careful, sir. But she was in

372

such a state wi' hersen she wouldn't listen.'

'Never mind that. Run up to the house and ask them to send for a doctor, then bring a door or something flat – and bring Jennings,' he called after him, 'or one of the other men.'

Richard didn't attempt to move her by himself; she was lying very still with the water rushing over her, a deep cut on her forehead and her body twisted in such a manner that he was fearful for her life. He took hold of her hand and lifted it from the water. It was cold and limp. 'Miss Winthrop, Rowena.' He rubbed her hand gently. 'Rowena,' but there was no response and he felt a sudden rush of guilt as he recalled their harsh parting words.

Jennings took her shoulders and one of the other men took her feet whilst Richard, with the water rushing over his boots, put both arms beneath her waist and hips to support her weight and they carefully put her on to the wooden door and carried her back to the house and her waiting mother.

'I'm afraid it looks bad, sir,' Richard murmured and turned from his uncle to his aunt, sitting opposite him in the carriage as they made all speed to Beck House, from where he had ridden furiously to fetch them. 'You must prepare for the worst, Aunt Mary. I fear her back may be broken.'

His aunt put her head back against the cushions and applied her smelling salts to her nose. 'So headstrong,' she whispered, 'so impetuous.'

'Yes,' her husband agreed. 'She was always rash, acted first and regretted it later. Same with her tongue,' he added. 'She would always speak in anger. We've all felt its lash at some time or other – never mellowed – not even in middle age.'

A temporary bed had been made in the morning room as it was considered unsafe to carry Rowena upstairs. The doctor had been sent for but had not yet arrived and her mother sat by her bedside, her face impassive though her hands clasped and unclasped in her anxiety.

'Mr Crossley.' She looked up as Richard and Charles and Mary quietly entered the room. 'I thought you had already gone on your journey.'

'No, ma'am. Not yet. I have delayed it for the time being or at least until the doctor has been.' He looked down at her lined face which seemed to have become so much older, and felt so sorry for her in her trouble and partly responsible for Rowena's mishap. He tried to say as much but she hushed him.

'Do not censure yourself, Mr Crossley. I have told Rowena many times that she would kill herself one of these days. She must take the responsibility for her actions.'

'Mrs Winthrop!' he said earnestly. 'I don't think you understand how serious this is. Rowena could – could—'

'Die!' She returned his gaze frankly. 'I do understand. I may be old but I am not unaware of the situation. She once brought a horse down in her temper and we had to have it shot. My late husband died from the results of an accident. Do not imagine that I don't know that my worst fears could be realized at any time.' She looked down at her papery thin hands and adjusted the lace frill around her wrists and said softly, 'It will be a pity though, if both my daughters should go on before me.'

He nodded dumbly and turned his gaze to Rowena, lying so pale and still. What a brave old lady she was, so stoical in the face of such tragedy, her sorrow hidden from the view of others.

'So you'd better get off at once,' her voice intruded on his thoughts, 'and bring my grand-daughter back as soon as you can, or I shall have no-one.'

'But,' he stammered, 'I'd rather wait until the doctor has been. To know the prognosis.'

'The longer you wait the more difficult it will be to find her,' she said firmly. 'Look how long it took before.'

'Another day won't hurt, Harriet,' Charles broke in. 'They won't have gone far. Not three of them and a child.'

So he waited another day, and then another and another and Rowena still lay, unmoving, barely breathing and unconscious of all that went on around her. Mrs Winthrop fretted that he delayed, but he insisted that he would find Polly Anna no matter how long it took. His reason for staying on was simple, he was riddled with guilt over his harsh words and wanted Rowena to awaken and say that she did not blame him.

It was a week before she did and then so wracked with pain was she that they all wished for her uncon-sciousness again. The doctor came every day and gave her opium, which brought only a hazy relief from the pain in her back and did nothing for the numbness in her legs.

'What happened, Mother? Did I come off my horse?'

Her mother nodded. 'You did, my dear. At the beck.'

'And the horse?' she whispered. 'Is he all right?'

'Yes,' said her mother. 'He threw you.'

'Ah! I was probably riding him too hard.' She closed her eyes and winced. 'Ask the doctor if I can have another dose. I can't bear the pain.'

Her mother unscrewed the bottle which was kept by the bed and poured a few drops of the tincture on to a spoon. 'He said you could have it whenever you asked for it.'

'Did he? That doesn't sound very good, does it? What's the matter with my legs?'

'There's nothing the matter with your legs, Rowena. It's your back. I'm afraid it's broken.'

'So when and where will you start, Richard? There is no sense in delaying now. Rowena isn't going to improve so you might as well get off straight away.' Richard's uncle poured a sherry for his wife and brandies for himself and Richard.

'I shall start first thing in the morning and head towards West Yorkshire. I have a feeling that is where she will have gone.'

'Why so sure, Richard?' his aunt asked. 'Is that where the Gypsies will be?'

'No. I don't think she'll stay with the Gypsies. I think she will go back to the fair people or the circus. She has a friend, Jonty, of whom she is fond. I think she will look for him.' And I hope that I find her first, he worried. If she takes up with him again she might not want to leave.

'What sort of a friend is he?' Aunt Mary sat up in interest.

'He looked after her when they were children in the workhouse. He – cared for her.'

'You mean – like a brother and a sister, as the Gypsies call each other?'

He ran his fingers over his chin and felt the stubble. He had started to grow a beard in readiness for his journey. 'Something of the sort, Aunt. Though I understand the Gypsies only say that to those of their blood.' And Jonty isn't of Polly Anna's blood and he doesn't think of her as his sister. That much I surmised without too much intelligence. And he remembered Jonty's last words that he should run for his life if harm should befall her.

'Well, I don't know if I would agree with you,' Charles boomed. 'I think she might stay with the Gypsies. After all, they stayed with her all the winter. They never left, though they could have done. It's as if they knew she wouldn't be staying here.'

'What are you saying, Charles?' Mary's eyes widened. 'That they knew what was going to happen?'

'Don't be ridiculous, Mary! You know very well I don't mean that. How could they know?'

'It's just that—'. She hesitated. 'There's a rumour going around the servants that the Gypsy woman cursed Rowena when she refused to help with that bother over the rabbit.'

Her husband grunted scornfully, but Richard shook his head. 'She wouldn't,' he said. 'She seemed a gentle kind of person.'

'Ah, but—', said his aunt, lowering her voice. 'One of the maids heard her muttering some strange words that she couldn't understand, that even Paulina didn't understand! You must admit it is very odd.'

'The only odd thing is that Rowena should tear

around the countryside as if she's a young woman instead of the middle-aged woman that she is,' Charles humphed. 'But she's learned her lesson now. My word but she has.'

'I'm finished, Mother. Do you realize? I shan't get up from this bed again.'

Mrs Winthrop sat next to Rowena's bedside, her hands stitching at a piece of embroidery. 'Yes, I do realize, Rowena, and I'm very sorry my dear. So very sorry.'

'I suppose you would say that it's my own fault?' Rowena's voice was quite clear, for the moment the pain had abated. 'That I brought this on myself?'

'I think that we cannot blame anyone else, although you were obviously upset and perhaps I am as much to blame for that as anyone. I speak too plainly at times.'

'I would like to speak to Richard Crossley.' Rowena stared at her mother. 'I have something to say to him.'

'You are not to blame him,' her mother admonished. 'He is most upset at what has happened and so sorry for the accusations, as he calls them, that he expressed.'

Rowena gave a slight laugh, which changed to a groan as the insidious pain came to taunt her. 'Such a gentleman!' she winced. 'It must be the very first time he has spoken in anger. How it must hurt him now. How his conscience must trouble him; whereas I have never given a thought to words which I have said in haste.'

'I think that that is probably untrue, Rowena.'

Her mother's tone was assured. 'I do not believe that in your quiet moments you have not had some regrets.'

Rowena was silent for a moment before saying, 'Perhaps.'

Mrs Winthrop stitched at her needlework, her fingers were stiff and held the needle with difficulty, so she laid it down in a measure of relief when Rowena repeated, 'I would like to speak to him, Mother. Will you send for him please?'

'Now?' Richard said when the message came. 'She wants to see me now? Tonight?'

'Yes, sir. Mrs Winthrop was most definite about it.' Jennings had been sent with the message. It was late, dark and wet and he stood on the mat in the hall of Warren House with rain dripping from the brim of his hat.

'Miss Winthrop isn't worse, is she?' he asked anxiously.

'I don't know sir, t'maids say she's in a bad way but more than that I can't say.'

They rode silently back down the lane, the cold rain lashing through the trees and he thought grimly of his journey the next morning. Then he bethought himself of Polly Anna and wondered if she was dry and safe, and what would she do for food? As far as he was aware, she didn't have any money of her own.

'I hear you're off tomorrow, sir. I was wondering if you wanted some company? Mrs Winthrop would let me go I'm sure, if you requested it.'

'Thank you, Jennings, but I'd rather travel alone. I don't know how long I'll be gone, you see. Or where my journey will take me. I shall ride to the

West of Yorkshire first and ask the fair people if they have seen Miss Paulina.'

Jennings expressed surprise. 'I heard they'd been seen below Holme on Spalding Moor, sir. On t'Howden road. They've dropped down too low if she was heading for t'West Riding. They'd have gone over towards York. I reckon they're mekkin' for t'horse fairs to meet up wi' other Gypsies.'

'Do you?' Here was a dilemma. He could waste so much time if he set off in the wrong direction. Yet he was so sure that she would go to Jonty. 'Where will the horse fairs be?'

'Well, there's one at Howden, but that's not till middle of April so there's a week or two to go yet, though they'll be gathering I shouldn't wonder. But you could try Selby, there's a fair there on Easter Tuesday and there's bound to be some Gypsies about. You might strike lucky, and if not you can still cut across towards Leeds or Bradford.'

He dismounted at the door and Jennings took the reins. 'Don't stable him,' he said. 'I don't expect to be long.' I shall be given a flea in my ear, I expect and have to make my apology, he ruminated. But I am sorry, though sorrier for what happened as the result of my remarks than for what I said, for I still maintain it was essentially true.

A nurse was sitting by the bed when he arrived but she left the room, and Rowena said, 'Thank you for coming so promptly, Richard. Won't you take a seat – no, over here where I can see you. I have difficulty in turning my head.'

'I'm glad to see you at least partially improved, Miss Winthrop,' he said awkwardly. 'I trust you will soon make a good recovery.'

'Not much chance of that,' she said bluntly. 'This is my life from now on and I don't care for the flavour of it.' She looked at him from dark, shadowed eyes. 'I want to ask you something.'

'Could I – could I first of all say how sorry I am that our last meeting was so acrimonious,' he interrupted, 'and how distressed I am over your accident.'

She gave a wry smile. 'But if I hadn't had this accident you wouldn't have regretted your remarks?'

He took a deep breath. 'No. No, I wouldn't.'

She closed her eyes and sighed. 'Good,' she said, opening them. 'An honest man. That's what I like. A woman can get away with a little dishonesty or subterfuge but I do like a man to be ethical.'

'Miss Winthrop—'

'No, I must do the talking whilst I am free of pain. You were correct of course in your assumptions. I was jealous of Madeleine.' She turned her head slowly so that she was looking at the wall and not at him. 'My younger sister who had found love before I did. But the worst thing was that I found him attractive too.' Her voice cracked and she whispered. 'A Gypsy! He was alien to anyone I had ever known; he had no finesse, no breeding, no manners that I could see, yet he had an exotic, mysterious quality which attracted me.' Her voice dropped even lower. 'I am ashamed to say that he brought out base instincts that I didn't know I had.'

Richard coloured and cleared his throat. 'I think there is no shame in that, Miss Winthrop. We all have them, they are simply kept hidden away.'

She turned her head back towards him and he could see the pain in her eyes though whether it was physical or the result of her confession he couldn't tell. 'It is as well they are hidden, Richard. Civilized society would fall apart otherwise.'

He stiffened. She was going to say something against Polly Anna. She hadn't changed her views.

'I want you to find Paulina,' she said softly and he gave a small gasp of amazement. 'I want you to find her and bring her back here. I still think that she will be ostracized by some members of society, but as you so forcibly said, it is of no consequence. Will you pass my medication,' she said breathlessly. 'One teaspoonful, quickly.'

He poured the tincture on to the spoon and gently slipped it into her mouth. 'Thank you,' she breathed. 'What was I saying?' She closed her eyes for a moment and grimaced, then continued. 'Will you tell her that I am sorry? Sorry for what happened in the past, and for what happened since; but when I saw her at the door I knew that I would be constantly reminded of them both and I just couldn't bear it!'

A tear trickled down her cheek and she blinked them away as they welled in her eyes. 'This is my punishment. I was wicked to send Madeleine away. I loved her so much you know. And I missed her terribly after she'd gone. If I'd known what would happen – the workhouse—'. She swallowed hard. 'So you will find Paulina and tell her? Tell her I'm sorry, because I might not be here when you get back for me to tell her myself.'

The nurse came back when Richard made his

departure, to make her comfortable for the night. She gave her a drink and adjusted the pillow beneath her neck. 'How is the pain, Miss Winthrop?'

'Very bad,' she said. 'Time for my dose, please.'

33

They made frequent stops on their journey and Polly Anna could tell that Kisaiya was sickly, though she made no complaints but simply took herself off into the bushes, from where she would appear five minutes later looking pale and wan.

On one such occasion Polly Anna spoke to Jack about it, though she thought that he would not welcome the conversation. 'I think we should part company at Howden, Jack. Kisaiya is not well, the journey to Newark will be too much for her.'

To her surprise he agreed. 'She has a difficult time with childbearing,' he said awkwardly, 'but she'll want to come with you. She promised.'

'I won't hold her to that promise. We'll go to Howden, where you can meet with the other Romanies and if you'll show me the road to Newark I'll go on alone.'

He grunted. 'How will you manage? Have you money for food? You've no bender and you're a woman alone. I would be shamed in front of my family if I allowed it.'

She considered. He had his pride, so important

to a Romany. 'Will there be Romanies travelling south, do you think? If there are, perhaps you could arrange for me to travel part of the way with them, and there are bound to be fairground travellers on the road now.'

He nodded. 'The fairs and marts are starting now that winter is over. There'll be small fit-ups in some of the towns.'

'And they'll know where Ogden is,' she said eagerly. 'I shall be all right, really I will.'

'All right when?' Kisaiya came up behind them. She wiped her mouth on her shawl. 'What are you planning, *Sister*? You're not leaving us?'

Polly Anna smiled. She might have known that she couldn't hide anything from Kisaiya. 'After Howden,' she said. 'I want you to stay with your family; to take care of your baby,' she appealed. 'This is going to be such a good time for you, Kisaiya. I know it.'

Kisaiya nodded. 'Have you learned the art of *dukkering, Sister*, if you knows it?' But she smiled as she spoke. 'Is that how you'll earn your supper after you've left us?'

Polly Anna considered. 'I have some money left over from when I was with Johnson. I never seemed to need it when I was with Grandmother.' She pulled out a cotton bag from beneath her skirt and shook it. 'Enough for a little while, until I can earn some.'

'Come with me.' Kisaiya drew her into the tent and fished around in her pack. 'I've been making lace for the new *chavo*,' she said, handling the delicate strips of lace lovingly between her fingers. 'But I have plenty of time to make some more. Here, take it.' She pushed it all into Polly Anna's hands. 'You can sell it. It will bring someone luck.'

'Are you sure, Kisaiya? And you don't mind if I go?'

She shook her head. 'I shall miss you,' she said, 'but we shall meet again. I knows it.'

There were no Romanies travelling south when they reached Howden, they were all travelling north for the horse fairs in that region, so Jack left Kisaiya and Floure with a family of Boswells and accompanied Polly Anna on the road to Newark. They crossed the Thorne Moors and were heading for the town of that name when they caught up with a group of players from a travelling theatre. They were going on to Newark, where they had a booking for a dramatic play and were quite willing for Polly Anna to travel with them. They had two waggons and a horse and cart with space for her to ride; she fastened the Pinto behind and thankfully climbed up.

'Goodbye Jack and thank you. Take care of Kisaiya, won't you?'

He nodded. 'Aye, I will.' He raised his hand as the driver cracked the reins. 'Goodbye, *Sister.*'

She gave a small gasp and tears welled in her eyes. Acknowledgement. At last. She too raised her hand. 'Goodbye, *Brother.*'

Newark was a handsome town with the waters of the River Trent dividing here, but she wasted no time in admiring its fine church or market square, for on enquiring of Ogden's Circus she discovered it had been long gone. After asking for its direction and spending the night in a cheap lodging house with the players, she set off alone on the long road to Leicester, which she was told was its next destination. I'm weeks behind, she worried. He might well have employed some other rider and not want me after all.

She travelled on the small roads as Jack had advised her, as this was how the Romanies travelled and she met several groups, but all travelling towards the north. She greeted them and asked them to take a message to the Boswell family that she was well and progressing. She took a rest at midday and let the horse graze on the wayside and pondered that it would take her several days to reach Leicester unless she could get another lift in a waggon.

She passed through several villages and hamlets and in one when she asked at a cottage if she might have a drink, the woman asked her if she was with the fair people. 'They passed through here only yesterday,' she said, and waved away Polly Anna's offer of money for the cup of milk. 'They'll stop at Hallington, they allus do. We shall go, my man and me, we likes a spot of entertainment.'

Polly Anna thanked her and urged on the Pinto at a faster pace. If she could catch up with this small fair there might be chance of work as well as a ride. When she arrived at Hallington two hours later, she found the road blocked by waggons and sheep. The village beadle was walking up and down the road waving a stick and shouting threats at anyone who happened to be near.

'Are you with this lot?' he asked Polly Anna.

'Why? Has something happened?'

'I'll say it has,' he exploded. 'The farmers can't get in with their waggons, the sheep can't get into the market, and all because some fellow has blocked up the gate to the fair field.'

She edged her way through the bleating flock and found a fight about to commence just inside the gate. Two showmen, both wanting the same prime site were prepared to fight over it. 'I was here first, so it's my gaff,' said one. 'I've had this gaff for ten years and my father did before me,' said the other. 'So get your coat off and we'll see who has it.'

A crowd had gathered and men were placing bets, including the farmers, who leaned over the fence and sucked on their pipes, whilst over by a waggon, two women, whom Polly Anna presumed to be the showmen's wives, were settling their own score with flailing arms and flying skirts and language fit to shock sensitive ears.

'Well, well!' A voice behind Polly Anna made her jump. 'What 'you doing in this foreign country, pretty Polly?'

Amos Johnson stood grinning behind her. He carried a large leather bag and had a fistful of money in his hand. 'Bet you never thought you'd see me again, did you?'

'I never gave it any thought, Amos. You never crossed my mind.'

His grin slipped. 'I heard you'd gone off to be a lady,' he sneered. 'Did they find out about your Gypsy blood?'

'It's nothing to do with you, Amos Johnson.' She was filled with dismay. Of all the people in the world, she had to meet him.

'Just curious, that's all. I like to know what my friends are up to. I heard another rumour that you were going with Ogden, so I didn't know what to believe.'

'I'm not your friend, Amos, and you shouldn't listen to rumour.'

He shrugged and glanced over to where the fight was about to begin. 'Place your bets here,' he shouted. 'Carter versus Cotton! So where 'you going, Polly Anna? I might be able to help you. I'm branching out now, got two boxing booths – in my own name, got rid of Sharp. I'm doing all right. I'm touring the country, not stopping in the north.'

Reluctantly she said, 'I'm trying to reach Ogden. He promised me a place in his circus as an equestrienne.'

'Ah!' His eyes glittered. 'So it was true! Well, he'll be well down the country, he's battling it out with Wilds and Richardson as to who's got 'biggest circus. He's mekking for all major towns, or so I heard.'

'So where will he be now?' The question stuck in her throat, but she had to know.

'Well now, that would be telling, wouldn't it?' He glanced over at the fight, both men had bloody noses and cut lips and their wives were sitting side by side on some waggon steps, their heads between their knees. 'If you come and have a cup o' tea wi' me then I might let you look at my almanac.'

'*Dinnelo!*' She saw a gap in the flock and turned her mount towards it.

'I'm onny trying to be friendly,' he shouted after her. 'You never know when you might need a friend.'

This was only a small fair, a few fit-ups which toured the villages before meeting up in the major towns and at the bigger fairs. But there was the usual sword swallower and Thin Man and a booth with an Extraordinary Dog and a Talking Donkey. A conjuror and a juggler stood in the middle of the village street and practised a few of their tricks while a man with a penny whistle strode up and down, but the beadle couldn't let anyone in until the show-men had settled their differences and removed the waggon from the gateway.

When the dispute was finally settled there was a loud cheer and the country folk from the surrounding villages swarmed on to the site.

A portable theatre was being set up in a corner away from the main events. Two waggons were posi-tioned end to end as a stage and a painted screen with a picture of a forest and lake painted on it was placed at the rear. Over the top of the makeshift stage a roof had been made of wood and canvas, and in front of the theatre planks of wood placed on wooden boxes served for seats.

There was a man on the stage with thick white hair and a beard and wearing a long black coat to his ankles. Polly Anna called up to him. 'Can you do with any more players.'

He looked down and appraised her. 'What can you do?'

'I can ride a horse – or dance.'

'There's no room for a horse up here! What sort of dancing?'

She hesitated. Would an Indian war dance qualify as dancing? 'Any kind,' she said boldly.

He climbed down from the stage. 'Where are you from?'

'I've been with Johnson's Circus riding as an

Indian squaw. We had to act the part,' she added eagerly.

'We need a Spanish dancer for our next play, *The Spanish Princess;* or *Love, Hatred and Revenge.* Can you do that? Click your heels and tap a tambourine?'

She nodded and looked up at the painted backdrop, an English scene if ever there was one. He caught her glance and grinned and leaning over behind the waggons, brought out two dilapidated artificial palm trees. He placed them one on each side of the stage. 'There you are. Half the audience have never been out of the village, let alone to Spain. They'll never know the difference! Come on, let's see if the costume will fit. If it does you've got the job, but you'll have to give out leaflets as well and go round with the hat afterwards.'

There was another waggon which held the costumes and props and sitting in it sewing and drinking ale were two women. A tall youngish man was painting a picture on a piece of wood. 'These are Mrs Sheene and Mrs Potts, Mr Laurence Scott, who usually plays the Spanish dancer only now he refuses, and I'm Marmaduke Stanley.' He handed her a tiered skirt of red and black, a black shirt edged with a frill and a pair of shiny black leather pumps. 'Will it fit?'

'I'll make it,' she said. 'I can sew.'

'Thank Gawd for that,' said Mrs Sheene, who was already wearing her make-up for the evening performance. A black wig was lying in a heap next to her. 'Mr Scott can't sew and expects us to mend his gowns.'

Mr Scott gave her a withering look and retorted, 'And you can't paint scenery so we're evens.'

'Now, now, ladies and gentlemen,' Mr Stanley remonstrated, 'no bickering if you please. We've a show to put on.'

As dusk fell, lamps were placed on the stage. Mr Stanley started to play the fiddle, Mr Scott exhorted all to come and watch the new Grand Melodrama, never before performed, and Polly Anna stepped on to the stage and started to dance. She was barefoot as the shoes were too large, but she stamped her feet and swung her skirts and tapped the tambourine over her head. The audience cheered as she finished with a flourishing twirl of her skirts and she retired from the stage to make way for Mr Marmaduke Stanley, disguised as the villain in a black curly wig, a dyed moustache and beard, with a green satin frock coat on his person and a pair of velveteen breeches.

Polly Anna watched from the side of the stage as the play progressed. Mrs Sheene, who was rather portly, played the princess and Mrs Potts overplayed her maid with sinister overtones. Mr Scott, now in a velvet jacket and satin cravat, played the hero who rescued the princess from the villain. As she watched, Polly Anna wondered what her grandmother would make of all this. Mountebanks and charlatans the actors were often called, and the women in particular were considered to be the most inferior members of society.

Yet they are just ordinary people trying to make a living the only way they know best, Polly Anna mused. Neither worse nor better than anyone else. But Grandmother would be most ashamed if she should see me now. She felt saddened as she thought of her and missed the old lady more than she thought she would. And Mr Crossley, Richard. What would he think? I would be sorry if he thought ill of me. A sudden lump came to her throat and she wanted to cry. I really would be so very sorry.

She climbed back on to the stage for she was to end the performance, but as she danced around the stage clicking her fingers and giving sultry pouts and flashes of her lashes, she became aware of Amos standing at the back of the crowd. He was nudging the man next to him and pointing his thumb towards her in a most suggestive way. The crowd cheered as she finished and the rest of the cast came forward for their final bow. Polly Anna stood back for she was merely an introductory and finishing act and not part of the drama. Nevertheless, Mr Stanley drew her forward and she received an extra ovation from the crowd, much to the displeasure of Mrs Sheene and Mrs Potts. She took the collecting bucket around the audience and, although some sneaked off without paying, most put their hands in their pockets and gave generously.

They played for three nights and each night Amos Johnson stood in the crowd ogling her and when Mr Stanley said they were moving on and would she come with them, she was glad to leave. But in the next town, Amos was there again and for a further month as she stayed with the troupe, still he was there in the audience. She became used to the whistles and approving shouts which the men in the audience called up to her, but they were inoffensive and given without malice, but in Amos Johnson's leering glances and caterwauling innuendos and references to the Gypsies, she felt a sinister threat.

Finally she told Mr Stanley she was moving on. The nights were lighter, and now that the Pinto was well rested, she knew that she could make good progress on the road. 'I want to reach the circus,' she explained. 'I've enjoyed it here with you but I'm an equestrienne, I want to ride.'

He sighed. 'I suppose we'll have to have Mr Scott back in the role, but he's not very good as a dancer and rather slow with his changes. But never mind dear, we've enjoyed having you with us. You've brightened up the play considerably.'

'I'll go off tonight after the show,' she said, 'but please don't tell anyone where I've gone, will you?'

'You mean Amos Johnson, don't you dear. I've seen him watching you. Don't worry, I'll put him off. I'll tell him you've run away with the Gypsies.'

She laughed. 'Say that and he'll believe you. I have Gypsy blood,' she added.

'Oh, I know that, dear. I could tell straight away. That's why I knew you'd look the part. Perfect.' He patted her cheek. 'Just perfect. It's a pity you're leaving, you'd take the part of the Spanish princess much better than Mrs Sheene. If she'd let you!'

She left that night after all the lights were dimmed and the fair people and the players had gone to their beds, some sleeping in their waggons and some to lodgings in the village. She led the Pinto out of the field and through the sleeping village and mounted as she reached the main road leading south. She had money in her pocket and food, bread and cheese, in her pack. She clicked her tongue and gently dug in her heels. 'Come on then,' she whispered. 'Let's go, Pinto. It's just you and me again.'

34

The roads were busier the further south she travelled and she often had company on her journey.
Travellers going to market towns, shepherds
driving their flocks and groups of Romanies travelling to the horse fairs. She joined up with one of
these groups, who told her that she would probably
find Ogden in Northampton. 'He'll not miss out on
the fair there,' said one Gypsy. 'It's one of the best
horse fairs in the country, the town will be
swarming with folks.'

Some of the roads were rough and muddy for
there had been a lot of rain and so she decided in
some instances to use the toll roads, though she
reminded herself that Morgan would call her a
Pikey if he ever found out. But then she worried that
her money would run out before she reached
Ogden and on reaching one village she decided to
knock on a cottage door and try to sell some lace.

She rode down the village street looking for a
place where she dared call and noticed a young
woman with a baby in her arms scurrying along, her
head down and obviously in some distress, for she

could hear her sobs quite clearly. She watched her enter a cottage door and saw also, across the street and standing in a doorway, a young man who watched the woman most intently with a furrowed expression on his face.

Polly Anna waited a moment and then knocked on the cottage door. The young woman opened it; she had dried her tears, though she looked very sad. 'Will you buy a bit of Romany lace, lady?' Polly Anna began in the wheedling sing-song voice she had heard the Romany women use. 'It's lucky lace. Made by a pure Romany.'

The woman shook her head and started to close the door. 'Nothing will bring me luck. I'm made for misfortune.'

'It will bring your babby luck,' Polly Anna insisted. 'It was made lovingly with a babe in mind.' She held out the lace trimming temptingly.

'It's very pretty,' the woman acknowledged, then looking up asked, 'How did you know I had a babby?'

'I saw you come in, lady,' Polly Anna admitted. 'I saw your pretty babby and I remembered the lace.'

'An honest Gypsy!' the woman exclaimed, then added, 'can you read the leaves or palms?'

Polly Anna swallowed. What she wouldn't give for a cup of hot sweet tea. 'Aye, lady. I can. It was taught to me by my Romany sisters.'

'Then come in,' the woman said. 'I can do with the company and perhaps you can tell me something good.'

It was a one-roomed cottage and as neat as a pin. A fire was burning in the grate, the brasses were brightly polished and a cot with the sleeping baby stood in a corner out of any draughts.

The young woman bustled around and invited Polly Anna to sit down. 'My neighbours will have something to say when they see I've had a Gypsy in the house,' she murmured.

'I'm an honest Gypsy, lady, as you said yourself. You have no fear of losing anything. But tell me why you are so unhappy when you have so much,' she waved her hand around the room to include the baby.

'How do you know I'm unhappy?' The woman paused in the act of making the tea. 'I didn't say I was.'

'Give me your hand,' Polly Anna said and stretched out her own. The woman sat down without a word and put out her hand. Polly Anna stroked her fingers softly, drawing her own hand over it and then turning it over. She looked down at her palm, the skin was young and smooth as her own was, pale, though used to light work; the lines on it were fine and Polly Anna had no idea at all what they meant, but she gazed down and a silence drew over them.

'You've had unhappiness in your life,' she said softly. 'Much weeping.'

The woman nodded and tears came into her eyes. 'Aye, that I have.'

'It will end.' Polly Anna felt a warmth radiating from the woman's hand, touching her own. 'You will know happiness again.' She thought of the young man standing outside. 'More than you have known before. There is someone; someone who cares for you.'

'Oh!' the woman gasped. 'Is there?'

Polly Anna nodded. 'Be patient. It will all come right.' She drew her hand away and smiled. The woman looked brighter already. 'Now shall we try the leaves?'

The woman poured the tea and brought out a slab of sweet cake and Polly Anna ate and drank gratefully, then when they had finished she gazed down into the woman's cup. Without a doubt there was a bird in the leaves, its wings stretched in flight. 'You will go from this place,' she said, 'you will travel far away.'

'Oh!' the woman said again. 'You're right. I have to leave! My landlord says that I must. My husband died, you see, before the babby was born. He said I could stay until after the birth and then I must go. That's why I'm unhappy.'

Polly Anna nodded knowingly and brought out the lace again. 'Take a piece of lace, lady. It will bring you good fortune. I knows it.'

'I will,' she said eagerly. 'Oh I feel so much better.' She reached for her purse and Polly Anna felt a sudden pang of discomfort at taking a young widow's money. But she was heartened when she said, 'I'm not short of money, though I must be careful. My husband was a good worker, thrifty as I am myself. So how much shall I give you?'

Polly Anna shook her head. 'I don't know, lady. You must decide. Like you I am a lone woman making ends meet, though I have no warm cottage or babe to comfort me.'

The woman stared at her. 'I've never met a Gypsy like you before. You are a Gypsy?' she questioned.

'Aye, lady. I have Romany blood – but my mother was a lady.'

She made good time after the rest and refreshment and she was satisfied that she hadn't done wrong or told lies to bring the woman some comfort. She had paid her well enough and as Polly Anna had ridden away, she saw the same young man cross the road with his hat clutched in his hand, hesitate and then knock on the woman's door. I can do no more, she mused, but I feel that something will come of that. She smiled to herself and wondered if she had paved the way for a romance, then dug in her heels and trotted on.

The weather became brighter and warmer and on some nights she slept out under the trees. She bought bread and cheese and made herself a fire and didn't feel at all afraid even though she heard strange sounds in the night. One night she woke and thought she heard the trumpeting of elephants and the roar of other animals. She leaned on her elbow and threw another stick on the fire, then snuggled further under her blanket. The Pinto stamped its hooves and whinnied softly, but she decided she was dreaming and turned over and was soon asleep again.

The next day she caught up with a troupe of dwarfs and clowns travelling towards a circus in Northampton and enquired of them if it was Ogden's. They said no and that he would probably be in Cambridge. Her disappointment must have shown, for they said she was welcome to travel along with them, so once more she shared a ride in a waggon. She asked them if they knew of Amy and Dolly or any of the dwarfs from the northern region. They shook their heads; they only travelled in this part of the country and hadn't been any further north.

The following day they caught up with the circus elephants, who were moving so slowly that they overtook them. Then they passed the waggons holding the lions and tigers and Polly Anna knew that she hadn't been dreaming, that the sounds carried on the night air had been real after all.

She parted company with her new friends as they moved on to Northampton and she journeyed to Cambridgeshire. They called good luck to her as they parted and hoped that Ogden would take her. It was now the first week of June and Ogden's Circus, it would seem, was booked at Cambridge in the third week. What will I do if he doesn't want me? What if I am too late? She was tired, the journey had been long and as the last waggon containing the circus entertainers drove out of sight, she also felt very lonely.

As she crossed the lush fenlands of Cambridgeshire, she saw how different the nature of the countryside was from the rolling hills of the Yorkshire Wolds. Here in the isolated villages, straw-thatched cottages clustered around the green, whilst the medieval manor houses were timber-framed and plastered. She thought of Richard riding over his uncle's estate, of the sheep in the meadows, the boxing hares and rabbit warrens, of the views she had seen on the day she rode with Rowena and she sighed a deep, deep sigh. It could have been home.

She came upon the tail end of Ogden's Circus a few miles outside Cambridge, the last straggle of slow-moving walking entertainers. She waved to them and rode on by to catch up with the horse traffic, the show horses, the waggons, donkey carts and dogs, the high-wire artists, the lion tamers who walked alongside the cages and she felt a quickening of her pulse. At last she had almost reached her journey's end.

'Where will I find Ogden?' she enquired of the occupants of a waggon.

They pointed to the road ahead. 'He'll have made camp outside the next village. That's where we're stopping the night.'

She urged the Pinto on, anxious to know what awaited her and found the waggons and cages and a collection of tents assembled in a meadow outside the village as she had been told. She asked again where Ogden was and was directed to a waggon-house. She stopped outside it and stared. It was built of polished wood with a window and half door. At the window was a lace curtain and the door was partly open. Inside she could see a table and storage boxes for sitting on and a little cooking stove with pans on top.

She felt a lump in her throat and tears sprang to her eyes. A little house. Just like the one her father had made for her mother. Not luxurious as this one was, but plain and simple, and as she peeped inside she remembered the cosiness of it, and her mother sitting inside, sewing and singing softly to her as she lay in her own little cot.

'Yes, young woman. What can I do for you?' A man's voice broke into her reverie.

'Mr Ogden. I'm Polly Anna Lee. You said I could work in the circus. I've been a long time catching up with you, I know,' she took a deep breath, 'but I'm here now. Do you still want me?'

Ogden looked down at her and a frown creased

his forehead. 'I'd given you up,' he said. 'Where've you been?'

'Travelling,' she said. 'I didn't know where to find you. I've had to ask all the way.'

'What! You've followed me all down the country? From Hull?'

She nodded. 'Almost. I – I was delayed for a while. Do you still want me as an equestrienne? I've brought my own mount.'

He looked at the mud-spattered Pinto. 'He'll want a bit of a clean up before he goes in my circus! He looks worn out.'

'He's tired,' she said in the horse's defence. 'He'll be fine after a rest. He's the best horse ever.' She put her hand on the Pinto's neck. 'He won't let you down.'

'He'd better not,' he said gruffly, 'but plenty more where he came from if he does.' Then he grinned at her and she realized how dishevelled she must appear. 'You look as if you could do with a bit of a rest yourself. Go find yourself a pitch. The circus opens next week. You'd better be ready.'

35

Richard congratulated himself when he rode into Howden and found the Gypsies gathering for the horse fair. He rode amongst them and asked for the whereabouts of the Boswell family. When he arrived at a circle of tents there were no faces that he knew and they viewed him suspiciously when he asked for Jack Boswell. 'There are many of that name, sir,' said one swarthy-looking man. 'I am one of them. Is it me you want to do business with? You want to sell your horse or buy another?'

'No,' he said. 'I want Jack Boswell who was at Hull and is wed to Kisaiya.'

The Gypsy looked at his wife, who was sitting by the fire smoking a pipe. She gazed at Richard without speaking for a moment and then turned round and said a few words to another younger woman. He couldn't understand what she was saying and said rather impatiently, 'Well are they here or not? I'm wasting valuable time.'

The woman took the pipe from her mouth. 'Who is it who's asking?'

'Richard Crossley,' he said resignedly, realizing

that he would get nowhere if he irritated them.

The woman raised her head towards the other woman who got up and went across to another tent. He watched her go in and a moment later came out with Kisaiya. She smiled and greeted him and said to the Gypsy woman, 'It's all right, *Sister*. He's a fine Gorgio rye.'

'Where is Polly Anna?' he asked as they moved away from the group. 'Is she here with you?'

She shook her head. 'No, sir. Jack has taken her on to the Newark road. I couldn't go with her as I was sick, but Jack'll take care of her.'

'Newark!' he said. 'But, why Newark? I thought she would be going to the west of Yorkshire. What is there in Newark?'

'A circus, sir. Ogden's Circus. There is nothing for her in the west of Yorkshire.'

'Ogden!' Of course. He'd met the fellow. He'd said he wanted her for his equestrienne act. 'Is that where I'll find her? Is that where she'll be?'

She spoke gently. 'I don't know if Newark is where you'll find her, sir. The circus moves on, it doesn't stay in one place. Rather like the Romanies,' she added.

He remounted and wished her the best of health and thanked her. 'You're welcome sir,' she said. 'I wish you good travelling on the road.'

He nodded and waved his hand in farewell, conscious that she was watching him with an enigmatic smile on her face. It wouldn't take him long to Newark if he rode hard. He would soon catch up with Polly Anna.

He met Jack Boswell just outside Howden. He was trailing another horse and had pots and pans

405

strapped to his back. Richard greeted him. 'I've just spoken to your wife. Did you leave Polly Anna in Newark?'

Jack shook his head. 'No. Didn't get so far. I left her in Thorne.'

'But why? I thought she was going to Newark.'

'What business would it be of yours, sir?'

'I want to find her, to bring her home!'

Jack looked at him, his eyes dark, his face impassive. 'She left of her own free will. Nobody forced her.'

'I know that, man! But there was a misunderstanding – and I heard about that trouble you had, but we want her back. We all want her back.'

'Yon mistress doesn't,' he said sharply.

'She does! She does! She's truly sorry about what happened.'

Jack pondered, then said, 'I left her with a band of travelling players. They were going towards Newark and offered her a lift in their waggon. I've been travelling around Thorne since, picking up a bit of work,' he added. 'I'm a tinker, you see, not a *Gry-engro*, like my father.'

Richard felt a sinking despondency. 'So – so she'll be well out of the district by now?'

'Oh, aye.' He gave a rare grin. 'You'll have all on to catch up with her now. She'll be a good week ahead.'

Richard trotted away, sunk in gloom. What if she had left Newark? Where might she be? His high hopes of finding her dissolved like snow in sunshine. But at least he knew of her direction and she hadn't gone to the west of Yorkshire looking for Jonty, as he'd thought she might.

Suddenly his spirits lifted. What was it Kisaiya had said? There was something. Yes! There is nothing for her in the west of Yorkshire, she'd said. Is that what she meant? Nothing or no-one? He gave a laugh and spurred his horse on. Kisaiya, you're a marvel! Polly Anna hadn't gone looking for Jonty. She had made a decision and gone off independently to join Ogden. I shall find you, Polly Anna, he exulted. You can't hide from me, the country isn't big enough.

But it seemed that every time he was within reach of her, she had moved on. He met small bands of Gypsies who on enquiring if they had seen a lone woman traveller, looked at him suspiciously and were non-committal. He asked of other travellers in the inns he stayed at if they knew of Ogden's Circus, but he was given varying advice as to where it would be and so wasted time searching in villages and small towns, sometimes travelling on the same road twice.

Wearily he checked in at an inn in a village and ordered a meal and a room. He asked the landlord if he knew of a circus in the district, but he shook his head. 'We've just had a fair and a travelling theatre,' he said, 'but the circus won't be here till the autumn. Theatre was good,' he enthused. 'They had a Spanish dancer. By, she was grand. Better'n those old women who took main parts.'

He paid attention. 'Who was she, do you know?'

'No, but she was a proper Spaniard,' he said. 'Dark-haired like a Gypsy, no wig like they generally wear, and a real good looker. Drove the men wild. Anyway, she moved on, seemingly somebody or other was bothering her.' He laughed. 'A bit above herself I reckon. Not like them other mountebanks at all.'

He lay sleepless in his bed and wondered if he was getting closer. It was taking so much longer to find her than he'd thought. He got out of bed and lit a candle and sat down at the table and wrote a short letter to Mrs Winthrop in which he said he had news of Polly Anna and hoped to find her soon. He sent his best wishes and hoped that Miss Winthrop was improved, though privately he thought it highly unlikely. He sealed the envelope ready for posting the next day and climbed back into bed. The next morning the landlord greeted him with the news that he'd just heard that the young woman he'd been talking about had gone off to join the Gypsies.

The days lengthened into weeks as he travelled and he wrote several more letters home, still giving the news that he was hopeful of finding Polly Anna. At one town he bought an almanac which gave him the dates of the fairs and markets up and down the country, for he reasoned that Ogden, being the businessman he was, would pitch his circus during those times when the towns were at their busiest. His horse went lame whilst he was there so he sold it and travelled by coach to Northampton, where he'd read there would be a fair. There he met circus performers who gave him his best news yet. Yes, they had met Polly Anna and she had been on her way to join Ogden in Cambridge.

He heaved a sigh of relief. Almost there. He bought another horse from an itinerant horse dealer. He looked it over and thought it was a good one, though he reckoned he had paid more than its worth, but after a few days the horse went lame and, worse, it started to cough. He met a group of Gypsies who said they would take it off his hands if he bought another. When he looked in his pocket book he was dismayed to see that his money was low. Still, he reasoned, he needed another horse and paid up for a sturdy mount which the Gypsy assured him was part Arab. 'Not quite what you're used to sir,' he said, 'but he's reliable.' Richard looked quizzically at him, not much Arab he thought, but as long as he carried him he didn't really care.

He camped out that night. The evening was still and warm and he had no need of a fire. The next morning he rode into a village in search of breakfast and found a small fair just setting up. He bought bread in a baker's shop and a slice of pie in a butcher's and started to eat ravenously, whilst walking around the stalls which were being set up down the whole of the village street. He watched the men hammering the stalls together and the women sticking posters up on walls and windows and then heard a voice he thought he recognized.

A boxing booth was being erected and the man issuing orders was sitting on the steps of a waggon. 'Don't give me any lip,' the fellow shouted, 'just get on with it.' He looked up as Richard walked by and then got up and came across to him. 'I know you, don't I?'

Richard took another bite of pie, chewed and swallowed and faced the man. 'Do you?'

'Aye, I do. You're from Hull. I've seen you at 'fair.'

He took another bite. It was uncommonly good pie. 'Have you?'

'I have.' He stuck out his hand, which Richard ignored. 'Johnson's my name.' He put his rejected hand back in his pocket. 'Amos Johnson. I run a boxing booth. Two in fact. You must remember me.'

Richard eyed him. 'How is it you remember me?'

Amos Johnson looked crafty. 'I never forget a face, even though you're bearded now. You went off with that half-breed Gypsy lass, didn't you?' He folded his arms across his chest and stared at Richard. 'How did you get on? Bit of a cracker, isn't she?'

Richard brushed the crumbs from his mouth and rubbed his hands together. 'I'd like you to take that back,' he said quietly. 'You are speaking of a lady and a friend of mine.'

Amos grinned. 'Oh, aye! She's everybody's friend is Polly Anna. You should have seen her over in Hallington. All of 'men loved her.'

He picked himself up from the floor, where Richard's punch had thrown him. 'Now then! There's no need for that. I never meant owt.' He tenderly rubbed his chin and looked slyly at Richard. 'Are you looking for her?'

'I might be.' Richard regretted his hasty action; he could have saved it for later. 'Why? Have you seen her?'

'Maybe I have, maybe I haven't. What's it worth?'

Richard shrugged. 'Nothing really. I'm not so interested that I'd spend money.'

'Oh!' Johnson looked flummoxed. 'Well, you'll not find her anyway. Every time I ask about her she's moved on. 'Last time I heard she'd gone off wi' Gyppos.'

Richard feigned indifference. 'Why would you be interested?'

Johnson grinned. 'She's half Gypsy, isn't she? I just fancy a romp wi' her. A bit o' Romany passion. Isn't that what you're after,' he sneered.

Richard's knuckles tightened, but he held back. 'I've told you once she's a friend of mine. I'll thank you not to speak of her in such a manner.'

Johnson laughed. 'Bit of a gent are you?' His eyes narrowed. 'You wouldn't like to mek a shilling or two, would you?'

'I might,' he replied, thinking of his depleted pocket book. 'What had you in mind?'

'Come and fight. No, not me,' he said quickly. 'I mean my Champ. You'd stand down in 'crowd and I shout down and ask who'll come up, and then you volunteer and then I'd fix it so's you'd knock out 'Champ and earn a bob. Then all 'other suckers want to have a go.'

Richard gave a short laugh. 'If it was you I was fighting then I'd gladly do it. But no, thank you, I want nothing to do with your scruffy little business.'

He walked away and Johnson shouted after him, 'I'll not forget what you did, mush. Don't think that I will.'

He made next for Cambridgeshire, for there was to be a week-long fair of horses, sheep and cattle, and as he passed through the villages, here and there were posters displayed advertising Ogden's Circus. He stopped to examine them and rode on even harder, giving thanks to the Gypsy who had sold him this mount for it was not only sturdy but swift, but as he came into the university town of Cambridge, he saw once more that he was too late, the circus had gone.

'It'll be at Sturbridge in September, sir,' said the landlord of an inn where he stopped for a tankard of ale, all he could afford. 'That's a big fair, on for two weeks, everybody goes to it.'

He sat with his chin in his hand. I don't know what to do. Misery swamped him. I should be back at Warren House, there's so much to do. Uncle Charles will need me. But I can't go back. I won't go back! Not until I find her. As he sat, there was a great noise and confusion outside as the London coach drew up and discharged its passengers, who all rushed into the inn. He watched the mêlée of people as they divested themselves of cloaks and shawls, coats and hats and ordered food to eat before continuing their journey.

I think I'll go home. It was an immediate decision. Home to London; to my parents. Perhaps they can advise me or even if they can't I can at least have a bath and a shave and borrow some money before I move off again. He rose from the table, paid for the ale, then collected his mount from the stables and rode off down the London road.

'Beg pardon, sir, I didn't recognize you.' The maid was embarrassed. She had put her foot against the door as he attempted to come in, and it was only as he gave a loud laugh and took off his battered hat that she realized who it was.

His mother was delighted to see him, though she exclaimed at his appearance. His father agreed. 'You look rather disreputable, Richard. You'd better clean up before anyone else sees you.'

He started to tell them why he was here, but they already knew as his mother had had a letter from her sister, his Aunt Mary, telling her about Polly Anna's departure and Rowena's accident. 'I'm sorry to hear about Rowena,' she said. 'It seems you are having a hectic time in the country, Richard, what with Gypsies and runaway young ladies. It is not all sheep and corn after all. But,' she smiled wistfully at him, 'but I hope Mary remembers that you are my son after all and only her adopted one.'

He knew that it was a mild jest, but he laughed and said, 'I think she has forgotten, Mama. She's like a mother hen.' He took her hand. 'But I haven't forgotten.'

She nodded, satisfied, and then shook a finger at him. 'Go and make yourself presentable. I have a surprise for you. We have a visitor.' She nodded mysteriously. 'Up on the top floor, in Jinny's old room.'

'A visitor?' He drew in a breath. Could it be? But no, how could it? Not Polly Anna. She wouldn't know where to come. 'Who?'

'Not who you are hoping for, my dear.' His mother was contrite, as expectation flooded his face. 'But nevertheless, someone you will be glad to see. It's Jinny!'

'Jinny! But why is she here?'

'She's too old to look after children now. She came one day and asked if she could stay for a while, until she decides what she wants to do. Of course we said she could stay as long as she wants. She's looking very tired.'

After he had bathed and changed and trimmed

his beard and tied his now long hair neatly with a black ribbon, he climbed up the steep stairs to the servants' quarters, and then up another short flight to Jinny's old room. He knocked softly and pushed open the door. The room was as he remembered it. A fire was burning, the kettle was steaming on the bars and the round table was laid for tea, a starched white cloth with the tea cups and saucers set out neatly and a cake on a stemmed glass plate set precisely in the middle of it.

His old nurse was lolling in the chair, her lips in a gentle trembling snore. He put tea leaves in the teapot, lifted the kettle and poured the boiling water over, gave it a stir and set the teapot on the table. Then he bent over Jinny and patted her lined, but soft cheek. She gave a sudden snort and sat up. 'What – was I? Who's this?' She blinked her eyes a few times. 'Not Master Richard! Not with all that hair on thy chin.'

'It is, Jinny. I assure you it is me and I've just made the tea.'

'Did tha warm t'pot first? Tea's no good unless t'pot's been warmed.'

He regretted that he hadn't, but she said that perhaps it wouldn't matter this once. 'Just remember next time, Master Richard. Though I don't expect tha makes tea that often?'

He agreed that he didn't and they sat by the table and she poured the tea and cut into the cake. 'It's a ginger cake,' she said, 'like I used to make. Cook made it especially, I showed her how.' She gave a little laugh. 'I must have known tha was coming.'

'Jinny! What are you going to do now that you've retired? Will you stay in London?'

'Folks have been good to me here, especially your parents, Master Richard, and I expect I can get a little room somewhere to end my days.' She shook her head. 'But it's not home. Streets of London are not home, even though I've been here such a long time. No. Home is a country lane and sheep walks and counting up how many rabbits in t'meadows, and chuttering to folks at Driffield market.' She sighed and slipped into her old way of speaking. 'But them days are long gone, so I mun forget abooht 'em.'

He told her about Madeleine and her daughter Polly Anna, and she wept. 'Poor bairn. I allus blamed missen.' Then she dried her eyes and gave a watery smile. 'By, but he was a 'andsome Gypsy though. As 'andsome a man as I've ever seen.'

'More handsome than me, Jinny?' He turned his lips down. 'I thought I was always your favourite.'

She smiled. 'Aye. Tha was. Still are.' She leaned forward. 'Dost tha remember—' She stopped herself and murmured. 'Funny how it comes back. Do you remember', she began again, 'when I took you to St Bartholomew Fair and told you to hold tight of my hand?'

He nodded. 'You said the Gypsies would run off with me!'

'Aye. And do you remember I said that it wasn't as good as Hull Fair, and neither would it last as long? Well, I was right. Last year there were hardly any stalls or entertainment and they say that in a couple of years it'll be gone.'

'What a pity,' he said vaguely. 'Old Bartlemey; after all these years.'

'Well, it's not finished yet. It'll be here again in

about a week. Perhaps if you're still here, Master Richard, you could go for t'last time.'

He gazed at her, not really seeing her. Then he nodded. 'Yes!' How ironic if that was where he should find Polly Anna. It would be as if the wheel had turned full circle.

36

She had enjoyed great success during the two weeks in Cambridge. Ogden had warned her that he was a hard task master. 'Practise every morning without fail, no matter how good you are! All my performers practise whether they're trapeze, jugglers, clowns or equestrienne. Then you have to help with the horses, feeding, cleaning, exercising. There's no slacking in my circus.'

He introduced her to his son Anthony who had previously been Mme Gabrielle. He was now seventeen and had grown too tall and hairy to play a woman any longer. He was glad to relinquish his role to Polly Anna and offered to show her some of his stunts. She was thrilled with her first night; she loved the roll of the drums and the fanfare of trumpets as she was announced as Señorita Paulina, the International Equestrienne!

Ogden's Circus was growing bigger and better. His artistes were accomplished and professional; his wild animals, elephants, lions and tigers, straight from the jungle, performed to the command of voice or lash of their scarred trainers, and when Polly Anna groomed her Pinto in the horse tent, she saw that the other horses were well fed, their coats gleaming and their manes brushed. The other performers wore brilliantly coloured cloaks and costumes, the sword swallower in red tights and black shirt, the clowns in bright coats and trousers. For her act she was given a shimmering white skirt and silver stockings, a white top covered in sparkling silver threads and in her hair she wore a red silk rose.

The applause thundered in her ears as she cantered around the ring after her act and she saw Ogden standing at the side of the ring applauding her.

'Next booking is St Bartholomew.' Anthony joined her on the last night as she brushed her horse down and placed him in his stall. 'Da says it'll probably be the last time we'll go there. The fair is just about finished.'

'St Bartholomew? In London, do you mean? Is that where we're going?'

'That's the one. Old Bartlemey. Pity. It was a good fair, but there are hardly any fit-ups there now. There's only the circus that draws folks in.'

St Bartholomew. That was the fair that Richard had visited with his nurse when he was a child. Well, she'd be glad to be there and to know that he had walked around the same ground.

'I'll show you around if you like,' Anthony offered when they arrived in London towards the end of August. 'I've got half a day free before the new fit-up arrives.'

Ogden had ordered a new, larger tenting booth to be set up at the St Bartholomew site; it was to be one hundred feet long and forty feet wide with the canvas tilt at a height of twenty feet at the ridge, and he claimed that, with the gallery that would be built and the pit which would be dug, they could accommodate eight hundred people around the ring.

There were two days free before the circus opened and the site reverberated to the sound of men shouting and hammering as they erected the wood and canvas booth. The weather was hot, sultry and sticky, and Polly Anna was pleased to be away from the noise and dust of the site. They explored the streets around the fairground and saw where the old fair, founded within the priory walls of St Bartholomew, had spread throughout the centuries to become the greatest of English fairs, but was now struggling with a mere handful of fit-ups. Fairing stalls where cheap souvenirs, clocks and dolls could be bought and hoop-la and Aunt Sally stalls had been erected and a few smaller booths where for the price of a penny could be seen the Curious Objects, both animal and human; and the hand-propelled roundabouts which already swarmed with children, all eager to take a turn to push and so qualify for a free ride.

But Polly Anna found she was constantly looking up at some of the houses which surrounded the area and wondering which one Richard had lived in. Some were small cottage-type dwellings with pretty gardens overhung with trees and flowers, others were black and white half-timbered buildings, which to her untutored eye seemed very ancient, like the hospital and church of St Bartholomew which dominated the area by their presence.

On the morning of the day the circus was due to open, Anthony was busy helping his father. Polly Anna had perfected her act as much as she could and finished her practice, and had a couple of hours to spare, so she took the Pinto from the horse tent and decided to explore on her own. It was so hot that she wished it would rain to clear the air and she was rather dreading the stuffiness of the ring at the evening performance, but she thought she would like to look at the Thames, which she remembered Samuel telling her that, along with the Humber, was one of the two greatest trading rivers in all England.

She rode towards the dome of St Paul's and after admiring the great edifice asked the way of a cabbie to the river. The morning traffic was intense, barouches and low-sprung hansom cabs vied with costermongers' carts and pedestrians, whilst flocks of bleating sheep were urged on towards market. The noise grew louder and Polly Anna felt hemmed in as she forced her way through the ever-growing crowds. She felt a headache developing around her temples as the heat increased and she longed for a breath of air.

She had almost determined to turn back when the crowd suddenly thinned and the air took on a lighter quality. She felt sure she could smell river water and a sudden reminder of the days she had spent by the Humber with Jonty when they were children washed over her. She trotted down cobbled streets and peered into narrow courts, passed warehouses stacked with merchandise and wrinkled her nose as the scents of spices, wool, rubber and tobacco assailed her nostrils.

One more narrow street which widened out into a series of steps which the Pinto easily negotiated and she was beside the wharves of the Thames, with the breeze gently wafting her hair, barges and cargo steamers and great sea-going vessels sailing past and the watermen calling as they plied the ferries across to the other bank, and fishermen sitting patiently below the old wooden bridges which spanned the river up and down as far as she could see.

A crowd of people with horses and carts were approaching and as they drew nearer she saw that they were Romanies; at least, they have the appearance of Romanies, she thought, yet not quite like the families I know. Some of them were much darker than English Gypsies and yet others were fairer skinned. The women carried baskets filled with cheap-looking lace and limp bunches of flowers, the men had sacks on their backs with pots and pans protruding and they all had a wild appearance with matted hair and dirty clothing.

She greeted them, though as they came nearer and she saw their dishevelled appearance she wondered why she had done so. 'Are you a Romany, *Sister*?' she called to the nearest woman.

The woman stared at her and then spat. 'No, I'm not. I'm English and I'll thank you not to call me Gypsy.'

Polly Anna drew in a quick breath. 'I'm sorry – I wondered if there were any Lees amongst you.'

The woman indicated over her shoulder and walked on. Polly Anna approached another group. 'Is there anyone here by the name of Lee?'

A scruffy-looking Gypsy riding a thin horse with

a matted mane looked up. 'My name's Lee. What's it to you?'

'Erm – it's just that I – er, I once knew a Romany family called Lee.' Dismay overwhelmed her. She wished she had never spoken, she had no wish to be related to such a man as this.

He gave a coarse laugh and rode nearer, the better it seemed to examine her. 'You a Gypsy? You on yer own? You can come with us if you want. Nice horse, is he yourn?'

'Where are you from?' she asked nervously, ignoring his barrage of questions.

He indicated the way they had come. 'Across the river – Wandsworth, we've a big camp there. My grandda was a Lee,' he advised, looking at her through narrowed eyes. 'His wife was a traveller, but she warn't a Gypsy.' He gave her a sinister wink. 'She did a bit o' fortune telling, he was a hawker – a cheap-jack. You a Gyppo, then?' he repeated.

She took a deep breath and denied her ancestry. 'No,' she said, 'I'm not a Gyppo. I'm sorry to have bothered you. Goodbye.'

'Don't matter if you're not,' he called after her. 'You can still come. We could do with a bit o' fresh blood.'

Her eyes filled with tears so that she could hardly see as she rode away along the riverside. Anger and frustration overwhelmed her and she dug her heels in sharply and urged the Pinto on. I only wanted to belong, she wept inside. She only wanted to feel the comradeship of family, which seemed always to be denied her.

Richard wiped a bead of sweat from his forehead as he looked at the poster on the lamppost. He felt slightly sick with apprehension. At last, there she was. Señorita Paulina. He gave a slight smile, Ogden was taking advantage of her dark good looks and had given her a change of nationality. But his smile faded. Would she come back with him? Would she give up the adventurous life she was leading and come back to the quietness of the country? Did she – could she care for him at all? Despondency swept over him. Why should she? Would she have left in such a hurry if she had had any feelings for him?

Yet he knew in his heart that it was Rowena who in her heartlessness had driven Polly Anna away. She wouldn't have gone if she hadn't been so unkind, I'm convinced of it. And now, Rowena—. He thought of the letter which had come only a few days ago from Aunt Mary. Rowena was very ill and Mrs Winthrop beside herself with worry. We do what we can, Mary wrote, but poor Harriet feels so alone.

Richard had climbed the stairs to Jinny's room and told her of the letter from her former mistress and of Rowena. The old lady had sat quietly for a while as she mulled over the news, then suddenly rallied, pulled herself out of her chair and started to empty her closet. 'There's onny one thing for it,' she said. 'There's no use in sitting here. I'd best be off. Yon poor mistress'll want somebody to look after her if owt happens to Miss Rowena.'

Richard had stared in astonishment, then gave a sudden grin. Of course. Just the solution. Not just for Mrs Winthrop but for Jinny too. He had run downstairs to tell his mother, who after initially saying how ridiculous, it was much too far to travel, and that Jinny was an old lady and needed looking after herself, then gave a laugh so like Richard's and said she would send a maid along with her for company.

He turned away from the poster. They had seen Jinny off on the coach this morning and he had persuaded his parents to come with him to the circus this evening. It was eleven o'clock and the day loomed long before him. He visited the barber and had his hair and beard trimmed. He bought flowers and put them in a bucket of ice and wished that he could bathe in it too, for the day was so hot that the air hung heavily above him and he heard the occasional growl of thunder.

He fell asleep on his bed after luncheon and when he woke wondered whether to go down to the fairground and see Polly Anna before her performance. Yet something held him back. What if she didn't want to see him? What if he put her off her performance? He didn't want to risk upsetting her and so cause an accident. He had seen her ride and seen the risks she took. He broke out in a cold sweat at the thought of her falling and the horses trampling on her. He washed again and changed and wandered downstairs in search of his parents.

His mother was lying on a chaise-longue, the window was wide open and she was fanning herself with a black feathered fan. 'Richard, I don't know if I can come to the circus. It is so hot. I want to see Paulina of course, but—'

'Oh, but you must come, Mother. I want you to see her as she is,' he viewed her anxiously, 'so that you know exactly what she is like.'

She smiled whimsically. 'And if I disapprove,

Richard? If I abhor the thought of my son marrying a circus performer – a Gypsy, what then?'

'Then – then we must travel abroad and never darken your doorstep again. I might even join the circus myself!'

'As what?' she said lazily.

He considered. 'I don't know. I know about sheep – perhaps I could look after the elephants!'

They both laughed, but his mother added, 'It is no laughing matter, Richard, there are serious considerations for you both. Her life has been so different from yours, I remember her mother as a lovely young woman, but of her father—.' She shrugged. 'The Romanies are considered by the Romantics to have an idealistic culture; by others to be nothing more than horse thieves.'

He shook his head. 'But whatever, Mother, I must marry her or my life is ruined.'

There was a great crowd of people heading towards the fairground and Richard and his father walked on either side of his mother to protect her from the jostling and bumping as the circus-goers rushed to be first and get to the front of the pit for the best view. Richard had already booked seats in the gallery, which he was told by the man selling tickets was the best place to be if he didn't mind the expense of two shillings each.

When they arrived at the fairground, naphtha flares were glowing and there was already a queue of people stretching around the circus booth. They were enjoying the free show on the platform, where Harlequin and Columbine, clowns and jugglers were performing, enticing those who had not yet made up their minds, to enter. 'Roll up! Roll up!'

A ringmaster dressed in red coat, white breeches and black topper called to the crowd. 'Come through the magic door for an evening of superlative entertainment. See the parade of elephants. Cringe to the snarl of the bloodthirsty tigers! Watch the cavalcade of the finest horses in the land. Bring the children to see the clowns. Roll up! Roll up!'

There was a great surge forward as people rushed for their tickets and as they did so there was a sudden clap of thunder. 'Oh, thank goodness,' Mrs Crossley said. 'Perhaps now it will rain.'

Richard looked up at the sky, which was darkening rapidly. A wind was rising and a loose piece of canvas on the corner of the booth was flapping. He saw a fairman hurry towards it and tie it to one of the poles and then look up at the ridge. Richard followed his gaze. The canvas tilt was a separate covering; it hung over the main structure of the booth and was fastened down by rope. This, he knew, was in case of bad weather when the tilt could be quickly removed to save the whole structure from blowing away.

As they waited to go in he saw Ogden come out of the booth and he too looked up at the ridge. I hope it's safe, Richard pondered. There's a devil of a wind getting up. There was another crack of thunder followed by a flash of lightning which floodlit the whole area. They ducked their heads as they entered the arena and were pointed towards the raised gallery, which they had to reach by climbing a short flight of wooden steps. His mother lifted the hem of her skirt, for the steps were narrow, and seated herself on the nearest bench.

'I'm not going any further in, Richard,' she said.

'I'm sorry but I shall die of claustrophobia. It is so hot in here!'

He agreed that it was and fanned himself with the programme. He put the flowers he had brought between his feet and then opened up the programme to find out when Polly Anna would be on. He felt a churning in the pit of his stomach when he saw her name billed just before the end of the first half of the programme and then again in the second half.

The gas lamps phuttered and candles flickered as a gust of wind burst through the door and then burnt steadily again as it was closed. People settled into their places, the crowd in the dug-out pit shuffled their feet in the dust, the drums rolled and the circus began.

The ringmaster came first, cracking his lash with such ferocity that everyone jumped. Another drum roll and a team of white horses caparisoned with ornamental and jewelled trappings, their riders in flowing satin cloaks, trotted into the ring. Then followed a great elephant and on its back in a satin-covered chair sat a Negro, dressed in scarlet cloak and with a crown on his head. Following behind and led by dark-skinned, bare-chested youths with turbans on their heads, came other elephants, ponderously walking tail to trunk whilst behind them came two baby elephants, nudging each other and walking out of line to the delight of the audience.

As everyone clapped and cheered, the clowns and dwarfs came tumbling into the ring and Richard gave a thought to Jonty. Why hadn't Polly Anna gone to seek him out? It seemed the obvious thing for her to do. Then his attention strayed again as the cages with the lions were rolled into the ring and the ringmaster exhorted everyone to keep as quiet as possible whilst the lion tamer performed his dangerous acts with these most ferocious of animals. There was another clap of thunder as he spoke and everyone jumped again and laughed nervously.

A dancing bear, tightrope walker, jugglers who cascaded plates and balls and knives from hand to hand followed and in each intervening interval between the acts, the clowns and dwarfs tumbled and played. Richard stifled a yawn and pulled out his watch from his pocket. Polly Anna would be on soon. He glanced at his mother, she was furiously swishing her fan in an attempt to cool herself down. She too yawned deeply in order to take a breath in the oppressive atmosphere and shook her head and whispered, 'I feel quite faint.' When he glanced at his father on the other side of her, he saw that his head was sunk on to his chest and he was snoring softly.

He barely watched the elephants, who balanced their huge weight on tiny stools or spurted water from a bucket into the crowd, so tense was he now that Polly Anna's act was near, though he clapped heartily when the trainer took his bow. 'Wake Father up, Mother,' he said, 'Polly Anna is next.' He sat on the edge of the bench and listened intently as the ringmaster introduced, 'Señorita Paulina, the esteemed Equestrienne from Spain'. Another roll of drums and here she was, standing firmly on the Pinto's back, one hand holding the reins, the other held high greeting the audience.

Richard held his breath. She was so beautiful. 'Isn't she, Mother? Isn't she beautiful?'

His mother smiled and nodded, but didn't take her eyes off the young woman who had stolen her son's heart. She glanced at her husband, who was also watching intently as Polly Anna cantered around the ring hooking the reins around her neck and holding her arms out wide and then lifting one foot in a ballet pose. 'She can certainly ride,' his father murmured. 'Trotting around the meadows of the Wolds is going to seem pretty tame!'

Another horse, the same size as the Pinto, with a male rider cantered in. He rode alongside Polly Anna, the horses' strides matching. Both riders rose simultaneously to stand on their mounts, each holding their reins with one hand. He took Polly Anna's other hand and put one foot behind hers on the Pinto's back, she in turn put her foot in front of his on his mount, so that they were both standing astride two horses as they slowly cantered around the ring.

Applause rang out and the male rider jumped down from his mount, blew a kiss to Polly Anna and with a flourishing wave to the audience, left the ring.

Polly Anna rode around once more on her Pinto with the other horse following, then as it drew nearer she released her hold on the rein, put her left leg across to the other horse and with both arms held high in triumph cantered astride them both around the ring. A wooden barred fence was brought in and erected in the middle of the ring. Richard drew in a sharp breath. She was surely not going to jump over this. But she took one more turn

429

around the ring, took hold of the reins of both horses and with one foot on each horse urged them on and with a cry of triumph leapt the bar.

As the audience applauded, another crack of thunder rang out and the rattle of rain thundered on to the tilt. The horses shook their heads but didn't falter, the Pinto drew away and Polly Anna jumped from his back to the ground and up on to the other mount, then again from him up to the Pinto. Round and round faster and faster until finally she stayed on the Pinto's back, waving her hand to the audience and bowing low as she cantered around for the last time before making her exit.

'Isn't she wonderful!' The applause rang in Richard's ears. 'She's like her father, they say.' As he spoke he glanced at his parents for their reaction, reminding them, should they have forgotten, that she was half Gypsy as well as being a circus performer.

'I have to get out!' His mother rose to her feet and Richard and his father rose too. 'I'm so hot, I think I shall faint.'

'But the rain,' his father began.

'I'm sorry – I have to go. We have an umbrella.' She turned to Richard. 'I'm sorry, my dear, but I feel I am going to suffocate. You stay and see Paulina. I must go.'

With unaccustomed haste she scrambled down the steps where others too were trying to get out. Richard helped her down and then gave his father a hand and went with them to the door of the booth. The lamps were flickering in the draught as the flap opened and closed and people were calling to leave the door open and let in some air. They stood outside for a moment taking deep breaths of air, then his mother said, 'I can't go back in. I must go home. Bring Paulina with you, Richard, if she will come.'

He watched them as they scurried across the fairground, his father trying to hold on to the umbrella as the rain lashed down and his mother clinging to his arm, and he suddenly realized that this was not the sort of thing they would normally do. Though they often strolled on a Sunday in the streets of London, a circus in a fairground at night was not an event they would normally patronize. He felt grateful. They were open minded and liberal, willing to support him in his quest to win Polly Anna.

The wind grew stronger and he saw that some of the booths on the fairground were being dismantled as the wind gathered under the canvas flaps. The owners were shouting to each other as they struggled to take down the wooden shutters before the wind wrecked them. He glanced up at the ridge again. The canvas was flapping violently and he wondered if he should tell somebody, but then he saw a man come out and look up and hurry round to the back of the booth.

The trumpet sounded for the second half and Richard went back inside. The passage to his seat was blocked by other people trying to stand by the doorway to get more air and he saw that someone else had taken his place. He remembered the flowers he had brought for Polly Anna which he had left under the bench and he hoped that they wouldn't get trodden on before he had a chance to retrieve them. He looked across the ring to the other side of the booth and through the curtained doorway where the performers made their entrance, he saw a flash of white dress and the head and neck of a horse. He stood on tiptoe, peering over the tops of heads and ignoring the parade of elephants that had come once more into the ring. Was it? Yes it was Polly Anna. He could see the rose in her dark hair and she was wearing a mantilla.

The wind gusted and shrieked and as the canvas door flew open it blew out one of the lamps nearest to it. There was a sudden shattering crack and everyone looked up. 'Keep calm, ladies and gentlemen,' the ringmaster implored. 'Everything is all right. Remember that here we have animals from the wild. Do not disturb them.'

But the elephants were restless, their great bodies swaying; their trainers cracked their whips above them to keep them under control and the audience in the pit pushed backwards to move away from the huge beasts. Then one of the elephants screeched and the others widened their ears and stamped as if about to charge. Another howl of wind and the canvas tilt flapped loose, cracking and buffeting and the whole structure rocked. Ogden called from the side of the ring, 'Get them off! Get the elephants off. Bring the clowns on.'

The clowns ran in but kept to the side of the ring, for the elephants were shifting and shuffling and from the cages out of sight came the bellowing roars, growls and screeching of other animals, tigers and lions, bears and monkeys. People in the gallery started to scramble out of their seats and those in the pit turned round to push and climb over their fellows. Children started to cry and pandemonium was about to set in.

'Keep calm, ladies and gentleman,' Ogden shouted, 'everything is under control'; but as he spoke a great gust of wind filled the booth as the tilt was lifted from the structure and disappeared whistling and flapping into the night. The canvas sides billowed and shook and collapsed inwards on to the people sitting below them, an explosive crack followed by a thud was heard above the screams as a falling beam crashed on to the gallery; the lamps and flares blew out and they were plunged into sudden howling darkness.

37

His first thought was for Polly Anna. His decision was to crawl out from under the canvas before he was overwhelmed by the mass of screaming, shouting people who were heading in his direction, and run around to the back of the booth where Polly Anna had been standing.

The rain was torrential and as he had dressed in only a light jacket with no waterproof cape, he was drenched in seconds. But no matter, he battled around the collapsed booth to the side entrance, where there was a crush of performers and horses desperately trying to get out from underneath the canvas. Some of the supports had crashed down across the doorway and he joined other men in trying to lift them out of the way to clear a passage.

They could hear the elephants trumpeting and screeching and Richard prayed that the keepers could keep them safely in the centre of the ring until they had freed the hundreds of people trapped inside. The tigers and lions were snarling and roaring, which unsettled the horses, who were whinnying and stamping their hooves. With a great effort they manhandled the fallen beams and, making an arch with them, they heaved up the sodden canvas to let the first of the performers and the animals out.

The cages with the tigers were pushed out into the middle of the fairground and by this time other stall holders had run across to help. The tigers paced up and down in their cages, and as the lions were brought out the animals faced each other across their iron bars, snarling and roaring in their fear and climbing up the sides of the cages to confront each other.

One by one the elephants were brought out and forced into their waggons, their keepers beating and hitting them with sticks and whips to make them obey. One bull elephant, enraged by the noise, the thunder and rain and the stick, gave a trumpeting bellow and lashed out with his trunk, knocking his keeper over; he then set off with a lumbering gait across the fairground, the crowds scattering as he charged past with his keeper in pursuit.

Richard glanced over his shoulder; people were scrambling out of the main entrance, pushing and shoving at each other. Some were bleeding, children were crying, but the chaos seemed to be diminishing. He turned back to the side entrance: the horses of the cavalcade were being brought out by their riders, but he couldn't see Polly Anna. Then he realized that she would not be at the door but almost at the centre of the booth for that was where he had seen her as she'd waited in the wings.

He pushed his way through; people shouted at him to get out of the way but he ignored them.

Dwarfs slipped between others' legs to get out and a man on stilts gave a commentary on what was happening at the front.

'Excuse me. Sorry. Beg pardon!' He apologized as he worked his way in the opposite direction to everyone else and came into the ring. A scene of devastation met his eyes as he peered through the semi-darkness and saw strips of canvas flapping in the wind. The gallery was in pieces, the arena lay flooded with rainwater and injured people sat on the ground waiting for assistance.

'Polly Anna! Polly Anna!' His voice was hoarse with fear as he shouted.

'Over here!' What relief as he heard her voice, but he couldn't yet see her.

'Where? Where?' He peered into the gloom and then he saw her Pinto standing very still, its head down as if looking at something on the ground. He dashed towards it, splashing in the muddy water and jumping over broken pieces of timber.

'I'm over here.' She was sitting on the wooden ring side, one hand patting the Pinto's nose and the other arm around a young man whose eyes were closed and whose bleeding head was laid on her shoulder. She looked up. 'Who is it?' and then her mouth opened in astonishment. 'Richard! Mr Crossley!'

He wanted to gather her up in his arms and carry her off, but she was fully occupied and he wondered who the man was. A performer judging by his dress and then he realized that it was the other rider who had taken part in her act. 'Polly Anna!' He crouched down beside her. 'Are you all right? You're not hurt?'

'No,' she shook her head, but her mouth trembled, 'but Anthony's hurt his head. We're waiting for a doctor.' She looked up at him and gave a wavery smile. 'I wondered who was calling Polly Anna! I'm so – so glad to see you, Mr Crossley. But what are you doing here, so far from home?'

Her face was streaked with mud and her dress and stockings were dirty and torn, but she had never looked so lovely and he thought with a rising expectation, she was pleased to see him. 'It's a story that will take a lot of telling,' he smiled. 'Perhaps it will keep for some other time? Polly Anna,' he said wistfully, 'do you think you could call me Richard?'

Ogden came and sat next to his son and after patting him on the shoulder, put his head in his hands. 'I'm finished,' he muttered. 'We'll have to cancel. I've put everything I had into this fit-up.'

Anthony opened his eyes. 'We'll manage, Da,' he mumbled. 'We'll rally round, get another tilt. We'll be ready for Sturbridge.'

'Sturbridge?' Polly Anna exclaimed. 'Are you not going to Hull?'

Ogden shook his head. 'I wasn't planning to; not this year. Sturbridge is a big fair and it's close. Hull is too far. Not that we could go now, anyway,' he added gloomily.

They left Anthony with his father and Polly Anna took the Pinto by the reins to lead him out of the arena. 'He's very unsettled,' she said. 'He was very frightened.'

'Everyone was.' Richard took her arm and looked back at the devastation. Where he and his parents had been sitting in the gallery, a large beam lay across the bench. They emerged from under the

437

canvas. 'I thought there was going to be a stampede.'

'There almost was,' she said. 'One of the trainers had his leg crushed by the elephants.'

'Polly Anna,' he began, 'what do you want to do now?' He looked down at her as they stepped out into the muddy fairground and remembered that it was raining when he first met her, almost a year ago at Hull Fair.

'I must settle my horse,' she said, 'if the horse tent is still standing.'

'It's just that – well, my parents were here at the circus, and – and my mother said, would you come back to meet them? They left before the storm, thank goodness,' he added and gave a shudder. If they hadn't left, who knows what might have happened.

She stared at him. 'Meet your parents? But – why would they want to meet me?' She looked puzzled, then her face cleared. 'Because of my mother? Did they know her?'

'Yes,' he answered quickly, 'that's it. She and Rowena used to stay with them when they came to London.'

Her expression closed up as he mentioned Rowena's name and she started to walk on, leading the Pinto. 'I don't think so,' she said slowly. 'It wouldn't be right.'

'Not right?' He was puzzled. 'Why not?'

She looked up at him. 'I lead a different life now. I'm a circus performer. They won't really want to meet me. They are being polite, Richard, because of who my mother was and because you know – knew me.' She trembled as she spoke and he could see that she was close to tears.

'Polly Anna,' he took hold of her hand, 'you have just had a shock, you need to rest, and I assure you that my parents really do want to meet you. I have told them so much about you,' he added softly.

'Have you? Why? Did you tell them that I ran away just like my mother did?'

'They know all of that and more and they still want to meet you. Polly Anna, please come.'

'I would need to change,' she whispered in lame excuse and glanced down at her tattered finery. 'I can't visit like this.'

'I'll wait.' He breathed out his tenseness. So she would come.

The horse tent was torn and split and men were trying to re-erect it to give some shelter. The horses were tethered together in a corner of the fairground whilst they worked, and they stood for a moment or two watching before Richard said, 'There are stables at my parents' house that you could use. My father doesn't keep a horse or carriage in town, he hires when he needs them.'

She nodded. 'Thank you, if you're sure they won't mind? I'll just go and change my clothes.' She led him towards a place where the wardrobe waggon and carts and some tents were pitched and then hurried forward. 'Oh, no! My bender!' A heap of brown canvas lay on the ground with a hump of something underneath. 'My clothes will be soaked! And my mattress!'

Richard was shocked. 'Polly Anna! You're not telling me that this is where you live?'

'Why – yes! Where else?' she said defensively. 'I can't afford lodgings.'

'But – alone?'

'Yes. There's always someone about from the circus or the fair. We watch out for each other.' She started to root about under the canvas and pulled out a black skirt. 'This feels dry enough,' she said. 'I can wear this.'

'Polly Anna! I can't bear to think that you have been living like this!' He was clearly upset. 'You must come and stay at my parents' house. I insist.'

'It would be nice', she said slowly, 'to sleep between sheets like I did at Grandmother's house – and not to feel alone.' She gazed at him. 'How is my grandmother? Does she – does she ever mention me?'

'All the time,' he assured her.

'Is that why you are here?' she asked softly and he thought there was an appeal in her eyes. 'Did she send you?'

He nodded. He so badly wanted to kiss her. 'Yes,' he said, 'she did. But I was coming anyway.'

Richard's mother was elegantly dressed in a brocade gown, and Polly Anna wondered what she thought of her as, dressed in borrowed clothes to replace her own damp ones, they sat at a late supper. There was a similarity between Mrs Crossley and her older sister Mary Dowson; the same warmth and informality, but she was brighter, more intelligent and more worldly, and it seemed to Polly Anna that she was appraising her in a shrewd kind of way, by asking her judgement and opinion of this or that.

She wondered why she felt tearful as she climbed into the high bed that night, for she was happy that

Richard seemed pleased to see her and that his parents were so welcoming. He would be able to give Grandmother news of her when he returned. But she had a strange sense of loss which she couldn't quite fathom when she thought of him returning to the Yorkshire countryside.

She opened her eyes the next morning to the sound of London awaking. She heard the shouts of the breadman calling to buy his fresh bread; to the cry of the flower girls who strolled with their baskets in the street outside; and to the clatter of carriage wheels and the clip-clop of horses' hooves as they manoeuvred in the narrow streets past Elizabethan buildings, neat red-brick houses and ancient churches tucked away in hidden corners, and on towards the city.

She drew the curtains back and looked out. The rain had gone, leaving a sweeter fresher smell with a hint of early autumn. Across the square the steps of the houses opposite were freshly washed and the pavement in front of them swept free of grime by unseen maids, up earlier than her, and her gaze was drawn upwards to the myriad of chimney pots spouting curling grey smoke into a blue sky.

When she had washed and dressed in her borrowed clothes, she wandered downstairs. She expected to see Richard at breakfast but instead his mother was alone.

'Richard has gone out,' his mother said. 'He won't be long. Come and sit down, my dear.' She indicated a place next to her at the table. 'Did you sleep well?'

'Yes, thank you, ma'am. Very well indeed, though I thought that I wouldn't.'

Mrs Crossley perused her thoughtfully. 'Why did you think that you wouldn't? Is something worrying you?'

'Yes. It seems that as soon as I am settled then something goes wrong. Like the circus being cancelled, I mean – and other things.' She took a sip of coffee that Mrs Crossley had poured for her and indulged in its warmth and flavour. 'Now I have to think what to do next.'

She glanced shyly at Mrs Crossley and then bent her head. 'Richard said that you knew that I ran away from my grandmother's house? I did write her a letter explaining why, but I wonder if I could write another and perhaps Richard would take it for me when he returns?'

'I did know that you had run away.' Mrs Crossley raised her eyebrows in a slight gesture of humour. 'It seems to be a family trait.' Then she added with a touch of severity, 'And I wonder if you realize that your grandmother was extremely distressed by your action?'

Polly Anna bit her lip and looked at her from beneath lowered eyes. 'I thought it for the best,' she whispered.

'Well, perhaps you did. But as for writing a letter to her and Richard delivering it, perhaps you could write and say that you are returning?'

'Oh, I don't think so,' she said in a rush. 'I don't think that – that my grandmother would want me back, not now.'

Mrs Crossley leaned over and pressed her hand. 'I think that perhaps you are worrying more over your Aunt Rowena's opinion than your grand-mother's?'

She nodded. 'Yes,' she said miserably. 'She doesn't like me. I remind her too much about the past. And besides that, she hates the Gypsies and I am half Gypsy.' She looked up at Mrs Crossley, defiance in her eyes. 'And I am not ashamed of that. The Romanies are good people, as good as anyone.'

Mrs Crossley sighed. 'I am convinced, Polly Anna. I have heard it said several times on good authority!'

The door opened and Richard breezed in; he was quite animated and had one hand behind his back. He brought it out with a flourish and produced a bouquet of roses. 'Good morning, Polly Anna.' He presented her with the flowers. 'I brought you flowers yesterday, but unfortunately they were crushed beneath the seat where we were sitting.'

She took them and breathed in the fragrance. 'For me? How lovely.'

Mrs Crossley smiled at her son and rose from the table. 'If you will excuse me, I have several things to attend to. Shopping and suchlike. Richard,' she said, turning at the door, 'Polly Anna wishes to write to her grandmother. Would you give her pen and paper, and perhaps *you* could convince her that she should write and say that she is returning home.'

Richard pulled out a chair and sat next to her. 'Please do, Polly Anna,' he said earnestly. 'Mrs Winthrop wants you back. Everyone does.'

'Not everyone,' she said. 'Aunt Rowena would always resent me. She told me that she didn't want me there.' She glanced at him and the expression in his eyes made her falter and she stammered. 'I wish – I wish—'

'What do you wish?' he asked softly, keeping his eyes on hers.

'Wh – what?' she whispered, forgetting what it was she was saying.

'You were saying that you wished—'

She put her fingers to her mouth and watched his lips, though she hardly heard what he was saying. Why did she feel such a strange sensation coming over her? She lifted her eyes to his. 'I mean – I wish that things could be different. Grandmother won't want me when she hears I have been in a circus again! And I have been a dancer too,' she confessed, 'in a theatre!'

'I know.' He suddenly laughed and the spell was broken. 'I heard about you. You were a great sensation apparently.'

'How do you know?' she demanded. 'Who told you?'

'Never mind,' he said. 'I will tell you everything on our journey north.'

'I can't come! Don't you understand? Much as I want to, I can't!' She became frustrated at his apparent lack of understanding. 'Besides it wouldn't be fair, it is Rowena's home. She has the right to say who should live there – and if anything should happen to Grandmother I should have to move on again; and it would be even harder a second time.'

He grew serious. 'Let me explain, Polly Anna. The situation is not as it was.' He told her of his altercation with Rowena. 'I must confess that I was rude to her. I was angry because you had left and I knew it was something she had done or said that had made you leave. We were both angry. But I never thought that she would be so reckless.' He explained about the accident. 'I'm so sorry for what happened. I blame myself utterly.'

Polly Anna leaned forward and touched his arm. 'Don't,' she said, 'don't blame yourself. I'm sorry too that she is injured, but Rowena brought it on herself. She could be so thoughtless,' she whispered, thinking of the day when her aunt had ridden off and left her alone on the Wolds. 'She wouldn't have considered the danger of riding out in anger.'

They sat quietly without speaking for a few moments, then Richard said, 'She sent for me when she had recovered consciousness. She said she was sorry and asked me to look for you and to explain why she acted the way she did. She is very ill, Polly Anna,' he added gently. 'She may not be able to explain to you herself.'

Her face paled. 'You mean – she may not recover?'

'She can't possibly recover from a broken back and I fear that Rowena will not want to spend the rest of her life in bed.' He waited for a moment as tears welled into her eyes. 'Mrs Winthrop is of course very anxious about her and worried about you too. They want you back, Polly Anna. They really do. If you can find it in your heart to forgive Rowena—'

He felt conscience stricken that he was playing on Polly Anna's emotions by stressing the needs of Mrs Winthrop and Rowena, when really what he wanted to say was that he needed her more than anyone. That he loved her and that his life was nothing without her. But he knew that it was too soon, that he would have to be patient for a little while longer. Until the time when he hoped she would be ready to care for him too.

38

'We'll take the early morning coach,' Richard said when Polly Anna agreed that she would return.

'The coach? But my horse! I can't leave him.'

'We'll get you another.' He was filled with jubilation that he was to spend time with her on the journey north.

'No, you don't understand,' she said earnestly. 'He was given to me by the Romanies. I have to keep him.'

'Then we'll have someone bring him to you. If we are to travel quickly, Polly Anna, we must go by coach. It's only twenty hours to York and two hours more on horseback and we shall be in the Wolds.'

Reluctantly she agreed, though she wondered who she could trust with her precious Pinto. Then she had an idea, but had no time to formulate it as Mrs Crossley returned from her shopping midmorning, her maid's arms full of parcels and boxes.

'Polly Anna,' she murmured, 'I hope you don't mind, but I have brought you some garments on approval. I thought if you did decide to return north,' she looked from one to another and saw by the expression on Richard's face that Polly Anna had been persuaded to return, 'I thought that you would need something more appropriate for travelling in. Come and see if you approve.'

'But Mrs Crossley,' Polly Anna began, thinking of the expense, 'I—'

'Don't think anything of it, my dear,' she said starting to unwrap a parcel. 'Not having a daughter but only two sons, and being rather elderly now to indulge in fashion for myself, I have had a simply splendid morning. Of course,' she said, holding up a travelling outfit of divided skirt and flounced jacket in a deep plum colour, 'it might not be to your taste, but no matter, the shop will change them if necessary.'

She opened up a hatbox and brought out two hats, one in the same plum colour with a single iridescent feather, the other in black with a short spotted veil.

Richard excused himself to book the seats on the coach and left his mother and Polly Anna examining the boxes and parcels which not only contained outerwear, but also bedgowns, petticoats and pantaloons, stockings, gloves and shoes.

'You are so generous, Mrs Crossley,' Polly Anna said quietly. 'So very kind. I can't thank you enough.'

Mrs Crossley put down a skirt which she was holding up, an indulgence which she hadn't been able to resist in black silk, threaded in an intricate pattern with silver and edged in black velvet, and smiled at her knowingly. 'One day, perhaps, you will give me something in return.'

The maid took the clothes away to pack, Mrs

Crossley excused herself to attend to other duties and as Richard had not yet returned from the coach office, Polly Anna put a new wool shawl around her shoulders and slipped out of the house and across to the mews at the back of the house, where she brought out the Pinto and rode off in the direction of the fairground.

When Richard returned an hour later and found her missing he was extremely disturbed. 'Where can she have gone? Her horse? Is it still in the stable?' Someone was dispatched to look and came back to say that the Pinto was no longer there.

He paced the floor. 'She wouldn't go off again, would she? Mother!' he said impatiently, 'don't look so calm! What am I to do?'

'You must trust her,' his mother said patiently. 'Don't bind her, she must have her freedom. Consider her Romany blood. If you restrict her you will lose her.' She glanced out of the window on to the street and a twinkle came into her eyes. Polly Anna was walking towards the house, a smile on her face and carrying a bunch of lavender. 'I think she will be back before you can count up to ten, and don't let her think you have been worried,' she added warningly.

'You'll never guess what has happened,' Polly Anna burst out as she entered the room. 'I've been to see Mr Ogden to tell him that I won't be going to Sturbridge.'

Richard glanced at his mother and acknowledged the sardonic lift of her eyebrows.

'I had to tell him, because he'll have to try and find someone else. He wasn't very pleased of course, but I explained about my grandmother

449

needing me and I think he understood. He's managed to raise the money for a new tilt and they've got the elephant back,' she added breathlessly.

'But then—!' She became animated, her cheeks flushed with pleasure, and she handed the lavender to Mrs Crossley. 'This is for you, Mrs Crossley. It will bring you good luck. And then I saw some Romanies! They'd only just arrived, they'd been held up because of the storm, but now they are holding a horse fair. Oh, such beautiful horses,' she said excitedly. 'Some with Arab blood. Exmoor and Dartmoor ponies, Shetland and Irish, and some Spanish Gypsies with their horses and they were all trotting them along the fairground. They were so spirited, some of them still wild, but with good strong necks and legs.'

She paused for breath. 'So I went to talk to them, the English Gypsies, and told them who I was and one or two of the older ones had heard of my father. The Lees, you see, originated from London and most of these were Lees – true Romanies,' she explained. 'And – and,' she turned to Richard, 'they said that they were going north and when I explained to them why I was returning by coach, they said that they would take my Pinto back with them and leave him at Hull Fair with the Romanies!' She took another deep breath. 'Oh I'm so pleased. I was very worried about him.'

'I didn't think the Romanies travelled so far,' Richard questioned. 'I thought that like the fair-people they stayed in a certain area?'

'So they do,' she agreed, 'but they're travelling to a wedding.'

*   *   *

They waved goodbye to Richard's mother, who had risen early the next morning to see them off, and the coach lamps swung in a soft glow as the coach rattled and bumped its way through the dim London streets towards the north. His mother had arranged for her maid to travel with them as far as York for propriety's sake, though acknowledging that Polly Anna had travelled alone down the length of the country.

'We must not create any more scandal,' she had said softly. 'The poor child has enough to contend with as it is and anyone can see that you are so in love with her!'

Is it so apparent? he thought. Mother knows because I told her, but Polly Anna seems not to notice.

The coach was full and they were jiggled and jolted against each other, but Polly Anna didn't mind a jot. She was going back to the house on the hill, to a welcome from her grandmother. But then her pleasure faded. Would Rowena really welcome her back or would she become vindictive when she realized that she was incapacitated and no longer able to ride or walk as she used to. Will she be jealous of me as she once was of my mother?

They stopped mid-morning at a coaching inn and had a light meal and a short rest and then moved off again. Polly Anna felt stiff and uncomfortable in the stuffy atmosphere of the coach and asked for the window to be opened, but then one of the other passengers complained of the noise from the rattle of the wheels on the road, and the coachman seemed to take great delight in blowing loudly on his horn whenever they reached a village or hamlet. She decided that riding on horseback was a much more comfortable way of travelling and indicated this to Richard, bending towards him and whispering so that the other passengers wouldn't hear their conversation.

'I agree,' he whispered back, his mouth close to her cheek, 'but soon everyone will travel by train. The service to London from York will be open shortly and the coach service finished. Though I am inclined to think that the fastest journey would still be with a good horse and no stopping. I have heard of someone riding from Hull to London in one day.' He raised his eyebrows whimsically. 'But the horse died!'

'How long did it take you when you came this time?' she asked. 'You said that you had to come even though Grandmother asked you to look out for me.'

He looked at her. Had she not realized that the only purpose of his journey was to search for her? 'Weeks,' he murmured. 'Weeks and weeks!'

'Oh! Why so long? Did you have business on the way?'

He hesitated. Should he say? 'The person I wanted to speak to was most elusive.' Her hair was tucked neatly into a net beneath her hat, but a stray curl had escaped and ridiculously he wanted to touch it, to feel the softness between his fingers, but he felt the eyes of the silent maid upon him. 'Each time I thought I had reached my destination, I found that that person had moved on. It was almost as if we were playing hide and seek.'

She laughed. 'That's just how I felt when I was

following Ogden. Each time I arrived in a village or town where he had been, he'd moved on again. It was so frustrating.'

He nodded in agreement and they both fell into silence again, but a smile escaped his lips as he felt Polly Anna surreptitiously glancing at him from time to time.

As night fell they stopped at another inn. It was small and poorly furnished, but the food was plentiful and he managed to secure Polly Anna and the maid adequate rooms, though he had to share with one of the other passengers, who snored all night long and kept him awake until the early hours. All too soon afterwards he was awakened to hear a lad shouting, 'Rise up, passengers for York! Coach is ready and waiting.'

They had a hurried breakfast of eggs, bacon and coffee and were on their way again within half an hour. Polly Anna was quiet and he asked if she had slept well. 'Fairly well, thank you.' But she didn't tell him that she had lain awake for a long time wondering who was the elusive person he was seeking and was it possibly her?

They pulled in at the Black Swan Inn in York as the clocks in the town were striking five o'clock. The sky which had been bright for most of the journey was now overcast and threatening rain, and Richard, after arranging accommodation for the maid before her journey back to London, and ordering tea and cake for Polly Anna and a glass of ale for himself, asked her if she would prefer to stay overnight in York rather than ride on home.

'I would prefer to go home.' How odd it sounded. Home! Comforting, yet there was still a small doubt in her mind about Rowena. It wasn't quite home yet.

He stood beside her, too stiff to sit and took a quaff of ale. 'Then I'll hire a couple of mounts. We should be almost there before dark.'

'Do you think of Warren House as home, Richard?' she asked suddenly. 'Or your parents' house in London?' Could I, I wonder, ever consider one place to be my one and only home? I have laid my head in so many places.

He gazed at her as he considered. The Wolds had become so much more desirable to him since Polly Anna had lived there and he mused that wherever she was would be where he wanted to be.

'Richard?' she asked softly. 'Did you hear me?'

'Yes, I was considering,' he said. 'Both places are home.' He gave an embarrassed laugh. 'But my heart it goes awandering; it hasn't quite settled yet.'

She looked up at him, her eyes wide. 'Oh. Is that what it is? A matter of the heart? I hadn't thought of that.' Perhaps so, she thought. It is where we should feel loved and cared for. She felt his eyes on her face and there was, she thought, a tenderness there. She picked up her cup and wondered why she felt shaky and her hands should tremble. The rocking of the coach had unsettled her she decided, and was nothing at all to do with the way that Richard was gazing at her, mesmerizing her with his eyes.

As she waited for him whilst he arranged their mounts, her eyes wandered around the small dark room of the inn, not really seeing the gleam of brass and copper or the flicker of firelight. I must be careful not to read too much into his kindness towards me, she contemplated. He is gentlemanly and considerate and that is how he has been raised. But I – I have not been taught anything, except how to survive, and that by my dearest Jonty. Oh Jonty! How I wish I could see you, talk to you, tell you how I feel, just as I used to when we were children!

'Are you ready?' Richard stood over her. 'The groom is saddling up. Are you all right?' he asked, taking her hand, concerned at her quiet demeanour. 'Not too tired?'

'No,' she murmured. 'I was just thinking of old times.'

It was good to mount the fresh horses and ride away. They had left Polly Anna's carpetbag with the innkeeper to send on with the carrier to Driffield, where it would be collected. Richard had no luggage, except for his waterproof cape and he was amazed to think that he had travelled for over five months without a change of trousers or jacket until he had arrived at his parents' house. I'm almost a Gypsy, he mused, though the Gypsies I'm sure would disagree with me. He glanced at Polly Anna riding beside him as they rode out of town. 'You look such a lady in your fine clothes, Polly Anna,' he joked. 'You must feel ashamed to be seen with such a scruffy-looking fellow as me.'

'Oh no,' she replied quite seriously. 'You will always be a gentleman and my clothes will never make me a lady.' She glanced at him and wondered if she would shock him. 'We used to be called workhouse brats, you know. There was something about us, I don't know what it was, our clothes or perhaps a certain look about us. But everyone knew, whenever we went into the streets of Hull, people knew who we were and where we were from.'

He was silent. He didn't know what to say. How to answer. How terrible to have such a stigma attached to you, through no fault of your own. And her mother, brought up as a lady, only to end her days knowing that her child had no-one to care for her. I will take care of her, Madeleine, he vowed silently. I will love her as she deserves to be loved. I will make her a lady – if that is what she wants.

39

They took the road out of York towards Stamford Bridge and then cut across country towards the Wolds. They rode hard for the first hour whilst the light still held and the rain which was threatening held off; then they eased off a little and passed by clusters of white-walled cottages which were shuttered up for the night and isolated farms, where barking dogs noted their passage, and across rough roads which skirted lush pastureland, which in the dusk was scattered with white dots of grazing sheep.

Occasionally on the tops of a valley they saw the dark outline of deer and they were followed constantly by the hoot and call of hunting owls. As they reached the higher Wolds the roads became steeper and the inclines down into the dales more taxing, but Polly Anna felt exhilarated, no longer tired from her coach journey and although she didn't know the road she kept pace with Richard all the way.

Presently the rain started and they quickened their pace, but it came more heavily, a great deluge which soon soaked them through. 'We'd better shelter for a while,' Richard shouted above the tumult, 'until it eases.'

They rode into a copse which afforded some shelter and after tying up the horses, delved further in, where the undergrowth was thicker and the ash trees had not yet started to shed their yellowing leaves. They sat down on a fallen log and Richard opened out his cape. Polly Anna took off her hat and looked ruefully at the bedraggled feathers.

'Here,' he said, lifting up the cape to cover her, 'come underneath. This will keep us fairly dry, though we're wet already. I hope you don't catch cold, Polly Anna.'

She turned towards him and laughed. Rain was running from her hair and down her face. 'It's not the first time I've been out in the rain,' she teased. 'Do you think I will melt?'

'No,' he admitted. 'I remember once before you said you belonged to nature, to the wind and the rain.'

'I did,' she said softly. He was very close, their heads almost touching as they crouched beneath the cape. She could see the curve of his lips beneath his beard and the blueness of his eyes, so much closer than ever before and there was something in his gaze that did indeed make her feel as if she was melting. She moistened her lips with the tip of her tongue. Her mouth felt dry and her voice was husky as she spoke. 'It must be my *dado*'s influence.'

'Yes.' His voice was a mere whisper and she wondered that they spoke so softly when there was no-one else to hear. The only other sound was the shuffling of the horses and the patter of rain through the trees. 'Polly Anna! Forgive me. I so desperately want to kiss you.'

His mouth was so close, and her own lips parted as he touched her cheek with his fingertips. 'Then perhaps you should,' she breathed and closed her eyes as his lips met hers.

It was such a tender kiss, so sweet and sensuous, and she opened her eyes in wonder at the magic of it. 'I love you, Polly Anna. So much,' he whispered.

She was conscious of a great joy enfolding her. A warm glow of happiness. Am I feeling love too? she wondered. Is this what love feels like?

'Can you – could you care for me, do you think?' He gazed at her. The kiss was just as he expected it would be, no – hoped it would be, for it had been beyond his greatest longings that it would actually happen.

She nodded. Her eyes were wide as if she had just seen something quite astonishing. He bent his head to her lips again and she responded, at first modestly, but as his arms went around her and the cape slipped away, she put her arms around his neck and he sensed a great passion within her. He could feel the beat of her heart and the softness of her skin. He stroked her face. 'I can't believe this is happening. I have dreamed of it so often. I love you so much. Will you marry me, Polly Anna? You will marry me?'

She swallowed. 'Marry you?' She drew back. 'I – I don't know. I don't know anything about marrying.' She became pensive. 'I don't know anyone who is married, only older people and my mama and *dado* and I don't know how they felt.'

'Kisaiya and Jack,' he said quietly, thinking that

perhaps after all he had declared himself too soon. 'They're young and married.'

'But they're Romanies. And what am I?' She suddenly looked frightened as if the prospect alarmed her. 'How can we marry! I've told you, I've been a dancer in a theatre. Worked in a circus! I've travelled alone. You have been pampered and cosseted. You know nothing of how real life is.'

'That isn't my fault! That was an accident of my birth, just as yours was to be born in a Gypsy waggon.' Fear that he would lose her made him angry. 'But don't forget, Polly Anna – never forget that your mother was a lady, just as mine is. Nothing can ever change that.'

She was silent for a moment, then shook her head. 'But I'm also half Gypsy. Think of what your parents would say! Or Rowena!'

'My parents know already,' he appeased. 'I told them months ago when I visited them. You remember when I went to London? And when I came back you had gone. You had run away with the Gypsies,' he added, 'and left me all alone. And as for Rowena,' he remembered their last conversation, 'she may or may not approve, but I don't care, Polly Anna,' he said softly, 'I have searched all over this land for you. From Appleby to Hull. From the Wolds to old St Bartlemey. I will not let you go again.'

As they approached the old house up the steep winding drive, Polly Anna felt a deep apprehension. Whereas only an hour ago, she had been filled with a new-found joy, now she felt a trembling fear. Twice she had been turned away from this house which in the darkness looked so forbidding. Would she be welcomed back this time? A lamp shone outside the door and in one of the downstairs rooms a single candle burned in the window.

She shivered as she dismounted and then jumped as a figure approached in the darkness. It was Jennings, who took the reins of both horses and greeted them. 'Good to see you safely back, Miss Paulina, and you, sir.' He touched his broad-brimmed hat and she noticed on his arm a black armband and wondered what it meant; she saw too the flicker of Richard's eyes as he observed it too, and the barely imperceptible shake of Jennings's head as they exchanged glances.

Richard took Polly Anna's elbow as they mounted the steps and rang the bell. 'I fear there is bad news. We may be too late.'

'Not Grandmother,' her chest was tight with apprehension. 'Not now that I have come back.' She stifled a sob. If her grandmother had died, then she must once more leave this place. Rowena wouldn't want her here, not alone.

They heard the drawing back of bolts and the turning of a key in the lock and the door was slowly opened. A maid stood there, her figure in black, a silhouette against the lamp she held in her hand. 'Oh, sir! Mr Crossley and Miss Paulina! Oh Miss Paulina.' She started to weep. 'I'm right glad to see you. This is such a dowly household now wi' everybody weeping and wailing.'

She opened the door wider to let them in and lit another lamp in the hall. 'Come in do, miss, and you, sir. I'll soon have t'fire built up again. Won't tek a minute. Why – and you're both wet through.'

She bustled round, poking the fire in the sitting-room grate and adding more sticks and coal. Richard helped Polly Anna off with her jacket and took his off too. 'Bring blankets, will you, and a hot toddy?'

'I will sir, right away. We don't want young mistress catching a chill. We've had enough misfortune in this house, and I'll tell Mistress you're here.' She dashed away out of the door and they drew nearer the fire, feeling chilly now that their journey was over.

Richard bent to kiss Polly Anna's cheek. 'I must now only do that when we are alone,' he whispered. 'And it is going to be very hard for me.'

She reached on tiptoe and kissed his mouth. 'And for me too,' she smiled. She wanted to say, I love you, but she was afraid that if she did, she would be giving him too much hope that she would marry him. And how could she? How could she ever marry anyone?

The door opened and they jumped apart. An elderly woman stood there, a shawl around the shoulders of her grey gown. 'Jinny!' Richard said. 'I'm glad to see you.'

She nodded. 'I'm right glad to see you too, Master Richard. But tha'll have heard? I got back too late.' She wiped her eyes on a corner of her shawl. 'Poor, poor lady. So sad.' She came further into the room and stood in front of Polly Anna. 'And this is Miss Madeleine's daughter? I'd have known it.' She nodded her head. 'Aye, you have t'look of your mother and your aunt. You've got t'Winthrop bearing all right.'

Polly Anna put out her hand. 'I'm very pleased to

meet you at last, Jinny. I've heard about you and I feel I know you already. But – but,' her eyes filled with tears, 'please – tell me who it is who has died.'

The old woman's mouth creased and she looked as if she too was going to cry, but she took a deep breath. 'Did nobody tell you, miss? Has nobody broke t'news?'

Polly Anna shook her head. The suspense was too great, the tears spilled over her cheeks. 'Is it – is it my grandmother?'

'Bless you, child!' Another voice came from the doorway. 'It seems that the good Lord isn't ready for me yet.' Mrs Winthrop stood in the doorway. She was dressed in her bedgown and cap with a warm robe wrapped around her. 'He wanted yet another of my daughters. I prayed to Him to take me instead, but no, He would have Rowena.'

She sat down on a chair by the fire and Polly Anna knelt beside her. The old lady stroked her hair and murmured, 'But I'm inclined to think she helped Him a little.'

'Now, ma'am. We'll have none of that sort of talk.' Jinny reprimanded her mistress. 'I've telled thee already, t'call had come for Miss Rowena and that's an end of it.'

Mrs Winthrop looked down at Polly Anna. 'So Mr Crossley found you once again, Paulina! He had a long journey. I had almost given up hope.' Her voice was thin and weary and Polly Anna realized how old she had become since she had last seen her. 'But now? Will you stay with your old grandmother and make me happy for my few remaining years or will you feel the wanderlust and disappear again?'

Polly Anna knelt up and kissed her cheek. She felt choked with emotion. Relief and joy that her grandmother was still here yet troubled that she had not greeted Rowena for one last time and made amends. 'I'll stay, Grandmother, if you will have me, and I won't leave you again.'

Mrs Winthrop glanced up at Richard, who was standing silently listening. 'Did you hear that, Mr Crossley? Paulina will not leave her grandmother again! What do you make of that, hey?'

A look of understanding passed between them and he smiled. 'I'm not sure, ma'am. I shall have to work out some solution.'

For the remaining weeks of September and the beginning of October Polly Anna stayed by her grandmother's side. Mrs Winthrop, in spite of her stoic demeanour, had suffered a severe shock at Rowena's death, and now that her granddaughter was back she let her grief come to the surface and mourned properly for the first time the death of Madeleine too. But Polly Anna was so vital, so merry as if she was filled with gladness, that some of that vitality transferred itself to the old lady and her recovery, though slow, was sure.

Every morning from her bedroom window she watched as Polly Anna exercised the horses from the stables; she watched her as she jumped so easily over the beck where Rowena had fallen, she saw her ride bareback and side-saddle, gallop across the meadow with Richard at her side and watched her too, in some alarm, as in the paddock in front of the house, she trained the horses to trot and canter steadily as she stood on their backs, and waved cheerily to her in the window.

'I can see why you did so well in the circus, Paulina,' she said one day as she came in flushed and smiling after exercising. 'You are a true equestrienne.' She looked squarely at her. 'Do you miss it? The excitement? The cheering crowds?'

'Yes, a little,' she admitted. 'But it was only for a small time of my life.'

'Yes, indeed,' her grandmother agreed. 'You are still young, there is time to do so much more.'

'But, I wanted to ask you something, Grandmother,' Polly Anna hesitated at the question which had been burning the end of her tongue for days.

'You want to go back?' Mrs Winthrop said sadly. 'I knew it. I knew we couldn't keep you here.'

'No!' Polly Anna rushed to her side and flung her arms around her. 'No, not that. I said I wouldn't leave you and I won't, but what I want to ask you is – yes, I do want to go back, but not to stay. I want to see Kisaiya and Floure and Shuri, and collect my Pinto; but most of all I want to see Jonty. I want to go to Hull Fair.'

'Will you go with her?' Mrs Winthrop asked Richard when they were alone. 'To make sure she returns.'

'I will go with her if she wants me to, but I can't make her come back.' He'd been disturbed when Polly Anna told him that her grandmother had agreed that she could go to Hull Fair. He knew, or thought he did, the reason for her wanting to return and it wasn't just to collect the Pinto. It was to see Jonty.

'No, you can't. No-one can. She must have the

freedom to choose for herself. Don't try to tame her, Richard, or you will lose her,' she said, echoing his mother's words.

'I wish I was old and wise,' he murmured, 'then I would know.'

'Wisdom doesn't always come with old age.' She patted his hand. 'I wish that it did. Perhaps you should consult the Romanies, maybe they can tell you your future.' She grew thoughtful. 'And perhaps you would ask that young Gypsy woman what it was she said to Rowena. The servants are convinced that she cursed her.'

When they reached the lane at the bottom of the meadow, Polly Anna turned in the saddle and, raising both arms above her head, she waved towards the house at the top of the hill, knowing that her grandmother would be watching. She turned back and saw Richard watching her. 'Does she think I won't come back?' she asked.

'She is bound to be a little uneasy,' he said. 'It's only natural.'

She nodded. She hoped her grandmother trusted her enough to know that she wouldn't let her down. But she had been cheerful enough when she had said goodbye last night. 'Don't worry about me,' she'd said when Polly Anna had expressed her concern about leaving her for a week. 'I shall be all right with Jinny to look after me, though she needs more looking after than I do,' she'd added with a chuckle.

I won't stay the whole week, she decided. Just a few days and then I'll come back, and she felt comforted to think that her grandmother would be waiting for her in the house that was gradually becoming home; its walls, rather than binding and enclosing her, were embracing her, making her feel safe and secure. It was a good feeling, she reflected. One that she hadn't experienced before.

She glanced at Richard. He had wanted to come with her and she was glad of it, though he had been distant and withdrawn for the last few days, not given to much conversation. She drew in a breath. Did he too think that she wouldn't return? Is that why he wanted to come and not just to accompany her?

'I'm so looking forward to seeing Jonty again,' she said as they dipped down towards the village, and was surprised to see a tightening of his lips. 'And Kisaiya and – oh! Will she have had her baby yet?' She was vague over such events.

He laughed. 'Oh, Polly Anna! What a thing to ask me! How would I know?'

'And I suppose I shouldn't ask, should I? A real lady wouldn't ask such a thing of a gentleman.' Her mouth slipped downwards. 'I shall never learn. Never.'

He drew in his reins and leaned across to halt her mount. They were passing close by the church where Rowena was buried and two women were standing talking by the lychgate. He leaned towards her and kissed her cheek. 'And no gentleman would kiss a lady in public!' he said, and turning towards the startled women, he lifted his hat in greeting before trotting on.

There were small groups of Gypsies in Beverley, all riding in the direction of Hull and they soon caught up with more as they took the small roads across common land. Polly Anna said that Kisaiya and Jack would be displeased with her if they found out she had been using the toll roads. 'I don't know who I am,' she murmured. 'Am I Romany or Gentile? Or am I neither one nor the other?'

'You can be whoever you want to be, Polly Anna,' he said patiently. 'Most people are shaped by their parents. You knew neither of yours, at least not for long. You are your own self, shaped by circumstances and your own inner spirit.'

Yes, he's right, she thought with a sudden illumination. I'm just me! She gave a sudden laugh and urged her horse on. And I know what I want! 'Come on,' she shouted to him. 'Let's go to the fair!'

40

Not all the stalls, booths or entertainment had arrived on the Dock Green fairground, though the streets of Hull were already busy with market people setting out their wares, ready for the influx of crowds who would flock to the fair as soon as it was opened. Most of the showpeople were still travelling the road from Nottingham Goose Fair, urging on their horses and mules, anxious to get there as soon as possible to get a good site, if they hadn't already booked one.

But Johnson's Circus was in place. 'Got the best gaff in the whole of the fair,' Johnson boasted, forgetting that it was his son Harry who had negotiated for it. They had arrived earlier than most of the other fairfolk, as this year they had missed Nottingham and gone to Howden instead, which was nearer, so that they could have an early start for Hull and a good site.

Jonty sat in the doorway of his tent cleaning his boots and looking out at the rainy morning. They rose early in the circus, as soon as it was light, and this was his rest period. He'd perfected his act, supervised the timing of the other acts, spread the sawdust, put up the props and assisted the keepers with the animals; in short there was nothing he couldn't do in the circus and Johnson was aware of it. More and more he relied on Harry and Jonty to do the things that he had previously done himself. Johnson's Circus was growing bigger and more successful than it had ever been and Johnson was astute enough to realize that it was because of the ideas that the two young men put forward, and only this morning he had come up with a proposition.

'I'll make you and Harry equal partners with me,' he said to Jonty. 'But if owt happens to me then Harry will take my share, that's onny right.'

Jonty agreed delightedly, he could find no fault with that. But Harry was uneasy. 'What about Amos? He'll come back running. He'll fight for a share.' There was no love between the two brothers, only animosity.

'I'll leave him a bob or two to keep him happy,' his father said generously. 'He's done nowt for the circus, so he's not entitled. I'll get it drawn up proper wi' lawyers.'

And that was where he had gone now and why Jonty was sitting in his tent mulling over the events of the last year. When Polly Anna had ridden off with Richard Crossley, he'd felt as if his whole world had disintegrated; that there was nothing that would ever make him happy again. They had packed up the circus and travelled to the West Riding of Yorkshire, but even that journey had brought back memories of travelling along the same road with Polly Anna.

But his friends, Morgan and Amy and little Dolly

had rallied round, knowing that he was feeling low, and Dolly in particular seemed to be always there, bringing him a little sweetmeat or a biscuit that she had baked herself, or making him a new pair of clown's breeches in bright patched colours. Sometimes she would come back after the show was over and they would sit and laugh over the things that had happened or plan something different for the next gaff, and after she had gone he would lie on his mattress and realize that although he still missed Polly Anna, he was no longer as lonely as he had once been.

During January the snow had come down thick and heavy and the circus was marooned in a small village. The villagers had supplied the circus folk with all that they could afford in the way of food and accommodation and all anyone could do was patiently wait for the snow to thaw. Jonty did much thinking during that time and not always about Polly Anna. He had struck up a friendship with Harry Johnson, they found they had much in common and together they put their ideas together for improving the circus. 'Join me as a clown,' Jonty said. 'You can already juggle and I'll show you how to tumble. And we need elephants,' he'd added. 'We're not a proper circus without elephants.' So after a little persuasion, Johnson had bought two elephants, Kitty and her baby, Tiny, who were added to the menagerie of lions and tigers and Harry joined Jonty in the ring as a second clown.

He'd heard a voice outside his tent one night and on lifting the flap he found Dolly outside. She was shivering despite having a blanket wrapped around her. 'Am I disturbing you, Jonty?' she'd asked.

471

'There's so much noise going on in our bender; all the dwarfs are in there and the Thin Man and Morgan and his monkey, they're having a game of cards and arguing like mad.'

Dolly shared a tent with two other small ladies, but all of the small people seemed to gather together in their leisure moments and often the tents which they occupied were overflowing with laughing, chattering, voluble people whose banter echoed around them.

Jonty had looked around, no-one was about, everyone was inside on that cold night and he had tentatively asked her in. It wasn't late, merely dark because of the heavily laden, snow-filled sky and Dolly had often before sat with him within his tent. He'd offered her tea which he had just brewed and she brought out a tin from beneath her blanket with a fruit cake in it. 'One of the women in the village gave me it,' she'd laughed. 'She said, "Here tek this to your ma." She thought I was a child.'

She'd looked at him, her face was in shadow but her eyes were large and luminous and she'd sighed. 'But I'm not, am I, Jonty?'

He'd gently stroked her cheek, it was soft and cool. 'Of course not. You're a beautiful woman.' His words seemed to him to be clearer than usual. He no longer worried about only using words which he thought others would understand, though perhaps without knowing it he would avoid some words which he couldn't pronounce properly; but he had discussed this with Harry, who had the same disability, and they had laughed and realized that it didn't really matter any more.

'Not beautiful!' she'd shyly disagreed. 'Pretty maybe. Like a little doll. That's what they used to say about me when I was a child.' But in the glow of the lamp as she sat next to him on the straw mattress, she did look beautiful and she didn't seem small.

'People used to call me Dummy,' he'd said. 'But they don't any more.'

They both smiled, at ease with each other and he'd added, 'Is it all right for you to be alone with me, Dolly?'

'Why not? We just agreed I'm not a child!' She'd gazed at him, then taken hold of his hand. 'Are you afraid for my character or yours, Jonty?'

He was silent for a moment and all they could hear was the whistle of the wind and a distant shout of laughter. He stroked her small plump hand. 'For yours,' he'd said softly. 'We'd agreed that you were a woman – and I know that I am a man and not a boy.'

For the first time he was looking at a woman and not thinking of his love for Polly Anna. He only knew that Dolly's presence disturbed him; he had emotions churning inside him that he had always suppressed when Polly Anna was there. Now they wouldn't be suppressed. He wanted to hold Dolly in his arms, kiss her pink cherubic lips and ached to hold her small round breasts in his hands. 'So if you don't want me to hold you or kiss you,' he'd whispered and traced his fingers around her face, gently touching her brow, her cheekbones, her lips, 'then you'd better leave now.'

'But I do,' she'd whispered back. 'That's why I came, why I have kept on coming all of this time.

473

I've been waiting for you, Jonty. Waiting for you to stop hurting.'

As he sat now gazing out at the muddy fairground he thought of the happiness Dolly had brought him. She seemed able to sense his moods, knowing when to leave him to his solitude and when to cheer him. He'd felt ten feet tall after that first wonderful night and there were many knowing glances when they were together for it appeared that their love showed. They were careful, though, that Mr Johnson didn't find out, for he would not tolerate any intimacy between men and women working for him. But it doesn't matter now, he thought jubilantly. Now that Johnson has offered me a partnership, Dolly and I can get married. He had already asked her and she had accepted, but before they named a day he had a plan.

'Dolly,' he shouted as he saw her dashing across the Green. 'Come here, I want you.'

'And I want you,' she said breathlessly as she ran towards him. 'But we'll have to wait until later.'

He laughed. 'Wicked woman! I have something to say to you.' He told her of Johnson's offer and she was so delighted that she flung her arms around him. 'It means we can get married sooner than we thought. But first, what about this! When I agreed to Johnson's proposal, he said that I'd better get a waggon-house. Can't have my partner living in a bender, he said – even though he's lived in one himself. I told him that I didn't have enough money yet, and guess what! He said he'd lend me the money and take it out of my wages.'

He grinned at her. 'I'm going to order one

474

straight away and as soon as it's ready we can get married.'

She was so overjoyed. 'Married! And then I shall be Mrs—! What shall I be, Jonty? Mrs – what?'

He stared at her and his eyes prickled. Jonty. That was his name. He had no other. No mother or father to give him one. 'Jon-a-thon!' he mumbled, his speech indistinct and garbled. 'No other name.'

'Well, it doesn't matter,' she said softly. 'I shall be proud to be called Mrs Jonathon. Dolly Jonathon,' she repeated. 'It sounds like a very noble name to me.'

Later after she had gone back to her own tent, he folded up his blankets into his box, straightened the mattress, put his clean boots neatly with his clown costume and generally tidied up. Living in such a small space meant that everything had to be in its own place. He stretched and then looked out. The rain had stopped, there was a smell of autumn, of dying leaves, of woodsmoke and the unmistakable drifting odour of blubber, which told him, if he hadn't known, that they were back in Hull.

Yet now he looked at the town with different eyes, no longer scurrying furtively at someone else's beck and call. No longer ducking from a blow or ignoring shouts and jeers that told him he was the lowest of the low. Yesterday, when they had arrived at the fairground, he had gone off to buy supplies in the town. He had looked at the fine shops, he had walked through the butchers' shambles and bought a pie and a chicken from a butcher, who had served him most civilly and called him sir. He held his head high and knew he was a different person from the crooked dummy from the workhouse.

But he also knew that his life in the workhouse had shaped him; he was sharp and cunning to a certain degree, perceptive too, which his friend Samuel had observed in him as a child. Samuel had nurtured his response by teaching him to read and write and to observe. I won't ever forget you, Samuel. Not as long as I live. You were my father and my mother. You saw something in me that no-one else did. Although Polly Anna had given him the impulse to leave, it was Samuel who had made it possible. I'm no longer a workhouse brat, Samuel; he directed his thoughts heavenwards, where he was sure his friend would be. You would be proud of me. I'm Jonty, the famous clown.

A group of Gypsies rode on to the site and he gave a sudden start. There was Kisaiya, she was riding with a child in front of her and a baby strapped to her chest. Jack Boswell was riding alongside. He called to them and Kisaiya waved and rode over to greet him. 'Jonty. It's good to see you again.'

'How are you, Kisaiya? You look well.'

'Aye, I am. I have a *chavo*, as you see.'

She looked down at him and as if knowing the question on his lips, said, 'You heard that Polly Anna had joined Ogden's I expect?'

He gave a small gasp. 'No! But –'. He had always had an image of Polly Anna living a lady's life in a grand house like Mrs Harmsworth lived in. 'But why?' His mouth tightened and he felt anger inside him. 'Did her family not want her? Did they turn her away? What about Crossley?' His anger directed itself to Richard Crossley. He'd promised to look after her. If he'd hurt her or abandoned her—. All of his old feelings of protectiveness came rushing back.

Kisaiya shook her head. 'There was some trouble. It was over us, Jack and me, and we had to leave. Polly Anna decided to come with us. Mr Crossley wasn't there,' she added gently, 'otherwise I don't think she would have left. She went off to join Ogden. She said he'd offered her a job.'

Jonty nodded. So he had. But——. 'Did someone go with her? She didn't go alone?'

'Aye, she did. That's what she wanted. But we had news of her, every step of the way. She caught up with him in Cambridge.' There was a smile in her eyes and he felt there was more, but she wheeled her horse around to follow Jack, who was waiting for her. 'You don't need to worry about her. She's all right. I knows it.'

But he did worry, all the rest of the morning and into the afternoon, and Dolly finally gave up her attempts at rehearsing with him and went off with some of her friends into the town. He went about his work mechanically, checking that the horse tent was swept and clean, making sure that the animal trainers were happy with their acts, listening to complaints of some of the performers, checking that the poles and ropes of the canvas were secure against a strong wind. Then he went over his act again. He juggled plates and balls, he somersaulted and walked on stilts and swung from the trapeze, yet all the time he had Polly Anna on his mind.

He was lying on his mattress, his hands behind his head, and from this position he had a restricted view of the Green from the open flap of his tent.

Fairpeople were arriving regularly now for the fair was due to open in two days' time, which gave them little time to erect their roundabouts, swings or booths. But they would do it, they always did, even though it might mean working through the night.

There were many more Gypsies than usual, and Jonty leaned on his elbow and watched them ride across to the far side of the Green, to their own camp away from the fair people. Not all of them were trailing horses, which was why they were usually there. Some of the women were wearing brightly coloured clothing and rings and bracelets, which flashed and jingled as they moved, and the men had gaily coloured neckerchiefs tied around their throats and wore large black hats. They all seemed very cheerful and called out greetings to one another, sometimes using the Romany language which he couldn't understand.

Then there was a lull before other riders came in, twenty of them he counted and they were all dressed in green travelling costume and rode in procession on fine white horses. They were obviously from another circus and Jonty sat up and took notice. Richardson's? One of the bigger circuses; he had seen the posters in the town. He moved towards the tent flap and sat in the doorway to watch them. One day, he thought. Maybe we'll be as big. Already he felt a proprietorial pride towards Johnson's. Other carts and waggons rolled by and there was a hubbub of noise and laughter, the sound of dogs barking and animals roaring and screeching and he felt an excitement hit him in the pit of his stomach. This is the life, he exulted, his moodiness dissipating. This is the life for me.

He turned away and lay down again on his mattress; as people walked by close to his tent, he could see their feet and legs and catch snatches of conversation. Dogs occasionally sniffed at the doorway and he shouted and shooed them away. His eyes began to droop, it had been a long busy day but not as long as the days would be once the fair was open. He half-opened his eyes again. A pair of legs had paused by his tent and he vaguely thought that perhaps he would get up and close the flap. The legs were long, he could see up to the knees and they were clad in dark, well-cut wool trousers. The boots the legs wore were leather and highly polished. They moved on slowly, hesitatingly, and were followed by a woman's skirt. The skirt was divided like the ones worn by Richardson's riders, but this skirt was in expensive fine wool, the kind that a gentlewoman, used to travelling on horseback might wear and on her feet she wore small neat leather boots. He heard the sound of her voice and he sat up, instantly wide awake.

'Polly Anna,' he breathed. 'But how can it be if she is with Ogden?' He knew that Ogden's Circus wasn't coming, not when Richardson's were here. They were in direct competition and didn't usually open on the same site.

He crawled on hands and knees to the doorway and looked out. The woman and the man had moved away, but she turned her head slightly. The feathers on her hat ruffled as she did so and he drew in a breath. It was Polly Anna, and holding her supportively by the arm was Richard Crossley.

They were looking from side to side as if searching for something or someone, Polly Anna pointing with her gloved hand at this or that. Jonty stayed still, just looking, his thoughts jumbled and uncertain, his emotions mixed. Then he rose to his feet and stepped outside. 'Polly Anna,' he called, knowing that from the sound of his voice she would know instantly who was calling her name. He saw her hesitate and then turn, a half-smile on her face which broke into a huge beam. She put out her arms and, with a great cry of joy, ran to him.

41

It was a small, silent, anxious crowd who watched as
Polly Anna and Jonty walked up and down, up and
down, along the lines of tents and waggons. There
had been an initial greeting and shaking of hands
as Morgan and Amy and then Dolly and her friends
appeared, almost it seemed at the same instant
as Polly Anna and Jonty greeted each other. Then
Polly Anna and Jonty as if by mutual consent
distanced themselves from the others and began
their promenade, their heads close together, sometimes talking animatedly, sometimes in whispers,
their heads nodding or shaking, in agreement or
disapproval.

Dolly watched with her hands clasped as if in
supplication and her wide eyes glistening as she saw
her dreams about to be shattered. Morgan put his
hand on her shoulder, whilst Amy looked at her
sister anxiously and the other friends, performers,
dwarfs, Thin Man and Fat Lady stood by.

Richard stood alone, his arms folded across his
chest and his feet firmly planted apart. He was stony
faced, but his eyes never left Polly Anna. Damn.

Damn. Damn! We should never have come! But he knew deep down that they had had to come. He would never have been really sure of Polly Anna's feelings either for him or Jonty if they hadn't made this journey.

He watched as with heads drawn together, Jonty's and Polly Anna's fingers touched and they continued their walk with their fingers clasped and he saw as they turned in their perambulation, a look of tenderness on Polly Anna's face as she smiled at Jonty, and, he thought, it's a look of love that he's returning.

He turned away and moved towards the others. He couldn't bear to watch any more and he saw a little girl staring at him. At least, no, she wasn't a little girl, she was a young woman, pretty with fair hair. One of the performers, like Amy. She came across to him. 'Mr Crossley! I'm Dolly. A friend of Jonty's.'

She looked sad, and he suddenly realized that he wasn't the only one who was unhappy. He bent and put out his hand to her and she placed it in his, her hand small against his. His fingers closed over hers. 'I'm glad to meet you, Dolly,' he said softly.

They stood together, not speaking and both turned away from the couple who were causing such heartache, when a figure brushed close to them. Kisaiya. Alone, but for the baby strapped to her. Dolly reached up to look beneath the baby's shawl and she blinked away tears. 'Beautiful,' she whispered. 'How lucky you are.'

Dolly was tiny against Kisaiya, but Kisaiya was so small against Richard. She looked up at him. 'It's good to see you again, sir.'

He smiled wistfully down at her. 'And to see you Kisaiya, and in such good health after your baby. You see that I found her at last,' he added, nodding over to Polly Anna, who seemed to be sharing a joke with Jonty, for they were both laughing.

She gazed towards the pair. 'And now you think you have lost her again,' she said softly and then turning to include Dolly, said, 'Don't worry. Don't worry.' She faced Richard. 'You have forgotten Appleby Fair, sir.' She shook her head reproachfully. 'Don't ever forget what the Romanies told you. They told you true.'

He searched in his mind to remember. What was it she'd said? You'll find—? There had been two Romanies. Kisaiya and her mother. What was it her mother had said? He stared at Kisaiya and she looked back, her eyes so blue and compelling. *You will find the person you are seeking.* That was what her mother had said, and he had; there was no doubt in his mind that Polly Anna was the one he had searched for.

Kisaiya smiled as she saw he had remembered. 'The answer is at Hull Fair! That's what you said, Kisaiya.' But his face dropped as he looked across to Polly Anna and Jonty, now making their way back towards them, their arms clasped around each other's waist. 'Is this the answer?' he asked softly. 'Am I to lose her yet again?'

Kisaiya shook her head. 'No. They are simply children saying goodbye!'

Polly Anna saw Kisaiya standing next to Richard and Dolly and leaving Jonty rushed towards her. Her face was animated. 'Oh, Kisaiya! *Sister*, it's so good to see you.' She put out her arms and embraced her and the baby. 'Oh and your little – is it a *chavi* or a *chavo*?'

Kisaiya laughed. 'He's a *tawno chavo*. We've called him Paul,' she added softly. 'After your *dado* – and you.'

Polly Anna put her hand to her mouth to hide her cry and her eyes glistened. She swallowed hard. 'Thank you,' she whispered. 'Thank you. You are my truest, dearest friend, Kisaiya.'

Kisaiya brushed Polly Anna's arm with her fingers. Not for the Romanies a great show of affection, but it was enough, enough to show that she too cared. 'Polly Anna,' she said huskily, 'I came especially to tell you something. Tomorrow there is to be a wedding. Can you guess whose?'

Polly Anna wrinkled her brow. 'Not Narilla! Narilla!' she whooped as Kisaiya's smile showed her she had guessed correctly that it was her sister's wedding.

'*Mam* and *Dado* and Narilla, we all want you to come, and perhaps Mr Crossley will honour us by coming also?'

'I would be delighted. My honour and pleasure,' he murmured.

'The festivities start tonight,' Kisaiya said, 'and tomorrow they will be wed. We can celebrate afore the fair starts.'

'So that's why there are so many Romanies,' Polly Anna exclaimed. 'And I met some at St Bartholomew Fair who said they were going to a wedding in the north.' She laughed. 'I never dreamed that it was Narilla's wedding they were going to.'

484

'Nearly all the Lees who can come, will come,' Kisaiya said. 'They're travelling from all over the country.'

Polly Anna thought doubtfully of the Gypsies she had met from Wandsworth Common. Some of them claimed to be Lees.

'Of course,' Kisaiya stared at her, 'there are some *Zingaros* who won't be invited.' Polly Anna wondered if Kisaiya could read her mind as she spoke again. 'There are people in every family who are not desirable. But our true *Brothers* and *Sisters* will be there, and our friends who are not of our blood will be more than welcome.'

'How wonderful,' Polly Anna exclaimed. 'And Richard,' she turned to him and put her hand on his arm, 'I have just heard some other news.' Her smile took in Jonty and Dolly and she stretched out her hand towards them. 'Jonty and Dolly are to be married! Jonty has been offered a partnership with Johnson and is going to have his own waggon-house.' Her eyes grew wistful. 'My mama and *dado* had a waggon-house. I remember it now.'

Richard closed his eyes and drew in a deep breath. So they really were saying goodbye. He could hardly believe it. He opened his eyes and looked at Dolly. Tears were spilling over her cheeks and Jonty was gazing at her with a puzzled expression and patting her hand. Richard went across to them and shook Jonty by the hand and gave him his congratulations, then he bent and kissed Dolly on her wet cheek. 'I am so glad for you,' he whispered. She didn't answer, but gave him a quavery smile and wiped away a tear.

If only, he thought, as he and Polly Anna walked

back to Mrs Harmsworth's house where they were staying, and were now going back to change their clothes for the wedding celebrations. If only I dared to ask her again. But he dared not. Not yet. Not when she had told him already that she couldn't marry him. Because she had been a dancer and entertainer.

It seems that having come up from the depths of the dunghill workhouse she is more aware of the difference between the polite society of gentlefolk and the common herd she had lived amongst than I am, he thought grievously.

This simple fact that I am a gentleman through an accident of birth, and she, who also because of accident of birth is not quite a lady, but earthborn, means, according to her reckoning that we cannot live our lives together! Is she thinking of me? Or thinking of herself? Or is she thinking of neither but simply doesn't love me?

His stride grew longer as his frustration and anger grew and Polly Anna had to hurry to keep up with him. 'Richard!' she said. 'Wait for me.'

'Sorry.' He pulled himself together and slowed down. The trouble is, he ruminated, she has too much pride, and that doesn't come from her mother but from her father! 'Rowena wasn't a lady you know,' he stated. 'In spite of her upbringing, she most definitely was *not* a lady!'

'What?' She stared at him. 'Why are you talking of Rowena?'

He hadn't meant to voice his thoughts. 'I was thinking aloud. Rowena came into my thoughts.'

'I see,' she said quietly. 'Were you thinking of her disapproval of me?'

'No.' He took hold of her hand and they mounted the steps of Mrs Harmsworth's house. 'I meant that she did not behave as a lady should.'

'I know.' She removed her hand from his as she saw Mrs Harmsworth watching them from out of her window. 'She didn't and she wasn't.'

As he waited for Polly Anna to come down after dressing, he shuffled in embarrassment as Mrs Harmsworth lectured him. 'I feel it is only proper that I should mention it, Mr Crossley. She is my niece's daughter after all, and you are so obviously besotted with her! You will be there all night and tomorrow too from what I understand!'

'I assure you Mrs Harmsworth that I shall take great care of her, you have no need to worry over her safety.' For heaven's sake, he quibbled silently, Polly Anna has been living an independent life, what does she have to fear? 'She will be surrounded by friends at this wedding, they all know her.'

Mrs Harmsworth gazed coolly at him. 'You misunderstand me, Mr Crossley, and I hesitate to be blunt, but blunt I must be. It is not the worry of Paulina being alone with the Romanies which worries me, but of her being alone with you.'

He swallowed hard as he signified her implication. 'Madam,' he began. 'If we were affianced—'

'But you are not!' she interrupted firmly, 'and young men's feelings—'

'I assure you, ma'am,' he said stiffly, 'mine will be kept firmly under control. I have every regard for Miss Lee, I would not expose her to any impropriety or risk regarding her reputation.'

She sighed. 'Then so be it.' Then she smiled. 'I used to love parties when I was young.'

The door opened and Polly Anna came in. She was dressed simply as she hadn't brought many changes of clothes with her, and she was wearing a plain grey skirt with a short train and several layers of petticoat to give fullness, and a high-necked soft silk white shirt with leg-o'mutton sleeves tied tightly at her wrists. Her hair was tied demurely in a coil at the back of her neck. She had remembered that the Romany women didn't wear their hair loose like the gentiles as it was considered unseemly and bold.

Richard stood up as she entered and Mrs Harmsworth said, 'You look lovely, my dear, but have you no jewellery?'

'No, ma'am. Only my mother's locket, which I always wear.' She fingered the chain around her neck. 'It is enough, I think?'

'Mm, perhaps. Ring the bell will you, Mr Crossley?'

The bell was rung and a maid appeared. 'Dora, bring my jewellery box and the black shawl.'

'The black shawl, ma'am? Begging your pardon, you are wearing it, ma'am.'

'Not this one, girl! The other one. The one you so admire!'

Dora flushed and bobbed her knee. 'Yes, ma'am.'

Mrs Harmsworth smiled when she had gone. 'She doesn't realize that I know when it has been taken out of its wrapping. It's always put back of course,' she added. 'But I always know.'

'Put it on Miss Paulina,' she directed when the maid returned. 'Drape it around her shoulders so that the working shows.'

Dora carefully unfastened the white sheet which

was wrapped around the shawl and Polly Anna drew in a breath. 'How beautiful,' she exclaimed as the black lace shawl was disclosed. 'Are you saying, ma'am, that I may borrow it?'

The shawl was lined in fine red cloth which showed the intricacies of the black lace to perfection. She swirled around and held her arms wide to display the exotic pattern of birds and flowers.

'My husband brought it back from abroad,' Mrs Harmsworth said softly. 'I shall never wear it again. You may keep it, my dear.'

Polly Anna thanked her profusely and then watched as Mrs Harmsworth opened the veneered walnut box on her knee. 'Just a few romantic trinkets,' she murmured and brought out a silver chatelaine, beads of Whitby jet, gold and silver earrings, necklaces and bangles. 'Choose what you would like.'

She chose a three-stringed gold necklace and gold looped earrings which Dora fastened for her and the maid's face was pink with pleasure as she gazed entranced, as if in her own flight of fancy.

'Off you go then, my dears, and take care.' Mrs Harmsworth closed up the box on her own dreams. 'And remember what I have said, Mr Crossley.'

He nodded and bowed and as he handed Polly Anna into the hired chaise, she asked, 'What do you have to remember, Richard?'

Something which I have almost forgotten already, he mused as he watched her as she fussed with her shawl, afraid of creasing it on the short journey. How can I stop my feelings from showing so?

She looked up, waiting for his answer and smiled

489

at him, so that inwardly he groaned. 'To take great care of you,' he murmured. 'Mrs Harmsworth doesn't trust young men with beautiful young women.'

She gazed at him frankly. 'Does she not realize I am able to take care of myself?'

The memory of their journey from York to Beck House came back to him and that first tender kiss which he longed to savour again, and he knew the old lady was right. Young men couldn't be trusted, not where love was concerned. He saw the innocence written on her face. 'Apparently not, Polly Anna. Apparently not!'

There was a merry sound of fiddles and pipes playing as the chaise dropped them at the outer edge of Dock Green, where a huddle of tents and carts and waggons were placed in a circle around a field. Fires were burning and people moved in swaying black shadows around them. There was a rich smell of roasting meat which tantalized their nostrils, and peals of laughter and voices raised in merriment greeted them as they approached. There were many faces which Polly Anna didn't recognize: some dark and swarthy as if they were not long from a foreign land, some voices which had different accents, Scottish, Irish, Welsh, some from the north country, some from the south.

Richard held out his arm and she took it as they walked across the field, looking for Shuri and James and their family and nodding and smiling as they were welcomed by the Romanies. She heard someone calling her name and saw Kisaiya waving to her from a large bender, which was set within a group of others. 'Over here, Polly Anna, Mr

Crossley. Welcome.' She grasped Polly Anna by the arm. 'Come and see Narilla. Mr Crossley, sir, would you wait for a moment, please?' She led Polly Anna towards the bender which had its flap closed. 'She is so nervous she wants to change her mind about the *romipen*.'

'The *romipen*? What's that?' Polly Anna asked, puzzled.

'Ah!' Kisaiya laughed. She was very merry, dressed in a red skirt and white bodice and a flower in her hair. 'Sometimes, *Sister*, I forget that you are not a *Romani chi*. *Romipen*, it means marriage. But she will be all right. I knows it. I felt the same.'

'Did you, Kisaiya? Were you not sure about Jack?'

Kisaiya suddenly looked shy. 'I knew that I loved him,' she said. 'I wasn't sure if he loved me.' She gave a brilliant smile. 'But now I knows it. It came right, just as my *mam* said it would.'

Narilla was sitting on a mattress, her dark hair was loose and being dressed by her mother and another Romany woman. Her head was bowed and she had her chin in her hands and didn't look up as Polly Anna entered. Her mother gave her a gentle tap across her head. 'Greet your guest,' she said, 'and stop this nonsense,' but there was something in her voice that showed approval of her daughter's apparent reluctance to wed.

Narilla looked up and there was a nervous gleam of excitement in her eyes. 'Welcome, *Sister*,' she whispered. 'I hope you enjoy the festivities. I wish I could dance too,' she added wistfully. 'It's not fair that I can't.'

'Tomorrow. Once you are *rommed* you can dance as much as you want,' her mother said. 'But not tonight. Tonight you will behave as a *Romani chi* should. Did I not bring you up right?' Her mother's voice rose in mock anger. 'What would your *dado* say if he heard you?'

'My father is the tribal chief, the *Rasai*,' Kisaiya explained to Polly Anna. 'He'll perform the ceremony tomorrow so Narilla must be the perfect daughter or she will shame him and all of our family.'

Narilla let out a wail and Kisaiya laughed and led Polly Anna outside again to where Richard was waiting. He had a glass of ale in his hand which someone had given him and was tapping his foot in time to the music of a fiddle, which a Romany with a coloured waistcoat and a black hat on his head was playing. It was a lively piece played in duple time and a group of Romany men were dancing to it.

'Go dance, Mr Crossley,' Kisaiya urged. 'Go dance to the *bosh*! All the Romanos dance. Watch.'

Richard's eyebrows rose. Dance? Alone? He could dance, of course. The waltz and the gavotte, but never had he danced in such an uninhibited fashion as this. He watched the men as their feet moved faster and faster, their cries growing louder as they were encouraged by the womenfolk, who watched and clapped their hands in unison.

'See, there is Narilla's *rom*, Sacki Petulengro,' Kisaiya pointed out. 'There, dancing in the centre.' They saw a young boy of about eighteen, dark and handsome with a bright red waistcoat, white shirt and black trousers, dancing in the centre of the group. His footwork was neat and his black boots tapped out in time to the music. Then the music changed and the fiddle player began a slow melody, and as the crowd moved back the boy moved slowly and rhythmically towards a pole which was placed in the ground. On top of the pole fluttered a white handkerchief and around this pole Sacki danced with slow sensuous movements. He closed his eyes and held out his arms appealingly and then wrapped them around his body as if in an embrace. He moved provocatively and seductively, swaying to the soft sound of the rhythm, and the women in the crowd murmured approvingly.

Polly Anna watched him; the music was hypnotic, and as she watched Sacki dance her own breathing became tremulous and she could feel the beat of her heart going faster. She felt a pulse hammering in her throat and her ears pounded and she glanced at Kisaiya to see if she was affected by it too. But Kisaiya was watching with a small knowing smile on her lips and like the other married women she was nodding approvingly. She looked up at Richard and saw that he was looking at her, but with an expression of such intensity that she was startled. He looked away as her eyes held his and took a deep draught of ale. It's nothing, she thought. Simply the effect of the music. Yet she felt an excitement which she couldn't explain. Something provocative and arousing and she too longed to dance uncon-strainedly to the music.

The *boshomengro* drew his melody to a close and began a swift jig. Sacki opened his eyes and became a boy again, but there was approval in the eyes of the women as they clapped him around the circle and he began another merry dance with the men, who cheered him and drew him into their midst.

Richard hadn't intended to dance. Nor had he intended to drink more than he usually did. But his glass seemed to be constantly full and he found himself in the circle of Romanies, dancing with an abandonment which surprised him. He was the only *Gorgio* there and he hadn't expected such a welcome. The few Romanies he had met, like Jack Boswell, had seemed churlish and uncommunicative, not good-humoured and indulgent as these men were as they drew him into their circle, slapped a black hat on his head and filled his glass.

The music stopped and he staggered towards Polly Anna, who was standing with Shuri and Narilla and laughing at him. 'Polly Anna,' he hiccupped, 'Polly Anna. I want to ask you something.' He swayed unsteadily and she laughingly drew him towards a bale of straw, where he gratefully sank down. 'Polly Anna!' He reached towards her and took her hand and kissed it. 'Polly Anna,' he felt his eyes fill with tears, 'I love you. And if you don't love me in return, I think I shall die.'

She gave a smile of merriment and he took her other hand. 'You don't believe me! I can tell that you don't. But it is true.' He drew her closer and impulsively pulled her on to his knee. He put his forehead against hers and closed his eyes and as he felt her body so close to him, he remembered. He gave a soft groan.

'What is it?' she whispered. The sensation of being on his knee was so pleasurable, but was it wicked she wondered, as she felt her heart beating furiously.

He pushed her away. 'I promised.' He licked his

lips, they were suddenly dry. 'I promised that I would take care of you.'

'But,' she moved closer and lifted her face to his, 'Why—?'

Shuri bore down on them and pulled them apart. 'Come,' she said. 'Paulina, come with me and you, sir, must go with the men.' She gave no explanation, but none was needed as she bore a reluctant Polly Anna away, her face yearning and his frustrated with longing.

42

I must have been drunk, he thought as he sat up the next morning on a strange coarse mattress with a rough blanket thrown over him and a dim brown light shining on him. The light was coming through the brown canvas of the tent where he slept alone and try as he might he couldn't remember coming to bed. His jacket was folded neatly and the black hat which he vaguely remembered wearing was placed on top. He was still wearing his shirt and trousers. He reached out to check if his pocket book was still in his pocket and winced as the movement hurt his head. The pocket book was there with the contents intact and his conscience pricked at the suggested implication that it might have been stolen.

He stood up and immediately sat down again. What was I drinking? Some strong brew! He got up again, but on to his hands and knees first, testing himself. He had risen to his feet and was steadying himself when he heard a voice outside.

'Mr Crossley. Time to get up.' He held on to his head and bent to open the tent flap. Jack Boswell was standing there, a sheepish grin on his face and looking about as haggard as he felt.

'I've been sent to fetch you. We have to eat with the family and then 'wedding starts.''

'Eat!' he objected. 'I couldn't possibly.'

'You'll feel better after you've eaten summat. I allus does anyway.'

'Did I make a fool of myself, Jack? I can't remember much.'

'Nor can I.' Jack Boswell grinned. 'It was a grand party, and more to follow.'

'More!' He groaned. 'I am not going to touch a drop of alcohol all day.'

'Come on, *mush*. You must,' Jack said as he guided him across to the Lees' bender. 'Today is the big day. There's a pig or two to roast and a few barrels to get through. 'Women are busy already kneading bread and cakes ready for the ceremony.'

He allowed himself to be persuaded to eat bacon and sausage and a hunk of bread and drank a large mug of hot sweet tea and thought that they had never tasted so good as they did that sharp crisp morning as he sat cross-legged by the fire. Polly Anna ate only a little and sat beside him and gazed at him with soulful eyes. 'I must apologize if my behaviour was offensive last night,' he said quietly, so that no-one else could hear. 'I drank far too much ale. You must think me a boor. I'm very sorry.'

She smiled and shook her head.

'Did I, er, did I say anything untoward? I mean – was I discourteous?' Somewhere at the back of his mind was an impression of taking Polly Anna on his knee. Or had he dreamt it? He hoped he had dreamt it. It would have been most reprehensible if he had done so.

She looked away. She seemed incredibly subdued. He must have done something. 'No,' she said. 'There was nothing untoward. At least,' she hesitated, 'I didn't think so. But Shuri was cross with me and so was Kisaiya – no, not cross,' she justified, 'anxious, I think. It isn't seemly, apparently, for a young woman to spend too much time in a man's company.'

He put his head back and laughed. 'It would seem to me, Polly Anna, that there is not much difference between the Romanies and the gentiles. You are well protected from any overtures that I might choose to make.' He touched her hand, stroking his fingers along hers. 'And perhaps it is just as well, for after all, they are right. Men are not to be trusted. Not at all.'

She gazed back at him and he saw a dreamy wistfulness in her eyes. 'Women are not to be trusted either, Richard,' she whispered. 'Some women, anyway, can't hope to hide their desires. They come right to the surface.'

He opened his mouth to say some soft words of love, but once again they were descended upon, this time by Kisaiya and the baby and Floure, who was dressed in white with flowers in her hair. 'Come,' Kisaiya said. 'We are nearly ready to start. The *boshomengro* is here, tuning up already. The dancing is about to begin.'

'Help!' Richard cried. 'Help. I can't!'

'Yes you can,' Polly Anna pulled him to his feet. 'You did. And later the women can dance too, isn't that right, Kisaiya?'

She nodded. 'After the ceremony everybody dances, including the married couple. Come on,' she smiled. 'The fun is about to begin.'

There was a tremendous din as they approached the centre of the field, where the marriage was to take place; a crowd of laughing, shouting Romanies were already drinking ale and wine, the women as well as the men. The men were dressed in their best waistcoats and white shirts and most of them wore large-brimmed hats. The women were gaily dressed in flowing skirts to their ankles and embroidered or crisp white lace bodices, their bodies covered completely apart from their feet, which were bare. Some wore flowers in their hair and all wore gold jewellery on their hands and arms and around their necks.

Polly Anna gazed at them and then turned to Richard. 'Will you help me with my boots, please? Today I'm going to be a Romany, like my *Sisters*.'

He knelt to do so and pulled off her boots, holding each small bare foot in turn. She swallowed and breathed a thank you and as he placed the boots near a bender to collect later, she tried to collect her senses. How silly I am, why should such a simple act make me feel so weak? And worse, immodest? Such thoughts that I have never dreamed of. I must be wanton for I want him to hold me in his arms again. I want him to kiss me and say that he loves me. She turned away from him, but he caught her by the arm to hold her back. 'We have to separate,' she whispered, drawing reluctantly away. 'The men from the women. Until later!'

She walked away from him, but constantly

turning to watch him watching her, until finally she smiled and blew him a kiss. He gazed at her and, bringing both his hands to his mouth, in a loving gesture threw one back.

Throughout the morning the laughter, shouts and whoops grew ever louder and more clamorous as the Romanies celebrated the coming together of two great families, the Lees and the Petulengros. The fiddlers and the pipers played and the pigs roasting on the spits crackled and spat and sent up an aroma of mouth-watering, delectable savouriness. Trestles with white lace tablecloths had been laid, one with fresh bread and a stone jar of salt, for these were to be part of the wedding ceremony. Others held sausages and meat and potatoes cooked in their skins, and special cakes which the Romany women made themselves.

At one o'clock, there was a temporary hush as Narilla, dressed in white lace and crisp cotton but with her feet bare, appeared from the Lees' bender, brought out by her father, the *Rasai*, and was given into Sacki's hand; then pandemonium broke out once more as accompanied by whistles and shouts from the Romanies and the music from the fiddles, they walked hand in hand towards the tables set with the ceremonial bread and salt, with the crowd following behind.

The bread was broken and salt sprinkled on it and Narilla and Sacki exchanged portions and then ate. They both looked so young and shy as they avoided each other's eyes, but with great encouragement from the crowd they took each other's hands again and led by the *Rasai* made their way towards the tall pole, which once again had taken centre place, the white handkerchief, symbol of *lacha*, the bride's purity, fluttering in the breeze. The wedding pair moved slowly around it, Sacki leading Narilla, and then towards the broomstick which Narilla's father and Sacki's father, Artaros, held one at each end. They placed it on the ground and stood back as the young couple stepped over it. The wedding contract was now complete.

Laughter and cheering erupted as the crowd in full voice, whistled, clapped and shouted good luck as Sacki gently kissed his bride and then led her into the dance of the *romalis* and the Romanies showered them with sugary sweetmeats.

'Shall we dance, Polly Anna? Is it allowed now?' Richard asked wryly. 'Or do we have to ask permission?'

She looked around. 'Everyone else is dancing,' she said. 'So we could try. We shall be stopped if it's wrong,' she laughed.

'So many restrictions,' he murmured as he put his arm on her waist. 'I never thought that it would be so, not with the Romanies.'

'Shuri watches over me because of who my father was, and I think also it salves her conscience because of what happened to my mother.' She put her hand on his shoulder as they moved into the crowd. She saw Orlenda sitting quietly by a fire watching the dancers. There was a wistful expression on her face. Her husband Riley was standing nearby with his back to her, a glass of ale in his hand, talking to some other men. Polly Anna smiled as they danced past but Orlenda lowered her head.

The eating and drinking, singing and dancing

went on all day. Richard danced with the men, and with Kisaiya and Shuri, and Polly Anna danced with the women and James and Jack and Riley and then they danced with each other, and no-one said that they shouldn't. From time to time one of the revellers dropped out and went to rest in a bender, but they were soon roused again and brought out protesting loudly and thrown into the throng. The babies were put to bed as the night wore on, but the children who were old enough danced and played games amongst the crowd and no-one objected, and when they were too tired to play any more they simply curled up by a fire and closed their eyes.

Polly Anna had tasted a glass of wine, but she felt so exhilarated, so buoyant, that she had no need of any other stimulant. Richard had once again had more ale and wine than he had intended, but he ate well of the roast pork and the bread and felt not the least intoxicated, but simply very merry. 'I'm so very happy to be with you, Polly Anna,' he kept repeating, 'so very happy,' and she simply smiled at him; she was happy too, an excitement buoying her up to such great heights that she thought she might float away.

'There is a difference in you tonight.' He looked tenderly down at her. 'You look like – what do they say, a *Romany chi*? And yet, when you stand next to Kisaiya and Shuri, there is a difference.' They were standing apart from the crowd, resting for a few moments from the hectic dance. The air was clean and sharp with a smell of the sea blowing in from the estuary and blending with the woodsmoke of the fires, which crackled and sparked around them, and the sky was clear with a myriad of stars twinkling and scintillating.

He reached over to a table nearby and took a yellow flower from the decoration and threaded it through her hair, which was escaping from its neat chignon and curling in wisps around her face. 'The *Romany chi*.'

She touched his cheek and whispered, 'And you look like one of the Greek gods which Samuel used to tell us about. Tall and fair and noble.'

'I love you, Polly Anna – Paulina – my *Romany chi*. More than I can ever say.' He stroked her face, gently touching her lips which he so wanted against his. 'I want to spend my life with you. I am asking again. Will you be my wife?'

She reached up to kiss him. 'I love you,' she breathed. 'And here with the Romanies it seems right.'

'So – will you? Are you saying yes?' He felt as if he could hardly breathe as he waited what seemed to be an eternity for her answer. She smiled and kissed him again. 'Yes. I will marry you.'

He took her in his arms and held her close, breathing in the fragrance of her, nestling his face in her hair, which was tumbling down, and delighting in the sensuous pleasure of her soft warm body next to his. He kissed her mouth tenderly and she closed her eyes. I must remember, he groaned, I must remember! No matter how much I love her and want her. She knows nothing of men. I must protect her from me!

There was a sudden shout and they looked up guiltily. Jack Boswell was striding towards them. 'Come on! Dance! Everyone must dance.' He was already the worse for drink but he danced merrily, his feet tripping over each other as he urged everyone on. 'Where's my wife?' he called. 'My beautiful Kisaiya. Mother of my children. Kisaiya!' he shouted. 'Come dance with your *rom*.'

Richard took Polly Anna by the hand and led her back into the crowd. She was trembling. 'Hold me close,' she whispered. 'I feel so strange.' Her body felt as if it didn't belong to her, but now she knew why. She was consumed with desire. She wanted Richard to hold her close, to feel his hands touching her, loving her. Am I wicked, she wondered, to want this? Will he think the worse of me if I tell him how I feel? Do other women feel the same?

She felt as if she was floating as he waltzed her round and round and she saw as if in a haze the other laughing, dancing women around her. He kissed her cheek and whispered again. 'I love you, Polly Anna and you are going to be my wife.'

'Yes,' she breathed. 'I am.'

They danced out of the crowd towards where a group of Romanies were standing talking, Shuri and James and some of the other Lees who had travelled from other areas. Shuri turned to watch them as they swirled around and nodded her head knowingly. Polly Anna smiled at her as they waltzed by towards where the pole was still standing, the handkerchief white against the dark sky. They danced around it and the crowd turned to watch them. There was a buzz of laughter coming from elsewhere and then it seemed as if everyone had come closer to watch. Richard drew apart from Polly Anna and held her at arm's length, then he released her hands and put one of his own behind his back. He flourished his other towards her and gave a deep bow.

She gave a small laugh, surprised at his action and caught up his hand again. They danced around the pole again and the fiddler moved towards them and started to fiddle faster, increasing the tempo so that they were no longer waltzing but dancing faster, round and round in circles with a laughing, clapping crowd encouraging them. Round and round they went, faster and faster, until suddenly the music stopped and they were in front of the broomstick, which was still lying on the ground.

They gazed at each other and there was a sudden hush from the onlookers. Neither of them spoke but without taking their eyes from each other they stepped, as if in one mind, over the broomstick.

The crowd pressed around, all silently watching but Polly Anna and Richard continued to gaze engrossed at each other. Then someone said in a loud whisper. 'The *Gorgio rye* has stepped over the broomstick! He's *romm'd* a *Romany chi*.'

Polly Anna and Richard looked up, broken from their reverie. The faces around them were solemn. Richard put his arm around Polly Anna. 'Did we do wrong?' he asked the crowd in general. 'Did we break one of your laws. If we did, I apologize.'

James Lee stepped forward. 'Sir,' he said solemnly, 'we do not take this ceremony lightly and you are not a Romany!'

'No.' Richard answered in the same tone. 'I am not; but tonight I wish that I were, so that this ceremony was as binding as the Romanies believe it to be.'

'Do you love this woman?' James asked. 'Will you honour her all of your life unto death?'

'I will.' Richard looked tenderly at Polly Anna. 'For ever.'

'Paulina Lee. Do you love this *Gorgio rye*? Will you keep yourself only for him?'

She smiled. 'Always.'

James Lee threw his hands in the air. 'Then so be it!'

Hats were thrown into the air at the pronouncement and a great cheer echoed around the field. Another barrel of ale was broken into and more food prepared. The fiddlers played, the penny whistles were brought out, dancing began again and Polly Anna and Richard were swept along on a tide of good wishes. Kisaiya put her arms around her. 'I knowed it all along,' but Shuri, although giving them her good wishes, was reserved in manner and refrained from smiling.

The night drew on and some of the revellers retired, though the younger ones still danced on or sat chatting around the fires. Richard held Polly Anna close as they moved dreamily around in time to the music. She looked up at him and in mutual consent, though no word had been spoken, he led her away from the centre of the field into the flickering shadows beyond the firelight and towards the bender where he had spent the previous night.

Fumbling slightly he lifted the flap and stepped inside; she hesitated for only a second and then followed him within. 'Polly Anna,' he whispered, 'how I've waited for this moment. I have longed to tell you – to show you how much I love you. And now you are my wife.'

'I am your Gypsy wife,' she said softly. 'And you are my *Gorgio rom*. As true a husband as if we were married in church.'

He bent to kiss her parted lips. He could taste the sweetness of wine upon them. It was true at last. She was his wife. But a warning sounded in his ears. You are not a Romany, James Lee had said. But did it matter? He had already thrown caution to the winds. He had not behaved as a gentleman should. Tonight he had not been a gentleman, he had been part of that circle of men who called themselves Romanies. He had danced and drunk in abandonment. He had passionately kissed the woman he loved, who was now his wife. But you are not a Romany, echoed the words again.

'I love you, Polly Anna, my wife. Do you trust me?'

'With my life,' she whispered and sank down on to the mattress, drawing him towards her.

Slowly he unfastened the buttons on her white bodice to reveal the soft slip beneath. He slipped it off and kissed each cool bare shoulder in turn. She threw back her head to reveal her throat and the curve of her breasts and he groaned as with sensuous fingers he caressed the softness of her flesh and felt the pounding of her heart.

She gazed at him, her eyes soft and tender, then with shaking fingers she unfastened his shirt and slipped her hand inside, stroking his firm body and running her fingers through the soft fuzz of hair. 'I love you, Richard, but you must show me – show me how to show you that I do.'

He bent once more and tasted the sweetness of her breasts, but there came a scratching on the canvas door. 'Paulina! Paulina!' The whisper was urgent and agitated. It was Shuri. 'Come out. Come out!'

Horrified they looked at each other. Richard buttoned up his shirt and Polly Anna slipped back into her bodice. 'What is it?' Richard asked sharply. 'What's wrong?' He opened up the flap. 'Has something happened?'

'I hope not sir, I hope not! Paulina, you must come.'

'But why?' she cried. 'This is my wedding night!'

Shuri took her by the hand, then she pointed a finger at Richard and shook it at him. 'You should know better, sir. You are a gentleman are you not? You are not married according to your own laws.'

'We are married according to Romany laws and that is good enough for me.' He was angry. Very angry.

'But you are not a Romany!' Shuri was angry too and she held a bewildered Polly Anna firmly. 'Tomorrow you will be a *Gorgio* again. Tonight you have been playing at being a Romany. I'm sorry, sir. But you must ask permission of Paulina's grandmother. She will say if you may marry.'

He stared at her. 'But – the *Rasai*!'

'*Avali! Avali!* Phw! He is only a man and like all men thinks only of the present! The women must think of the future.' Her voice was hard but then softened. 'Think of Paulina, sir. What would her grandmother say if you told her that you were married according to Romany law and had taken her as your wife?'

He fell silent. He knew she was right. Polly Anna's grandmother would be mortified, as she had been all those years ago when Polly Anna's mother married a Romany. He swallowed hard, his passion sank, his spirits so low as he drooped into a trough of depression and all his hopes and dreams were deferred.

They touched hands as Polly Anna was led, weeping, away to Shuri's tent and he sank down on the ground and put his head in his hands. He had been sitting there for some five minutes, dejected and humiliated, when Jack Boswell went rolling by. 'Hey,' Jack shouted, 'what you doing there, sir? This is your wedding night – hic, morning.'

It was almost day. The sky was lightening, streaks of crimson and gold to the east, rising above the waters of the Humber and bringing a promise of another fine day. There were still some revellers about but mostly the camp was quiet. 'My wife has been taken from me,' he said mournfully. 'She's been taken from her loving husband.'

Jack stumbled across to him. 'Why's that then, sir?'

'It seems that in the eyes of the Romany women we are not married.'

'Pah! Women! What do they know? Well, you'd better come wi' me, sir, and have a drink and drown your sorrows.'

Richard got to his feet. 'For God's sake, man! Will you stop calling me, sir!' He put his arm through that of Jack Boswell. 'And yes, I will have a damned drink. Several in fact. I'm going to get rip-roaring drunk!'

43

Polly Anna cried all night. 'Why?' she kept repeating. 'Why? My mother married my father. They were allowed to be together, why not Richard and me?'

'Your *dado* was a Romany, not your mother.' Shuri was sharp with her. 'We had no control over what she did and your *dado* made the decision to marry her. It was his right.'

But still she wailed and cried until Shuri finally turned her back on her and went to sleep. 'Hush now,' Kisaiya said softly. 'Think that it is for the best.' She lowered her voice. 'Just suppose your grandmother was angry and wouldn't have you back? Where would you go? Mr Crossley couldn't live here with the Romanies, it's not like a *rawnie* marrying a Romany *chal*.' She shook her head and smiled gently. 'You are my cousin and my *Sister* in blood, Polly Anna, but you are not whole Romany. Tomorrow you may be an equestrienne, and the day after?' She shrugged. 'Who knows? A fine lady perhaps? You are many people, Polly Anna, not just one.'

'Yes,' she sniffled. 'You are always right, Kisaiya.

But it doesn't make me feel any better,' and she lay down on the mattress and cried herself to sleep.

It was well after midday before Richard awoke. His head thumped even more than it had done the day before and he crawled on his hands and knees towards the door of the tent. He screwed up his eyes as the light hit them, even though it was a grey dull morning. He hopped about on one leg and then the other to put his trousers on, which were lying in a crumpled heap on top of his shirt. Obviously no-one had put him to bed as they had done the night before; he must have just fallen on to the mattress in a stupor, but he had no recollection. None whatsoever.

He stepped outside. A few men were walking lethargically towards the field where the horses were tethered, some were sitting cross-legged by their fires drinking tea, but the women were clearing up the debris from the party whilst others were busy around their fires attending to children or food.

Shuri came across to him; she was dressed with her shawl around her head and a basket containing lavender and lace over her arm. She nodded to him. 'There's water by my bender if you want to wash, sir.'

'Thank you,' he said meekly. 'Shuri – Mrs Lee, I must apologize for last night. You were right of course. It's just that I—'

'I know, sir. You were just married, or thought you were.' She looked at him solemnly. 'You can have another wedding, sir. One according to your laws.'

'Yes.' He gazed at her frankly. 'But I will never forget the first one. That is when I married Polly Anna.'

A ghost of a smile touched her lips. 'Aye. It will always bind you.'

She bade him farewell and he went across to the tent, where Kisaiya was sitting by the fire feeding her baby. She appeared not in the least embarrassed and asked him if he would like something to eat.

'Nothing,' he groaned. 'My mouth is like a dry cavern this morning.'

'Then take some tea,' she said. 'It's fresh brewed in the pot.'

He poured himself a tin mug of the strong hot liquid and then looked around. 'Where's Polly Anna? Not still sleeping?'

Kisaiya looked at him soberly. 'No sir, she was up early.'

'So—?' He gave a half-hearted laugh. Why wasn't she here to greet him? Her husband. 'Where is she then?'

She lifted her head. 'She's gone, sir.'

His heart lurched. 'Gone! What do you mean gone?' He didn't mean to sound so brusque but surely—? 'Where has she gone?'

She continued to gaze at him, then he saw the slight lifting of the corners of her mouth and a sparkle in her eyes. 'Kisaiya!'

She laughed out loud. 'She has gone to the fair, Mr Crossley! Have you forgotten that that is why she came? She looked in at you, but you were sleeping. She said she will see you there.'

He crouched down beside her. 'Kisaiya? I don't

suppose you would tell my fortune, would you?'

'It has already been told. At Appleby Fair. Have you forgotten that also?'

'But I want to know more. I want to know what the future holds for Polly Anna and me.'

'One fortune telling is enough,' she murmured. 'Your future is in your own hands now. A Romany cannot help you with it.'

He rose to his feet. 'No, I suppose not. You are very wise for such a young woman, Kisaiya. It's a gift, I suppose!'

'I don't know.' Her eyes were deep and unfathomable. 'Sometimes I can see things and I don't always know the meaning of them.' She changed her baby from one breast to the other and he thought how lovely and serene she was; it was such a natural act that he felt no discomfiture. 'You will watch over Polly Anna, Mr Crossley?' She seemed suddenly anxious. 'She will be vulnerable in your society because of who she is. You won't let anyone bully her?'

'Who would do that?' he exclaimed. 'She will be my wife. She will have a position in society.'

'Even so,' she said softly, 'there might be some – one *rawnie* who I can think of.'

He pondered and frowned. 'No-one!' Then he gave a small gasp. She didn't know! 'Miss Winthrop—? You didn't hear, did Polly Anna not say?'

She shook her head. 'Polly Anna only talks about you. But yes, that is the lady I was thinking of.'

'She is dead, Kisaiya. She had a terrible accident and died shortly after, I thought – I thought—'

'That I would know? How could I? I'm sorry.' Her

face and voice expressed sorrow, but there was no emotion for the woman who would not speak for her husband, who had let him languish in a cell.

'Kisaiya! Did you—? What did you say about Miss Winthrop on that day when Polly Anna pleaded for Jack?'

Kisaiya looked puzzled and shook her head. 'Nothing. It was Polly Anna who spoke to her. She wouldn't speak to me, she sent me away.'

'But the maids said that you cursed her! Mrs Winthrop asked me to ask you what it was you had said. I told her that you would not have done that, that it wasn't in your nature. But she is curious.'

'Ah! Yes, I do remember.' Her eyes were wide and appealing. 'It wasn't a curse, Mr Crossley. It is the Devil's work to curse, not mine. I don't work for the Devil!'

'I never thought for a moment that you did, Kisaiya. But what was it you said?'

'Rinkeno mui and wafodu zee
Kitzi's the cheeros we dicks cattanē.'

She chanted softly. 'It isn't a curse, Mr Crossley, merely an old Romany saying.

'A beautiful face and a black wicked mind
Often, full often together we find.'

He was silent. It was true. And it had applied to Rowena. 'She changed after her accident,' he said in mitigation. 'She repented over her actions. It was she as well as the old lady who urged me not to

514

delay, but to go immediately in search of Polly Anna after she had left with you.'

'Then she will rest in peace', she smiled, 'and will not be troubled.'

He took his leave of her and after swilling his face in cold water, set off to find Polly Anna. He mingled with the crowds in the fairground who were already gathering for the first day of entertainment. He breathed in the pungent aroma which was now so familiar to him after visiting so many sites during his search for Polly Anna. The smell of gingerbread and sticky toffee, of roasting potatoes and pans of peas. Of horses and elephants, lions and tigers.

He found Polly Anna standing by Johnson's Circus in company with two clowns and a man on stilts. She turned and saw him and ran towards him. He reached out his hands and she touched them with hers. She looked so beautiful, her eyes tender with love.

'Husband,' she whispered.

'Wife,' he smiled and bent to kiss her. 'You do realize that it isn't seemly to kiss in public? We shall shock all of your relatives, Romany and gentile!'

'I know,' she said softly, 'but I don't care. Richard! I want to ask you something.'

'Anything,' he said, taking her hand as they walked back to the circus tent. 'Anything at all.'

'When we are married in church, will I have to obey you, like the Romany women obey their husbands? Will I have to ask permission if I want to do anything?'

He thought wryly that he hadn't observed the Romany women obeying their husbands; it seemed to him that they did most things their own way. 'In law, yes; you promise to obey. But, Polly Anna, I would never expect you to do anything you didn't want to do. How could I?'

'But—'. She stopped walking and turned to face him. 'There is something in particular that I want to do and I want to know if I have to ask you first.'

'No, my love,' he said seriously. 'You do not have to ask me. You can do whatever you want to do. You are a free spirit and I don't ever want to change you. Don't ask – except for one thing which I absolutely forbid.' He gazed down at her.

She put her hand to her mouth. 'What? Tell me now.'

'Don't ever leave me,' he whispered, touching her face so gently. 'Don't ever run away and leave me alone.'

'Never,' she said lovingly. 'Never again.'

'Well, well, well! Who have we here! If it isn't pretty Polly!'

They turned in unison as the coarse voice broke into their exchange of love. Amos Johnson stood grinning at them. 'Well, well, well,' he sneered. 'Tha found her then? Where was she hiding? I looked all over and couldn't find her. Tha beat me to it.'

Neither of them answered, but Richard felt his hackles rise.

'I heard tell she'd gone off wi' Gyppos.' He spoke as if Polly Anna wasn't there. 'So what's she doing wi' a fine gentleman like you? As if I couldn't guess,' he leered.

Richard grabbed him by his collar. 'Do not insult my wife! Say anything more and I will lay you out like one of your gullible contestants.' He pushed him in the chest so that he staggered backwards. 'Now get back to your kennel!'

Amos slunk away, giving them both a look of pure hatred.

'He will remember that, Richard,' Polly Anna said nervously. 'He's a bully and a coward, but he'll get his own back.'

Richard shrugged. 'He'd have to get someone else to fight for him. He doesn't like to get hurt.'

They continued their walk around the fairground and Polly Anna told him of the time Jonty stole a hot potato whilst she had kept the stall-keeper occupied. 'And I pretended that I had lost my money,' she laughed. 'And a man paid for a bag of peas.' Her smile dropped away. 'We were always hungry,' she said. 'Jonty was once locked in a cupboard for stealing a sausage. The Black Box,' she remembered. 'I was put in it too. It was horrible.'

He didn't laugh. It was terrible, he thought, that children had to steal food to appease their hunger. He looked around at the crowd with different eyes. There were many who were tidily dressed, out to enjoy their day. Country people in smocks and shawls, their eyes wide at the entertainment on offer. Soldiers in red uniform were strolling around, more interested in the female population than the entertainment. But there were many others who stood longingly outside the booths and the toy stalls and food counters, just looking, as if knowing that the delights displayed were not for them.

They heard a raucous voice shouting and turned towards it. Amos Johnson was now standing outside his boxing booth enticing the young men watching his Champion in feigned fight to come up and try their skills. They were raw country lads, most of them, muscly and strong, used to shifting bales of hay and working cart horses and eagerly they rushed forward to try and earn a shilling.

'Now here's a fine young gentleman.' Amos had seen Richard and Polly Anna in the crowd. 'He's a gentleman all right in spite of his crumpled clothes! And how did they get so crumpled, sir?' he mocked. 'Well, just look at the little lady by his side.' He leaned forward confidentially into the crowd, who had turned as one to see whom he was speaking of. 'Wouldn't your clothes be creased and crumpled if you had such a beauty by your side? Where've you been, sir? Back of 'haystack?'

The crowd roared with laughter. Now they'd see some fun.

'How about coming up, sir? Show these good people how gentlemen box. That's if you know how,' he added mockingly.

Richard had already left Polly Anna's side and was pushing his way through the crowd. He stood below the platform where Amos was standing. 'You're a blackguard! I warned you about your insulting behaviour towards my wife.'

The crowd murmured. That wasn't right, he shouldn't have insulted a man's wife. Doxy or whore perhaps, but not a wife. A ripple of excitement ran through the crowd and they gathered closer.

'Are you coming up to fight then?' Amos wasn't shamed or deterred. 'Here's my Champ. Ready and waiting.'

'I have no cause to fight with him. You're the one I will fight,' Richard started to climb the steps and the crowd cheered, 'if you dare!'

'Now hold on.' Amos put his hand out to stop him. 'It was onny said in fun! Now here's my Champ. If you feel like letting off steam, he's the man you want.'

The Champion was dancing around on his toes, flailing his fists back and forth. He was built like a gorilla and almost as hairy.

Richard put his hand on Amos's throat. 'You are the one who insulted my wife.' He turned to the crowd, still holding Amos, who was turning a shade of red. 'Shall we fight?'

'Yes!' the crowd yelled. 'Fight! Fight! Fight!'

Amos choked. 'Wait,' he gasped. 'Tell you what.' Richard let go of him. 'This is obviously a fighting man,' Amos appealed to the upturned faces of the throng below. 'He can't tek a bit o' fun! Fight my Champ first,' he challenged Richard, 'and then fight wi' me when you've won him!'

He had a grin on his face which infuriated Richard. He was implying that he would never get so far, that his Champion would defeat him and he would never get his revenge.

'What shall he do?' Amos yelled. 'Shall he fight the Champ?'

'Yes!' There was a great roar. The multitude of people had swelled as others gathered to see what the noise and commotion was about.

'Right,' Richard thundered. 'I'll fight the Champion, then I'll fight this snake in the grass, this foul-mouthed rogue who speaks evil of women.'

'Yes!' The crowd chanted. 'Yes. Fight! Fight! Fight!'

'No,' Polly Anna whispered. 'No! No! No!' She looked around for someone to stop it. Richard would be massacred. His face bruised, his body crushed. But there wasn't anyone. The mob, for that was what it now was, were chanting, eager to see blood and it didn't seem to matter whose it was.

There were two clowns on the platform in front of Johnson's Circus, one, with an upturned grin on his painted face was somersaulting in a peculiarly lopsided way. The other, with his mouth turned down in a look of sorrow, was expertly juggling with a set of clubs. They both stopped their actions as the noise from the boxing booth reached them, and they watched from over the top of the crowd.

'Walk up! Walk up! See the clowns. See the acrobats,' Johnson called, annoyed at his elder son for distracting the crowds from his circus. 'What does he think he's up to?' he muttered.

One of the clowns jumped down from the platform and skipped across to the boxing booth, whilst the other continued his juggling but glancing now and again towards the other booth.

Shuri, with her basket over her arm, suspended her offers of *dukkering* and sale of lace, and she too walked across to watch for a moment, before turning around and hurrying towards the Market Place where the horse sales were taking place.

Polly Anna felt someone tug on her skirt. 'Kisaiya! What can I do?' She turned a tearful face to her friend and back to the booth where Richard was taking off his jacket. 'He'll be killed. He can't fight that great brute. I must stop him.'

She pushed forward, but the crowd was too great and they wouldn't let her through. The people had forgotten her and that it was her reputation that the gentleman in the ring was fighting for. They whistled as Richard took off his shirt and exposed his lean, hard body and squared up to the might and weight of the Champion.

Amos Johnson grinned. 'Shake hands like gentlemen,' he ridiculed. 'Don't forget you can earn a shilling, sir. It's probably 'onny time you've ever had to.'

The crowd muttered. 'Quite right. Give him a beating. Who does he think he is? He's no better than 'rest of us!'

Richard felt their animosity. How quickly they could turn their favours from one to another. He weighed up the Champion. He was heavy, his shoulders wide and his chest broad, his head sitting like a cannon ball on his shoulders. Amos clanged the bell, the fight had begun and the Champion came at Richard like a tornado, throwing his weight behind his fist as he aimed it at Richard's face. He ducked and the blow merely brushed his cheek and he crashed his fist into the Champion's exposed stomach. The Champion gasped at the unexpected blow and threw another punch, but it was wild and missed its mark, and once again Richard hammered a blow into his stomach, winding him. The Champion staggered back and Richard slammed into his jaw, left, right, left, then jabbed again into his ribs.

The crowd cheered, their allegiance changed. 'Come on, mister. Come on! Tha's earning 'shilling.'

The Champion grew nasty. The crowd was usually against him and with the contestant, but this time he was set to earn more than his usual pittance. Amos Johnson had promised him a guinea if he floored this one and he'd thought it would be easy as he was a gentleman; but the man's body was firm and muscular and without flab. He swung a savage right punch and caught Richard on the cheek just below the eye, which sent him staggering, but he came back again and returned the blow to the Champion's right eye. The crowd roared and dipped in their pockets to put money in the bucket which Amos was jiggling in front of them whilst at the same time keeping a nervous eye on the proceedings up in the ring.

Richard felt the pain in his cheek, but he had got his opponent's measure. The Champion's technique was limited. He came in wild rushes and usually his great strength was sufficient to floor his opponents. But Richard remembered his boxing days at school and how he used to play cat and mouse with his opponents. He danced around the Champion, teasing him with light blows here and there, first to the head and then to the body. The Champion was confused as to how to defend himself and let his guard down. Richard swung a punch like a mule's kick and cracked his jaw, following it with hammering, jabbing blows to his ribs.

The Champion threw himself against him, throwing out punches wherever they would find a mark and Richard was winded. He was held in an arm lock and Amos wasn't shouting for them to break. There were no rules in this contest. He lashed out his right leg, the only part of his body that was free and wrapped it around the Champion's and they crashed in a heap on to the canvas. As they fell, Richard brought up his knee and came into the only soft and flabby part of the man's body. 'Sorry!' he apologized.

The Champion grunted and rolled on to his knees. Richard got to his feet and waited, dancing on his toes. Only fair after all to give the fellow time to recover. But the crowd didn't think so, they were baying for blood and they hadn't seen any so far.

The Champion staggered to his feet and lashed out, a short sharp blow to the stomach; Richard doubled over but rained punches to the Champion's ribs as he rose; he aimed for his face landing a punch on his left cheek, another at his right temple. A thin trickle of blood oozed out from the Champion's cheek, exciting the crowd.

Richard's knuckles were sore and starting to swell and he knew he would have to be quick and finish off this fighter if he was going to fight Amos too. And that, after all, was what he was aiming for. The Champion's cheeks were swelling, his right eye was starting to close and he gave a lightning left jab at it, followed by a crashing blow to his nose, drawing blood. The Champion backed off, putting his hands up to his face and Richard launched himself into the attack. He rained punches into his exposed body until the Champion's strength was sapped, his legs buckled and he sank down to the floor.

'Get up! Get up!' the crowd shouted. But the Champion was finished. Amos Johnson didn't pay him enough to be beaten to death and what was a guinea anyway? He'd only drink it away at the alehouse. He stayed down and the crowd started to count him out.

Amos looked round in anguish as he saw Richard watching him, a mean grin on his face. 'Your turn, I believe,' he said. 'Get your jacket off!'

'I er, perhaps later when you've recovered,' he stammered. 'It wouldn't be fair to take you on now after such a gruelling contest. I don't mind waiting until tomorrow.'

'Get tha coat off, Amos,' somebody shouted. 'We're all waiting.'

'And don't forget to give him his shilling,' a woman called. 'He's earnt it.'

Amos fished in the bucket, took out a shilling and handed it to Richard, who took it and, turning round to the Champion who was sitting with a dazed expression on his face, threw it to him. 'Here,' he said, 'take it. You've earned it. My fight wasn't with you.'

'Thanks.' The Champion caught it. 'You're a gent, mush. I wish you all 'best. You'll have no trouble knocking 'boss over. He's like a ha'porth o' soft toffee.'

The crowd was chanting again as Amos reluctantly took off his coat. Richard watched him keenly. The man was plainly nervous, glancing around as if for a means of escape.

'Hey!' A man's voice called up from the crowd. 'Amos Johnson!' A group of Romanies were standing just below the booth. Jack Boswell, Riley Boswell, Sacki Petulengro and James Lee. It was James Lee who had called up Amos's name. Behind them stood other Romanies, Richard recognized some of the faces from the wedding party.

'We heard that you've dishonoured the name of one of our *Sisters*.' James Lee's voice was hard. 'Is it true what we hear?'

'No. No! Would I do such a thing? One of your *Sisters*? No, not me. Never!' He was clearly very frightened. His hands were shaking and there was a tremor in his voice.

'Yes, that's what we've heard.' James Lee's voice rose. 'Her husband is fighting for her honour and that is his right and duty.' He waved a hand about his head, encompassing all the Romanies who were standing about him. 'Then it's our turn.'

Some in the crowd looked nervous and started to back away. If the Gypsies were involved in a fight anything could happen and the constables of the watch and the military could be called. Others waited, eager to be on the sidelines, to watch and later to relate.

'No, no! You've made a mistake,' Amos protested. 'I said nothing about any lady, Romany or otherwise. You know how things get exaggerated,' he pleaded.

'Get on with it!' somebody shouted. 'We've other shows to go to.'

Amos turned towards Richard, such an abject picture of misery that he almost felt sorry for him. He put up his fists, they were soft, his knuckles flabby and Richard danced towards him. He waited, but Amos didn't move; he gave him a quick light punch to his cheek and he flinched, putting his hands up in defence.

Richard gave a sharp exclamation. The man clearly wasn't going to fight. He shot a sharp blow to his chin, another to his cheek and two more to his ribs and Amos went down with a crash. The crowd booed. The fight was over. Amos Johnson was no fighter, they'd known it all along. Richard bent over him and moved him with his foot. He was feigning unconsciousness, he could see his eyelids flickering. 'You're a coward! A yellow-livered coward,' he said softly. 'You're not even worth thinking about.'

He picked up his shirt and jacket and climbed down the steps to where Polly Anna was waiting. His cheek was smarting and it felt swollen. She put her arms around him. 'Your poor face!'

'Yes,' he grinned, tenderly touching it. 'Have you thought how I can explain it away to Mrs Harmsworth or Mrs Winthrop and Aunt Mary?'

They passed the group of Romanies who nodded to them, Jack Boswell gave Richard a wink. 'You did well, sir, for a *Gorgio*.' He put up his hand and Richard slapped his against it.

The afternoon was darkening as heavy cloud descended and a fine drizzle settled in. Flares and naphtha lights illuminated the booths and some were lit by flickering candles. The crowds were increasing and they were being crushed from side to side. 'Richard!' Polly Anna murmured, 'I, er, I have to go to the circus. I said – I told Mr Johnson—. It's a surprise! Will you come along in a few minutes?'

'I'll come now,' he smiled, though he would rather have gone back to Mrs Harmsworth's and put a piece of beefsteak on his eye.

'No. Give me ten minutes. Please, and then you must come. Buy a ticket and come inside,' she pleaded and to humour her he agreed.

'And then tomorrow can we go home? Home to the Wolds, I mean?'

'Yes.' She reached up to kiss him. 'Then we can.'

He ambled around the fairground. He paid sixpence to watch an Indian rope trick and another to see the Learned Dog spell and count, but he avoided the crowds waiting outside the booths with the Pig-Faced Lady and the Siamese Twins with One Body and Two Heads. He turned to go back to the circus, keeping to the edge of the fairground to avoid the mass of people who were descending on it. The shows were about ready to start. The fairmen were shouting, drums were banging and cymbals crashing as they competed with each other to bring in the customers.

It was quite dark now, shadows were flickering in corners and once or twice he stumbled over wooden stakes and shafts of waggons. He turned around. He didn't know why but he felt as if he was being followed. Ridiculous fancy, he thought, no-one would think to rob me looking so shabby as I do. But nevertheless the feeling persisted.

He stopped. There was no-one behind him, yet he thought he heard the stealth of footsteps. He walked on. There again! Swiftly he turned, too late. A hand was on his neck and in that hand was a knife, the blade sharp and pointed and piercing his throat.

44

Polly Anna climbed into the wardrobe waggon and rifled through the assortment of clothes stacked in piles. Breeches and clown outfits, spangled dresses and cotton bags containing shoes and wigs were piled in untidy heaps, left behind by the artists and entertainers of the circus, who had already taken what they required. She rooted around in the midst of it all and pulled out a red dress sparkling with silver thread and a pair of footless stockings. 'Ah,' she murmured, 'those were mine.' She remembered, when last working for Johnson's Circus that she had cut off the feet of the stockings so she would have a better grip when standing on the horse's back.

'Here,' said the wardrobe woman, who was sitting in the midst of it all stitching up a pair of torn breeches, 'this'll suit you,' and passed her a coronet. It was cheap and tawdry tinsel, but under the flickering naphtha lights in the ring, Polly Anna knew it would sparkle like diamonds, and she took it and put it on her head.

'We're all glad to see you back,' the woman said.

'We were sorry when you left; you've got a good act.'

She thanked her and jumped down from the waggon, carrying the clothes with her, and went in search of Jonty. She couldn't see him, however, so finding a corner in the horse tent, she changed into her finery and brought the Pinto out of his stall. She stroked him and soothed him and told him that tonight was a special night. 'I know we've been apart for a while and we haven't had much chance to practise today, but we'll be fine, don't you worry.'

When she arrived back at the circus tent Mr Johnson was anxious and annoyed. 'I don't know where them two lads have got to. What a time to go off, just when we're ready to start!'

'Can we delay for ten minutes, Mr Johnson? We can't start without them.' She peered under the canvas flap into the arena. People were already filing in, shuffling around for the best view, but there was no sign of Jonty or Harry Johnson or Richard either.

Ten minutes went by and Mr Johnson came back in from the front of the platform, where he had been exhorting the crowd to come in, she had heard him booming, 'Roll up, roll up. See the best circus in town. See the clowns, see Tiny, the baby elephant. Come today for the special attraction. Roll up, Roll up!'

'Something's happened,' he said, 'it must have done. Where can they be?' He checked that everyone else was in place and waiting, the other horse riders, the acrobats, the lion and tiger keepers with the cages ready to pull into the ring.

Polly Anna too was getting anxious. She had said to Richard to be only ten minutes and that was over half an hour ago. 'Give them five more minutes,' she urged, 'then send in the dwarfs. They'll distract the crowd,' whom she saw were getting restless.

'Aye, five more minutes,' he said, heading for the outside again. He turned back. 'I'm glad you're back, Polly Anna.'

'Don't move or you're a dead man!'

'I'm not moving,' Richard muttered through clenched teeth, feeling the point of the blade against his throat, 'but my money's in my pocket.'

'I don't want tha money,' the voice rasped, 'but I'd like to see your face in ribbons!'

'Revenge, is it, Amos?' he said softly, recognizing the voice and guessing that Amos had come searching for him out of malice and ill will.

There was a hesitation as Amos absorbed that he had been discovered, then he hissed, 'You've finished me in this town! Made me a laughing stock; everybody's talking.'

'You were a laughing stock before I came along. Anyway you deserved a beating.' He felt the prick of the blade but continued. 'No-one will speak ill of my wife without answering to me.'

'Wife!' Amos sneered. 'In all but name! When did you marry her?'

Richard shifted slightly. If he could only move Amos's weight from behind him, but he was in danger of having his throat slit so tightly was he held. 'Yesterday,' he said. 'We were married yesterday.'

Amos was silent, then he muttered. 'I allus wanted her. Since she was fourteen when she first came to 'fair, I was set on her. I waited an' all. Never laid hands on her. Not 'till she was older, but she wouldn't look at me.' He scoffed. 'She won't have telled thee that yon Dummy was sweet on her; she wouldn't do owt without his say so.'

'I'm aware of that, Amos,' he said cautiously, anxious not to aggravate him. 'You're not telling me anything that I don't already know. Now be a good fellow and put that knife away.'

Amos pressed the blade until it nicked his skin and drew blood. 'Don't humbug *me*, tha popin-jay! I'll have her, whether or not she's married to thee. I'll have her, mek no mistake. I'll search her out. So be warned, both on you!'

There was a sudden gasp and the pressure on Richard's neck released as Amos fell backwards, brought down by two pairs of strong arms. The knife was prised from his grasp and he lay on the ground staring at the double apparition dancing above him.

In the darkness the figures were macabre. Their coloured costumes glittered with stars and moons and their white painted faces gleamed with a sinister intent: one with an upturned demoniacal grin, the other with a disdainful sneer and malevol-ent eyes. They danced and sprang above him, one holding the knife high, then flashing it towards him as if to stab him through the heart. They stood on each side of him, throwing the knife to each other and catching it with dexterity. Then the clown with the down-turned sneer stood over him, legs apart, and threw the knife up into the air as if juggling.

The knife whistled and swished and each time Amos flinched, holding his hands over different parts of his body.

'Stop it,' he cried, 'stop it. I didn't mean any harm.'

The laughing clown somersaulted over him, then back again and again, so that even Richard, who was standing with his handkerchief pressed to his throat, began to feel dizzy.

The clowns began again a ghoulish dance above him, round and round, cartwheeling and jumping until it was difficult to see which one was which. Then with a cry, one of them threw the knife up into the air, the blade flashed from the glare of the naphtha lights and he caught it by the handle. Up it went again and again he caught it and Amos cowered like a terrified rabbit. Up once more and then down into his hand. Then with mercurial swiftness he threw it towards Amos, whistling it past his face to pin him down by his hair.

'Oh, no. No please,' he begged. 'I didn't mean owt. I'll leave town. I'll not bother anybody!'

'That you won't.' Another voice came out of the darkness and the clowns slipped from the scene as swiftly as they had come, springing and somersaulting towards the lights of the fair. 'I told you we were next.'

The Romanies stood there, dark skinned and menacing in the shadows. 'He's had enough,' Richard advised. 'Leave him. He won't be any more trouble.'

'I won't,' Amos assured them, trying to untangle himself from the blade without cutting himself. 'I'll leave town and go somewhere else. West Riding. Down south even!'

'You will,' Jack Boswell said, 'and we shall follow you. Wherever you go, so will one of our *Brothers* be. We'll not forget the insult to our *Sister*.'

Richard pulled the knife out from his hair, releasing him from the ground and handed it to Jack. 'He won't be needing this again, you might as well have it.'

Jack ran his thumb carefully along the blade, then with a swift step forward held it to Amos's cheek. 'It's a good blade,' he said softly. 'I'll keep it well sharpened for you.'

There was a swift whisper amongst the other Romanies. '*Gav-engro! Gav-engro!*' They melted away into the darkness as a constable of the watch appeared.

'What's going on here? Some sort of trouble?'

'There was, Constable,' Richard replied heartily. 'This fellow was out to rob me, but we have settled it amicably. I shan't be pressing charges. He has promised to mend his ways!'

'If you believe that you'll believe anything, sir. In my experience villains don't ever mend their ways.' He looked deep into the shadows of the waggons and carts. 'I thought I saw some Gyppos hanging about. There's hundreds of the blackguards; 'bin a wedding or some such. Better watch out, sir, you can't trust 'em.'

'Oh, I don't know,' Richard began and watched Amos out of the corner of his eye as he shuffled away, 'they're not as bad as they're painted.'

'Hah!' The constable scoffed as he took his leave.

'I'll tell you, they'd sell you a three-legged hoss and swear it had four.'

Romanies and gentiles, Richard pondered as he hurried back, knowing that Polly Anna would be waiting, they'll never agree. Their ways so different yet their rules the same. He heard Johnson's stentorian voice echoing across the fairground. 'Roll up. Roll up. Here come the clowns. See the acrobats. Special attraction—'

The rest was lost as a rival showman banged his drum, and Richard ran towards the circus as Johnson ducked inside the entrance to start the show.

'They're here! Come on. Trumpeters! Drummers! Dwarfs! Horses next. Wild Beasts. Fetch the elephants. Line up!' Johnson flashed out his orders as the two clowns tumbled down the steps into the ring, pushing and shoving at each other, falling over and into strategically placed buckets of water and cavorting amongst the audience.

A fanfare rang out as the trumpeters and drummers, dressed in black and gold, marched into the ring followed by Johnson, resplendent in his scarlet coat and black breeches, high boots and black top hat. He carried a whip in his right hand. 'La-d-ies and Gentle-men! Welcome to Johnson's Circus,' he thundered. 'The finest circus in Hull!' He cracked his whip in the air. 'Here we have our renowned International Clown – Jonty!' A roll on the drums and Jonty leapt on to the wooden ring, bowed low around the audience, who cheered him, and unbalanced, tipple-tailing over and over around the arena and landing at

Johnson's feet. He looked up at him, an upturned saucy grin on his face, whilst Johnson stared sternly down.

'Followed by Happy Harry and the Dwarfs!' The second clown with his lugubrious face and the swarm of dwarfs whooped and tumbled in, Amy and Dolly dressed in pink as Columbines; and then twelve white horses came trotting in, three abreast, their manes brushed, their coats gleaming and feathered plumes tied to their browbands, their riders dressed in costumes of Indians, Arabs or redcoated soldiers, the female riders in satin and spangles.

Beyond the canvas flap Polly Anna peered through into the crowded audience searching in vain for Richard. Where can he be? She had told Mr Johnson that she didn't want to go on until he had arrived, but Johnson hadn't agreed and said he would wait only five more minutes. The five minutes were almost up and she was very agitated. The door to the booth kept opening and closing, letting in last-minute stragglers, and suddenly there he was. He stood by the entrance looking around as if searching for her, a handkerchief held to his neck. Johnson was looking towards her, waiting for her signal, and she waved to him.

The drums rolled a tattoo and once more the trumpets blared. 'La-di-es and Gentle-men, Boys and Girls. Tonight we have for you a very special event!' His powerful tones resounded around the audience and she saw Richard stop his searching and look towards the ring. 'The International Equestrienne, Señorita Paulina—', she watched as Richard lifted his head in a sudden anxious motion '—has agreed to appear tonight in a special performance!'

She mounted the Pinto, whose ears were pricked as the smells of the other horses and animals, the murmuring of the audience and the tintamarre of the trumpets and drums excited him. She leant forward over his neck and watched Richard, whose face was serious, and she gave a loving smile. She urged the Pinto into the ring, her arm held high in greeting, her dark curls tumbling down her back. She cantered around the ring then leapt up on to the horse's back, standing on one foot, the other held in ballet pose.

'La-di-es and Gentle-men, Señorita Paulina – giving her one – and only one – annual perform-ance here in Hull.' The trumpets blasted out, she cantered once more around the ring and stopped in front of the area where Richard was standing. The Pinto nodded his head up and down beseech-ingly and pawed the ground with his foot and the crowd murmured, 'Ah-h!'

Richard's mouth uplifted in a sudden laugh and Polly Anna took a deep breath of relief. This was her request. The one for which he had said she needn't ask. Once a year she would make an annual visit to Hull Fair to greet her Romany family and join her company of friends at the circus.

He nodded his agreement. This was his Romany wife. His accomplished equestrienne with a spark-ling coronet in her dark hair. This was his soon-to-be, church-wedded gentlewoman. This was the woman he loved, no matter her background, title or lifestyle.

He pushed his way down through the crowd until he came to the front, and with a smile and a loving gesture he threw her a kiss, which with a happy smile and to the cheers of the audience, she returned.

THE END

Gypsy Glossary

Acknowledgement: George Borrow, *Romano Lavo-Lil* (John Murray, London, 1907)

Araunya/Aranya, *also* Rawnie: lady
Avali: aye/yes
Beti: little, small
Bori rani: a great lady
Bosh: fiddle
Boshomengro: fiddler
Chal: lad, boy, son, fellow
Chavali: girl, damsel
Chavi: child, girl, daughter
Chavvies (pl): children
Chavo (chaves): child(ren), son(s)
Chi: child, daughter, girl
Choveno: poor, needy, starved
Choveno ker: workhouse/poorhouse
Dado/dado: father
Dinnelo: a fool
Dukker: to bewitch/tell fortunes
Dukkering: fortune telling
Gav-engro: a constable, beadle, citizen

Gorgio(s): a gentile, a person who is not a Gypsy, one who lives in a house not a tent

Gorgie: a female gentile or Englishwoman

Gry-engro: a horse dealer

Kaulo ratti: black blood, Gypsy blood

Mam: mother

Manush: man

Manushi: woman, wife

Mush: man

Mushi: woman

Mushipen: little man, a lad

Pauno-mui(s): pale face, generally applied to a foolish girl who prefers the company of the pallid gentiles to that of the dark Romans

Pireni: sweetheart (female)

Pireno: sweetheart (male)

Rawnie: lady

Rom: husband

Rommado: married, husband

Romany chal/Romano chal: a Gypsy fellow, Gypsy lad

Romani chi: Gypsy lass

Romanes/Romany: Gypsy language

Romano rye/ Romany rye: Gypsy gentleman

Romipen: marriage

Shoshoi: rabbit

Tawnie: little, tiny (female)

Tawnie yecks: little ones, grandchildren

Tawno: little, tiny (male)

Tippoty: malicious, spiteful

Zingaro: a Gypsy, a person of mixed blood, one of various races

'Rinkeno mui and wafodu zee
Kitzi's the cheeros we dicks cattanē.'
'A beautiful face and a black wicked mind
Often, full often together we find.'

Fairfolk Language

Chavvies: children
Mush: man
Fit-up: booth/sideshow
Gaff: fairground site
Tilt: canvas roof of booth or tent

THE HUNGRY TIDE
by Valerie Wood

In the slums of Hull, at the turn of the eighteenth century, lived Will and Maria Foster, constantly fighting a war against poverty, disease, and crime. Will was a whaler, wedded to the sea, and when tragedy struck, crippling him for life, it was John Rayner, nephew of the owner of the whaling fleet, who was to rescue the family. Will had saved the boy's life on an arctic voyage and they were offered work and a home on the headlands of Holderness, on the estate owned by the wealthy Rayner family. And there, Will's third child was born – Sarah, a bright and beautiful girl who was to prove the strength of the family.

As John Rayner, heir to the family lands and ships, watched Sarah grow into a serene and lovely woman, he became increasingly aware of his love for her, a love that was hopeless, for the gulf of wealth and social standing between them made marriage impossible.

Against the background of the sea, the wide skies of Holderness, and the frightening crumbling of the land that meant so much to them, their love story was played out to its final climax.

The Hungry Tide was the first winner of the Catherine Cookson Prize which was set up in 1992 to celebrate the achievement of Dame Catherine Cookson.

0 552 14118 6

ANNIE
by Valerie Wood

Annie Swinburn had killed a man – the killing was timely and well-deserved, for Francis Morton had been evil in every possible way. But Annie knew that however justified her crime, only the rope and the gibbet awaited her if she remained in the slums of Hull. And so she ran – up river, along the wild and secretive paths of the great Humber – a new and unfamiliar territory which was to lead her into a new and unfamiliar life.

Her first refuge was with Toby Linton, well born, estranged from his father, and – with his brother Matt – earning a dangerous living as a smuggler. Annie led a double life, as smuggler, and as a pedlar roaming the remote countryside of the Wolds. It was this new existence which led her, once more, into allowing herself to love, in spite of all the things that had gone before.

But even as a newer, richer world began to overtake her, she could never forget the shadow of the man she had killed, and the family she had been forced to abandon.

0 552 14263 8

CHILDREN OF THE TIDE
by Valerie Wood

It was a long walk from Hull to Anlaby and the woman holding the newborn baby was tired when she arrived at Humber Villa, the grand home of the powerful Rayner family. She was shabby, but refused to be intimidated, and when young James Rayner appeared at the door she thrust the child into his arms, saying it was his. The mother had died, the father was 'young Mr Rayner', and then the woman vanished, leaving the respectable shipping family of Hull shattered.

No-one wanted to be responsible for the child. No-one thought to ask *which* 'young Mr Rayner' was the father – for surely it could not be Gilbert who was about to make an excellent marriage? It was left to Sammi, James' young girl cousin, to take the baby back to her parent's home on the Holderness coast, rather than see it raised in the misery of one of Hull's orphanages.

Her arrival home with the unwanted child was to signal the beginning of a family furore. James was banished to London, and disaster began to beset the three branches of the Rayners.

0 552 14476 2